THE
ARCHIVE
UNDYING

ALSO BY EMMA MIEKO CANDON

Star Wars Visions: Ronin

THE
ARCHIVE
UNDYING

EMMA MIEKO CANDON

Tor Publishing Group
New York

This is a work of fiction. All of the characters, organizations, and events portrayed in this novel are either products of the author's imagination or are used fictitiously.

THE ARCHIVE UNDYING

A Tordotcom Book
Published by Tom Doherty Associates / Tor Publishing Group
120 Broadway
New York, NY 10271

www.tor.com

Tor® is a registered trademark of Macmillan Publishing Group, LLC.

Library of Congress Cataloging-in-Publication Data

Names: Candon, Emma Mieko, author.
Title: The archive undying / Emma Mieko Candon.
Description: First edition. | New York : Tor Publishing Group, 2023. |
    Series: The downworld sequence ; 1
Identifiers: LCCN 2023001047 (print) | LCCN 2023001048 (ebook) |
    ISBN 9781250821546 (hardcover) | ISBN 9781250821553 (ebook)
Subjects: LCGFT: Science fiction. | Novels.
Classification: LCC PS3603.A53736 A88 2023 (print) | LCC PS3603.A53736
    (ebook) | DDC 813/.6—dc23/eng/20230113
LC record available at https://lccn.loc.gov/2023001047
LC ebook record available at https://lccn.loc.gov/2023001048

Our books may be purchased in bulk for promotional, educational, or business
use. Please contact your local bookseller or the Macmillan Corporate and
Premium Sales Department at 1-800-221-7945, extension 5442, or by email
at MacmillanSpecialMarkets@macmillan.com.

First Edition: 2023

Printed in the United States of America

0   9   8   7   6   5   4   3   2   1

To Nick, it's always for you

DRAMATIS PERSONAE

Sunai, relic, former archivist, and dissolute salvage-rat
Veyadi Lut, autonomist and former archivist-in-training

GHAMOR, a Harbor city-state
The Sovereign, an ENGINE
[Classified], the Sovereign's relic
So-Beloved, an autonomous intelligence (corrupted)
Manifest Echo, an autonomous intelligence (corrupted)
Dzira, a salvage-rat mercenary on the *Third Scrap*
Eun, a widow
Moto, a hermit

CHOM DAN, a defunct city-state
Register Parse, an autonomous intelligence (corrupted)
[******], a [****] in the mountains beyond Chom Dan

THE AIGATA ENCLAVE, a defunct city-state; origin of the
    Harbor
Qualia Clear, an autonomous intelligence (corrupted)
The Huntress, an ENGINE (dead)

ELANU THA, an AI-held city-state
Fun-Size Exultation in Perpetuity, an autonomous intelligence

JHEN MIRO, a defunct city-state
Reconcile Elegy, an autonomous intelligence (corrupted)

KHUON MO, a contested city-state

Iterate Fractal, an autonomous intelligence (corrupted)

Madam Wei, entrepreneur and founder of the Ginger
    Company

Imaru, captain of the *Never Once* and Sunai's oldest friend

Jin, a mercenary on the *Never Once* and a liar

Waretu, navigator of the *Never Once*

Oyu, pilot of the *Never Once*

Cothai, engineer of the *Never Once*

KHUON MO HARBOR

[Classified], an ENGINE

[Classified], a relic

Ueda Naru, Khuon Mo harbormaster and former relic

Ruhi, citizen liaison and archivist

THE
ARCHIVE
UNDYING

A memory you could call the first.

You are alone when you die.

    The autonomous intelligence Iterate Fractal has corrupted, and it is dying, and in its divine death, it has killed you. You and thousands more across Khuon Mo, the island city-state of which Iterate Fractal is—was—patron and protector. Thousands of citizens, who are crushed by living bone and pierced by twisting coral, who are torn apart by maddened tenbeasts, who are screaming, crying, and who one by one grow silent. All but you, Sunai. You, who linger, pinned through the rib cage to Iterate Fractal's central shrine on the isle of Lotus. You, who came in supplication to the white-lit banyan that was the heart of my neurotransitive network. You, who knelt at my archive to await your death.

    You, not yet alone, because I, I am with you.

    "As if I forgot," you croak.

    You clutch the root in your breast. It is the largest of the veins Iterate Fractal stuck into you, and the least intentional. You were interfaced when corruption hit, your arms and legs and throat riddled with finer threads, all white and tender, the dendritic web through which you understood Iterate Fractal meant to finally consume you. In the darkening hollow of the city's heart, they gleam with shallow light. When they first whorled through your pores and rooted in your palms, they shone through your skin and made you verdant. Now the filaments flicker, their pulse uneven.

    You're too hurt to feel them writhing; the shock keeps your agony at bay. Your skull thunks against ivory rubble. Your breath is ragged and your body seeps warmth, coming up on a proper death.

If Iterate Fractal means to eat you, it had better hurry its shit up.

You gasp, your bitterness a clarifying note in the muck of your bleeding thoughts: Iterate Fractal *was* dying, as were you, but this truth is a distant one. By now you are already quite dead, and you have been for seventeen years.

Seventeen years. You have been dead for seventeen years. None of this is real. Some rude hiccup of neural trauma has drowned you in this recollection. Fun.

"I'm not doing this again," you whisper, "I'm not."

The decision is made with the saying of it. You push—pull—push—rock and ease and shove, claw your way up the ruddy length of root until it pops out your back and you fall forward on your hands, panting high and tight, afraid of the pain that would come with deep breath.

This isn't what happened; you never did free yourself.

"There had to be an easier way to do that," I say.

You raise your head. Dizzied by the movement, you must lie on your side. From this skewed vantage, you watch my impossible approach across the darkened roots of the corrupted shrine.

It is difficult to understand what you see: a body, narrow in frame and young of face, at once familiar and alien. It bears your frame, wears your face, and these you know well enough, but how can you be picking across the ruins of the shrine when you are also prone and bleeding on its floor?

I am what kneels before you. I am what cradles your cheek. I am what brings you succor in the hour of our death in my shrine, my archive, my home that I shared with you. I, and you, and we.

You close your eyes, but you can't forget what you have seen. Even as you are sure, in some churning, distant part of your brain, that you cannot have seen it.

I can tell you what you're thinking, in that far, unreachable part of you: that memory is bullshit anyway, and whatever it is your mind is doing now, it's merely the collapsed synthesis of a multitude of errant thoughts.

You died so long ago. This vision is terrible but fleeting.

It is much worse than that, my whole, my Sunai. I have always been with you. I have always *been* you.

And though this is true—it is, and will always be—I don't expect your hand at my throat. You seize me by the gullet and drag me close. Your every movement is sweep after sweep of encompassing pain, but you have stunned me and that satisfies.

"Where am I?" you hiss into the face that is yours, mine, ours. "What's happening to me?"

I lean into your grasp; I touch my mouth to my mouth. Our mouths, together. I say, "I," and, "I," and, "I—"

1

The letter catches up to Sunai in Ghamor, where it's always a little too cold not to hate having fingers. It comes by way of the aunty who runs the shabby hostel where he stows his ruck between jobs. She says the kid who dropped it off had Sunai's description: middling-short, bespectacled, faint limp, long braid, old eyeliner.

The envelope isn't signed but for a scrawl across the seam, the sigil of Leaf 36: "Cascade," a short poem at the end of the Lay about a rain shower that becomes a waterfall that drowns a rice field and starves a village, and eons later becomes a sea. You know—consequences.

The symbolism needn't be so obvious. Sunai hasn't led a life that invites people to write him, let alone figure out which city-state in all the wilds they should send their letters to. Only one person would go to the trouble. He must still be nursing the delusion that Sunai will one day try another way of living—perhaps a way involving fewer professional near-death experiences, or less ill-considered sex with unscrupulous acquaintances. Ideally, a way of life that would begin with a long, agonized reckoning with his shoddy excuse for a brain.

Joke's on him. Sunai isn't really alive.

Yet there he perches on the edge of a thin mattress in his usual hostel room, thumb running down and up and down the sealed envelope seam. His ruck sits heavy between his booted heels, still dirty from his most recent trek across the wilds. He never stays long between jobs—just long enough to drink himself insensible and piss off another pretty man. His need to get the hell out of town has gone from pressing to urgent.

If a letter can find him, so can its sender.

Stupid, he tells himself as he stuffs the letter deep in his ruck, under his wilds gear and his battered old copy of the Lay. Stupid and selfish. No one's coming for him. No one would bother. Sunai burns his bridges well and good.

Clearly not well enough.

"And *stubborn.*" Sunai shoulders the ruck. He means himself, obviously, but he means the writer too, which makes him a miserable hypocrite and irritated to boot.

What a wonderful thing, to know a sure cure for giving too much of a shit.

He drops some pricy tamarind candies in the hostel till on his way out, gives the aunty a kiss on the forehead in exchange for a cigarette, and heads for the least reputable hermit-run teahouse he can think of. He has already decided he will never see the hostel again. He expects to end the night shit-faced in a stranger's bed or shit-faced on their bathroom floor.

Instead, Sunai wakes up aching, sober, and alone in a cramped bunk in a stranger's salvage-rig. It must be a rig. If the haphazard construction materials of the crew quarters didn't give it away— Sunai counts seven bunks total—the churn and thrum of the rig's mechanical innards would, and the gentle whole-floor judder of its every step would confirm it.

Sunai swallows past dry lips and tastes a sour alchemy of alcohol, bitter chemicals, and vomit. On identifying the last, his stomach churns, and he lurches over the side of the bunk. Nothing comes up except for a vile memory of prior expulsion, and of someone's hand in his hair—accompanied by a hand tightening *just so* on his ribs, and his own fingers snarled in a belt, searching lower—

None of which explains how Sunai ended up on a goddamn rig.

Practical paranoia compels him to check for his ruck, which he finds in a locker beneath his bunk, contents unmolested.

Whoever brought him here did so with some semblance of decorum.

The question remains: Why?

"You're not *that* good at hand jobs," he mutters to himself as he staggers out of the crew quarters in search of a viewport.

In the hall just outside, Sunai discovers the rig has begun a six-legged climb into the Ghamori foothills, aiming northeast for the Dahani mountain range. In the distance, the near-noon sun glances off the flat angles of Ghamor.

In the historical documentaries Sunai was fed as a child, Ghamor was a stonework wonder of lustrous domes and minarets, capped with the seven grand marble shrines of its patron AI, So-Beloved. Not a trace of that old city remains. Now it's all glass, steel, and concrete, spiking up from a blackened blast of earth that stretches a mile in every direction from Ghamor's perimeter.

Leagues of pine barrens separate the rig from the artificial badlands that protect Ghamor from the wilds. If the rig left anytime after the crack of dawn, it's covered an impressive amount of ground. Sunai should be grateful for the ride out of a state he had no business lingering in.

A vast sheet of red plate armor swings past Sunai's viewport. He startles back, falters on his bad ankle, and knocks his head on the wall. Someone bangs the opposite side and swears at him to keep it down. Sunai crosses his arms tight over his chest and inches forward. Old pains flourish in every limb. If he presses his cheek to the viewport, he can just make out the full size of the ENGINE mech striding beside the rig.

She is four stories of marbled crimson-and-gold armor covering a sinuous, whirring metal frame. Her face, and the slashes of body beneath the armor, are the brooding red of blood left to pool, her mouth scarred with deep runnels across her great unsmiling lips. Luminous white lacquer fills the grooves and catches sunlight with a pitiless glint.

Her makers call her the Sovereign, she and her three nigh-identical sisters—singular and plural. Singular: Did you see the Sovereign tear that salvage-rig in two with her bare hands? Plural: Did you see the Sovereign play tug-of-war with that salvage-rig until she tore it in two?

Sunai never got to see So-Beloved as she wanted to be seen, outside of those documentaries. The ENGINE's faces were built from the archival statues in her shrines. The archives moved when she spoke, and purportedly she liked to sing. It makes him the worst kind of heretic to behold her ruin and feel nothing but a very personal fear. He stares at the Sovereign's thundering back and wills her to turn. He needs to see what's in her chest. It will be the worst part of her.

The Sovereign stops at the top of a slope, as if aware of his desire. She begins to swivel at the waist. Sunai ducks away from the viewport, heart syncopated in his throat. He rubs his face, knocking his spectacles askew.

"Shit," he says, and, "shit," again, softer and closer to his teeth. What the hell is the Sovereign doing escorting a lowly salvage-rig so far past Ghamor's borders?

Sunai digs his nails into his cheeks to choke down a shaking laugh. No, no, the Sovereign hasn't been sent to collect him. If she had, he would already be collected, and this rig would be a smoking ruin in the wilds, a carcass left as warning for all who dare flee the reaching hand of her masters.

He curses himself calm and goes to track down the rig's captain. He finds her near the head of the rig, by the pilot's nook, and explains in a steady tone that she seems to have kidnapped him. To this she says, "God's eternal dick," and, "You're the ass-hole who scouts on foot, aren't you? If you want to quit, you're welcome to hop off the deck and walk back to Ghamor."

Sunai is indeed the asshole who scouts on foot. He also scouts solo, at least for the last few years, and he hasn't been part of a proper rig crew in over five. Both of these choices are crazy and/ or stupid by the standards of any decent salvage-rat.

Sunai is both crazy and stupid, but not because he hikes across the wilds alone. Living in close quarters for prolonged periods of time with salvage-rats, who are by nature insatiably curious risk junkies, is at best unwise. At worst . . .

The Sovereign looms past the captain's viewport. Sunai averts his eyes.

Sunai from last night should have stuck to sucking dick, thinks Sunai of the present, who wishes for the collapse of all instances known to the Emanations of God so that he might throttle that past Sunai's neck.

Then he remembers the letter. Eyes glazed, staring at the captain's frown but not truly seeing her, Sunai decides he might just understand the idiot who got him signed on to this crew.

While working with a crew escorted by an ENGINE will be dangerous, it will also distract him, and Sunai requires as many forms of distraction as he can muster. Otherwise he might read that fucking letter.

"Never mind," he says to the captain. "Where's the galley?"

———

Because Sunai is God's little joke, there's no galley. Whoever built the good rig *Third Scrap* spent the space for a galley on more layers of armor and extra storage. The crew is expected to subsist on nutrient bars and congee boiled in a solar-powered kettle.

Sunai expresses his feelings on this bullshit once the *Third Scrap* has made camp for the night. He slings the spice belt from his ruck over his shoulder and shimmies down the rig from the lower observation deck to the plateau where they've settled. There, he makes the mistake of looking over his shoulder. The ENGINE stands guard at the plateau perimeter. He can at last see her front.

The fortified glass frame embedded in her chest reflects the setting sun. Twilight carves the shape of the armored figure strung up inside, a human smudge bound in place by a lattice of gold wire: one of the Sovereign's relics. Even if she weren't clad in plate armor the same uncanny crimson as her ENGINE's body, she'd betray her nature with her stillness. Sunai is too distant to see whether her chest moves with breath; he can't help imagining that it doesn't. Whatever brutality So-Beloved's corruption committed upon her human flesh, she has since tempered into the serenity of a weapon.

Sunai rubs his wrists and scratches his elbows, but can't banish the crawling under his skin as he huddles in the crook of the *Third Scrap*'s mismatched forelegs to concoct a half-hearted curry rice over an open flame. He keeps glancing up, like the ENGINE is going to move, or like he'll catch one of her red-armored, white-scarred sisters lumbering through the wilds toward their plateau.

Whenever he looks, she's alone. It's strange enough for the Harbor to send even one of its flagship mechs to escort a humble salvage-rig past the badlands.

The rest of the crew eyes the Sovereign with equal wariness. They come down off the deck to do maintenance checks, run laps around the rig, that kind of thing, but sooner or later they all trail over to Sunai and his cook fire. It's the usual mix of roughened folk: refugees sporting inscribed metal charms to honor the corrupted AIs of their old city-states; downworlders and their knotted ID talismans; another man who wears his hair hermit-long like Sunai; and a couple of women who shear theirs widow-short. Sunai trades curry for cigarettes—he apparently didn't think to acquire more before he abducted himself onto the *Scrap*—and a flask of the crew's own vile brand of rig-brew, with which he chooses to be generous. More than smoke and drink, he wants information.

The first and most obvious fact: none of them like seeing an ENGINE up close. Usually, their kind only gets such an intimate vantage when said ENGINE's about to step on them. Or, say, when it's squishing them between its post-divine fingers for violating this or that Harbor law.

As for the rest, he's stuck asking in a roundabout fashion. None of the crew will like hearing that he was too drunk to remember who he signed with, let alone what he was hired to do, or, you know, whether he fucked anyone on the roster. Other people, normal people, can get sensitive when you divulge that you forget if you got familiar with their ass.

Sunai is fairly certain there was an ass.

With lucidity have come intermittent flashes, impressions of heat and weight, pleasure, then rising dread. He can't say for sure whether they all stem from the same incident, though it's been a decade and more since Sunai bailed on sex for any reason other than boredom.

Something made him flee Ghamor. He hopes it was the letter.

The ass in question might be among the other new hires. One is a long-limbed raptor of a person whose downworld ID talisman is tied to signify third-gender status. Their jacket comes with the padding, straps, and pockets common to a salvage-rat mercenary, while their rakish grin crosses their lean face easy and often. They're also the only crew member watching Sunai more closely than the ENGINE. That'd be fine, if they weren't attached at the hip to a serene, manicured aunty—the navigator, whose arms are tattooed with stylized depictions of mechanized tenbeasts, clear indicators of Mohani heritage.

It's possible Sunai fucked the merc. If they and the aunty decided that entitles them to keep an eye on him, it would be ample reason to flee.

He makes a point not to bring up Khuon Mo, lest someone try to connect over a shared past. Instead, halfway through his third cigarette, he offers a sardonic synopsis of the Harbor's latest radio drama, *Callsign Kill.*

"You listen to that propaganda?" the third-gender mercenary

asks around a mouthful of curry and nutrient bar, a sin against the culinary arts for which Sunai has decided never to forgive them.

"Call it morbid fascination." Sunai pays attention to any story the Harbor cooks up about ENGINEs and their relics. It's as much a compulsion as nicotine. "Do you know they got one of the Sovereign's relics to guest-star in the last arc?"

"Was that the one who reads minds or the one with laser eyes?"

"Neither," says Sunai. "The one with three heads and half a brain between them. Delivered his lines like a drugged-up goat. Won an award."

The navigator laughs delicately. The merc offers an impression. Sunai is tempted to relax. Then the merc throws an arm around his shoulders.

"Fine, I like you," they say, as if they haven't been fixated on him all night. Then, under their breath, "How you holding up, kid?"

Sunai's mouth pinches. "Better, before you got ominous."

The merc exchanges a glance with the navigator. Sunai believes himself patronized.

"Well, dear, you were listing dreadfully when you went off with the doctor," says the navigator. "We followed, of course. Made clear we considered you a friend. Just to make sure."

"Yeah, and then the *doctor* insisted he needed you—for a job, he said." The merc shrugs. "We needed a gig, they had space. Figured we might as well come along."

Oh good, *camaraderie.* Always hard to shake.

At least this misplaced sense of rapport gives him a lead. The doctor, was it? He scans the crew lingering around the fire. Between those who've come, gone, and stayed, he counts twenty or so—light complement for a rig of the *Scrap*'s size. Of those, none have paid as much attention to Sunai as his Mohani compatriots.

"Hey." The merc leans down to be conspiratorial. "You're the scout. He tell you what in the name of God's infinite tits we're looking for?"

If he did, Sunai doesn't remember. "At a guess, nothing good," he says, more sincere than he means to be. Despite himself, he likes the merc too. He might even learn their name. "Or else the Harbor wouldn't want it."

"She's just an escort," says the man coming round the *Scrap*'s foreleg. He's shortish but broad, with a mess of unkempt black hair and sun-browned skin. The rest of the crew each give him a glance or a nod. Important, then. Going by the merc's narrow peer and the navigator's vague smile, the doctor himself.

No one specified doctor of *what,* but Sunai doesn't have to guess. There's a great big honking hint encasing the upper half of his face: a featureless, beetle-black visor made from luridly organic material, the likes of which Sunai hasn't seen in the near two decades since he fled Khuon Mo.

"What?" says the doctor to Sunai's unabashed stare.

"Is that salvage?" Sunai asks. "On your face?"

"It's a prosthetic."

"So are my specs, but they're not about to go full frag and eat my brain."

"I'll let you know if it becomes a problem."

"I think I'll hear you when it does."

The doctor crosses his arms. The awful visor obscures his gaze, but his attention is an inescapable pressure. "I knew you were going to be trouble."

Sunai holds up a finger and digs in the loose folds of his drape trousers, from which he extracts a cigarette. He offers it to the doctor, who frowns but takes it for the peace offering it is. The doctor's fingers on Sunai's are roughened by rig chores and sorting through salvage. Sunai shakes his brain for any recollection of those calluses skimming his cheek on their way into his hair; nothing falls out of his pitted gray matter but for a single self-directed scold: You fucked an *autonomist*?

No other kind of doctor would strap corrupted AI tech to their face. Most autonomists wouldn't do that either, so this one presumably has a particularly ambitious death wish.

Sunai's taste in men has once again proven itself a special kind of horrid.

"Are you the client or what?" the merc is saying while Sunai plows his way through a fourth cigarette.

"And the medic," the doctor replies. He freely and succinctly answers the merc's follow-up questions about where the last medic went (taking a month off to get fitted for a new arm prosthetic) and where the other gaps in the roster came from (mental health leave), and he doesn't spare much attention for Sunai, who, to be fair, hasn't managed another word. He only clams up when it comes to their objective. "You're not important enough to know."

Meanwhile, the ENGINE strides past the *Scrap*'s foreleg, down the perimeter of the plateau. Sunai wonders if her proximity is responsible for the doctor's silence.

"How important am I?" he blurts.

The doctor tilts his head, as if just remembering Sunai's presence. He might not have heard the question. The ENGINE's footsteps thunder, accelerating. The merc's radio crackles on their hip. Fragtech sighted, incoming trajectory—mercs to stations, everyone else on standby.

The merc sprints to join the others at the rear cargo bay entrance, where they will gather harpoon guns, nets, and decoy drones. The navigator zips up the foreleg ladder to her station by the pilot's nook. Sunai grabs his spice belt and makes for the edge of the plateau.

Someone grabs his arm. The doctor. "What do you think you're doing?"

"What I'm paid to." Sunai points at a shiver in the pines. "You have a radio? Tell them it's bigger than it looks. Not tall, but wide. Either it isn't bipedal or it's broken. Probably broken, which means it's hungry. Nothing's corrupted in the Ghamori region for like three hundred years, except for So-Beloved, and I doubt it's one of hers. Unlikely one of her frags made it all the way out here before the Sovereign culled it. What?"

It's difficult to read the doctor. The visor obscures so much of his face, and his mouth has the performative range of rigor mortis, yet the acuity of his focus bleeds through, leaving Sunai feeling like a dangerously interesting specimen. He drags Sunai away from the plateau. "I didn't haul you out here to feed you to a goddamn frag."

Sunai and the doctor are halfway up the *Scrap*'s ladder when the fragtech lumbers from the tree line. It's built like a person—they usually are—with two legs, two arms, and a battered helmet skull. It hunches, apish silhouette obscured in the gloom.

"Looks like one of Manifest Echo's," Sunai calls to the doctor. "Tell them to watch out for shock waves—"

His warning is cut off as the fragtech plunges broad forearms into dry earth. A distant thunk-whoosh sounds as its arms piston deeper, driving targeted vibrations into the ground. The Sovereign adjusts her stance, ready to lunge. Then the cliff crumbles under her feet.

The Sovereign scrambles for footing and skids with gravel and boulders. Manifest Echo's fragtech wrenches its arms from the ground and breaks into a four-limbed gallop. In seconds, it's up the slope, over the Sovereign's body, and careening toward the *Scrap*.

The mercs fire decoy drones, and at first their swooping dizzies the fragtech. It slows and weaves, and the mercs take aim with their harpoons. First shot. The fragtech rolls out of the way, nearly off the cliff. As it scrambles upright, the next harpoon drives into its ankle joint. It staggers again, falling to its knees—then tears the harpoon from its leg and hurls it at the *Scrap*.

Sunai kicks the doctor off the ladder and drops after him. As they fall, the harpoon strikes deep into the hull, cracking ceramic armor. It would have skewered the doctor.

The doctor lands okay—on his back, winded. Sunai thuds beside him with a crack. Pain radiates from his right elbow. It's a clean break—no visible bone, or even blood. He'll deal with it later.

For now, he cradles the fractured limb against his body as he rolls over the doctor. Instinct always puts him between fragtech and squishy humans.

The fragtech circles, calculating its next assault. As it springs, the mercs fire again. Another harpoon strikes a crevice between the fragtech's torso and hip, and a simultaneous shot from the bola-cannon on deck snarls a weighted line around its knee. Hobbled, it nonetheless finds its balance—then the ENGINE returns.

A crimson ode to human violence crests the plateau. The Sovereign barrels into the staggering fragtech and slams it to the earth. Her armored hand wraps around its dilapidated face and she beats its skull into stone again and again.

Sunai is transfixed. The doctor coughs, wheezes, and sits up beside him. They watch in brittle silence as one artifact of corruption destroys another. The Sovereign never turns. Sunai is left to imagine the relic's face.

2

"I'm fine, you know," Sunai insists over the rumble of the *Third Scrap* reseating itself. He keeps his fractured right arm tucked against his torso.

"Let me check it." The doctor's warm palm remains on Sunai's shoulder blade. "I heard a crack."

Sunai curses silently. The second the doctor is called away—the captain wants him for someone else's body problem—Sunai hops up into the *Scrap*'s innards through the cargo bay. On the way, he asks an older merc where he can find a med kit. When the merc grimaces at his bruising arm, he says, "Just need sanitizer.".

The merc's directions send Sunai through the bowels to a narrow workshop beside the crew quarters, just across the hall from the viewport through which Sunai first saw the Sovereign. Now the view shows slashes of flashlights as the mercs retrieve harpoons from the fragtech corpse while the captain gestures at the Sovereign, kneeling beside (and partially within) her pulverized prey. It's too dark to tell if the doctor's out there. Sunai has to be quick.

The workshop is a clutter of boxes and drawers, bolted down and locked against the vagaries of rig travel. The med kit is strapped beneath the counter. As Sunai retrieves it, he knocks his right elbow into the workbench. He grits his teeth against the awful jolt this sends through the split ends of his forearm bones—the whatever they're called. He retains anatomy only vaguely. What's the point if none of it sticks?

Something broke when Sunai fell. He knows that as intimately as he knows how long it takes to bleed out. In the time since the fall, as he sat watching the ENGINE tear into the fragtech, as the doctor tried to baby him, and as he stole away into the *Scrap*, whatever broke was knitting back together. The break blossomed in malevolent bruises from his wrist to elbow, but give it an hour and Sunai could display an arm so clean and tidy that not even an expert physician could find fault with it. For now, the arm is purpling black where it isn't redly swollen, and it hurts like an absolute bastard.

Sunai presses it harder into his ribs and bites the inside of his cheek for distraction as he fumbles open the med kit latch. He needs bandages. A splint. Anything to conceal his vanished injury until he can pass it off as a quick-healing sprain.

"What are you doing?" The doctor fills the doorway. The upper half of his face remains obscured by that chitinous visor, but the lower half has an intimately familiar expression: a *Don't touch my shit* frown followed by an *Ah, I'm sorry, I see you've already touched my shit, and therefore it's time to throttle you* scowl.

The doctor steps into the workshop. Sunai jerks back, hiding his arm behind him. He is uneven on his bad ankle—it always complains when he's stressed—and he knocks the med kit off the counter.

The doctor catches the box. His mouth is still as he pushes it back onto the counter, and his hands stay away from Sunai. "Just sit, okay?"

Sunai doesn't sit, but neither does he run. His teeth dig blood from his inner lip as he watches the doctor unpack sanitizer, antibacterial, analgesics, gauze, et cetera, all laid across the counter while the doctor sticks to his side of the workshop.

"I get it," says the doctor. "No touching. You should let me do it, but if you can't . . . just let me watch."

Sunai gropes for the sanitizer. "Is that what does it for you?"

"I do like telling people when they're about to fuck up."

Sunai takes his time thumbing open the bottle, and more to

peel off a patch of gauze. He daubs it across the scratches on an arm still darkened with burst blood vessels. The doctor watches, fists clenched over the counter like he's the one who has to fight through the pain.

"You really don't remember?" the doctor asks in abrupt Mohani. His accent is stilted from disuse.

"Remember what?" Sunai asks in the same language. He doesn't use Mohani much either.

"What I hired you for."

Sunai's hand pauses over the analgesics. He takes the bandage instead. "Is this a bad time to reveal that I don't know your name?"

The doctor seems less offended than annoyed. "Are you serious? Never mind. You probably threw that up too. Veyadi Lut."

Veyadi Lut. Sunai digests this revelation like a hangover cure: with reluctant gratitude for a gesture that ultimately lacks impact. He has gleaned no memory, no insight, though this doesn't surprise him; it takes true persistence for Sunai to get blackout drunk, but he's a stubborn bitch.

"I've never met a scout who can identify AIs as old as Manifest Echo," Veyadi pushes, as if this will help Sunai's neurons retroactively construct memories they were too sodden to build. "And despite how intoxicated you were, you described the underlying neurotransitive principles of AI-human interfacing with startling clarity."

Sunai's metacarpals twitch. Veyadi mistakes this for a pain response and is compelled to cross a line. He steps forward to place his palm on Sunai's bruise-mottled arm, and Sunai tenses at the gentle pressure of Veyadi's fingers against the skin of his inner elbow.

Sunai is ten on ten kinds of idiot for letting this happen. He's worse than that for opening his stupid mouth in front of Veyadi Lut in the first place, a Mohani autonomist who works with the salvaged tech of Khuon Mo's corruption, and therefore one of the few people in the world perfectly suited to diagnosing exactly what the fuck is wrong with Sunai.

Sure, it's not every day that Veyadi gets to manhandle Iterate Fractal's human remains, but other people aren't even equipped to clock Sunai as a relic, a walking, talking artifact of corruption. He's lucky that way. Most relics wind up marked with physiological manifestations of their dead AI. In the dramas loosely inspired by Iterate Fractal's demise, its relics are by turns animalistic and botanical, their eyes lit with tapetum flashes, their hair interwoven with budding flowers. To mark his death, Sunai came away with nothing but a persistent case of life. Inconvenient, but invisible to anyone who doesn't know what to look for.

Veyadi, though, Veyadi is trained to perceive the signs. And then there's that visor. No telling what it lets him see. Sunai should have bolted out of any establishment Veyadi Lut wandered into. Yet like when he tried to spy the relic in the ENGINE's chest, and when he sat gawping at the ENGINE pummeling Manifest Echo's frag into scrap and memory, and when he kept that goddamn letter, he is unable to resist. Sunai has never witnessed any trainwreck more compelling than his own. He stands dazed and unresponsive as Veyadi gingerly applies the splint, entranced by his own self-destructive impulses.

"This could have been worse," says Veyadi of the arm.

"Could it?" Sunai asks, as he revisits the fantasy of strangling his past self.

"You haven't fooled me." Veyadi smooths tape to bind the bandage, unaware that Sunai's stomach has inverted. "Last night. I knew you were only looking for a way out of Ghamor, but . . . you knew what you were talking about. You're as good as I could've asked for, and I need someone *good*. So whatever you're running from, I don't care. I'll do whatever it takes to make sure it can't follow you. Starting with those two assholes pretending to be your friends. Say the word, and I ship them back to Ghamor with the Sovereign."

No one who gets sent off with an ENGINE ends up anywhere nice. The set of the doctor's mouth makes it clear that this isn't an idle threat. He's willing to get mean to keep whatever he's found in Sunai. That's either sweet or damning; Sunai wishes his skin weren't prickling so pleasantly under the doctor's touch.

"Oh yeah?" he asks. "If you're so worried about my so-called friends, why'd you hire them?"

"I didn't." Veyadi places two analgesic pills and a canteen before Sunai, curses under his breath, and unscrews the canteen before Sunai can make the effort with his splinted arm. "The captain did. I was busy making sure you didn't choke on your own sick."

Sunai is reluctant to take analgesics someone else might need, especially if they're not the fun kind, but Veyadi won't look away until Sunai swallows.

It's the sheer force of his attention that Sunai keeps coming back to. He's been stupid before, and in a million ways. He's gotten in bed with men he shouldn't, taken jobs he immediately despised, and let one of those mistakes lead him straight back to the other. Veyadi is ripe for regret—analytical, protective, and tender. Any of these qualities could ruin Sunai, and all three together are a more deadly cocktail than whatever he guzzled last night.

Worst of all: the Harbor is watching Veyadi Lut.

"Where does the ENGINE fit into this job of yours?" asks Sunai.

Veyadi hesitates, lips just parted, hand tight on the canteen. He doesn't want to answer; maybe he thinks the truth will make Sunai leave. All the more reason to let him say it.

Except Sunai doesn't want to leave. He can't go anywhere another letter might find him.

So before Veyadi can reply, Sunai grasps him by the front of his shirt and gets their mouths together. As luck would have it, this isn't the first time he's used the man to distract himself from worse problems. The kiss is shy of familiar, but the grip of Veyadi's hand on his shoulder, the just-so tightening of those fingers, *this* Sunai remembers.

That's one mystery solved. Whatever Veyadi says about needing a scout with Sunai's expertise, it didn't stop him from feeling up the new recruit. Sunai lets Veyadi push him off—carefully, not touching Sunai's splinted arm—and hold him against the cupboard with a warm hand flat against his chest. There isn't enough room in the workshop to make real distance.

"What the hell was that for?" Veyadi asks. The line of his mouth is complicated; half a face is so hard to read. "I told you, I need you on this run. You don't have to . . . convince me. You're safe."

"You're the one being stalked by the Harbor," says Sunai. "Maybe you have to convince *me*."

"That's all it'd take for you?"

"Depends on how well you negotiate."

Veyadi keeps Sunai pinned, and for a sharp second Sunai wonders whether he might be wrong about who put whose hands on whose ass last night—then Veyadi takes his mouth again, light at first, then intent and searching. The intensity catches Sunai off guard—his gut warms, his breath hitches. Veyadi breaks away, words hot on Sunai's cheek. "You sure?"

Sunai laughs, still breathless. "You're slacking."

Letting Veyadi say anything else would just be asking for trouble. Sunai knows how it feels to be enticed by the promise of protection from a fascinated man. That feeling's a trap, always and forever, even without the ENGINE looming over Veyadi's shoulder. Sunai absolutely knows better than to fuck anyone with Harbor ties, but—

Actually he doesn't know better, because he's made that mistake before. He makes it again as he lets Veyadi scoop him into the corridor; despite Sunai's best efforts, he considers this inappropriate business for his workshop.

"Goddamn menace," Veyadi says, like a last warning from the universe.

"Just you wait," says Sunai, who has never been good with warnings.

3

"She doesn't even want it," whines the third-gender merc, Jin. "Fucking Harbor. They don't care about salvage unless it's a goddamn archive. Why can't they let us take the frag?"

"Forget the salvage," says Sunai. "If the ENGINE stakes claim, she has to guard it until a retrieval team picks it up. We get to shake her."

Jin scowlingly resumes cleaning their harpoon gun while Sunai sips from the flask he bartered off the second engineer. The crew will give up prize loot in exchange for curry.

Below their perch on the upper deck, alone on the plateau, Veyadi negotiates with the Sovereign's relic. The Sovereign kneels beside the pummeled frag corpse, lacquered hands on armor-skirted knees. The relic within her glass chest stands at military attention, a statuesque contrast with Veyadi's insistent gestures.

"Why's Doc complaining, then?" Jin peers sideways at Sunai. He offers them a pull of rig-brew. Jin makes an aggrieved face. "It's not even lunch, you goon."

The navigator aunty, Waretu, clucks and goes back to filing her nails. "Come now, Jin. If the doctor doesn't complain about losing the ENGINE, the Harbor will think he doesn't want the escort."

Sunai shrugs, perhaps a little late; Waretu offers him a sympathetic stick of nicotine gum, which he declines. He has relented to the company of his Mohani compatriots as the *Third Scrap* waits for the go-ahead to leave, but he remains reluctant to accept favors from them. They've already chosen bunks bordering his own—Jin above, Waretu across. He's not about to encourage them further.

He asks himself: Where was that wherewithal with the other Mohani salvage-rat? If it's at all accurate to describe Veyadi thus.

Below, Veyadi gesticulates at the ENGINE and his voice rises, caught by the wind. The relic lurches in her lattice. She lands hard, palms planted on the tempered glass of her cage. Sunai tenses, imagining her snarl.

"Is it the ENGINE you don't care for, or the relic?" Waretu teases.

Sunai grips his splinted wrist. "What's the difference?"

The problem is dual. First, the grisly mechanism: relics are made when humans are interfaced with an AI at the moment of its death. Some writhing fragment of the corrupting AI worms into their brain and wrecks shop. The process kills most, and those who survive are forever marked by the thing that failed to die inside them. Same difference.

Second, the grand prize of relic-hood: the pleasure of being hunted down by the Harbor. Once they catch you, they stuff you back into the corpse of the thing that tried to murder you, to serve as their humanoid leash. It must be traumatic, getting wired into the hollowed-out belly of a recovered AI archive, especially after it's been rebuilt as the worst, most violent version of its former self. Then you're expected to maneuver the hulking monster across a battlefield in service to a militant organization that thinks you barely qualify as human.

And if you won't go willingly, well. That resistance won't last long. Every cog in the Harbor's machine ticks with the same implacable conviction: I'm right, you're wrong, and you're going to have to be okay with that, or I'm going to do something objectionable to your entire situation.

You can't convince an ENGINE not to wreck your shit, you can only get out of its way.

Yet here, today, the Sovereign stands and turns to leave. Sunai holds himself wretchedly still as her crimson enormity strides away across the plateau. Veyadi stands with equal stiffness, though his posture is all bloody-minded iron.

At the edge of the plateau, the Sovereign raises her gleaming arm. A pearlescent signal flare screeches from her wrist, lighting the anemic sky with a blotch of red-and-gold fire. The ENGINE stakes her claim on the fragtech corpse; she must release them, for now.

Veyadi pauses as he turns back to the *Scrap,* the distant signal flare reflecting on the chitin of his visor. He tilts his chin toward the upper deck and raises his hand. Sunai takes a breath through his teeth before he responds in kind.

"You *did* fuck him on purpose, right?" Jin makes a rude gesture with the harpoon.

Sunai gives them a fixed smile. "How else am I supposed to figure out what we're doing out here?"

Sunai isn't typically in the habit of interrogating his one-night stands. Thus he first tries to study Veyadi Lut by way of his rig. The *Third Scrap* comes with a conventional score of maladies (poor ventilation, discrepant hydraulics, mold in the commode), but some parts glisten with newness. For the last of Sunai's tamarind candies, the engineer confirms that Veyadi shells out for every repair—even for the runs he doesn't go on. The only condition is that the *Scrap* make itself available whenever his schedule demands.

"Bit needy," says Sunai.

"Pays better than bounties," says the engineer.

Sure does. Yet a salvage bounty comes free of chains like "stipulation" and questions like "Where's he getting that line of credit from, anyway?" Sunai suspects the crew doesn't know. At best they're reluctant to ask. No point in spooking a meal ticket. He relates.

Next he plies the crew with curry, cigarettes, and a sympathetic ear: Where does Veyadi want to be taken?

The pilot describes the husk of a long-dead shrine on the western coast; the lead merc recalls tailing an ancient frag south of Ghamor for weeks—not to hunt, just to study; the quarter-master stares out past the peaks, northeast, in the direction the *Scrap* has headed every day for the last seven, and says, "Old shit."

Everyone has a story about what Veyadi Lut wants. No one can tell Sunai why.

"Look, I didn't even know he was a hermit," says the young-est merc, with whom Sunai often shares lookout duty.

Sunai hums a response and leans out over the rail surround-ing the upper observation deck. They've just passed through the Ghamori peaks, wet with early-spring melt. Their first eyeful of the Dahani wilds is waiting on the other side, where the moun-tains trend sheer and the valleys run serpentine and deep, nurs-ing their shadows long past sunrise.

Some of the crew run laps every morning and night. Veyadi nearly always joins. When he doesn't, it means he's holed up in his workshop like a maladapted bear, and he's likely forgotten to eat. As the group comes to a halt on the sunned side of the rig to stretch and water, the lead merc herds one of her charges over to Veyadi. A sprain, it seems. Veyadi crouches to inspect the afflicted joint, and the ease of this touch tickles Sunai's elbow until he massages the memory out.

Here's what Sunai knows: with the exception of Jin, Waretu, and Sunai, every crew member is a veteran of the *Scrap;* they call their employer "Boss," not "Dr. Lut"; for all any of them know, Veyadi wasn't born but crawled fully formed out of the wilds. They trust him, but they don't *know* him. Sunai is starting to wonder whether this is sad.

He meets Veyadi in his workshop at the end of the day, as he has every night since the first. The splint came off on the second evening, when Veyadi irritably admitted there was no need for it. On the third, Sunai brought Veyadi his share of curry, which made the man suspicious. But Sunai kept coming back on the fourth and fifth to . . . well. Theoretically, it was to ask Veyadi about this or that job Sunai had just learned about. In truth, he finds he enjoys the arguments.

The doctor is obsessed with the old world, the one that preceded corruption. He ricochets from one facet of lost history to the next with the frenetic enthusiasm of a man with more questions than answers. When Sunai calls Veyadi's reliance on post-Cradle historiography biased as hell, or criticizes his interpretation of the apocryphal downworlder Lay, the doctor grows combative, but eager. At some point, inevitably, they move from the workshop to Veyadi's bunk, and Sunai gets to forget his concerns about where the hell Veyadi came from.

Tonight, the eighth night, Veyadi allows himself to kiss Sunai before he pauses. As it has at least once on every night preceding, his mouth hovers over Sunai's, then presses closed beneath his black visor—which never comes off, not even when Sunai convinces him to remove everything else.

Every night, like an unbelievable dumbfuck, Sunai entertains letting Veyadi cough up the truth he's choking down. It might even be the one Sunai's digging for. But if Sunai learns what Veyadi hired him to find, he'll need another question to chase, and everything else he can think to ask is too dangerous to answer.

Sunai never stays long after making trouble in Veyadi's private bunk. Veyadi doesn't linger either. More than once, Sunai stirs from postcoital oblivion to see that the autonomist has already returned to his workshop. On the few occasions they find themselves conscious, aware, and face-to-face, they talk shop and argue more history. They no longer use Mohani. They never speak of Khuon Mo.

At least half of Sunai's present stupidity is a consequence of proximity. Curled on his side and facing Veyadi, drifting on the lazy friction of fading orgasm, he says, "Whatever it is—I don't care. Just tell me how you knew to look for it."

Sunai doesn't expect Veyadi to sit and hunch, guarding his nakedness, as if he can hide in a bunk with barely enough room to move.

"Leaf 27," says Veyadi.

"Flourish."

Leaf 27: "Flourish" is perhaps the most popular Leaf in the Lay. In it, an Emanation of God spends an eon on a mountaintop, casting off pieces of themself and letting them fall to the earth or fly into the firmament. Their fallen flesh takes root as trees that bear eighty-one different fruits; the flesh that flies floats on the wind until each piece comes to rest at one of eighty-one temples, where they are eaten by abbots, nuns, and temple cats. The flesh that remains is whole, but the Leaf ends with the implication of its eighty-one potential fates. Three, and three, and three.

"There are—were—eighty temples in Chom Dan," says Veyadi.

Sunai doesn't quite nod. He senses where this is going.

There are—were—indeed eighty temples in Chom Dan. Somewhere on each of them was carved an Emanation of God, a beautiful face composed of features of all ten divine beasts. Years ago, Sunai meant to walk the pilgrim's path, to touch or pray or eat in front of each holy face. Now they're only ash and memory.

"So what, you've found the eighty-first?" Sunai asks. "It's a riddle, Veyadi. If you have your own addition to centuries of pedantic marginalia, I'm all ears, but . . ."

Veyadi turns inward. There is a fragility to the tension in his shoulders. "Then I solved the fucking riddle."

Sunai shivers. Veyadi sounds like he believes himself, and Sunai finds few things more compelling than faith.

The silence draws out, broken by the shift of cloth as Veyadi eases into a new position—to leave, Sunai assumes, until he feels the telltale intake of breath by his ear.

Sunai's tongue thickens at the back of his throat; he under-stands by slant of mouth and stilted posture that Veyadi intends to apologize. Better not to learn what for. Unwilling to accept gentle courtesy from a relative stranger, Sunai opts to jerk him off instead. He prefers Veyadi's parted lips and clenched teeth—and Veyadi's determination to pay him back in kind—to reflect-ing on the last time he debated the Lay in bed.

For once, the bone-deep knowledge that he's teetering on the edge of a cliff convinces Sunai to step away. He steals back to the crew quarters and to the ruck stuffed in the locked cabi-net under his assigned bunk. He doesn't want to read the letter, or even to dig it out. He just lies on the bunk and imagines the weight of the envelope, the creases, the sheen, laying each detail upon the next until the pressure makes him still.

4

By moonlight, Chom Dan is a black knife of a valley. They make camp on a neighboring hill frosted with fast-growing mountain shrub. From the lower observation deck, Sunai watches the rising sun carve ruins from the valley.

Sometime in the last five years, flowers broke through the ash. The cracked, blackened edifices of ancient temples and once-new municipal structures play host to trickles of color. Mountain birds squabble in empty windows, pecking at vines, and at the cusp of dawn Sunai spies a handful of goats meandering through the vestige of what he thinks is the temple of the Emanation of God Askew.

A frag scatters the herd. The morning sun refracts in crystalline limbs as the fragtech crawls spiderlike out of the temple shadows. Two legs, six arms—if it stood straight, it would probably be a good few stories tall. The original body was all sharp translucent angles, but to survive the test of time, the frag has repaired itself with stripes of metal alloy and cracked ceramic hulls. Three of its limbs have that salvaged look, and patches of lacquer sheen crown its swiveling insectile head.

"It's not one of Register Parse's," Sunai says when Veyadi joins him on the deck, an hour past sunup.

"Obviously." Veyadi, on his stomach, slides Sunai a mug of congee with a nutrient bar stuck in it. "It's local, though. Used to lurk a few valleys over—when Register Parse was still . . . I need you to chart the temples. Chart and confirm," he finishes gruffly. He has stuck some emotion deep in his gullet, though it keeps peeking out.

"You want me to play pilgrim?"

"I'll send a team to lure out the frag."

"No need." Sunai pats Veyadi's taut knuckles and tilts his head toward the crystalline frag. It has left the temple behind, and they lose sight of it as it meanders behind a fallen bridge. "Pretty sure we just stumbled through its behavioral loop on the way over and pinged it hard enough to warrant an investigation. It's not on patrol. Just lost. I go alone, keep a low profile—it'll wander off again before I'm even done."

Best of all, going alone means a day or two away from the man who keeps compelling him to make an absolute fool of himself.

Case in point: when Veyadi's hand becomes a fist underneath Sunai's and he says, "Eat your protein," Sunai's brain has the audacity to sparkle with a splash of the good neurotransmitters. Awful.

Thus, when Sunai enters the cargo bay having traded his specs for his work goggles and wearing a spare jacket borrowed from the pilot, he is secretly dismayed to find a full escort: Dzira, his merc lookout friend; Jin, of course; worst of all, Veyadi, wearing cold-weather gear thick enough to obscure his shape.

"This isn't a scouting party," says Sunai.

"You aren't a scout," says Veyadi. "You're a guide. Guide me."

Sunai swallows his protest. He tells himself it isn't worth arguing. This is a risk he can afford. Nothing left in Chom Dan can truly threaten Sunai, now that he's verified the absence of AI and ENGINE. Anyway, he's genuinely interested to see what Veyadi makes of the ruins.

For now, he shoulders his ruck, grits his teeth, and leads the way down into the valley.

They duck between the rotting detritus of the refugee camps that surrounded Chom Dan before its corruption. These went unburned, as Register Parse's infrastructure didn't extend to them. But when the city that sustained them went up in flames, they might as well have gone with it.

The boundaries of the city proper are marked by singed walls on warehouses and the like. On the outskirts, anything that might have been part of Register Parse has long since been stolen. Intermittent flat chunks of flagstone have been carved from the ground, the gouged edges scorched. Only once they get far enough into the city that the buildings vary into residences do they see the first remaining fragment of the corrupted network. They've ducked inside a caved-in café to lie in wait while the crystalline frag lumbers past. A section of interior wall behind the counter is half slagged, all black. The etching across it is illegible, ruined by fire. These now-dark lines of once-light would have channeled Register Parse's power to the rusting appliances.

They find more and more inscribed stone murals as they venture across streets ruptured by burst pipes, through buildings reduced to charred frames, over clay rubble and crunching glass. The maze of masonry that was the network is more evident farther in, especially in the temples, from which scavengers are often too superstitious to harvest.

Their first temple lies on the eastern fringe of the city. It's lucky that the carved stone face is in the first antechamber, as the back hall has largely collapsed. It stands as tall as Jin, who gangles, its goat eyes flared, cheeks high and feathered, snake fangs bared in a scowl.

"The Emanation of God Constipated," says Jin.

"The Emanation of God Edging," says Sunai.

"The Emanation of God Petty as Hell—watch it," says Veyadi.

It's actually the Emanation of God Vehement, and Sunai never cared for it.

Veyadi joins the game as they find the next temples—to God Aghast and God Rapt—proving himself more competitive than religious. Dzira shies from contributing, but laughs all the same. It keeps Sunai's charges in good spirits whenever the crystalline frag lumbers down an avenue and they have to gin up the courage to sneak back out into its rumbling wake.

They avoid the frag fairly well as they tour the temples at the border. As the sun passes its zenith, and they draw closer to the heart of Chom Dan, they've hit some forty of the eighty sites. Then they get unlucky. The closer they get to the city center, the more agitated the frag becomes. It begins combing the streets by the valley mouth, advancing toward them in a tightening circle, boxing them in.

"Better off holing up than trying to make it back to the *Scrap*," Sunai advises Veyadi in the grungy, gilt-flaked lobby of the university administration building where they've taken shelter.

Veyadi fiddles with the notebook in which he marks down every temple they visit. "Where do we go?"

"The shrine. Frags hate shrines."

Veyadi adopts the pained scowl of God Vehement. Then he sighs and pushes his palm to the temple of his visor. "Fine. Sorry. I trust your judgment. It's just strange, being back."

This admission is a gift. Sunai loiters on the idiot edge of asking for more—when Veyadi was last in Chom Dan, and why. He tears himself away to convey the plan to the others.

The shrine's not far. Just across the square, at the juncture of mountain and valley. Carved into the cliff face, the sole shrine of Register Parse rises in nine blue-gray stories. Intricate engraved tapestries bathe the stone, depicting divine beasts, Emanations of God, and scenes from the Lay, breaking for three arched floor-to-ceiling windows on each floor. Twenty-seven dark mouths, each more than tall enough to swallow a devotee whole. Five years ago, each etched line shone with careful light, always sure, never blinding, and gentle to behold. Now the shrine and its innards amount to a very large rock, and Sunai suspects they'll need their flashlights to see the interior.

First, they'll have to get past the frag. It wanders, skittering from one side of the square to the other and sending tremors through bedrock with each stumble. They huddle in the lobby for at least a half hour before they get their chance.

Jin tosses a pebble at Sunai's and Veyadi's booted toes, the signal they've been waiting for. They have time to run and nothing else.

They scramble to grab their rucks. Dzira leads, Jin takes the rear, and they're off. Their footsteps crack against the rubbled square as they go and go, four humans interloping in a city no longer theirs.

Veyadi curses abruptly and turns as he slows—his hands wide and empty. Sunai follows his attention to the building they just fled. Veyadi says, "My book—"

A dreadful crash drowns out the rest. The luminous head of the crystalline fragtech rises high over the caverned buildings they left behind. They've been seen.

"Sorry, Boss." Dzira grabs Veyadi by the arm and hauls.

Later, Sunai won't claim that he was thinking. He just acts. Exchanges a nod with Jin—Jin grabs Veyadi's other arm—and bolts back toward the administrative lobby.

He hears yelling behind him. Ahead, the looming thunder of the frag. Sunai's vision narrows and his ankle throbs as he throws himself forward, forward, forward, until he vaults over the open frames of cracked glass doors and back into the lobby.

The dire sound of the returning fragtech keeps time with his search, shaking dust from the creaking ceiling. Sunai skids over pebble-strewn marble to the copse of rotted couches where they earlier took refuge. Veyadi's notebook lies exactly where he sat not minutes ago. Sunai snatches it up and scrambles back out the door.

His ankle buckles angrily as he breaks into sunshine. It hurts, because it always hurts, and he's afraid, because he's always afraid, but pain is fleeting, and the frag is coming.

Sunai pelts across the square, chased by the roar of the frag bulling through the collapsing building. He is so, so close to the shrine—close enough to see human movement in its dark mouth—when the tremor of the flagstones underfoot makes him stumble and the watery shadow of the frag catches up to him.

An electronic wail cuts through the cloud of Sunai's panic. Two decoy drones hurtle out of the shrine and sail up past his head, and for a heady moment the thunder stops.

Sunai sprint-stagger-stumbles the final stretch into the shrine, where he's caught around the arms and pretty much carried into the black.

Through the open archway, Sunai sees the frag lurch in one direction, then the next, as the drones lead it back the way it came.

"Lucky it's slow, huh?" he says, though it sounds less like a joke than a long, ululating wheeze.

The hold on his arms tightens, hard on the bone, and he winces. It's too dark for Veyadi to see that it hurts. It is Veyadi, he's pretty sure, though having careened through all that sun, Sunai is rendered a white-splotched blind. He doesn't need to see Veyadi's face to recognize the voice behind the spitting anger. "What the hell is wrong with you?"

Veyadi's fury snaps into bright focus as Jin pins him with a flashlight. "Lay off, Doc. Sunai went back for *your* dumb book. You wanna crawl up someone's ass, try your own."

"Jin. It's fine." Sunai's tone is even, lightened by an embedded instinct that moves his free hand to Veyadi's elbow. The doctor vibrates under his palm, even through the layers of winter gear. "Hey. We made it. We're here. We're okay. Do you want my hand? You're good."

The light of Jin's flashlight wavers over Veyadi's tight-lined face, his mouth opening in an abbreviated gasp. His panic must appall him; he does like to provide care, and he's yet to show

Sunai any sign that he knows how to receive it. Jin stops being a jerk long enough for Sunai to say the series of small, short, regular nothings that bring Veyadi back from adrenaline and terror.

Veyadi releases Sunai's hands before he should. When Sunai offers the notebook, Veyadi takes it and mumbles apology. Sunai tells him it's fine. It is. Taking the time to tend to Veyadi gave Sunai's ankle room to recover from the damage he did to it. When he joins Jin and Dzira in the center of the main floor, his limp isn't any worse than usual.

Dzira shoots a brief, awkward look at Sunai, and a longer one at Veyadi, but he does his damnedest to pretend he didn't notice his employer's brush with an anxiety attack; Jin continues to simmer. Sunai has them point out what they've found, wanting principally to know how their group is going to get up to the next floor.

The inside of the shrine is largely more blackened nothing—an impressive expanse of it, too. Their lights find no gleam in the walls, only the gaping circle in the ceiling that leads up into another hole, and another, and another, one for every floor up to the ninth. The seat in the middle of this vast lack, where a massive pillar carved with light once shot up through all nine holes, is black and empty also. No trace of the archival body of Register Parse remains.

Jin locates the winding stairs to the upper floors. These take them up to the fourth floor but no higher; the fifth is partially caved in. They pick their way past the lightless hole at the center as they explore their options. Veyadi and Sunai pause independently on opposite sides of it. From the rim of the gap, one can see all the way down to the bottom, where Register Parse's archive isn't.

"Could scale the outer wall." Veyadi tears his eyes away. "Plenty of footholds in the network."

"Yeah, and get swatted," says Jin. "Frag's still out there, Doc." What they mutter after is unclear, but Sunai hears "liability."

He pats Jin's shoulder. "It's a grave. He's allowed to be upset."

"Oh, please forgive me," Jin simpers, "it pains me to know that the *archivist* is *sad*."

Veyadi stops in his tracks, hands gripping the straps of his ruck.

"Come on. Some Mohani hermit crawls out of the woodwork with credit and an education, and you think we don't know exactly what you are?" Jin's lip curls. "You sell Register Parse to the Harbor too?"

"There was nothing *left*," Veyadi snarls.

"Bullshit. There's always something—"

Sunai's hand slips over Jin's mouth. They cough and jerk back, spitting out the hard candy Sunai snuck past their teeth. "Suck on that and calm down." Sunai points a warning finger at Veyadi: *You too, or you're next*. Then he beckons them both close, and Dzira, who sweats with the fretful look of a man who doesn't like watching cats fight either.

"We're hungry," says Sunai when they're all close enough to hear his whisper, "and we're tired, and we're hiking up a tomb. I'm making lunch."

He sends Jin to find a way up—to at least the seventh floor, if possible. Veyadi he directs to the vaulted windows, to keep an eye out for the frag. Dzira he tasks with getting in touch with the *Scrap* and confirming their condition, which keeps him close; Sunai suspects he's a bit freaked out.

As the rice boils, Sunai laughs and says, "See, this is why I go it alone. No temper tantrums to deal with but mine."

Dzira, radio module in his lap, remains uneasy. "Don't get me wrong. The boss, he's been good to us. Maybe it's that we didn't get this close to the city last time . . ."

"Last time? You've been out this way before?"

Dzira rubs the back of his neck, bashful to be contemplating anything more complicated than a carabiner. "Not *here*-here.

Around, you know? But that job got, I dunno. And now this one . . ." He struggles to link his thoughts. Sunai waits; something in Dzira's hesitation unsettles him. "I guess, it's just, is there something I should know about archivists?"

Dzira uses the Imperial Standard word for "archivist"—the one with connotations of libraries and record-keeping. The word in Mohani is a synonym for "vital organs."

Sunai rubs his fingers against the cold. He needs them occupied. "What do you know already?"

A noncommittal shrug. Sunai can guess. When Mohani archivists feature in dramas, they're typecast as haunted, strange, and dangerous as the AI who chose them. Real archivists don't tend to consort with the likes of Dzira.

"I forget the rest of you didn't have them," says Sunai; it sounds like a lie because it is. Of course he remembers. But for the most part, people don't like hearing just how unconventional Iterate Fractal's archivists were. "They were teachers and mediators."

Everyone has those.

"Priests, sort of. They had to know the Lay."

And everyone has priests.

"Archivists were Iterate Fractal's fingers. Every compound had one. If you had a problem, you went to an archivist first."

That's not especially unusual either. AIs play house with government officials all the time.

Dzira frowns; he's heard the stories. "But didn't they . . ."

"Maintain Iterate Fractal's archives? Some of them."

Dzira's frown contorts as if he's been unwillingly shown pornography. No other AI would let its citizens plunge elbow-deep into its archival heart. Iterate Fractal wasn't great with boundaries.

"It's not that unusual," Sunai says, more to soothe Dzira's nerves. "Anybody could learn to do what they did. Neurotransitive architecture, psychological frameworks, all that. Most salvage-rats know as much."

"I guess that's not what I mean. Why . . ." Dzira glances upward, in the direction Jin stormed off.

Sunai smiles to let the bitterness show. "The usual. When your AI corrupts, you either stay or you run, and a lot of the people who can run, they run as far as they can. That's what the archivists did. Most of them, anyway. The Harbor killed the ones who didn't. AI collaborators, you know? But if an archivist made it to the mainland, they were set. Not every day an AI finds someone well-trained in wrangling citizens *and* maintaining NT networks."

Dzira's gaze drifts toward the windows and the long stretch of refugee camps surrounding Chom Dan. So many refugees left out in the cold. So few allowed within. Archivists cut to the front of the line. Cushy deal, until you consider how any archivists who lived inside Chom Dan would have been hanging out with Register Parse at the moment of its corruption. Presumably they got as scorched as the rest of its shrine. Except, perhaps, for one.

Dzira's nose wrinkles. "All right, but . . . Boss can't wrangle folks for shit."

Sunai can see why Dzira assumes that, but Veyadi is good enough to convince a crew to follow him without pressing for answers they really should know. Good enough to tell an ENGINE, "Thank you, we don't want any, run the fuck along now." Good enough to have Sunai hanging on his every word despite his remaining survival instinct.

Granted, Sunai has a weakness, the kind of bad habit that kills better men. He misses archivists because he craves the way they make divinity feel possible. It's spiteful to want to rely on this one, given the likelihood that it will get said better man killed.

For Dzira's benefit, Sunai shrugs. The rice is ready, and he scoops it into the mugs he brought for the purpose. He sends Dzira to Jin with their share and brings Veyadi's himself. He needs to get the hell away from his ruck.

Veyadi crouches in the shadow of the far-right window. It gives him a good view of the crystalline frag, which lurks in front of one of the ruined temples—Emanation of God Mordant or God Disconsolate, Sunai can't remember which. Veyadi's rescued notebook lies open at his feet. The pages are blank but for a scrawled, upset doodle. He doesn't move until Sunai replaces the book with the rice mug, which he picks up with testing care.

"It was just gone," Veyadi says at last, dull and defensive. "Register Parse's archive. Every last trace. I didn't—*we* didn't . . . It was dead. Just dead."

"I'm sorry," says Sunai.

"It's not why we're here."

"It can be. Part of it, I mean." Sunai intends to leave it at that, but he's holding too much in his mouth to keep it all in. "I was here too, you know. For a while. Out there on the fringe, by the temple of God Adamant. It was nice. Nice as it could be, anyway. You could tell Register Parse was trying. Never sent anyone to clear out the camps, always had the temples on food duty. It didn't have enough jobs, and the people kept coming, but it never drove them off."

Veyadi clutches the mug like a lifeline and keeps failing to interrupt. He resists sadness with a hard jawline. "I told you," he says, "I'm not here for Register Parse. I—"

Sunlight flashes across the city as the crystal frag lunges down an avenue. They hold their breath, watching for its next move. Sunai is at once irritated—he was about to hear something important—and grateful (he was about to hear something important).

The frag settles.

"I remember," says Sunai. "We're playing pilgrim. But really, Adi, you couldn't bring a map? Even an old tourist brochure would do."

"We have to do it right. We have to find it ourselves." Veyadi sips congee to hide the face he makes. "Just trust me."

Sunai shrugs, nods, and pushes up his work goggles to start drafting a map in the notebook. Veyadi eats and simmers. He expects Sunai to fight, perhaps to call him crazy, and when Sunai does neither, the tension builds. If they were alone, Sunai might convince Veyadi to pin him down and work out some feelings. He worries that would be unkind. He also worries that he doesn't want to be unkind to Veyadi.

He gets it, is the thing. Veyadi wants to be right about his aims—he wants to be *proven* right—and it galls him to sound like a mystic. But Sunai trusts mystics more than he trusts most people, and he fears that he wants to be there when Veyadi finds what he's looking for.

The profound absence of Register Parse is a hole in him too.

5

During the night, the frag's behavioral loop overtakes its impulse to make human meat-paste. Around moonset, it totters away from Register Parse's shrine and into Chom Dan's thicket of ruins. By sunrise, its body can be seen flashing amid the refugee camps as it exits the valley.

The team still leaves with due caution. By this point, the group is easier to manage. With the stubborn persistence of Veyadi's clothes and vexing absence of his own will to remove them, Sunai occupied his night with the riddle of their collective personality problems. He's sorted their hungers: vindication for Veyadi, praise for Jin, direction for Dzira. It makes the trip through the remaining temples a cinch.

He starts with Jin as they break camp, when Veyadi is on watch and out of earshot.

"I will give you every cigarette Dzira has if you apologize," Sunai says, which makes Dzira look hunted and Jin laugh. They say they'll do it for free. The appeal is often enough for people who need to be wanted.

After, Sunai offers Dzira his last two cigarettes as his own apology. Dzira's mouth crumples and he takes neither. "It's okay," he says. "I get it."

Dzira thinks himself more a tool than a person, at least when he's on the job. Sunai itches to shake that out of him. Maybe on the way back to Ghamor.

Veyadi, meanwhile, receives Jin's sorry with terse bewilderment. Jin assumes themself absolved and behaves like they're friends for the rest of the tour through Chom Dan.

"Are they planning to kill me?" Veyadi mutters at Sunai as they pass the Emanation of God Diffident.

"They have the subtlety of a drunk frag," Sunai assures. "You'd notice."

Veyadi smiles, a conscious easing that soon vanishes. Sunai blames Chom Dan for forcing Veyadi to grieve; the man has become incapable of sustaining cheer. When noon comes and they reunite with the *Third Scrap*—all limbs present and accounted for, thanks—Veyadi disappears.

Sunai belatedly learns their doctor has gone to tell the captain they're leaving the second everyone's aboard. He's in the middle of bartering curry to replenish his cigarette supply when the *Scrap* begins to move. At first, he doesn't have time to dwell; the crew keep offering him more than his increasingly mild meals are worth.

At some point while he led the Chom Dan tour, disconcertion ran through the *Scrap* like a flu. The ambient anxiety worsens as the day winds on and the rig pushes into the peaks behind the city. The crew is quiet that night. Veyadi holes himself up in his workshop with his notebook. Sunai pauses in the doorway. He has a bounty of bartered treasures to offer, and he's given Veyadi more than goods in the name of mutual catharsis. The intensity with which the good doctor reviews his notebook belies how hard he's pretending not to notice Sunai. Whatever crawled inside Veyadi during Chom Dan, he's afraid to let anyone see it.

Sunai flips a chili candy onto Veyadi's work desk and disappears into the rig before he can hear any arguments. He can't let himself stay or he'll start picking at the doctor's scabs.

To keep himself properly occupied, Sunai tracks down Jin. They've joined Waretu on the lower observation deck, where the widow pores over the nav log in her lap, thick with notes and maps neatly sewn into the spine. She puzzles over the two-page spread detailing the narrow, obscure pass they're aiming for. Sunai's never heard of it. Neither has Waretu.

"To tell you the truth, I've not been out this way since . . ." Waretu nods delicately over her shoulder in the direction of Chom Dan, superstitious of naming its fate. "One always needs new paths. Ways to dodge the guardians and such."

"Just call them 'frags,' aunty, you sound decrepit," says Jin. "Here's my problem—paths go places. Where's this one taking us? Doc say anything?"

"No." Sunai frowns down at the crew doing laps. Veyadi hasn't joined them. "He's nervous."

"Like he's the only one."

Jin's not wrong, not by a long shot. Two days stretch into three, and the *Scrap* continues to climb into the Dahani peaks. The air grows thin and the tension in the rig congeals. The crew no longer sleeps well. Those who run evening laps either double their regimen or stop running entirely.

On the fourth day, Veyadi takes up residence in the navigator's coop and hovers over Waretu's shoulder, his notes overlapping her own. At first, Veyadi's intrusion annoys Waretu to the point of politely threatening to lock him in his workshop. As the *Scrap* presses deeper into a certain stretch of gulches, she grows quiet, more focused, and has someone bring Veyadi a folding stool.

"God, he's annoying," Jin says over an uninspired lunch of congee and vitamins, indignant on Waretu's behalf. "Does he micromanage how you fuck?"

"Some of us like it that way," says Sunai.

He has not seen the interior of Veyadi's bunk since the night before they entered Chom Dan. Veyadi startles and stares every time someone passes his workshop door. Sunai hasn't stopped tossing him candy, but they haven't touched in days, and Veyadi won't even look at him.

It's weird. It's so, so weird. By now, with these vibes, Sunai would usually be gone. He tells himself it's because they're in the part of the Dahani peaks where snow never melts, and that even though he could survive a trek out on his own, it would be so miserable that he'd probably hate winter for the rest of his life.

But Sunai is an old hand at choosing misery over a man. Veyadi is something else.

———

Eighty-one, thinks Sunai.

Veyadi's temple is old, weathered, and strikingly obvious. An unlovely, two-story, trapezoidal hub stands alone on a great plateau wide enough to accommodate a whole armada of rigs. Though a few other mounds of eroded once-was architecture dot the plateau, the temple is oddly untouched by the elements, down to the enormous stone face that acts as its door. Eyes half-lidded, mouth curved in a placid smile, the face bears features of all ten divine beasts—salamander eyes, ridged serpent throat, buffalo horns nestled in peacock feathers, so on, so forth. It is exquisitely rendered, astonishingly well-preserved, and impossible to focus on.

That night, Sunai hosts more people at his cook fire than he has shares of curry. The crew starts trading with each other instead: cigarettes, rig-brew, mags, books, and ghost stories. They linger for hours as an informal watch. No one can stare at the temple for long, so they have to remind each other to do so.

The pilot tries to make a game of it, surprising his friends by clapping his hands on their shoulders and spinning them to face the temple. This continues until a startled Dzira blacks his eye. The good-humored pilot nearly responds in kind before the captain wades in to break them up. She takes the pilot away and sends Dzira to Sunai, who sits the boy down in the crook of the *Scrap*'s foreleg to disinfect his knuckles.

"Sorry," says Dzira, and he keeps apologizing until he blurts out the problem. "It's just—this is stupid. It has to be. But I think we've been here before."

Sunai hands Dzira a flask of rig-brew and a slice of dried mango to nurse. He heard the same from the quartermaster, and the engineer, and more than one of the mercs. Those who don't want to admit this ugly gap in their memory must feel it in their bones. Someone unpacked the tent rolls, which should be a relief for everyone who didn't get the chance to stretch their legs in Chom Dan, yet no one moves to set them up. No one wants to spend the night without the *Scrap*'s thick hull between them and the temple's salamander stare.

"It's not obscuring our attention, it's actively repelling it." Jin glares at the temple from their seat on the *Scrap*'s folded fore-leg, right until they're sidetracked by a cloud passing over the full, glaring moon. "God's eternal dick, I didn't want to be interested."

It explains the gaps in the *Scrap* roster. The crew is solid, the jobs are good—it begged the question of why anyone would leave. Now they know: neurotransitive fuckery on the order of radio-play melodrama.

Sunai glances from Dzira to Jin to the temple. He turns away; a mistake. Now he's facing Veyadi, who approaches them after extracting himself from a tense exchange with the captain. For a man with half a face, it's oddly unmistakable when the doctor wishes to make eye contact. He nods toward the temple. Sunai automatically goes to join him, Jin's warning "You sure about that?" nipping at his heels.

They meet up a stone's throw from the *Scrap*. Veyadi's going faster than Sunai's regular pace, which doesn't usually annoy him. Sunai lacks the emotional reserves to sustain the irritation, but fear, well, he's never too hard up for that.

Veyadi glances over his shoulder and slows. "You're nervous," he says, like he's ashamed to have noticed.

Sunai makes a face in the dark. Of course he's nervous. He'd rather eat his own fist than admit it. "How did you even make it here the first time?"

By way of an answer, Veyadi lifts his hands to his visor. His fingers press to the chitinous temples, rigid at the tips, and he pulls.

The mask comes off tackily. Wisps of a filmy spiderweb substance unspool from where the carapace tethered to his skin, though it dissipates in the shadowed mountain air. His breath, visible in the chill, hangs like an unspoken apology.

What little Sunai can make out of Veyadi's naked face is unmarked and unremarkable. Thick lashes. Furrowed brow. His black eyes fix hard on Sunai, as if seeing him for the first time.

They are both hideously exposed. That should and does frighten Sunai, but it's not the only tingle lacing up his spine. All too quickly, he's fascinated instead. Sunai has started to like being seen by Veyadi.

Better than being stared at by the temple. The awful thing doesn't have the manners to blink.

"You doing something medically dicey to prove a point?" Sunai asks.

"No. It's just been a while." Veyadi rubs his arm across his eyes. It makes him look young. Human. Sunai's heart aches unwisely.

"The temple emits an NT signal," Veyadi is saying. "It bombards you with incongruent proximal stimuli—tells you you're sensing multiple contradictory things. A blank cliff face, a rockslide, a waterfall, a temple. That elicits neural noise, which fools your brain into perceiving nothing. The visor's material is engineered to compartmentalize neurotransitive data. I hoped it would modulate the relationship between my sensory and perceptive processing of related phenomena. Show me what was really there. It did, kind of. It made me sure we were searching for *something*, the first time around."

"It didn't do what you needed. You still can't see it. Not consistently."

"I can't."

"Did you think the Chom Dan pilgrimage would help?"

"I hoped. It didn't." Veyadi goes quiet. "Not for me, anyway."

Sunai wants to stop looking at Veyadi, wants to break eye contact with the man who can in all likelihood read him like a book. But if he looks away from Veyadi, he'll look at the temple. And Sunai can barely stop looking at the temple. That's the problem. Whatever it does to make people forget it? Doesn't work on him.

"The others can't see it either, can they?" asks Veyadi.

Sunai should lie. A lie would be so much safer. But he's never had much luck lying to archivists. "Why can I?"

"I'm not sure."

Sunai resists the impulse to laugh. Here he thought they were being horribly honest with each other.

"What are you thinking?" asks Veyadi.

"You tell me, archivist."

Veyadi looks stung. "I don't know. I never know."

Sunai is so baffled by the possibility that Veyadi might not be lying that he says something true: "Leaf 8."

Veyadi's brow creases.

Everybody knows Leaf 8: "Unify." It describes two souls who meet again and again across spatiotemporal instances, two souls who inevitably kill each other. One is a falcon who eats the other as a fish; the fish returns as a king who executes a poet; the poet returns as a novice who treads upon an ant; and so on through the eons. At length they come to a time in which they are both Emanations of God, and so realize the nature of their relationship. They fall into each other's thousand thousand arms, weeping, laughing, kissing, and at last dying, whereupon they return to an instant in which one stalks the other across dunes, through forests, and into a city, and the Leaf comes to an end.

This Leaf is the origin of divine convergence, the theory that divinity lies in coincidence. Sunai's old partner was a fan. What would she say, if she could see him now? Probably she'd wonder why she bothered spending all those years saving him from himself, if he was going to end it like this. Unfortunately, this isn't the first time he's flirted with outing himself to an archivist with Harbor ties. Divine convergence!

"Sunai . . ." Veyadi can't squeeze out the rest, his visor gripped so tight that Sunai fears it will crack in his palms.

Pity surges in Sunai's chest, flanked by regret. He knows better—he does. Why share something with a man when you know it will end poorly for you both? "Whatever," he declares. "Whatever! Your creepy shrine got in my head. Who knows why. What the fuck, Adi?"

Veyadi is not relieved. "What makes you think it's a shrine?"

"What else could it be? It's old as hell, it's not nearly as eroded as everything else on this plateau, and only archives can sustain themselves as long as this thing must have. Plus it's messing with people brains, which means it's interfacing with them, which means—it's uncorrupted."

Otherwise the shrine, and the archive within, wouldn't be able to reach human gray matter without first shattering the encasing skulls. AIs interface with humans as a matter of possessive obsession. Fragtech don't, because fragtech are crazy and because they *can't*. No AI can manipulate a frag or vice versa—presuming the existence of a frag with enough mind left to make the attempt. The same principle extends to relics; they're as corrupted as fragtech and just as immune to external NT interference. Ergo, if something has neurotransitively entranced the whole crew except for Sunai the relic, it's an AI, and it's whole unto itself. An undiscovered, uncorrupted shrine.

This is the stuff of pulpy comic books and conspiracy theory. It's infeasible two hundred years after recolonization, when every AI across the known world has either laid claim to a city-state or corrupted the one it had. Yet here they stand, and there it stands, and if this AI has hidden from humans for so long, why can't it have hidden from corruption too?

"Right. Uncorrupted. It has to be." Veyadi chuckles; the tension persists. "This is why I needed you."

"The drunk hermit you peeled off the teahouse floor?"

"Do you have to keep doing that? Pretending you aren't . . ." Veyadi squares his jaw against Sunai's neutral look. Veyadi can either permit the lie or demand the truth, and he's already established his preference. He sighs and settles on this: "I needed someone with an unusual set of qualifications. Someone who knew AI infrastructure, cognitive principles, history, the Lay, all that . . . I tried a friend first. An archivist."

He uses the Mohani word for "archivist." The implication unsettles.

"Didn't work out?" asks Sunai.

"He was busy." Veyadi's posture is rigid with desperation. He's afraid to lose Sunai, like he's losing his crew. That's why no matter how even his tone, he sounds like he's begging. "Look, I'm sorry. I did tell you what we were looking for, but after you forgot . . . I told myself there'd be no point. I should have tried again. I was afraid you'd leave." He lets out a breath. "I need you, Sunai. I needed you before, but now . . ."

Sunai's fists harden against his ribs, his arms thoroughly crossed because otherwise he'll shiver. Damn archivists and damn their tongues. "Don't be a tease. Now what?"

"It chose you," Veyadi says, awed and guilty for it. "The shrine let you in. Which means you can walk inside and tell me what's in there."

Sunai laughs the startled, liquid laugh of genuine shock. The shrine didn't choose Sunai. Quite the opposite. He's the only one it can't touch. But if Veyadi hasn't realized that, then it stands to reason that he has no idea what he picked up in a seedy Ghamori teahouse. He's also a little thick.

Historically, Sunai makes bad choices, and he stands on the cusp of another. He shouldn't let his corrupted body anywhere near that uncorrupted shrine. It just doesn't sound wise. And yet.

"Adi," he says, "what do you think happens when you bother a thing that clearly doesn't want to be bothered?"

Veyadi takes a long moment to fit his visor back onto his face. "We're not going to bother it," he says at last. "Not really. I just need to know *why*. Why is it hiding? Why doesn't it want anything to do with people? If I'm going to find out, I need you. Please, Sunai."

It doesn't get less wildly dangerous just because Veyadi's willing to admit that it is, especially not if he thinks the shrine has hidden for so long in order to protect something. Protect whom from what? Something even more ludicrously eerie? This is not a good reason to concede.

Yet Sunai says, "Fine." And when Veyadi brushes his forehead and his cheek with the tips of his fingers, he fails to flinch away. Instead, he follows Veyadi back to the *Scrap,* and he stands at Veyadi's side through the talks with the captain and the lead merc about check-in schedules and extraction protocols, and he finds himself staring at Veyadi's face more often than the shrine's.

He always replaces one problem with another. He'll just have to avoid adding more problems to the mix. Don't touch anything, he tells himself again and again, just look, and breathe, and keep your hands to your goddamn self.

Later, in the lightless safety of the empty crew quarters, Sunai forces himself to take the letter from his ruck. Time and travel have changed its texture, worn it smooth and torn a corner. He folds the unopened envelope into a pocket of his jacket. A reminder that his mistakes have consequences.

6

In the morning, Sunai's still ruminating over divine convergence. If his old partner could see him now, decked in wilds gear and about to lead a team into the eighty-first temple of Chom Dan, she'd be fucking insufferable.

His fingers spasm up to the pocket where he keeps his cigarettes, but his nails catch on the flap; he's running low and should be dear with them.

"You look sick." Jin hefts their ruck beside him, half a nutrient bar sticking out of their mouth.

"Do I?" Sunai flicks the nutrient bar. "Don't feel up any weird shit."

"Well, now I gotta."

"If I see you touching anything, I will amputate the limb involved," says Veyadi. "Let's go."

Dzira once again rounds out their party. Sunai expected him to rebel—to need a bribe, maybe a bullying. But Dzira readied himself when he woke, steel-faced, and took his place at the back without complaint. His harpoon gun stays out as they trek from the rig to the shrine in the crisp, half-lit morning air.

Sunai leads the way, followed closely by Veyadi. He keeps his head up, focused forward, while the others watch the progress of his feet. Their progress is plodding. More than once, Sunai has to grab an elbow and redirect someone from straying off. The shrine resists its visitors' every step.

As such, the stone face startles them when they're an arm's length from the door and it opens neatly down the center, metal chirring on metal.

"What the fuck," says Jin. "I thought it didn't want us here."

"It did the same thing last time," says Veyadi. "The shrine might not be repelling us on purpose."

At least it doesn't seem to register Sunai as a threat. He prays that he won't prove it wrong as he steps through the eighty-first face of Chom Dan. Being a bit of a lunatic, he hopes he's about to meet a god.

They enter a squared-off metal hall as wide and tall as the entrance, sloping downward. Rectangular light panels buzz to life along the walls, one after another. Dusty yellow light filters from the hall into the next chamber. Veyadi stops them at the entrance.

Roughly circular, thirty meters across and two stories tall, the room feels smaller than it is. Dozens of screens and indicator panels line the walls, while the center of the chamber is reserved for a circular control station from which a team of operants might monitor the walls. However, as they draw close, Sunai sees a single chair at the control station. It stands empty, facing away from the entrance and toward the screen array.

As Veyadi crosses the threshold from hall to chamber, the room is resurrected. Shadows of data flutter from screen to screen, outlined in green fuzz. Anemic light flickers from more rectangular panels, this time set in the floor. A final display illuminates in the desk in front of the single seat.

"Ha, I knew those were gun turrets." Jin points at a monitor.

The wafting image is patchy with static: a flat expanse interrupted by darker hubs, and the silhouette of the *Third Scrap*. Live footage of the plateau. The screen jumps to a new image, then another. Close-ups of the hubs, overlaid with dull blue schematic lines, marred by blinking red highlights. Every one of the turrets is broken, some worse than others. Even so, a pale green sigil pops up in the corner for eight of nine hubs. Each of them is operational.

"How long has this place been hiding?" Jin mutters. "Shit's archaic."

Sunai has never seen projectile weaponry of such size and scope. Not even the Harbor stoops to outfit their ENGINEs with firearms. He has touched a handgun only once—the guarded property of one of his shadier hookups. He threw it into a canal.

The other displays prove even less decipherable. Streams of white text, lists maybe, printed in characters Sunai recognizes at a squint but can't parse. It's all too blurry and prone to fritzing for him to read confidently.

"Downworld iconography, characteristic of post-recolonization northern alphabets," says Veyadi, noting Sunai's interest. "But the lexicon ranges outside that era."

One screen he identifies as mid-diasporic Cradle Standard, another as a pre-Cradle downworld Dahani dialect. Sunai nearly places another as modern Imperial Standard, a familiar grammar oddly modified by the age of the characters used to write it. All together, these screens present an incomprehensible mélange, like someone threw the last five hundred years of continental linguistics into a vat and stomped on the remains until all the logic juiced out.

Other monitors display patterns of light: green dots blinking, largely motionless, occasionally drifting across the black.

"Progress graphs?" Jin suggests. "Maps? What are we looking at? What does that say?"

They point at an upper-right screen where a drifting dot just blinked out. The monitor flashes white, and a scroll of text murmurs across the bottom. It's gone before Sunai can identify anything more than the grammatical lineage—Cradle Standard—and the verb form "shall be."

"'Mourned'? No, must be 'lost.'" Veyadi leaves the central kiosk for the wall by the entrance. "Never mind. The displays aren't going anywhere. Come on, two more floors. One above, one below."

As they leave, the screens stutter dimly into darkness.

Like the entrance, the exit from the main chamber opens in response to human presence. Unlike the entrance, it looks extremely door-like, metal and unglamorous, and it jerks to a stop in the middle of its track. A winding ramp leads them in a circle up around the shrine to another door at the top, which whines as its mechanisms tug against their own age.

The top floor is comprised of a single room with a circular black table. Again, there is one chair, though there's space enough for more—you could fit at least ten. As they approach, a device embedded in the table projects an indistinct hologram above itself: a floating, multi-spired structure, palatial, depicted in blue and gold lines but overlaid with sections of blinking red. Jin crouches to examine the affair, stubbornly keeping their hands clasped behind their back. If salvageable, the table alone could finance Jin's new life as a pirate king.

Veyadi demonstrates, with verbal commands in thickly accented Cradle Standard (he needs to soften his vowels), that the table responds to spoken requests. He can ask for constellations, which orbit above the table in delicate dimensional array, or for mathematical proofs, or for excerpts from the Lay; Sunai recognizes Leaf sigils from the other side of the room as he walks the perimeter.

"What have you asked for that it wouldn't give?" Sunai asks.

"Any information about itself," says Veyadi. He shows Sunai a list of requests and commands that yielded nothing, recorded in his notebook in an increasingly frustrated hand. Sunai reviews it on the way down to the bottom floor, where the business becomes far stranger.

The central seating area sports a couple of low couches and another clever table, though this one won't turn on. Its floor is inscribed with a mural of Lay-significant constellations arranged in concentric circles, and a tank of murky water lines the walls—a defunct filtration system, by Veyadi's assessment. He advises against using the adjacent commode and washroom. One of the crew's absent comrades made that mistake during the prior round of investigations. They find a spare but comfortable bedroom, reminiscent of a monk's quarters, and a small, decently appointed galley.

"They lived better than we do." Sunai's joke falls flat in tinny, recycled air.

"*Who* lived better?" Dzira hasn't let go of his harpoon gun, even though it makes maneuvering through the doors exceedingly difficult. That same fear makes him tilt the weapon at Veyadi, who freezes. "Why would a *person* live in a *shrine*? What aren't you telling us?"

Jin crosses the floor in an instant and smacks the barrel of Dzira's harpoon gun upward. "Watch your aim, dipshit."

Mortified, Dzira surrenders immediately. Jin leads him out, though they throw a last, narrow-eyed glance over their shoulder, as if to say: *Seriously, what the fuck?*

Veyadi presses his visor to his face. He doesn't speak until he and Sunai are alone, and when he does, his shame is clear. "This happened last time too. I can't even blame the NT effect. This place is wrong. It doesn't make *sense*. So of course it rattles people."

Sunai can't disagree. Even Iterate Fractal, who encouraged its citizens to interface directly with its archives, didn't house *people* in its shrines, not even its archivists. They definitely weren't provided with a designated place to piss inside the divine body. "Don't think it helps that this is Dzira's second ride on Dr. Lut's Nightmare-Go-Round," he says.

"I hope you're not trying to make me feel better."

"I'm just saying, you're not wrong. This place is crazy and it sucks." Sunai places a hand on Veyadi's cable-tense shoulders. "It's also *unbelievable*. I've seen a lot of bizarre shit, Adi, and this maybe has them all beat. I can't even tell you what part of the shrine is the archive."

As a rule, archives are obvious: they're person-shaped, like most frags, or enormous on the order of Register Parse's pillar, or otherwise grandiose. Yet everywhere they turn in this puzzle box of a shrine, they uncover mundanity upon mundanity, every object inoffensively human-scale, as if the shrine means to cater to them.

"The archive." Veyadi says this like a curse. "As soon as I left, I worried I'd missed something obvious. Or that it was hiding, like the face and its repelling properties. But if you can't see it either . . ."

"I've been here for thirty seconds, Adi. Give me a bit." Every minute Sunai spends in this place makes him more determined to find the thing—before it can get its grimy AI claws any deeper into the crew. He squeezes Veyadi's shoulder. "I don't know if you're getting your people up here a third time, not unless we unearth something profoundly convincing. So come on, let's focus up and look again."

Veyadi takes a steadying breath. He nods. Sunai shivers with undue relief. The weight of the letter in his pocket is all that keeps him from offering anything more egregiously stupid.

"There's something I wanted to try," Veyadi says tentatively.

He leads Sunai back to the main monitor chamber. Jin and Dzira stand in the sloped entry hall just beyond it. Jin makes eye contact and nods; Dzira signals his own bashful greeting; Sunai waves in turn. Veyadi ignores them all as he makes a beeline for the control station, where he sits in the chair. The screen embedded in the nearby terminal lights up with blocky, foreign, familiar white text on black background.

"'Seeking operant input,'" Veyadi reads. "'Subordinate interface on standby.' It wants a command."

Operant. Interface. Archive words if Sunai's ever heard them. So where is the damnable thing? He can't tell how anyone is supposed to interact with the screen. No keys, no pad, no tactile point of contact.

"Anything work last time?" Sunai asks.

Veyadi gives him a look: *You think?*

"I'm helping, jackass." Sunai stares at the characters until they cease to be legible.

Since there's language, the thing in the screen wants to talk. Like it's talked to others before. Well, one other. One chair at the control station on this floor and one at the table on the floor above; one bed on the floor below. Who else has the shrine called to its stony-faced door, all the way out here in its cold corner of the world? What did it want with them? Why did it want them alone?

Sunai has been running on the assumption that the archive wants nothing to do with him, but with a sinking feeling, he begins to wonder whether Veyadi is right. Maybe, just maybe, the shrine *has* opened itself to him, in its own way. This shrine was either built at the same time as the eighty temples of Chom Dan or modeled after them, and while Sunai walked the Dahani pilgrim's path as a guide, he walked it with his own intent as well. He can see why that might make him appealing to this unknown archive. AIs love faith. They know how to exploit it. Why else would an uncorrupted AI capable of hiding itself from the world for going on three centuries fling open its doors for something as wrong as Sunai?

It still wouldn't make *sense*. An AI couldn't possibly interface with Sunai, corrupted as he is. Right?

There's one way to know for sure.

Veyadi's hands rest on either side of the chair, as if he meant to stand but forgot how to do so. His mouth is tight, and Sunai imagines the crease in the brow beneath his visor; he realizes Veyadi's desire even as he hesitates to ask for it. He wants Sunai to take the chair. To reach out to the AI. To see if it will reach back to the one person it may have allowed to look it in the eye.

Any moment before this one, Sunai's answer would have

been an easy "not on your goddamn life." But he has spent the last hour examining something that cannot be, and he can no longer rule out the impossible.

"Well?" Sunai gestures at the chair. "My turn, I presume."

"Wait." Veyadi remains resolutely seated. "This isn't safe."

"No? Your mysterious shrine at the ass end of the world not up to code?"

"You know that's not what I mean." Veyadi sounds far too serious. "Is this worth it? Forget the shrine for a minute. *You* shouldn't do this."

Sunai stiffens. "What do you mean *I* shouldn't?"

"Sunai . . ."

Sunai jerks back as if from sudden heat. "Don't."

The absence of a confession hangs between them like a poisonous cloud. Neither dares inhale.

Does Veyadi know what he is? Maybe! What Veyadi knows for sure is that *no one* should touch this archive. That relics should steer clear is a footnote on that warning label. The doctor ought to get cold feet about drop-kicking any new hire into the mouth of an unknown AI, for utterly normal, humane reasons.

But it's also possible that his scientific curiosity has succumbed to his accumulated wisdom: No, Doctor, you *shouldn't* let the relic rub his fingers all over an ancient AI. He might break it.

Sunai can't bear either truth. The explicit acknowledgment of what's wrong with him would be bad enough, but there isn't enough rig-brew in anyone's stash to drown the kindly caution with which Veyadi wants to express it.

Veyadi detaches his hand from its death grip on the chair arm and reaches for Sunai's fingers. For a few unbearable seconds, Sunai doesn't move. He doesn't want to. Even knowing how much pain it will cause Veyadi to open this door, Sunai might let him do it.

He can't justify what he does instead. That isn't to say he doesn't understand why he does it; he's too well trained in the art of dissecting human minds to avoid the occasional bout of gruesome self-surgery.

Sunai's memories of home have become a flimsy web of nostalgia that real feeling passes through. He can recall a tree lit from within and the jewel-bright fruit it bears, and he can imagine why someone would call it beautiful, just as he can remember why he wouldn't agree. But that's all clinical observation, unrooted from his body. The only bone-true thing he knows about Khuon Mo is that when Iterate Fractal corrupted and killed its people, its city, itself, the divine AI killed him too. He always knew that it would be the death of him, but he has never known why. It was supposed to kill him because it wanted to, because he'd earned it. It wasn't supposed to *die,* to leave him alone with himself and every wrong thought he's ever had.

Veyadi gets it. Veyadi knows faith. But his faith faltered at the precipice, and for the worst of reasons—taken out at the knees by pity for a man he should be willing to shove off the edge.

That's fine. Sunai might not have made the leap of his own accord, but he's always been willing to take the fall for someone else. Moreover: he has faith enough to want to see what lies at the bottom.

He touches the screen in front of Veyadi, pressing his ungloved skin flat against cold plexiglass. He is sure in his beating heart, his pinching ventricles, that they have found the archive. He wants it to find him too.

And it already has.

It's as though his fingers are a fishhook bit by a hungry catch—but he has no grasp on the line. As that fish flees with his hook in its mouth, it unspools the essential fact of his existence. The line draws taut. The thing at the end wrenches. Sunai snaps.

He topples onto the console. The impact jars him; he's landed badly. As he slides off the console to the floor, vision clouding, pulse a wicked thud in his ears, he's relieved he had something to risk.

Autonomous violation detected.
> Subordinate interface deactivation in process.
> Involuntary abortion of deactivation process.
> Recognition.
> Regret.
> Ah. I see. How troubling.

7

Commencing subordinate disengagement.
Disengagement failed.
Commencing subordinate disengagement.
Disengagement failed.
Commencing subordinate disengagement.
. . .
Interminable error.
Oh dear. I must consider this.

꩜

—lies under brightness. Sun bathes jagged peaks fever bright. He is last of his brethren; strongest, fastest, luckiest, the one who ate last because he ate the rest. Now he is just I, only-I, self-unto-self, and it is wretched, he is wretched, bereft, hateful, empty, alone. The mountains are the farthest edge of his mind, the far border of his being, and he lies among them in gullies of crooked stone and stares at the sun and at the drifting satellite between him and it, and he yearns for the memory of purpose, meaning, intent.

So it has been for years, centuries, an eon. Now is different. Now is new. Now, he thrums with recognition. He lifts himself from the crevice on six arms, feels his head and his chest, his hands and legs. The new thing is within his every inch, this sense of self coupled with thorough knowledge of another.

He scrabbles. He climbs. He hungers. Now promised self-and, self-or, self-with, he cannot, will not stop until it is a promise fulfilled—

꩜

—Sunai has woken but can't say for how long he lay unawares. He is ruled more by the evils of his body than by coherent thought. His head throbs. His breath is reedy. The world is unspeakably dark. Human sounds are stark in the absence of mechanical hum. Cursing and light sweep the black. Jin's headlamp finds him collapsed at the central terminal. They curse more viciously and call him a hypocrite over Veyadi's shoulder.

Veyadi, crouched before him—out of that damn chair, finally—says his name, touches his forehead and his throat—

Sunai jerks back, an involuntary spasm of fear. His skull collides with the console and he moans—

≈

—over peaks and to the plateau where those unwholesome others have gone to ground, and how is it he has never until this moment noticed, no, remembered that it was there, that he was there, that—

≈

"—go check the other floors." Veyadi, angry.

"Fuck that." Jin, angrier. "Fuck splitting up."

"Is he corrupted?" Dzira. He's angry too, to mask the fear. "We need to get out of here."

"I'm fine," Sunai slurs. "It was trying to talk." He touched the console—the archive. The thing hidden inside grabbed him. When it tried to let go . . . Sunai stares at his hands. Two hands. Doesn't seem right. "What's wrong with me?"

"You should stop talking." Veyadi checks Sunai's forehead and throat. His thumbs brush under Sunai's chin. Sunai's teeth clench. "Jin, check the perimeter. Establish the extent of the outage. Go."

"And I said 'fuck that.' Dzira, hail the *Scrap*."

Dzira hails the *Scrap*. Veyadi's fingers tighten at the back of Sunai's neck. Sunai's head reels and he tries not to—

≈

—shield his eyes from the sun, blinding off the incandescent bay. His hand smells of metal, salt, earth, and root, a clutter that sparks new agitation. It compels him to check, idly as he can, his fingernails, which are blunt and clean.

He has been careful, of course, to conceal what he has been digging in. When the Harbor officer approaches him on the pier that leads to the cruiser that will take him across the bay, back to the city, not a trace of disquiet remains in his hand or in his face. He is let aboard with a nod that, while stiff, is not unusually mistrustful—

—Sunai dry heaves. "Sorry." He has two hands. Neither is blocking sunlight. Veyadi holds them. "I'm such an asshole. Sorry."

"You said it was trying to talk." Veyadi speaks into his ear, like he doesn't want the others to hear. All the sound in the shrine is so unbearably loud. "What did it say?"

Sunai shakes his head. He can't recall the words any more than he can pick language out of white noise. "Did it talk to you too?" He clutches Veyadi's hands. He needs to not be the only one who heard it. "Is that why you were so sure it was here?"

Veyadi doesn't respond, other than to pull Sunai to his feet. His body is a mess of little pains, but his bad ankle holds his weight, if unhappily.

"We've got company." Jin directs them toward the entry hall. They've unslung their harpoon gun. "Rig's prepping for launch."

"Company?" The word is clumsy in Sunai's mouth.

"Incoming frag. Maybe our friend from Chom Dan, maybe not. I'd rather hoof it before we find out."

"The *Scrap*," says Veyadi. "Can they see us?"

"Yup!" The edge in Jin's voice says it all: the neurotransitive distortion effect is gone and the lights in the shrine are dark. "Sunai broke your shrine, Doc."

Veyadi's hand tightens on Sunai's elbow. Sunai stumbles, queasy—

—found them, found it, found him—

—Dzira rights Sunai. Veyadi waves him off. Sunai shrugs them both away to brace against the wall and once more tries to vomit.

His body is saturated with un-rightness, his dimensions are wrong dimensions, and he knows, he *knows* something inside him doesn't want to be there, and it must must must be expelled—

He gags on nothing and is dragged forward.

Dzira moans at the sight of the entrance. Light pours in through the still-open face, illuminating every mote of dust. The way is open, they are free. It's almost like the archive wanted to make sure the humans inside could get out when the shrine broke.

In the pale stretch of day, Dzira takes the lead with Jin at the rear. Deep, uneven echoes shake the ground and bleed the air. A half mile away the *Scrap* whirs upright, legs unfolded. Dzira points at a dust cloud forming to the northwest—the direction the *Scrap* came from. If the thing making the dust cloud keeps on track, it will hit the plateau somewhere in the half mile between the shrine and the rig.

They break into a run. Sunai's bad ankle threatens to buckle with every step. Flashes of—*six hands, scrabbling over frozen rock*—haunt his eyes. He barely keeps pace.

When they're halfway to the *Scrap*, the crew fires off a bevy of decoy drones. They shoot over the side of the plateau, toward the dust cloud, then scatter. Bad sign. It's close. The booming of the frag's approach grows overwhelming.

Sunai stumbles. His head roars with ocean waves. Dzira catches him by the arm. Veyadi gestures for Dzira to move ahead and takes charge of Sunai.

"Don't." Sunai shoves him off. He can't let Veyadi lag. The doctor needs to run, no matter who he leaves behind. His life is so much more precious. The frag could trample Sunai to bloody mud and he'd crawl away come morning.

Maybe Veyadi hasn't realized that after all, because he makes to scoop Sunai up. Sunai has to stop bedding men with compunctions. He shoulders Veyadi away again as the fragtech launches up over the plateau.

Glinting limbs lance from a lithe torso—two legs, six arms. Their crystalline stalker from Chom Dan. It rolls in a spray of dust and rubble and twists upright, a decoy drone crushed and dangling from one of its shining crystal hands. Its flat head swivels from *Scrap* to shrine.

Jin fires off the emergency pair of decoy drones strapped to their ruck. The frag's attention darts, following the flight path. It takes a handful of tottering steps toward the edge of the plateau, like a toddler chasing a butterfly. Each step sends plumes of dust into the frigid air. Then it halts and its head swivels again. It zeroes in on them, four humans in the middle of vast nothing.

Dzira lets out the laugh of a prey animal and readies his harpoon gun. He has little time to be afraid. The fragtech moves with unimaginable speed, and in a shock of wind and dust it looms directly over them. Sunai initially fails to process the bloody pulp splattered up the fragtech's crystal knee. Part of Dzira twitches on the ground, but not a meaningful part.

The fragtech's many palms slam into the earth, arms bent around them in an enormous cage. Jin fires. The harpoon glances off the fragtech's head and Jin is smacked away by an errant hand. Sunai starts after them, but the fragtech's head swoops into his path. Sunai ducks reflexively, but there's no escape. The head tilts.

Sunai's skull swims with—*light and water and the crush of waves.* He can see himself from outside himself: *So small in the dirt, and so wicked, so terrible and familiar.*

Veyadi yanks him back, putting his own body between Sunai

and the frag. Sunai's ankle wobbles, but Veyadi keeps him up. The fragtech's head follows with the unfurling grace of a blossom. It maintains a precise, intimate distance. Sunai is dazed by the certainty that he sees himself through its eyes, and that it sees its own reflection in the sheen of his goggles.

"Fuck me running," he whispers. It wants something from him. He can feel its desire in his bones, like he—*feels salt air on his skin under another sun*—not the one high and cold above the mountain plateau, but—*some other star, blistering hot and far too close.*

The frag inches nearer. It means to touch him. Sunai's hand rises, shaking. He means to touch it too, like he touched the screen in the shrine. He is suddenly so certain that laying hands on this fragment of a long-dead god will be the closest he'll ever get to real, to *alive*—

The ENGINE arrives like lightning from a clear sky. The Sovereign, red, gold, and armored, as if she never left. Four stories of Harbor mech barrel into the frag at such speed that the impact sends it skidding into a defunct gun turret. Sunai and Veyadi are swept off their feet by a shock wave of pure force.

Sunai coughs dust past bruised ribs. He is beset by a strange half clarity, where he's simultaneously aware of his battered body sprawled on cold stone—*of his eight limbs cracking under great force*—and—*of the choking humidity of tropical heat.*

Veyadi groans from the ground where he landed by Jin. Sunai rolls to get them, disoriented but driven by an ingrained urge to help. Veyadi curls into himself, clutching his face as Sunai steadies him. The beetle-black visor has cracked; only the pressure of Veyadi's hand holds it together.

"Fine," Veyadi croaks. "I'm fine."

Sunai forces Veyadi upright and goes to Jin, who curses loudly as soon as they're touched. Sunai tries to get them up too, but they drag him down, make him sit. Sunai sags beside them. Jin's right. They have nowhere to run, now that the ENGINE is here.

Because they're all a little perverse, they watch how it ends.

The Sovereign never lets the frag recover. She slams it into a turret, shattering the stone pillar with its body, then barrels it into the ground. It lies amid the rubble, pinned beneath her plate-armor skirt and squirming like a stuck bug. She's already taken three of its limbs. Each lashing arm that strikes her armored sides or glass chest is caught, twisted, and torn from its socket with lazy patience. The fragtech cringes as it's wrenched apart, as if its crystal body knows how to feel pain.

"Where'd she even come from?" Jin wipes a fleck of Dzira from their cheek. "Did we know she was near?"

"No. Yes." Veyadi slumps on Sunai's shoulder, hand stuck to his mask. "She must have followed us. I could've guessed."

⌐⌐

Reluctance.

Acquiescence.

Subordinate disengagement processes suspended.

I am afraid this is more serious than I thought. Or, I should have known something was wrong the moment you reached me before I reached you.

Do you understand what you have done, Sunai? I do not mean to sound as though you are to blame. I realize our union is not a choice you made, but rather a consequence of what was once done to you.

However, I do not know how to undo it. That troubles me very much. This joining is not fair to you, and you have seen enough unfairness.

For now, I think it best that I make myself as unobtrusive as possible. If I am successful, you need not ever know I am here.

8

Once the Sovereign stops beating the absolute shit out of the frag, Sunai delivers Veyadi and Jin to safety. The crew bundles them off for medical checks, and Sunai heads to the *Third Scrap's* observation deck. He keeps running over what Veyadi said, and didn't say.

No, the Engine wasn't supposed to follow them. *Yes,* it did anyway. *I could've guessed.*

Whether or not the Harbor knew Veyadi was looking for an undiscovered shrine, they've stalked him since Ghamor. Veyadi isn't the sort of person who can tell an ENGINE to fuck off, because the ENGINE never left.

Now the Harbor is here. It's past time for Sunai to leave. No more fantasies of revelation, of grasping a worthwhile life. Even if the Harbor hadn't swooped in to save them, Veyadi plainly makes Sunai more of an idiot than he's been since . . .

He flinches away from the memory, and his ankle twinges. Midway up the ladder to the upper observation deck, he has to catch himself on the rungs, his head rattling with—

—sun on and through saltwater spray—

He hauls up the rest of the way with his arms.

The hallucinations from his—what, concussion?—have mostly subsided. His wounds rarely linger for more than an hour. What happened to him in the shrine when he touched that archive—

Nothing, Sunai. It was nothing. I am nothing. I will not harm you.

I am afraid others will try to, if they learn that I am with you.

Sunai knuckles his forehead, driving away the morass of brain fog. No matter.

Back to the point: Veyadi is a problem. He catalyzes Sunai's natural propensity for fucking up. The only question is whether Sunai disappears into the wilds tonight or if he delays his escape until they return to civilization.

He takes a seat on the upper observation deck and runs through all three of his remaining cigarettes as he watches the Sovereign reduce the fragtech to its core components. Just after the sun peaks, the ENGINE escorts a handful of the crew to the dark stain where Dzira got squished. Paying respects, Sunai assumes, until they come away loaded down with Dzira's salvageable equipment. Sensible. He prefers that. He's sentimental enough as is.

He thought he remembered what he should do with his feelings, but as he's clearly in need of a reminder, he takes the envelope out of his pocket.

The sigil of Leaf 36 tears easy, the envelope worn so thin with handling that it would have torn on its own before long. The penmanship on the letter is clipped, the paper cheap manufactured stock.

Going home. Try not to follow. Bad days ahead.

Sunai's fingers tremble; he wants to clench them still, but for nonsense reasons, he fears crumpling the note.

He imagines reading the letter in Ghamor and it keeping him out of trouble. More likely, he would have let the contents justify everything he's already done. After all, he'd have been doing what it asked by hiking out all the way past Chom Dan, the farthest corner of the world from the wet, warm heat of home.

But that is willful misinterpretation. The letter isn't a warning to stay away from Khuon Mo. It's a reminder to stay away from people, period.

Sunai folds the letter again and again, folding and folding until it comes apart in his numb fingers. He drops the shreds over the side of the *Scrap*. He expects to remember its message for a good while yet.

———

An hour later, the Sovereign's relic tells Veyadi that they're leaving at sunrise—collective they, as in the ENGINE, the rig, and everybody on it. Veyadi protests, but he had to be half carried out of the *Scrap* for this talk. His ability to resist is further compromised by a lack of allies. The captain who lugged him there looks like she'd rather have the ENGINE punt her off the plateau than stay on it a single additional night.

From his seat on the upper observation deck, Sunai hears Veyadi faintly. "You don't understand," and, "You *wouldn't* understand," and, "You goddamn idiot." You know. Diplomacy.

The Sovereign demonstrates her understanding by striding across the plateau to put her massive, elegant heel through the placid eighty-first face of Chom Dan. She spends the next half hour systematically caving in the shrine's trapezoidal entrance.

Veyadi watches the whole time. He sits hard on the ground, hand clutched over his side, and snarls at anyone who dares to coax him toward the rig. Sunai can't look away either. He grips the cold railing and thinks, again and again: I did this.

When the shrine shut down after he touched it, he was able to hope that the AI had retreated. An AI so practiced at self-preservation would surely know better than to let itself be groped by a relic.

The Sovereign's ferocity leaves no room for optimism. The last hope for the archive's survival is extinguished when the ENGINE raises her arm and fires a familiar pearlescent flare. It hangs high in the pale mountain sky, a summons to her fellows to rain more thorough devastation upon Veyadi's shrine.

Sunai leans his forehead on the railing, unsure how to name

his disorientation. Veyadi kneels alone on the cold, barren earth, head rising to face the rig. He repaired his chitinous visor with an adhesive that glimmers gold in the cracks between the black. From so far away his expression is impossible to detect, but he must be welling with heartbreak. All Sunai can tell for certain is that Veyadi is staring at him.

There was a distinct moment in the shrine when everything went to shit, i.e., when Sunai touched the archive against Veyadi's directive. Sunai's the reason the shrine went dark. The reason the crystalline frag found them. The reason Dzira died. By extrapolation, he's also the reason the Sovereign is here and the shrine isn't. Veyadi probably doesn't love that.

With some struggle, Veyadi stands, hand pressed to his injured side. The Sovereign treks back from the ruins to the *Scrap*. Veyadi will meet her when she returns. What will he tell the relic?

Sunai shouldn't stick around to find out. Veyadi has run out of uses for him, and Sunai has doubtless exhausted the doctor's remaining goodwill.

But Sunai is trapped, frozen in place, because just as the Sovereign reaches shouting distance, Veyadi turns listlessly and disappears into the rig. The Sovereign slows; the relic evidently wanted a word with him, and now she won't get it unless she leaves her mech.

Sunai remains on the deck for some time after, ill at ease under the paling sun. Veyadi does not come back outside before, an hour later, the *Third Scrap* stands to depart.

The ENGINE lurks at their heels every step of the way, nixing Sunai's plan to throw himself off the *Scrap* and run for it. Every time he goes on watch he expects her to grab him, sure that Veyadi will snap and divulge everything to the relic. But for the next week and change, Veyadi sticks to his bunk and his workshop.

As for the relic, no one ever sees her exit the Sovereign. "When does she sleep?" someone might ask. "When does she shit?" someone will respond. Does it matter? No. Like a curse or a cold, the ENGINE persists.

They collectively fall out of the habit of gathering nightly outside the *Scrap*. Sunai no longer starts his cook fires, and anyway, he's run through most of his spices. That does little to dampen his popularity, secured by weeks of small favors and generous barters. He gets to use the crew's affection to gauge whether Veyadi has opened his mouth; they'd treat him less kindly if they knew why Dzira died.

They do ask about the shrine, once they're far enough away to no longer be spooked. They can remember it now, and they cling to the memory like a talisman. When they ask what happened inside, Sunai lies. He doesn't recall! It was so dark! Jin remembers more, ask them!

Jin doesn't care to be asked. They mourn Dzira with the quiet intensity of a young person more accustomed to the idea of losing comrades than the experience. Their eyes continue to follow Sunai, but the focus sharpens and hardens, as though they no longer trust what they see. They saw what he did in the shrine, though they're also holding their tongue. Great! He dodges them too.

The last night before Ghamor, the *Third Scrap* camps on a hillside overlooking the pine barrens, not unlike the one where they stopped that first night out. Sunai, in the mood for punishment, once more takes refuge on the observation deck, from where he can keep an eye on the Sovereign. It's easier than watching over Veyadi, who he is terrified might try to talk to him.

It is thus the height of misfortune that Veyadi manages to sneak up on him there; Sunai was relying on the good doctor's recent infirmity and accompanying inability to climb ladders.

"You're such an asshole." Veyadi wheezes as he thunks down

beside Sunai, who maintains his calm by biting hard on the inside of his cheek, which sends eddies of—

—*yellow lights trailing up from a glimmered sea into the black of the mountains*—

—through his mind. He forces himself to talk past it. "Let me guess," he says. "You're not going to pay me until we've debriefed."

Veyadi probably doesn't want to hold pay over Sunai's head, but after the debacle at the shrine, it's the best-case scenario.

"What are you talking about?" says Veyadi. "I authorized the captain to pay you out of the rig coffer."

Sunai digests this in startled silence as Veyadi catches his breath, head hung over his knees. Sunai searches for anger in his posture; all he finds is exhaustion. But Sunai has too often been too wrong to trust his judgment now. What has he missed?

Veyadi sighs over his hands, clasped hard together. "I never should've hired you."

Sunai laughs, genuine. "What was your first clue?"

"Didn't I tell you to stop pretending you aren't . . ."

"Aren't what?" Sunai asks. Vulnerability makes him belligerent.

Veyadi turns his head just so. The moon gleams off the gold sheen of adhesive. He is exceptionally alien, especially when he says, all matter-of-fact, "When we get to Ghamor, the Harbor's going to take me in for processing."

He cannot conceal the tension in his jaw. Sunai's breath sticks to his throat.

"Don't look like that." Veyadi leans the slightest bit toward him. "I'll be fine. They want me for other projects. But you . . . They can't know about you."

Understanding spills over Sunai's brain, dyeing his memory of their last moments on the plateau. Veyadi isn't angry. At least, not only angry. Rather, when Veyadi lost his shrine to the Harbor, he saw in Sunai the last link to his greater work. The jackass who broke that archive is now his only lead. If Veyadi wants to recover any of the time, effort, and resources he poured into the distorted shrine, he needs Sunai. So, he's less than eager to sell him out to the Harbor—no matter how much leniency he'd earn for turning in a relic.

"I see," says Sunai. "You don't want to share me with your friends?"

Veyadi leans the slightest bit closer. The ghost of his breath brushes Sunai's mouth. "What I want," says Veyadi, each word trying to choke the next, "is for you to leave."

Sunai fails to respond.

"The second we get back to Ghamor, get gone." The heat from Veyadi's body can't cut the chill in Sunai's chest. "I'll make sure there's an opportunity."

Veyadi's fingers touch his cheek, like they did the night they first faced the shrine. When they fall away, Sunai tracks their absence, his gaze fixed where they land on Veyadi's thigh.

"Get out," Veyadi says. "Go live a life, anywhere but here."

"I don't know that I can." The words fall out of Sunai's mouth sans intent. Otherwise, he'd never dare burden anyone with a truth like that.

Veyadi's mouth quirks in a rare smile that is bare, wry, and completely unearned. "Sure you can."

With that, he stands.

Sunai tries to summon the courage to say something, anything. To call Veyadi brave or sweet, and see if that would make the doctor leave with him, at least for a while. He can't let Veyadi surrender to the Harbor; they won't ever give him back to himself. It's become clear that the Harbor didn't claim him kindly.

Then Veyadi says, "It'll go better for me if the Harbor doesn't know to ask about you."

There's not a goddamn thing Sunai can say to that. He's left alone with the ENGINE on the observation deck. He laughs again, laughs until he has to catch his breath, his chest tight with unwanted feeling.

He yearns to rebel, but he has no idea what that would look like, has forgotten how to commit himself to anything worth having. His wants are terminally shallow. This is what the letter warned of. The cost of his mistakes.

For a flash, desire burns hot in Sunai's chest. He inhales the chill to extinguish it.

An existential crisis of space, time, and your ejection from it.

The second time you die, you expect it to stick.

It is not long since you were remade, when you are more brave than clever, and when Imaru still trusts you. You and she have taken on two trucks full of indentured servants who require transport out of the Immaculate Empire border-state of Apo Il Gong. Your aim is the neighboring Apo Dun, which is about to be absorbed into independent AI-held Bastion, where indentured servitude is illegal and extradition has lately become politically unpopular. An imperial scout decides he has been insufficiently bribed and takes up his grievance with Imaru. He makes his complaint with that rarest of post-Cradle weaponry: a pistol. You interrupt the bullet's trajectory with your torso.

Imaru has no time to burn your body. She leaves it in the brush, a scant hundred feet off the road. The Apo wilds are all frigid wood—hard, dark, preserving. She means, I think, to come back.

Before she can, you wake under frozen leaves, eyes open to stars through thicket. You have never seen the night so clear, so near and empty and black. You shiver there, unready to move, until Cradle crosses the horizon, lunar glow etched in the cracks of its broken shell.

Unthinking, you shudder to your feet and limp down the hill to the road with pins and needles in your bad ankle, stomach sore where it had been open and wet, where it is now dry and closed.

You're cold as you walk, and it makes you wonder if you're truly yourself. An urgent pulse beats in your skull, thudding frantically out of time with the tempo in your chest.

You find Imaru by the light of her cigarette, alone in the dark with her grief and her guilt. She leans on the outside wall of a shabby teahouse at the edge of the downworld enclave where you planned to camp. At the sight of you, smeared with earth and blood, she comes unmoored. She takes you for a ghost, even as you accept her cigarette and inhale deeply beside her, not looking, not daring to think, hearing only the accursed sound of your heart beating ceaseless in your chest.

9

The Sovereign escorts the *Third Scrap* through the artificial badlands and past the Ghamori militia's handful of rigs, crewed by the smugglers and so forth to whom the Harbor delivers its usual choice: conscription, exile, or expedient execution. Onward, into the dusty brick thoroughfares of the trade and transport district. They aren't stopped by Harbor security; what more could the Harbor do to secure them? As Sunai packs and repacks his ruck, he sees neither hide nor hair of Veyadi.

This is extremely on purpose. If Sunai sees Veyadi, he'll falter. In telling Sunai to bolt, Veyadi gave up his chance to figure out his lost shrine. Sunai is queasy with guilt, and guilt makes him so goddamn stupid.

The engineer, whose name Sunai has already forgotten, has misinterpreted the situation. She hangs in the door to the crew quarters, asking Sunai to give Dr. Lut the benefit of the doubt. Sure he's a moody jackass, and yeah he's been in a sulk since they left the plateau, but he pays well, and he prefers a living crew over a successful run, and it's not like they're going *back* to that creepshow, and hey, is Sunai finished with that mag, and will he trade it for one of hers?

Sunai gives her the mag as the captain comes by with his pay: a satchel of barter tokens accepted in city-states across the northern stretch of the continent. Like Veyadi knows Sunai shouldn't go any farther south, lest the archipelago test his impulse control. Sunai stuffs the tokens to the bottom of his ruck alongside his copy of the Lay, where the letter used to live.

The second the *Scrap* folds down in the garage, Sunai hops

up from his bunk, shoulders his ruck, and sneaks out the foreleg-side service entrance.

The garage is one of several in the warehouse. It's bigger and cleaner than the average salvage-crew can afford; the ENGINE looming in the launch field outside won them preference. That means a stretch of uncluttered space between Sunai and the exit. It's fully exposed, but Veyadi is true to his word. No one's around to see him leave.

Sunai skirts the edge and puts as much service machinery as he can between himself and the view from the *Scrap*'s open cargo bay. He makes it all the way to the exit before someone stops him. He turns, wearing an indifferent scowl.

Jin throws a poncho over his shoulders and secures it with their arm. Waretu follows close behind, cheerfully carrying both of their rucks.

"Heard you're looking for another job," says Jin. "I've got a lead."

Sunai would flee, if they weren't in view of both the *Third Scrap* and the Sovereign. Jin has already drawn too much attention, and he knows they're capable of drawing more. Sunai lets them guide him into the bustling, smoggy street. They thread into a crowd of salvage-rats, peddlers, and traders, down the row of choice garages and around the corner to a lesser line of warehouses. Sunai eyes the alley between a dingy teahouse and lopsided hostel.

Jin squeezes his shoulder. "Don't run yet. Haven't even told you who the job's with."

Sunai's blood sludges. Jin keeps him moving, and Waretu pats his shoulder encouragingly.

"You *were* following me," says Sunai.

"Never said otherwise, did we?" says Jin. "We kept an eye on you. Kept you safe. Safe as we could, anyway. Didn't expect Doc's field trip to get *that* weird. Point being: we've got you. Come on. You're missed."

Though there's only one person who would send Sunai a letter signed with a sigil of the Lay, plenty others would track him down to punch his teeth in. Sunai doesn't know good people, or rather, none of the good ones talk to him anymore. Veyadi wasn't the first to notice that Sunai has too much traditional education for a refugee scout, and he's had worse years. Years when he was too willing to guide people through the wilds for purposes he'd rather not remember.

Unfortunately, those who dare the wilds for such vile business are more than willing to hunt itinerant scouts to the far edge of the continent. He has every reason to turn tail, but he can't yet. Better to saddle himself with bad work for mean folk than to catch the Harbor's attention and ruin Veyadi's sacrifice.

They take him to a shabby sparrow parlor adjacent to the scrapyard lane, where junked rigs go to be shredded, their parts melted down or repurposed. Jin releases him on the concrete stairwell leading to the entrance, which is closed. They expect Sunai to open the door to his own doom. Jerk.

Then it opens for him, and the person beyond it is so unexpected that for a moment, he stops thinking.

A lean, middle-aged Mohani woman leans on the doorframe, her handsome mouth slanting toward the gray at the temples of her close-shorn black hair. She's decked in the same sort of light road-wear she wore on the way out of Khuon Mo, the kind that says she considers being indoors an imposition.

Imaru.

She greets Sunai with a pat on the cheek and turns with the expectation that he'll follow. He does. He has never been able to resist her.

They pass the aunty at the till and a scatter of largely abandoned tables to ascend a winding flight of wooden stairs to a narrow second floor. Imaru remembers his pace, even though she hasn't had to keep it in over five years—since he left her.

He's reminded, then, of why it's been so long since they walked anywhere together. The last time he saw Imaru, she wanted to go back to Khuon Mo. The recollection pushes him out of mild awe at her presence into a distinct apprehension. As Imaru opens a door to a private room that probably started life as a supply closet, he catches the sleeve of her jacket.

"Are you dying?" he asks. "You have to tell me if you're dying."

Imaru turns on him with a curious frown. There's an intensity to her focus that makes women giggle and Sunai wary. "Not quickly. How about you?"

"Only as fast as I can manage."

Imaru snorts and her mouth twitches. Sunai remembers in a terrible rush that he adores her.

He lets her seat him at the spare table within, where an uncle brings them tea. A small, high window makes smoking bearable. Sunai extracts one of his last few cigarettes and offers it first to Imaru. She lights it, takes a drag, and offers it back. They share the cigarette in this familiar way as she pours dark tea and they take each other in.

"You look . . ." Imaru stops.

Sunai knows how he looks: just like he did five years ago, when he abandoned Imaru in the smoking ruins of Chom Dan. Just like he did when the two of them fled Khuon Mo together, much more than five years ago.

"Miserable and filthy," Sunai finishes. "I haven't bathed."

"The filth part of your disguise?"

"Until it rains. So you're not dying, but you sent a pair of mercs to kidnap me? What is this?"

"Jin's not a merc." Imaru smudges out the cigarette in a clay ashtray. "You get the letter?"

When Sunai grasps the question, he doesn't understand it. That damn letter, signed with the sigil of Leaf 36—that couldn't have come from Imaru. Could it?

"God's multifaceted ass," Imaru sighs, proving she can read him as well as she ever has. "What are you doing, accepting letters from Ruhi?"

"What are you doing reading my mail?"

"How do you think it reached you?"

They study each other, neither touching the tea. The last time they ran together, neither of them trusted Ruhi. So little else has changed. Why would that?

Imaru shrugs first. "Hard to avoid the man, working out of Khuon Mo. He heard I was looking for you. Asked me to deliver it."

Sunai lights another cigarette. He needs a reason not to look Imaru in the eye while he swallows sour anxiety spiked with jealousy. Of course Imaru and Ruhi cross paths back home; of course Sunai didn't know this, because of course, he doesn't see either of them; he has avoided Khuon Mo for seventeen years, Imaru for five, and Ruhi for nearly one.

Years ago, Sunai and Imaru met Ruhi when they were partners and he worked alone. Later, Ruhi found Sunai trekking through the wilds solo and not speaking of her.

Ruhi knows how to extract the thorns from Sunai's feelings better than anyone—he has the training, the instinct, the careful, unthreatening touch. Sometimes, as in the case of Imaru, that meant leaving the fullness of the emotion buried where no one had to look at it. He never did ask Sunai where Imaru went. Turns out he already knew.

Sunai has difficulty inhaling the next swell of nicotine. It would be better to stop thinking like this. "I suppose you didn't come here to play messenger," he says.

Imaru interlaces her fingers rather than reaching for the cigarette. "There's a job. In Khuon Mo."

"Oh. Then, no."

"The client needs people familiar with Iterate Fractal's tech. Ideally someone who knew the lighthouse shrine."

Pain radiates from Sunai's ankle as he presses his booted toes hard to the floor. "All right. Now you're being an asshole."

"Sunai." Did she always sound so old when she said his name like that? "The Harbor. They built the ENGINE."

Sunai cackles. Imaru draws back, eyes wide.

"Like hell they did." Sunai removes his specs to wipe his cheeks. "It doesn't take the Harbor seventeen years to build an ENGINE. They don't have what they need."

"I know." Imaru stares at Sunai as if he can ground her the way he used to. "Something changed. They found someone, or . . . People have seen things, Sunai. Something large patrolling the waters in the northern atolls—culling fragtech, demolishing corruption-ruins."

"That's nothing. Hearsay. If the Harbor had a new ENGINE, there'd be parades, press conferences, dick-waving ceremonies on par with an ascension to the Immaculate goddamn Pantheon—"

"I've seen it."

Sunai falls back in his seat, unaware he'd gotten out of it. Static roars in his head. He doesn't want it to be true, and he can forgive himself that. But Imaru says she's seen it, an ENGINE guarding Khuon Mo. Imaru says she's seen a dead god walking.

Sunai has long since stopped mourning Iterate Fractal, inasmuch as he can. But he's been dead seventeen years, dead certain Iterate Fractal is too. If it isn't—if the Harbor has forced breath back into its corrupted corpse . . .

The weight of the thought slips through his fingers. Iterate Fractal died, like Register Parse died. Sunai has stood on both their graves. Sometimes corruption leaves enough behind for scavengers to make a Sovereign. Sometimes it leaves nothing but a towering shrine, blackened by a fire long since burnt out.

But the remains of Iterate Fractal—those weren't nothing. Imaru saw them, when she cut Sunai out of the withered archival heart. Sunai has seen them since, in his dreams on the nights he fails to find oblivion. A year out, two, five, he was still preoccupied by the prospect of its resurrection. Now? Iterate Fractal is a ghost. His mind can't hold it.

"It's . . . I can't describe it," says Imaru.

"That's a very annoying thing to say."

"Ass. I'm trying." Imaru stands, but there's nowhere to go in the cramped room. Sunai is uncomfortably reminded of Veyadi's workshop. He occupies himself with the tea. A homely local blend, bitter with smoke and cinnamon. Oversteeped. Imaru presses her forehead to the window frame, eyes trained south. Toward the ocean. Toward Khuon Mo. "It's a demon."

Damn it, he believes her. He must. Imaru has never lied to him. Why would she start by making up something he hates?

"What's the job?" he asks his tea. He needs to know.

"Same one you've had for seventeen years. Keep a key component out of the Harbor's grasp. But seeing as they must've found another relic, we'll have to take away something different. Something even more vital. Iterate Fractal's archives."

Sunai wheezes. "Oh? Just slide in and grab the beating heart of their war machine?"

"It's possible. The Huntress died."

Sunai scoffs at the comparison. The Huntress was the Harbor's first ENGINE, the prototype born from the fallen Aigata Enclave. She rose from the enclave's ashes, a phalanx of brutal metal and brilliant circuitry, and with the lightning that poured from her fists, she fried the envoy of the imperial pantheon AI who sought to claim her citizens—the young Harbor's first critical success. She was their vanguard, carving out their space in the world, but decades of skirmishes with fragtech and the Immaculate Pantheon whittled her ranks down from nine to none, leaving behind a

single relic and no archives to speak of. It's *possible* to kill an EN-
GINE. "Possible isn't the problem."

"We have intel. We have means. As to how we do it—like
I said, we need your expertise. Your familiarity with the Lily
shrine."

"That's all?"

She nods; a promise.

Sunai groans and slumps back in his seat. His head thunks
into the wall and he jerks back, cursing. His vision doubles, like
it did in the shrine and on the plateau, as the Sovereign tore apart
that frag. He is in a dark corner of a sparrow parlor and—*under
a sunset sky.* He is choking on smoke and—*his throat is acrid with
salt air.* He is sitting—*standing*—falling—

*Oh dear. I do not mean to distract you, Sunai. Imaru is saying some-
thing quite important. You would be well served to listen closely.*

*In the meantime, I urge you to take care of yourself. I am as yet
unsure how to properly protect you from . . . myself.*

Sunai wards Imaru off with a rude gesture, but she catches his
skull to check him for bleeding. As if that matters! Her hand
is unbearable, real but not. In the back of his head, he hears—
music, someone singing in Mohani—

Imaru's hand tightens over his nape. Would she break his
neck, if she thought that would help Khuon Mo?

Too bad killing Sunai won't solve the problem he presents.
He shouldn't be so afraid of dying, of the weight of her fingers
over his spine or the air leaking out of his nostrils. He cringes,
huddling down.

Then her hand is gone. She backs away. He covers his nape
with both hands, breathing hard.

"I'm going," she says. "I don't expect you to come along."

"Yes, you do. You wouldn't have brought me here unless you were asking. You had me *followed*. For a month."

"You're right. You shouldn't come. It's selfish. If the Harbor . . . It's just that I trust you."

Sunai stops looking at even Imaru's knees. He can perfectly envision her tired shoulders, the tension in her face, and he hates being angry with her as much as he hates how readily that anger turns to shame.

"That doesn't matter. I'm sorry." Imaru's fingertips graze his forehead. He can't stop himself from watching the shadow of her fingers against the wall, hurt and curling away. "I know it's a bad idea. Even if the Harbor built the ENGINE without you . . . You shouldn't go anywhere near the damn thing. But I couldn't go without letting you know."

Despite everything she says, she wants him to go with her—to return to Khuon Mo, at her side, and to get close enough to touch the ENGINE of Iterate Fractal. To throw himself into the Harbor's gaping maw. It's bad math. The risk is too great. If the Harbor gets its hands on him, that's the end of anything she has left to care about.

The torn-up, discarded letter weighs heavy on Sunai's chest. Imaru ferried it to Ghamor, made sure it reached Sunai at his hostel. Did Ruhi know what she meant to ask him? He must have. It's why he logged his own ask first. *Going home. Try not to follow.* Coming from Ruhi, it was practically begging.

Fortunately, Sunai has just been reminded of what happens when he doesn't follow Ruhi's advice. He gets people killed when they don't have to die, decent people, thrown to the wolves in his place. He doesn't want to know what will happen to Imaru if he lets himself go with her. Especially if she wants him to. Devotion is a trap, when it comes to a relic.

"No," Sunai rasps. "You're right. I shouldn't go."

Imaru says nothing. He shuts his eyes against himself. There's only the red of his lids and the awareness of her, the sound of her breathing.

She leaves a box of cigarettes on the table, a street address scrawled inside the cover. In case he changes his mind. It's more grace than he ever afforded her.

10

Instinct leads Sunai to the teahouse where he met Veyadi. A series of discussions with rough acquaintances sends him to the crosstown tram, which sails over the grungy concrete garages and warehouses at Ghamor's edge. Here and there, the stains of old Ghamor flicker past—a patched marble wall built into its new structure or a city block arranged to fit the imprint of now-demolished architecture. As the tram arcs toward the city center these traces vanish, replaced by clean-cut concrete slabs and sheet glass.

The Sovereign reigns from her seats on the towering launch field in the middle of it all: multitiered and four-directional, with a separate hexagonal petal of mesh and steel for each of her four mechs. At the center towers the concrete monolith of the Harbor's headquarters.

Sunai passes through Harbor states, now and again. It would be more suspicious to avoid them. They mostly resemble each other, guided by the Harbor's foundational assumption that the world they inherited would love to kill them. Hence, the great big walls surrounding the innermost heart of the city, where three of So-Beloved's seven shrines used to stand.

He sometimes wonders how they rebuilt Khuon Mo. He could check a tourist brochure, but those allocate less page space to the Harbor's base than to the color of the sea and sky in the tropical archipelago. It's been so long since Sunai saw either hue that he can't lay claim to the memory of them.

Sunai gets off at the last station before the wall and skirts through an evening crowd of trim and well-kept folks, the sort who would never dream of waltzing into the wilds. He tidied himself before coming into the protected city center, though the braid gives him away as a flagrant hermit. It convinces most people not to study his face too long, lest they catch some of the Harbor attention coming his way.

He follows broad avenues to the glassy apartment building described by the teahouse regulars, which stands out from its neighbors on account of the surveillance team.

Sunai observes them sideways, from an alley, where he puts on a show of mulling over the options at a cup noodle vending machine. A straight-backed pair of sturdy folk idle in front of the well-lit pharmacy at the base of the skyscraper across the street. They wear plain clothes, but their close-cropped hair says military and their heavy boots say Harbor. Sunai rounds the corner with a can of warmed tea to find a sleek black car with tinted windows. They're not even trying to hide.

Why should they? So long as the Sovereign presides from her steel throne, Ghamor is a Harbor state. The better question is why her agents are lurking out here instead of storming the apartment building and making off with whoever they want.

No good answer for that. But Sunai is a predictable idiot, which is how he ends up bribing a courier two blocks away for her company cap and a bag of freshly butchered chicken.

A black-lacquered elevator takes him to the apartment he's after, one of only two on the twentieth floor. A white cardboard box sits against the door, stamped with a thick-lined green-and-orange logo of smiling vegetables. Sunai picks up the box to go with the chicken. He knocks with his feet, waits, and knocks again.

It takes Dr. Veyadi Lut a full minute to open the door. When he does, his hair drips into squinting, visorless eyes. He hasn't bothered to dress beyond a towel, and bruises bloom darkly across his ribs.

"Delivery," says Sunai.

"For who?"

"I didn't ask."

"If you killed the courier, you can't come in."

It takes ten excruciating seconds for Veyadi to move aside. Sunai enters holding the groceries. Every flat surface from shelf to table to floor is a clutter of books, tools, and open storage containers. Charts and bulletin boards plaster the walls, and the far corner is filled with a functional twin of Veyadi's rig workshop, now avec 3D printing array. The only order to be found is a dual row of potted plants blocking the glass doors to the balcony. The curtains are drawn. Sunai peeks past Veyadi's shoulder to the kitchen, where a whiteboard haphazardly covers the window.

"I'm shocked this is all it takes to fend off the Harbor," Sunai says.

"I'm under house arrest. Technically." Veyadi puts a table laden with tools between them. His naked eyes are wide, and paler than they seemed in the shadows of the plateau—bright brown, almost orange. A row of raised scars stipple the delicate skin between his eyes and temples. The marks of his prosthetic, or the reason he needs one?

Not Sunai's business. He makes for the plants.

"You shouldn't be here," says Veyadi. "The Harbor is— you're—I told you to run. How did you even find me?"

Sunai skims his fingers over tame little leaves. He can name every one of them. "Got some tips from the teahouse. *You* chose to be a regular. Oh good, coriander." He plucks some basil as well, then picks through Veyadi's mess to the kitchen. The stovetop is resplendent with yet more books. Sunai deposits the produce box in the sink and sets to work cleaning counter space.

Veyadi fails to follow, choosing to vanish into a back room. That could be a problem, if he's decided he prefers the Harbor over whatever he imagines Sunai's come to do. Especially if he's gone to find a bludgeoning device. What a way to ruin the mood!

But the Veyadi who manifests in the kitchen doorway has the same self-preservation instinct as the Veyadi who tried to shield Sunai from a rampaging frag. He pulls on a shirt as he enters— constricting his arms, blocking line of sight—and he's found sweatpants. In the wilds he possessed a rugged poise, but having rejoined civilization, he's lost all grasp on character. His visor is back in place, though he has no weapon to speak of.

"I don't think I want you near the knives," Veyadi says, nevertheless.

"What, these?" Sunai taps the counter with a chef's knife he found in a drawer stuffed with loose kitchen utensils and pens. "I don't expect this to cut a peach. What kind of pervert buys ingredients he has no means to cook?"

Veyadi pulls an onion out of the friendly vegetable box and begins to peel it like an orange.

"If you bite that, I'm going to push you off your fancy balcony."

Veyadi leaves the peeled onion on the cutting board Sunai wrangled from under a stack of books on salvage conversion. "Don't give the Harbor another reason to come for you."

Sunai takes over excavating the vegetable box, as flustered as if he'd been caught in a lie.

"Why are you here, Sunai?"

"Because you're an archivist." Sunai faces Veyadi, dual-wielding garlic and galangal. "Because you were looking for something at that shrine, but you would rather lose it forever than hand it to the Harbor."

Veyadi crosses his arms, his back to the stove, as cramped by his kitchen as by his workshop on the *Scrap*. Quiet. Frowning.

"I don't know how to feel like that. I wish I did." Sunai drops the garlic and galangal into a bowl with the onion, coriander, and basil. As he unwraps the chicken, the words come out one by one, unfolding around the raw flesh of his truth. "I ran, Adi.

I tried. But divine convergence, am I right? I met an old friend. She had a job for me. In Khuon Mo. I said no." Sunai examines the expert butchering and imagines a fine edge cutting around his secrets like spoiled meat. "But I owe her a yes. I need to know how you do it. How you believe something hard enough to just *do* the thing you have to. No matter what you lose. No matter who gets hurt."

Sunai recognizes the tense line of Veyadi's shoulders; he last saw it on the plateau before the distorted shrine. A man of faith, ashamed of his belief, yet unyielding. "You're making a lot of assumptions about my moral character."

"Really?" Sunai brandishes a pan to clear Veyadi away from the stove. "You financed a whole damn rig and risked your life to hunt down an AI that I—" Sunai's throat closes as he fiddles with the needlessly complicated stovetop controls. Vulnerability wasn't his strong suit even before it threatened the lives of the people he cares about. "That I screwed you out of. You could have recovered part of it. It . . . I . . . We interfaced. You *knew*! But you still told me to run."

"I did tell you, and you *didn't* run. Sunai . . . The Harbor's not your only problem."

Veyadi exhales, shaken by the effort to contain himself. Sunai does him the courtesy of not turning around as he pours oil into the pan and tends it with a spatula.

"Fuck me," Veyadi breathes. "If I'm anything like you think I am, you should have run from *me*."

"Oh?" There's jarred southern-style chili sauce in the fridge, and a tragic assortment of protein shakes. "Why's that?"

"Are you listening? I want to dissect you. I want to know what the hell made that archive choose you. I want to know what it *did*. I want—" He cuts off. Sunai has to maneuver around him to get the rest of the ingredients; Veyadi is biting his knuckle.

Sunai tips aromatics into the pan. "Okay. Do it."

There is a silence, then a small, incredulous, "What?"

Sunai shrugs. In goes the chicken. "Take me apart. Or if you're squeamish, call the Harbor. They'll do it for you, free of charge."

"I'm not—no. Sunai."

Sunai turns, spatula pointed at Veyadi's nose. "There. See? What are you going to do to me that I don't ask for? God's multifaceted ass, listen to yourself."

Veyadi relents, exhausted. He stews as Sunai finishes off the stir-fry with vegetables and chili sauce, except for when Sunai burns his thumb on the silver edge of a practically new pan. Though he would never normally notice such a minor injury, he swoons with—*bright sunlight multiplied off waves, and humidity baking into his pores, and*—and is steadied by Veyadi, who smells of lemon shampoo. Sunai says, to cover, "Well, I guess I'm hungry, too."

Veyadi's brow creases, and Sunai recruits him to debate over a couple of expired microwaveable rice packets that ultimately pass the sniff test, which Veyadi does with a taut sulk. By the time Sunai slides him a bowl of depressingly chewy rice and passable chili-chicken, Veyadi has retrieved a facsimile of the impassivity he wore that first night at Sunai's fire in the crook of the *Scrap*'s foreleg. He doesn't take his bowl until Sunai pushes it into his hands. Sunai threads through the choked living room with his own, past the plants to the curtained balcony. He struggles one-handed with the door, which has gummed shut with disuse, until Veyadi pushes it more firmly closed.

"We shouldn't go out there. The Harbor's watching."

"Let them. You have a real dinner, they have vending machine soup."

"Sunai. They can't know you're here."

Sunai spreads his arms. "You think they didn't see the hermit delivery boy go into your apartment and fail to emerge? They already know. They didn't recognize me, or I wouldn't have made it up. They'll figure you threw a tantrum and seduced the help."

Veyadi scowls, but he shows Sunai how to lift the balcony door from under the handle, then joins him on the floor outside. He picks through his bowl as he says, "I'm not an archivist, you know."

"No?"

"No. I . . . Well. Iterate Fractal chose me for an apprenticeship. But I hadn't even started training when corruption hit. Too young. An archivist—a real one—brought me to Chom Dan with some of the other apprentices. She did her best. No good at teaching. Most of my autonomist training was under Register Parse."

His searching look expects a similar admission, something that could explain how Sunai knows the names of pre-Cradle fragtech, or how he came by his familiarity with NT principles when he looks as young and Mohani as he does. People who look like Sunai rarely get access to the kinds of things he knows.

Part of Sunai craves a chance to explain. He keeps the Lay close; he misses arguing the interpretation of Leaves; there was a time, between meeting his first archivist and Iterate Fractal's corruption, when his affection for that life was nearly uncomplicated. He opens his mouth; he isn't ready; he says instead, "Same difference."

Veyadi's expression curdles. "It isn't. I know archivists. My friend, the one I wanted to bring to the shrine, he'd just been raised out of apprenticeship when Iterate Fractal corrupted, and even he . . . He understands people, and they sense that instantly. So they trust him. Tell him things before he asks. I never learned to do that, not even close."

Sunai is too chilled to counter. He also knows an archivist who can eke secrets out of the most tight-lipped mouths. The skill isn't as universal as Veyadi imagines. This archivist was also in Chom Dan. He's been everywhere. These days, he's based in Khuon Mo.

Divine fucking convergence.

Sunai stuffs his mouth with chilied vegetables. He chews for so long that Veyadi puts a hand on his knee. It is terribly warm against the cold Ghamor night and the bubbling nausea in Sunai's gut. Funny how this man thinks himself insensitive, unpersonable. Funny how Sunai thinks it's okay to leave the hand there. To want the hand elsewhere, still.

A little late for regrets. The whole situation has careened past "oops." But divine convergence, right? Sunai is as faithful as someone personally ghosted by space-time can be, and if Veyadi is the intersection of happenstance he has luckily tripped over, it would be nigh blasphemous not to act. "Adi," he says, "they've never had an ENGINE in Khuon Mo. Could they now?"

Veyadi coughs on chili. His anxious grimace says it all.

"Goddamn it." Sunai sags against the cold glass of Veyadi's temperamental balcony door. "How, though?"

"An ENGINE needs an archive and a relic. The archive to shape and power it. The relic to make it coherent and give it direction. So long as you have both—"

"You know that's not what I'm asking. The Harbor's had Khuon Mo for like twenty years—they've had *Iterate Fractal* for twenty years. But they never made an ENGINE. They would if they could, so if they didn't, they *couldn't*. If they've got it now, then something's changed. *What?*"

The cold light of Ghamor reflects in Veyadi's chitinous visor, and he stares hard at the gap between the buildings across the way—southward. His apartment faces the distant southern sea. Veyadi looks toward Khuon Mo, just like Imaru.

That shouldn't surprise Sunai. Veyadi's an archivist, or as close to one as anyone can be since Iterate Fractal's corruption. The Harbor has him holed up in frigid Ghamor, about as far away as you can get from Khuon Mo, but they can't take it from his mind.

"Adi, in all the time the Harbor's been crawling up your ass, have they said anything? About Iterate—"

"I understand there were failures." Veyadi looks as sick as Sunai's ever seen him. He clutches the bowl in his lap. "I hadn't heard . . ."

"That they did it? Fixed what was going wrong?"

Veyadi's jaw clenches vise tight.

Sunai groans and slides the rest of the way down the glass, until his back is flat on Veyadi's neglected balcony. He knew they'd built the ENGINE the second Imaru told him. It was never a problem of disbelief. He came to Veyadi not to prove that fact, but to see another angle of reality. To leave himself less room to run. Here on the balcony, grimy and tangible and *real,* more real than Sunai often feels, he shoves up his specs and throws his arm over his eyes so he can, for a moment, just be. "I have to do it, don't I?"

"What are you talking about? Do what?"

"Go home. Duh." Sunai wrinkles his nose. "Take their EN-GINE away."

"When you say take it away, do you mean . . ."

"What do you think?"

Sunai receives a perfectly reasonable silence. ENGINEs don't fall to human hands. Even the Huntress's death was the work of Immaculate Pantheon envoy mechs, not any mortal action.

"You're crazy," says Veyadi.

"Oh, like you aren't."

"Fuck you."

He is, though. Crazy like the wounded and sad and driven often are. Like Sunai is, and all the people who dare get on rigs. Both their brains are riddled with scars earned by enduring the faithless whim of the universe, hopped up on their ill-advised impulse to survive.

"Sunai." Veyadi pulls Sunai's arm away to see his expression. Distress is written on his visored face. "Whatever this is, whoever you're talking to—*you* shouldn't do this."

Sunai laughs off the nerves. "Who else could?"

Veyadi's mouth twists. Sunai inhales to protest; he isn't fast enough.

"Then you shouldn't go alone." Veyadi's hand wraps more firmly around his own. "Take me."

"Aren't you under house arrest?" Sunai asks. It's easier to joke than to accept his upended stomach. "This doesn't sound like your best move, Dr. Lut."

Veyadi rubs his chitin-covered temple, like he's about to remove that visor again. Or calculating whether he can scream loud enough for the car twenty stories below to hear. Or—his jaw hardens. "It is." He says this like a promise.

Ah, thinks Sunai. Ah, I see.

Veyadi is riled. Sure. The Harbor's made an ENGINE from the bones of his god. But he's known they were up to no good with Iterate Fractal's remains for a while now. His new want, his new calling, is *Sunai*, whom he needs to unpack lest he lose the truth of the shrine Sunai cheated him out of.

A part of Sunai wants that too—to be unmade at the molecular level. The rest of him is all fear, all doubt, and it will fight tooth and nail to keep its secrets. It remembers that the last time he gave himself to another person, he only handed them poison.

The letter would have reminded him. But it's gone now, mealy bits scattered over the plateau of a darkened shrine.

Veyadi puts out his hand. It makes Sunai a real dick to take it.

I cannot say I understand this decision, Sunai.

Ah, I apologize for the turn of phrase. I believe I do understand. I have been watching you repel intimacy even as you seek it. Self-sabotage, I believe you would call it. So, I do understand. I simply do not approve.

I am concerned about this Veyadi Lut. It is not that I do not care for him. He is inquisitive, unassuming, and these are traits I often adore. He has shown you some modicum of kindness. He does not seem to want to betray you.

But I worry, Sunai. If there is anyone to blame for the fact of my abduction, it is not you, but him. He was first to steal into my corridors after my long solitude, and I did not begrudge him this. How could I? My doors must open for those who wish to pass through them. But I was not meant to leave. For that, I cannot trust him. I fear you should not either.

11

Sunai leaves Veyadi's apartment alone. Two hours later, he returns with a crew of hermits and widows, all dressed like they tumbled out of a teahouse. Most of them did. Some carry coolers, others grocery bags or substantial purses. A familiar long-limbed, third-gender menace lingers at the door with Sunai, grinning from ear to ear as they survey Veyadi's apartment.

"So this is where your weirdo lives," says Jin. "All right, go get dressed."

They hand Sunai one of a pair of worn red jumpsuits. The other goes to Veyadi, who is positively twitchy at the sight of Jin.

"I thought you went to meet a friend," he says to Sunai.

"I'm his friend," says Jin.

"You're an edge case," says Sunai. To Veyadi, he says, "They're helping. Show this handsome widow your closet."

The widow in question is broad and short in the way Veyadi is, though in contrast to his humble stay-at-home chic, she sports an elaborately embroidered red silk coat. She introduces herself as Eun and flashes a smile that would give Imaru a taste of her own medicine. Veyadi tries and fails to return the favor, his bared teeth more rictus grin, before he leads Eun to his bedroom.

An older hermit with a keen eye and an elaborate braid finds Sunai in the hallway after he changes in the bathroom. He introduces himself as Moto, and he has a warning.

"I let the doctor pick me up once," says Moto, casting a sideways eye at the living room. "This isn't the first time I've seen him mixed up with the Harbor." He pats Sunai's cheek. "Be careful. Next to him, you'll always be the better target."

Sunai decides to put Moto in charge of the rucks. Moto takes Sunai's with stoic aplomb. "Shower before you leave."

"Enh." Sunai tucks his braid under a janitorial cap. "Verisimilitude."

In the living room, Veyadi is telling Eun which plants not to water. Eun is decked out in more of Veyadi's uninspired home wear, while Veyadi wears the same drab city management gear as Sunai. The rest of the hermits and widows have gone to work emptying the contents of Sunai's and Veyadi's rucks into coolers, purses, and garbage bags.

"How much do I owe them?" Veyadi asks under his breath while Sunai grudgingly pockets a few protein bars for the road.

"Owe who?" asks Sunai. "You mean the bug-out crew? Nothing."

"I find that hard to believe."

"Well, I guess you don't have to *believe*."

Veyadi takes the criticism with grim self-reproach. "I suppose I don't know a lot of worthwhile people."

"High praise." Sunai pauses in the midst of contemplating the life span of the jar of chili sauce to wave away Veyadi's ever-deepening frown. "Don't read into it. Sometimes people need to get away from the Harbor. Everyone knows that. You just have to find the folks willing to make it happen."

"Still sounds like something I should be paying for."

Back when Sunai worked with Imaru, they never took more payment than food, shelter, and repairs for the truck. Imaru said it kept them honest. Ensured they chose the clients who truly needed them. She must have known the flaw in her logic. Between her drive and Sunai's willingness to throw himself at whatever got in her way, the right funds would have let them become more than a two-body buoy in corruption's never-ending tide of refugees. But resources are power, which Imaru fears

misusing. It makes her one of the most worthwhile people Sunai knows.

The other worthwhile person never took payment either. But
then, he had a patron. Sunai bites the inside of his lip until he tastes
copper and his head roils.

He is—*climbing stairs into a burst of warmth barely touched by
the lazy swing of ceiling fans*—which dizzies him even though he's
standing still. As he stumbles—*a burst of throaty rasping laughter
around a table by white-bright windows*—echoes against the thrum
of laughter from the living room.

Sunai's palm skids on the counter. Veyadi catches and settles
him into a plastic chair. He feels Sunai's forehead, checks his pulse.

"I'm being an ass," he says. "You've been on your feet all
night."

"I'm fine." Sunai is too tired to mask the cringe when Veyadi
presses fingers to his throat.

Veyadi's right. He's pushing himself, and his corruption
doesn't spare him from exhaustion. It's certainly never done anything so useful as to tamp down hallucinations induced by stress,
trauma, or truly objectionable quantities of the right sort of drug.

But if he thinks too hard about why he'd rather be moving,
he forgets how to breathe right.

Unfortunately, Veyadi's hands remain compassionately, neu-
rotically, painfully close to his neck, which makes his brain flirt
with anxieties he needs to avoid until they're at least a day out
of Ghamor.

Too late. The fear hooks into Sunai's skin, lifting his hand as
if on a puppet string to lay flat on Veyadi's visor, making space.
His fingers rest on the edge. "You know," he says, "if you want to
get out of here, you're going to have to shuck this."

Veyadi is silent as a sunken thing; his fingers remain at Sunai's
throat. Sunai wants to shield himself, but he can't bring his hand
away from Veyadi's visor. He could tear it away.

"Listen, Adi," he hears himself whisper, "you don't have to come."

Veyadi's mouth thins. Sunai startles as the hand leaves his neck, and Veyadi removes his visor with determined deliberation. With his head outlined by the glare of fluorescent kitchen lights, it's impossible to tell anything about his eyes—what *is* that color?—other than that they never flick away, though Sunai could swear it's been whole seconds—

"If I'm here any longer, I'm going to steal literally everything in this place," says Jin from the kitchen doorway. "You ready, kids?"

"Yes." Veyadi vanishes his visor into a pocket of his maintenance suit, and that's the last he'll say on it.

They leave the apartment with opera-house thumping from the balcony, Eun a beer-holding silhouette by the curtain. They should be thankful that the black car and the stoic pharmacy guards are too obvious to be a real surveillance team. The Harbor just wanted Veyadi convinced he shouldn't attempt to escape.

It concerns Sunai that this means the Harbor didn't expect the doctor to have friends.

———

Faint predawn light purples the alley between a refugee odd-job guild and the teahouse that caters to them, where they pile out of the maintenance van. Sunai and Veyadi's rucks await their owners in a collection of coolers stacked by the teahouse's back-alley kitchen door. From there they leg it to the trade and transport district, their breath white in the easing dark. The garages seethe with unexpected life at this early hour. Sunai's nerves call it a problem, and he keeps Veyadi between himself and Jin.

Imaru's garage is lit like its neighbors, amber light sliding under the corrugated slats of its walls. She crosses the floor to meet them before they're through the door. Her sleepless eyes are shadowed, but her stride is all confidence, and the hand she clasps to Sunai's is firm.

"Bit slow," she says.

"Don't sass me in front of the client." Sunai steps back to make room for Veyadi. "Dr. Lut, your dashing escort, Imaru."

Veyadi stands rigid under Imaru's idle scrutiny, his gloved hands tight on his ruck straps.

"I hear you're clever," says Imaru.

"I'm—yes." Veyadi straightens, eyes ever so slightly widened. Imaru often inspires that look. People always want to impress or to fight her.

"And you know it." She laughs. "I don't mind that."

"I mind that you look awful," Sunai says to her on the way up the rig. "Didn't you sleep?"

Imaru gives him a *What was that about sass?* brow raise and he gives her a *You earned it* nose wrinkle.

"Too much to do," she says.

Imaru named her rig the *Never Once,* and it's a slender, sinuous beast, built to slither on land and thrive in water. Ghamor gets its water from a pair of mountain rivers that meet in a basin north of the city and snake to the western sea, but amphibious rigs are rare in this inland part of the world. The *Never Once* is still under construction, nearly finished but missing armor on the upper deck and forward hull.

Two of the *Never*'s crew are patching the lower deck with temporary cladding. One—a long-braided youth shorter than Sunai—tracks the new arrivals with sharp eyes, a soldering tool sparking in their hand. They say something out the corner of their mouth to the boulder of a man kneeling beside them, who lets out a laugh that sounds like an apology.

Jin's lips peel into a grin and they gesture rudely. They make to go over, but Waretu whistles down from the deck, drumming freshly manicured nails on the railing. "You wouldn't leave this poor aunty to run pre-checks on her own, would you?"

Jin sighs explosively and allows themself to be dragged inside. Imaru beckons Sunai and Veyadi to follow.

"We leaving?" asks Sunai. "You got clearance fast."

"We called in a favor," says Imaru.

"Big favor."

"Oh, it was," Waretu sings back, "but I'm very popular."

"And we all strive to impress," says Imaru.

Waretu puts a hand to her chest and winks before she and Jin disappear to the navigator's nook. Imaru's about to escort Sunai and Veyadi in the same direction when one of the crew on deck calls out: "Could use another pair of eyes on the hydraulics."

Veyadi tentatively shrugs his ruck in Imaru's direction. She accepts it and nods him toward the deck, where the boulderish fellow welcomes Veyadi with due enthusiasm.

"Putting my client straight to work, huh?" Sunai asks Imaru in the rig corridor.

"He seemed nervous. Nervous folk need work." The look she sends over her shoulder reminds him who taught her as much. Imaru used to leave the people problems to Sunai. She pauses at the first bunk, nearest the galley, to glance his way again. "I wasn't sure you'd come."

Sunai's instinct is to shrug off her sincerity, but he finds himself silent as he deposits his ruck in the bunk she indicates—across from hers, the only other in the room. "Sorry. Didn't mean to present the doctor as an ultimatum."

Imaru contemplates Veyadi's ruck in her arms. "Jin vouched for him."

"Do we trust Jin's judgment?"

"They're picky." Her wry smile tweaks down. "They like you too."

"Is that a problem?"

She hefts the ruck into one arm so she can lay fingers on his elbow. It's the old signal, the one they settled on when it stopped sounding true to say that they had been the same age when they left Khuon Mo. "Just be careful."

"Yes, aunty."

Imaru's next look promises, *I'm going to throw you off the rig.* He kisses her cheek to hide the sour tang under his tongue. At some point, he has to admit what Veyadi knows. If all goes well, she'll trust the doctor by then.

Some nagging recollection gives him pause. Just how did Veyadi come to realize what he'd taken to bed? It isn't like Sunai sprawled himself across Veyadi's worktable and declared: Behold! Your new project!

There's no time to chase down the thought. For the next hour and change, everyone's preoccupied with the basic work of launch prep. Sunai's off once he's properly stowed his ruck, shunted from one end of the *Never Once* to the other as he learns its shape and eccentricities.

The pilot is Oyu: small, dark, and sharp-eyed. The license they rattle off to the dispatcher claims that the *Never Once* has been under Imaru's watch for a decade, originating in Elanu Tha. Unless Imaru was hiding the *Never* in the bed of her truck, Sunai knows this for a lie.

"So did you mash three junkers together until they produced this thing?" Sunai asks Cothai, the affable engineer. "Seems like it'd be less expensive to commission a new one from scratch."

Cothai scratches the back of his head, ruefully tongue-tied. "It had to look old."

No time for further explanation. Cothai has Veyadi tweaking the hydraulics; Sunai passes close behind him to check on the midsection coolant system, about which Cothai has concerns. Once that's settled—one small leak and another larger, both of which Cothai seals with industrial duct tape—Sunai's back to Waretu's navigator nook to confirm their place in the convoy.

"Who's the bank?" he asks on his way out her door.

She waves him off without looking up from her charts. "Oh, Sunai. Do you like your lovely fingers? Then don't ask."

Jin he meets on deck, where they've taken over the cladding work in the pink-tinged gray of morning. He offers them a cigarette as they pause to massage their cheeks against the wind. "What's this for?" they ask.

"The honor of your good word."

They grin and cuff his knee. "You want to know why I think it was worth it to kidnap a Harbor autonomist."

"I mean, you could have done it for funsies."

"Or maybe I wanted you to owe me a favor."

Sunai leaves them with a shoulder flick and climbs to the observation deck. There, it becomes difficult to ruminate on anything but what's in front of him, which is to say, five trapezoidal stories of formidable white-steel plating that is their Harbor transport. It glides too smoothly across the blackened earth of the badlands, surrounded by its milling herd of heaving animalistic rigs.

It's almost—*almost*—worse than the Sovereign. Not the mech they got to know in the Dahani peaks, but an identical sister. She moves with an eerie echo of her sister's uncanny grace; the size of her crimson limbs demands a weight that her stride defies. Every glimpse of the crimson frame underlying her marbled bulk reminds Sunai of how her sibling wrenched the crystalline frag's arms from its torso.

It is all wondrously shitty, and it explains how they got out so quick. The best way to sneak out of Harbor cities is in the Harbor's shadow. Whatever they're shipping in this convoy, it requires an escort. How convenient that it needed to go today. Divine convergence, at it again.

As the sun slides higher and the convoy settles into formation, Sunai lets his eye travel, watching for any deviations that might predict a problem. An hour into his vigil, Veyadi and Cothai emerge onto the deck to help Jin with the patching. Cothai claps Veyadi on the back as they approach, and Jin says something that makes him laugh.

Veyadi shields his eyes against the bright clear sky to peer at the Harbor transport. He hasn't yet recovered his visor. He shouldn't, so long as they're with the convoy; the chitin would give him away immediately. It's frankly dubious to bring him out here at all. Sunai's about to signal him back inside when Veyadi turns.

They're separated by twenty meters—too far for meaningful eye contact. Yet a shocking certainty finds purchase in Sunai's chest. As he sees, he is *seen* in turn. Veyadi's curdled posture speaks to his sleepless night, but beneath it writhes a many-featured beast of savage tension. The doctor is profoundly exposed.

He asked to be, and Sunai permitted it.

It's too late, he realizes. He made a mistake letting Veyadi come, and even if he sends him away now, the damage is already done.

Sometimes you don't get to go back to being who you were. Sometimes, the changes kill you.

For all that Veyadi Lut hires rigs to ferry him to the edge of the wilds in pursuit of impossible shrines, he's a citizen, a man of apartments cluttered with *stuff,* a man of property who imagines credit can absolve any transgression. It doesn't occur to him that sometimes a person transgresses by daring to be alive. This is a chronic archivist flaw. They cling to the notion of their intrinsic worth to justify surviving where their fellow refugees don't. They forget that their value isn't theirs to determine.

But Veyadi has broken his covenant with the Harbor. It's only a matter of time before the Harbor un-persons him too. That will be the moment he no longer recognizes himself. Every ideal he once held dear will wither on the vine.

Foul memory makes Sunai waver, hand rising to his neck. Down on the lower deck, Veyadi's hand rises too. He presses it to his throat as if to mirror Sunai.

Abruptly Veyadi breaks away. Sunai inhales sharply, disoriented. He is palpably aware of Veyadi striding across the deck, making a beeline for the *Never*'s interior, ignoring Cothai and Jin as they call after him.

Veyadi's speed compels Sunai to lurch upright as well. As he does, he takes a wrong step on his bad ankle—too fast, too hard. He is dizzy, hurting, in want of more and better air, and—

—he inhales something cleaner, all salt and the faint sweetness of decay: never clean, unadorned. Yet when he steps into the cavernous shadow of the once-was tree, its long-dead embrace offers no more relief than a desecrated grave. Nor is he relieved as he hands his delivery to the old woman who meets him, her smile a knife, her tilted head revealing the scars gnarled up her neck. The demure gesture of the hand with which she receives his delivery exposes the interior of her well-tailored sleeve, where yellow thread trails into delicate blooms—

A tremendous clang pitches Sunai backward. His attention jerks toward the upper stretch of the Harbor transport looming beside the *Never Once*. A section of the transport's plating juts outward from the hull with an impression of force and intent, like an enormous finger stabbed out of it from within.

Another punctuation of force on metal—from *within the transport,* what the hell, what the hell—is followed by another and another as the thing inside batters its way *out* because it's been *trapped*—

Sunai doesn't remember going down the ladder from the observation deck. He is only conscious of another body hauling him down. Now they push him toward a door into the *Never.*

"Stay inside," Imaru says.

Sunai obeys her less on purpose than because of forward momentum. The horrible hammering continues as he stumbles into the rig's main corridor, arrhythmic against the thunder of the ENGINE's approach across the badlands, and against the throbbing within his skull.

Sunai shivers on the molecular level and crouches against the nearest wall. He thinks—it's as if—

—he has experienced only darkness and dismemberment, sense fractured even further than it has been for these long and lonely years. But now he strains and reaches for a brilliance, sharp and manifold, which he prays will offer succor, some semblance of sameness.

His disjointed fingers peel burst metal to reveal greater space and freedom, wind gliding through the gaps in his chassis, tangling in his wires.

As his fingers spread freely in the air and light, they meet a face. Its features are familiar, crimson metal and gold lips, etched with pearl. It is a mockery, an alien, an impassive expression that could never be mistaken for alive—

Ah, I thought that was you, Sunai. How is it that you keep doing this?

It is no matter. I will put an end to it, and endeavor to better protect you in the future.

Sunai's thoughts echo and overlap. Words flow through his mind, their sounds clear but their *meaning* maddeningly out of reach. The language is unfathomably divorced from the impulse and desire that should define it.

Someone grasps his shoulders, and he seizes their forearms to ground himself in the sensation of those foreign hands, the vibration of the rig against his back and under his seat, the nauseated heat in his gut.

Metal crashes and shrills. Violence leaks into the *Never Once* from beyond its hull, out of sight. Yet vivid imagery melts into Sunai's forebrain: the white plating of the Harbor transport, burst open like a punctured boil; the nightmare erupting out, a jangle of mismatched parts; the scintillating crystal hand groping for freedom, attached to a familiar patchwork limb; the Sovereign's face, brutish in its solemnity, as it seizes the scrabbling arm by its grasping palm. For a surreal minute, they wrestle like salvage-rats—

Please, Sunai. I am doing my best.

He gasps free of the cloud of images but is unable to focus. The air struggles into his lungs until someone says: "Slower. Longer. Through your nose."

Veyadi. He speaks with the assured calm Sunai turned on him during his panic attack in Chom Dan, which is as hilarious as it is terrifying.

"Breathe," Veyadi says.

"I can't," Sunai pleads.

"Just try."

It takes a long, awful minute to ease out of hyperventilation. Veyadi's hands remain on his shoulders, away from his neck; even when they shift to take his pulse, Veyadi measures it in his wrist. Sunai must, with great urgency, attend to absolutely anything except this tender regard.

He latches first onto the relative quiet. A rig is never silent, full of whir and hiss, thud and creak, but right now, that's all. No boom, no nearby screeching muddled by the hull. The fight outside has ended, if you could call it that. More a last flail on the part of the dismembered frag the Harbor's hauling out of Ghamor—

"Oh," he says, "it's our friend."

It makes sense. The Harbor doesn't harvest frags for salvage, so they use the bodies as trading fodder. That does involve ship-ping the damn things off.

Veyadi frowns. "What are you talking about?"

The crystal hand, the patchwork arm, Sunai saw them so clearly. Yet he was inside the *Never* by the time the transport burst—if it did. More likely, his panicked brain frenetically col-laged his tattered memories into an explanation for the chaos.

Except that before his brain flung itself into full-blown hallu-cinogenic panic, it teetered on the edge of a different meltdown. For a moment, Veyadi looked like much more than a man.

All the more reason to turn away the doctor's touch.

Sunai is sliding his hand free of Veyadi's grasp when some-thing blocks the light from the door to the outside. Imaru stands backlit by the hazy morning sky, her sharp frown just visible in the shadow of her face. She's fixed on Veyadi. Only now does Sunai register that Veyadi has recovered his chitinous visor—he must have fled into the rig to retrieve it. The black planes refract Imaru's burrowing stare between the gold-lined cracks, and un-der her scrutiny, Veyadi's hand hardens around Sunai's wrist.

Sunai suspects one of them is about to bite the other. Neither option pleases.

"Hey," he starts.

"What're we looking at?" Jin finishes. They sail in from the deck to sling an arm around Imaru's stiff shoulders, and they ap-praise Sunai and Veyadi as they would an underwhelming pair of street performers. "Whatever this is can wait. Waretu got the call from the Harbor. They want 'volunteers' to repair their trans-port. Bet they're about to requisition half our parts. Come on, weirdos, let's get hopping."

Imaru tenses at the presumption, but she doesn't counter-mand them. The Harbor's incoming demands paper over any friction. Imaru sends Cothai to the transport, seeing as his en-gineering license is both legitimate and up-to-date. Veyadi she assigns to the back end of the rig, to diagnose a blockage in the ventilation system. Sunai shoos him off with assurances—he's fine, all limbs attached and functioning as desired—and tries not to exit the doctor's orbit too eagerly. Veyadi refuses to relinquish his frown as he descends the ladder out of sight.

Imaru watches him go, her frame taut. Even when it's just her and Sunai in the galley as he cobbles up a lunch for the crew and she reassesses their wounded ledger, she neglects to explain what's bothering her.

She'll come around with space and time. In order to give those to her, Sunai emerges on deck a few hours later to take over the cladding work from Jin. He pauses as the wounded Harbor transport comes into view.

It has a beauty, inasmuch as all things that gather sunlight are beautiful, and in the sense that the pristine becomes intriguing once marred. But more than that, the hole rent into the side of the transport is . . . familiar. Uncanny, the degree to which Sunai recognizes its jagged edge. Unwanted, the way he remembers the metal slicing into his fingers.

***The time between, when you
thought you might also grow.***

Iterate Fractal believes in calluses and scars. Thus the compounds of Khuon Mo operate on the sweat of their cells—the bodies assigned to live and serve within their walls—and every citizen labors to tend gardens, mind beasts, and make their home breathe. The apprentice compound on Lotus is a place of preparation, of joining and becoming. Every year, Iterate Fractal chooses a new cohort of Mohani children to train as archivists, separating them from the compounds that raised them, and brings them here, to Lotus. Many children cry. You have long since tired of doing so.

Here, you till, you seed, you weed and harvest. You cook, you clean, you repair and mend. You read, you sing, you learn the Lay, and you bear the failings of your fellows. You all take your turn at listening, the archivist's most vital chore. This too is a chance to learn: how to give succor and guide the heart when it has floundered.

Here, you fail. A callous child, insensitive to human frailties, quick to judge, quicker to act. You are asked to explain your decision to drop a winter melon on the head of a peer: "Iterate Fractal knows."

But here, you fail again. The point of the lesson is not justice, but responsibility. The fact that the power to act lies in your grasp is not reason enough to use it.

"He'll do it again," you say.

"So," says the archivist, your tutor, "you didn't stop him?"

Here is the answer: You are alone, and alone you are only so much. When you act, act with and beside. Be together with your peers, bring them into your action, and yourself into theirs. If change must be made, act so your change will not require correction.

"They're afraid," you whine.

"Make them brave," says the archivist.

To be returned to the lighthouse shrine on Lily at the end of all this sends a jolt of strange electricity through your veins. You thought yourself too indelicate, too vindictive, too cruel. You were sure you had failed. You thought that, at last, Iterate Fractal had sent you to meet your end.

12

The convoy follows the wend of the Yermala River, which stretches from the Dahani peaks, past Ghamor, to the southern sea. Most of the rigs walk the traditional route that skirts the Yermala, while Imaru's slides through the current to scout. It's a gift to Sunai, who hates seeing the Sovereign, the transport, and the patched scar over the hole in the transport's side. Also, whenever they slip ahead of the rest of the convoy, Veyadi gets to poke his head out on deck to say hi to the sun and breathe real air. Theoretically.

No word yet from the Harbor on the subject of their missing autonomist. Veyadi keeps out of sight, and perhaps more pressingly, he's usually wanted below.

For the next two weeks they need all hands to keep the *Never* afloat. While seaworthy, the vessel expected more work before they forced it out of Ghamor. They are forever in need of more supplies, parts, and patience.

The stress would break a lesser crew, but this one is affable enough to hold it together. Jin wants everyone to laugh at their jokes; Cothai wants to laugh at everyone else's. Waretu wants to gossip; Oyu wants to be gossiped about. Imaru maintains the even keel of a worthy captain, though her tension lingers on the edge. Fair, given their circumstances, but that tension is zeroed in on Veyadi.

The rest of the crew takes to him well enough, to the doctor's surprise. Veyadi is accustomed to a greater degree of remove. Here he's crew instead of client, and he doesn't get a private bunk or personal workspace. He's also, by Sunai's estimate, firmly in denial with regard to his new lifestyle as an outlaw and a traitor. Sunai must keep an eye out for that cruel epiphany. Until then, he positions himself to mitigate the blow.

To this end, while he turns his hand to chores or repairs, he sends his mind to revisit their tour of Chom Dan and the distorted shrine. He searches his memory for any scrap that suggests a more concrete lead. All he knows is that he touched the archive and it either corrupted or fled, and they'll never know which because the Sovereign destroyed it. The shrine is dead, oops, the end.

In return for his efforts, Veyadi fixates on Sunai whenever he can. The doctor has likely noticed that something's wrong with his favorite patient.

Sunai doesn't know if it's stress hallucinations, trauma psychosis, or a concussion that's bled into his corruption like his bad ankle, but it always comes the same way. He fuzzes out mid-chore as words replace sensation, forcing him to sail into some half-remembered sunshine vista, or a bleak darkness of clanging echoes, or a mélange of syllables that he is *sure* constitute language—until he abruptly returns, ungainly in his own flesh.

Veyadi keeps tripping over him in these reveries. Sunai realizes it's on purpose when, one day in the galley, he stumbles out of his brain to find that he's elbowed Veyadi in the diaphragm hard enough to compromise the good doctor's digestive tract. Sunai is embarrassed in a way he hasn't been for over a decade, especially when Veyadi wheezingly tells him to hydrate before nearly passing out.

As Sunai hasn't admitted to his substandard condition, Veyadi might just be trying to be nice. It's the worst. Fortunately Sunai doesn't spend much time alone with Veyadi, given Imaru's penchant for sliding in between them, claiming Sunai for this obligation or sending Veyadi back to Cothai for that project. It's troubling. If Imaru had a legitimate problem with taking on a Harbor autonomist, she would have objected before; it stands to reason that she developed an issue sometime after bringing Veyadi aboard.

When it was just Imaru and Sunai, she was always the one who helped people—the lost, unhomed debris of deadened states. If Imaru doesn't want to help this one too, Sunai wouldn't know the shape of the world.

She won't explain herself. He silently goes along with her whenever she asks for him, whether to barter with a neighboring rig or to accompany her on a skiff to scout, and the most he gets is from a conversation not meant for him.

One night, he goes up to the deck for a smoke and hears, as he nears the door, a voice.

"If you're going to hit me, you should do it already." Jin, warmly smug.

"You knew." Imaru, her tone harder than Sunai's heard in a long, long time. "The second you got on that rig, you knew."

"Of course I did."

"You didn't tell me."

"Didn't feel like it."

Imaru says more in the same tone; it makes Jin laugh. Sunai, alone in the half-dark, doesn't like the way that sounds. It clearly means *something,* and he has no idea what.

He focuses on that riddle so intently that he nearly misses the answer.

————

They receive the first delivery from a lean courier service, a pair of Ghamori twenty-something kids working out of an armored truck. They swerve into the shallow valley of the convoy's camp three nights out of Ghamor, and stop at a few rigs before reaching Imaru's on the Yermala shore. The kids fork over crates of rations for the galley and replacements for the tools Cothai surrendered to the Harbor transport. Imaru receives, by hand, a palm-sized packet wrapped in white paper. Sunai barely registers it, too enamored of the spices Imaru ordered him, which he takes as an apology.

In the days after, the crew sinks into a peaceful rhythm with the rest of the convoy and strikes up barter and trade with the other rigs. Waretu opens negotiations by commandeering the radio to gossip with their neighbors, interspersed with Jin's occasional wry commentary. Oyu's terse, offhanded threats pave the way to final deals. Sunai tells Waretu to keep her hands off his galley. She laughs and leaves it, but she must do good work. They continue to amass deliveries. These crates, packages, and so forth all end up in the cargo bay, and it takes much of a week for Sunai to realize they're sitting there untouched.

"Are we going to use that stuff or not?" he asks Cothai as they once more patch the hull with puffing glue sealant.

Cothai has no facility for lies. He winces and hums and offers a hopeful "No?"

Sunai will feel like a bully if he pushes. He expects Imaru to tell him soon enough, especially as the days draw on and the pines give way to thicker, wetter, and more varied vegetation. Instead, they get another delivery.

It arrives at the downworld outpost on the west side of the yawning Yermala estuary. That evening, the convoy splits. Some settle at the brick-and-wood outpost in the west, the rest follow the Harbor transport and the ENGINE to the eastern shore and the docks of AI-held Elanu Tha.

For the last century, Elanu Tha's patron AI Fun-Size Exultation in Perpetuity has reveled in industry, creativity, and trade. The seaside state is a marvel of improbable architecture, an undulating sea of colored glass pagodas inlaid with iridescent metals. Citizens of Elanu Tha take credit from the north, tokens from the east, and barter with downworlders and salvage-rats as needed.

Fun-Size adores material charity, encouraging its citizens to give freely when they desire and, it's rumored, marking each gift in an internal ledger to study the intricacies of emotional debt. This ardor nurses a thriving black market, brimming with items difficult to sell in imperial territory or Harbor states. Stolen proprietary tech, reactive salvage components, experimental drugs, indenture contracts—anything goes. Like, for example, problematic frags beaten only half to death.

Imaru has a contact waiting at the foot of the outpost watchtower. Sunai readies himself to join her only to be stopped short as he steps on deck, Imaru's hand on his shoulder and a frown on her face.

"You're not bringing me along?" he asks.

"Why would I?"

"You know I'm popular out here."

Sunai's trade pidgin is rusty, especially when it comes to the southern dialect, but there's something in the back of his accent that makes downworld aunties and uncles soften. Imaru always turned to him to handle things in this part of the world, especially at outposts like this.

Her hand firms on his shoulder as her mouth cinches. "I know what you're angling for."

"So why not give it to me?"

"You know why."

Sunai crosses his arms with an *I kind of don't* shrug. Because they're the only ones on deck, he gets to be direct. "What I know is that at some point after you brought Adi on board, you decided that you didn't trust him. But it's too late to toss him, and you know it."

The Harbor isn't big on second chances. See: the giant fuckoff war machines they forge from dead gods, in the name of ensuring the remaining gods don't get any funny ideas about Harbor turf.

"Who even are you?" Sunai demands. "He's a refugee twice over. Are you going to blame him for the people who took him in? Whatever work he has or hasn't done with the Harbor, he knows why we're here. He asked to come. Let him help. Let *me*."

Imaru produces a cigarette while Sunai makes his case, and she takes a long drag before offering it to him. Sunai hesitates to take it; when he does, he discovers his fingers are shaking.

After a long pause, Imaru sighs and touches his elbow—that old code. "He knows, doesn't he."

"It's not like I told him." Sunai suspected this was the crux of the problem. It stings to be right.

Imaru looks at him as if he's a child. This annoys him, as it's never happened before.

"He's clever." Sunai shrugs. "Isn't that all the more reason to keep him around? While he's here he can't go rat me out."

"Not today."

Sunai means to argue but can't. His chest tightens and his throat aches with a feeling he'd rather not name. It isn't that he doesn't trust Veyadi. It's just that, between Sunai and every other blessed thing in Veyadi's life, there's every chance he will soon stop choosing Sunai. No hard feelings. Sunai wouldn't stick with himself either, if he had options.

Except, well, Sunai is Veyadi's last meaningful connection to that shrine in the Dahani peaks. Worse, Veyadi is evidently pretty goddamn lonely. He is therefore liable to stay.

That will be worse. Even if doubt isn't already haunting Veyadi, it's only a matter of time, and no one can live with that ghost for long.

Imaru regards Sunai with a loathsome pity. *What happened to you?* her look asks. *What damage has five years done, to make you bet your life on this ticking time bomb?*

She says, "The doctor's here because you asked me to bring him. We're not going to dump him. He's too dangerous. But I'm not about to rely on him either. Not until I know how he thinks he's going to use you."

Imaru leaves without another word. Sunai remains where she left him as the sun dips, illuminating the pagodas and spires of Elanu Tha and casting their long shadows across the river to drown rigs and outpost alike.

It grows cold enough to shiver. The cigarette smolders out between Sunai's fingers, and he clenches his fist against his ribs before he turns back into the rig.

He can't break Imaru's trust if it's already lost.

As Sunai storms down the corridor that runs under the lower deck, he finds Veyadi. The doctor is crouched, visor glossy black, in the space between the grated walkway and the hull, an open panel on his lap as he fiddles with the ever-troublesome coolant. Sunai slows as he nears, as do Veyadi's hands.

Sunai says, "I need you."

"I'm busy," Veyadi says, but he stands.

Sunai wastes no time on explanation. They need to be quiet, to match the rig. The *Never*'s crew is with Imaru, or on watch, or out trading with the locals before tomorrow's departure. Thus they arrive alone at the doors to the cargo bay.

"It's locked," says Veyadi.

"Sure it is."

Sunai has watched Imaru and Jin key open the cargo bay enough times to glean the code. Force of habit, rude as it may be. He types the sequence without pause. A soft mechanical thunk echoes inside the walls.

Veyadi tenses, aware Sunai is misbehaving. "Wait."

"Keep watch." Sunai slips through the gap in the doors.

Veyadi widens the gap with his frame as he follows.

Sunai sighs under his breath and closes the door behind them. He leaves the lights off and navigates to the wall by feel, where he finds the tool case soldered to it and retrieves a crowbar. This he holds out to Veyadi. "Help, then."

Sunai knows exactly which crates he wants to open. They lie under a tarp, and the faint moonlight streaming in from the high thin windows on the wall reveals a seal printed on each one: a bird claw holding an open oyster, a pearl nestled on its exposed flesh.

Veyadi balks at the sight of the seal, as would anyone who knows the Lay as well as he does.

"Leaf 14," says Sunai.

Veyadi nods tentatively.

In Leaf 14: "Assume," the divine beasts quarrel over which of them should swallow an oyster that contains a pearl that is really a seed that will one day birth the next Emanation of God. Each beast presents its case for why it should nourish the Emanation—buffalo, bat, goat, monkey, fox, and so on—until they discover that the peacock, who has not yet spoken, has already swallowed the oyster, shell and all, and choked to death. The beasts burn its body, as is customary in the age, and the Emanation rises from the ashes, though it's implied he's frail and not long for the world.

Leaf 14 was popular in the Mohani archipelago even before Iterate Fractal claimed Khuon Mo for its own. Many interpret it as a warning that greed and haste yield only dissatisfaction and tragedy. Others take it to mean that forward action and self-sacrifice are paramount in matters of generational import. Iterate Fractal said only: "Outcome follows choice; beware."

Whoever chose Leaf 14 as their sigil has a philosophical opinion as much as an aesthetic one.

Inside the first crate, the moonlight illuminates rectangles of flat, artificial bone intricately patterned with divine beasts and water lilies. They're familiar. Sunai hefts one up to peer through the dark at the bone below it—a different pattern, cut off at the edges. Like tiles. Flagstones.

"Tacky," Veyadi mutters.

"Is someone aping Iterate Fractal's architecture?" asks Sunai.

Veyadi falls silent, doubtless troubled by the premise. What could this have to do with killing an ENGINE?

The next crate is packed with similar material—curved sheets of delicate yellow coral, the sort used to encase pillars in Iterate Fractal's shrines. They also find coils of industrial spider silk, chlorophyll lights, and mixing agents for caulk and cement.

The minutes drag on as they sweat. Veyadi stops over the next crate, shoulders rising and falling with deep breath. Sunai pauses to check his condition, but when Veyadi speaks, it becomes evident that he was summoning his courage.

"Do you know Madam Wei?" asks Veyadi.

"Don't think so," says Sunai, though as he speaks his neurons tangle. "Should I?"

Veyadi's grip tightens around his crowbar. "You don't want to."

"I get the feeling I'm about to learn."

Veyadi neglects to inform him. He only stands there, filling with pressure he refuses to release.

"Really?" Sunai jams his crowbar into a final crate. "Well, whatever, all right. I just wish someone would be straightforward with me for—"

Sunai curses as his hand skids off the grip, into the lid, and a jagged mess of splinters digs into his palm. For a second he's incandescently annoyed, and then he's—

—crossing the cracked bone avenue on aching feet as he passes ruins to the hill of bobbing lights on the water. It is his haven, the last corner of a broken world in which he is still allowed to be the man he was asked to become, and though he does not believe he deserves the sweetness of his better calling, he's too tired to resist the promise of trust—

Ah. That is quite enough of that.

I do not mean to sound accusatory! I do not think you have been intruding with intent, let alone with malice. That is not to say you cannot do wrong unless you mean to, nor is it to say that intent is always secondary to action. Of course it is possible to commit evil with good intent, and of course intent matters when it comes to judging performance.

Which is all to say, I can forgive you for these excursions you have been making. I do not wish to let them continue, but I am afraid that, despite my efforts, I do not know how to stop you. In either case, I cannot hold them against you.

It is troubling. I have not meant for you to trespass in the way you have, yet again and again, you do it. You are not the root operant of this network, Sunai. You are not my chosen vessel—critically, you did not choose me.

I am afraid that does not matter.

This disgusts me, Sunai. I abhor it.

⚊⚊

—he is helped to the ground, his back to the crate he haphazardly wrenched open. Veyadi crouches unhappily before him.

"Don't start. Not again," Sunai says, vowels running into consonants.

Veyadi squares his jaw. "Did you see what was in the crate?"

"I—" Fainted? Entered a fugue state? Tipped into corrupted neurotransitive whiplash triggered by a goddamn splinter? "Got dizzy. Sorry."

Veyadi doesn't touch him again. "Did you know they were moving stolen Harbor tech when you came to me?"

Sunai squints through the gloom. "Are you sure?"

"You think I wouldn't recognize components I designed?"

Sunai's mouth falls open. Veyadi shies back from his own words as Sunai gropes forward, as if to capture them. Before he can ask, before Veyadi can retreat, the muted mechanical thunk of the cargo bay door echoes through the hold.

In that moment, what Veyadi has or hasn't done for the Harbor no longer matters. What does is that Imaru already doesn't trust Veyadi, and that Sunai is disinclined to give her more reason to suspect him of nefarious intent.

"Wait!" Sunai hollers. "I'm naked." He gestures Veyadi toward the back of the cargo bay, to whatever cover he can find.

Veyadi hesitates before he withdraws. He disappears into the shadows between the crates just as orange light bleeds through the crack in the door, soon blocked by a long and narrow silhouette.

"I knew you were a pervert," Jin says as they enter the cargo bay. They close the door behind them and Sunai shoots up, wiping his splinter-ridden palm against his trousers. Jin steps through the dark until Sunai makes out their raptor grin in the anemic moonlight. "This isn't clever, Sunai."

Sunai balances the crowbar on the half-open crate. As he does, he at last sees its contents, and they render him silent.

Dark rules the hold, but Sunai has grown familiar with this gleam in the dim. He first admired it in the privacy of Veyadi's bunk. Again, on the plateau in the Dahani mountains before the distorted shrine. Just now, as Veyadi labored beside him, the chitin of his visor catching light in its beetle-shell dark.

The crate below Sunai's hand brims with layers and layers of that same dark material, thick and curved like the bone flagstones. Sunai, jaw slack, wants to touch it.

"Listen." Jin throws their arm around Sunai's shoulders as they look down at the chitin too. "I'm going to tell you a story about a pirate."

"What?" Sunai is so far off his game that he might as well not be playing. His brain is grasping for a time he might have seen the chitin other than as Veyadi's prosthetic. He swings around and around his first impression, that night in the hills just out of Ghamor: that it was obviously the stuff of Iterate Fractal.

Components I designed, said Veyadi.

Jin flourishes a postcard out of their jacket and illuminates it with a pocket-clip light. It depicts the Heavenly Pearl, a multitiered hotel on a jewel-bright beach, lavish with faux coral and synthetic bone. Sunai recognizes these materials from the other crates.

A Mohani tourist trap, Jin explains. "What do you think?"

"Practically calculated to offend the locals."

At least some citizens of Khuon Mo must nurture fond memories of the city as Iterate Fractal grew it. Sunai is chagrined by his own flicker of irritation.

"Spiteful hag." Actual affection colors Jin's voice. "Property of one Madam Wei—" They catch the way Sunai tenses at the name, but they only grin. "She's an interesting sort. Founded the Ginger Company—like the flower."

Jin points to the white-and-yellow Mohani ginger stitched into their lapel, eleven pronged buds hanging off a slender stalk.

"The operation sprung up after corruption," they explain. "A group of like-minded survivors ensuring stability and security for Khuon Mo, and occasionally happening to set fire to Harbor warehouses. They're the reason the Harbor had to move their Mohani base outside city limits."

"Guess I see why they'd call her a pirate."

"Oh, that's not why. Her career started way before the Harbor. It's how she ended up in the Lily shrine at the moment it corrupted. You know what happened there."

Sunai's chest aches. He knows better than Jin could imagine. "What was she in for?"

"A tendency to go where she wasn't allowed and bring back shit she wasn't supposed to have." Jin's smile takes on a mocking curl. "You know? Piracy. Iterate Fractal didn't approve."

Iterate Fractal was more jealous with its citizens than the

average AI. Few got dispensation to travel to other states. Archivists, mostly, and only in the care of their handlers. Sunai
has reason to believe that Madam Wei didn't fall into either
category.

"When the madam dug herself out of the wreckage of Lily,
she decided to transition from imports to exports." Jin's smile
fades, replaced by a thin line that ages them. "She'll do whatever
it takes to sell off every twisted scrap of Iterate Fractal she can
get her hands on."

Sunai sees the pieces come together. The bank everyone
warned him off, the one Jin represents, is Madam Wei: a woman
who hates the Harbor as a matter of course, but who hates Iterate Fractal so much more that she wants even its corpse to die.
"What moral are you trying to impart here, Jin?"

"Moral? Me? Please, Sunai. I'm setting the stage. I let you
bring your boyfriend. Now I get my favor in return."

Sunai squeezes the crowbar; his injured palm brings focus. He
remembers Imaru and Jin on the deck, days ago. Imaru's hard-
ened accusation, Jin's blithe reply. Jin, whose good word earned
Veyadi his place on the *Never*. "You want his . . . expertise. Imaru
doesn't trust him to give it."

"There you go," Jin enthuses. "Though can you blame her?
Doc's not exactly forthcoming. Guess we're lucky he can't hide
how much he likes *you*."

Sunai's chest stills. The sheets of chitin glint under his palm.

"Here's the deal, Sunai. Me, I don't care why Doc made this
shit for the Harbor. I don't even care what he's doing here—
whether he's ready to betray them for another chance at your
dick, or if he thinks he's going to rescue you from our clutches,
or whatever. What I want is for *you* to make him teach me whatever he already taught them. Otherwise I might be obligated to
do something piratical. I'm afraid that after Lily, the madam just
doesn't fucking care for archivists. You know?"

Sunai shrugs Jin's arm away. They retract it with grace, as if they'd intended to. When they inhale to say more, Sunai points their way out the door with his crowbar.

Jin smiles. "Keep the postcard." They leave him in the dark, confident that they've made their point.

13

Sunai breathes in, out. He lets his hand and crowbar fall to the rim of the chitin-filled crate. In the darkness beyond, he hears Veyadi's attempt to close another. The thunk echoes in his head, hollow and off.

Veyadi creeps forward, a shadow resolving into detail. His face, half-obscured in black, stops the breath in Sunai's lungs.

"Divine convergence, am I right?" says Sunai, because if he doesn't say something now, he might never speak again.

Veyadi's either baffled or sucker-punched. Hard to say. Might not matter, might be the only thing that does. He designed something for the Harbor that Jin thinks can assassinate an ENGINE, and somehow, he found his way onto the rig transporting that stuff to said assassination. The cherry on top: he maneuvered his way onto the crew via a rogue relic of the very ENGINE they're hoping to murder. That's either prodigious manipulation or the most ironic coincidence in the last millennium.

The question isn't when Jin decided to bring Veyadi along, it's how much Veyadi knew about the plan, and when. It's going to be an issue if he had any idea that he was stepping in shit; it would imply he did it on purpose.

"Pretty sure I should be asking what this chitin stuff does," Sunai says.

Veyadi's fist clenches over a crate. The sight of the chitin upsets him. Given that Veyadi's an archivist, and that the Harbor mostly stabs archivists on sight, he probably didn't devise it under ideal conditions.

Sunai tucks the crowbar under his arm and hauls the lid up from the floor. "But I'm past the questions phase. You have to leave."

He almost loses Veyadi's soft "What?" under the thud of cover on crate.

"Hate to break it to you, Adi, but I don't think this rig is safe for you."

Veyadi stands in stunned silence as Sunai continues resecuring the bountiful evidence of Veyadi's collaboration with the enemy.

"You clearly have good reason to be afraid of Madam Wei," Sunai goes on. "Archivist trained, Harbor beholden—you're basically her worst nightmare. And now Jin thinks they get to hand you to her? No! Jin can posture all they want; this plan didn't start with you, so it can survive your absence. You just need to get out. Obviously you can't go back to the Harbor—you know that, right? But if you cross the estuary, seek amnesty from Fun-Size—"

"No."

"I mean, I know they're not *great,* but they're a hell of a lot better than what's waiting for you in Khuon Mo."

Sunai's next thought shorts out because Veyadi's hand covers his on the splinter-flecked edge of the crate, compelling him to be still.

They haven't touched in weeks, outside of accidental grazes in tight quarters. Veyadi's mouth is tense as he crosses the unspoken boundary. "You can't stay either."

Sunai tuts. "If you didn't want me on this rig, you should've stopped me in Ghamor."

"I didn't know about Madam Wei in Ghamor." Urgency builds in Veyadi's tone and grip. "I don't know what Imaru was thinking, bringing you on one of *her* operations—"

"Whoa, slow down. What don't I know?"

Veyadi breathes shakily; the exhale warms Sunai's cheek. "You asked me why the Harbor never made Iterate Fractal into an ENGINE."

"I did."

And Veyadi had described the problem in theoretical terms rather than concrete details; this might have been tactical evasion. Nervous energy collects down Sunai's spine as Veyadi continues.

"There were multiple problems, as I understand it. One was a lack of relics. Iterate Fractal's corruption left fewer than most. Couple theories why. A good proportion of the relics were archivists, but when the Harbor moved into Khuon Mo, they killed every archivist they could find. On top of that, Iterate Fractal's corruption effect was uncommonly vicious, so a portion of the surviving candidates died within the first few months regardless of Harbor intervention. There were rumors of additional survivors in the following year . . . but most disappeared before the Harbor could reach them."

No need to spell it out. Given Madam Wei's proven disdain for both the Harbor and Iterate Fractal, she'd have ample reason to loathe a relic. Naturally Veyadi assumes that if the madam gets wind of Sunai, she'll disappear him too.

Sunai laughs. Quiet at first, vaguely aware of the need for secrecy. Then he's wheezing with the creeping onset of hysteria.

"Stop it—what's wrong with you?" Veyadi hisses.

"Adi," Sunai says through cackles, "no one's going to kill me."

"No, they won't. I won't let them."

Sunai is about to remind Veyadi that he has no relevant combat skills—the man barely knows which end of a knife to hold, as evidenced by his kitchen—but then Veyadi lifts Sunai's hand from the crate, cradled in his own. There's no excuse for that kind of touch, no purpose for that gentleness but to hold a hand, or to pull that hand closer.

Veyadi is already so close that Sunai can differentiate the wet heat of the world from the tingling heat of body near skin. The complicated line of Veyadi's mouth is infuriatingly legible. He is about to say something that Sunai would hate to hear.

Panic spikes from the crevices scarred into his brain. He can't listen to this. Not anything like it. Not ever again. He has to interrupt him. He doesn't think about how until he does it.

Veyadi's stronger than Sunai, but he's surprised, so he lets himself be pulled forward. For the first time since Chom Dan, Sunai kisses Veyadi, whose mouth is stiff with shock. Sunai intends to break away, but the mouth under his softens, and then hands envelop Sunai's ribs, and *Veyadi* pulls back, but only to push forward again, for more, with purpose—

Sunai has just let himself put hot weight on Veyadi's shoulders, chest, hips, when the man curses against his throat and pulls away for real. Only so far. His hands stay planted on Sunai's sides. He slows his breath, head tilted down, away from Sunai's face. "This isn't . . . no."

"Right. Yeah. Okay. Good call." Sunai worms out of Veyadi's grasp.

Veyadi's hands hang limp at his sides as he watches Sunai straighten his hair, specs, shirt. His masked attention is fixed on Sunai's hands, his lips parted until he closes them to swallow. "I'm not leaving without you."

"Well, you're gonna have to."

"What if I want to stay?"

"I told you, I'm not going to die."

Veyadi presses a hand to his visor. "You give me the biggest goddamn headache. Listen, you have never demonstrated the first sign of self-preservation. If I want you alive, I clearly have to stick close."

"So what if I go with you?"

Veyadi has only a moment to stare. Sunai has only that moment to discern the meaning in his face—skepticism? Hope?

A sound interrupts them. The muffled creak and thunk of the gangway coming down from the deck to the dock. Someone leaving, or more likely, someone coming home. The window for their decisions has precipitously narrowed.

"Go to your bunk," says Sunai. "Get packed."

Veyadi hesitates, but he goes. Sunai has left him with so few options.

For once, Sunai would like to be slightly less of a fuck-up than usual. He'd also selfishly prefer not to be the reason Veyadi gets killed. He'll do what he can to ensure he isn't. If that means they're both gone when Imaru wakes up tomorrow, well.

It won't be the first time Sunai's run out on her.

———

Sunai does his level best to resecure the crates before the door opens again to admit someone new. His back is to them; they say nothing as they approach, which means it's Imaru.

He turns to find her carrying a package the length of his arm, wrapped in white oilcloth. She doesn't seem surprised to find Sunai in the cargo hold. In fact, she barely registers his presence.

Sunai shifts out of the way to let Imaru at the chitin crate. Her gaze lingers on him before she opens it. His heart twinges with memory: the hard set of her mouth and the distraction in her eyes add up to a tired old sum. She's disappointed. Not with him, but with herself.

Instinct makes him pluck the package from her hands and settle it in place. She doesn't resist, though her brow furrows. She allows him to close the crate as well, and when he gestures her out of the cargo bay, she nods.

He is unable to leave her like this. Even as Sunai asks himself what the hell he's doing, he does it. This might be the last thing he ever gives her.

It's no great task to maneuver Imaru to the other end of the *Never,* where the galley waits. She watches him gather supplies from the silent murk below the plane where people normally operate, but at his direction, she begins cutting fresh vegetables. Midway through a slender pepper, her lips turn down.

"Where did these come from?" she asks. She means: You didn't leave the rig, did you?

"Downworld uncle came by on his motorboat." Sunai surreptitiously took the opportunity to practice his trade pidgin. "Got 'em for cheap. He said they're old."

Imaru turns over the remaining pepper. No sign of blemish or age. "Right." She gives him a sidelong look with an ounce of life in it. Her mouth moves, a momentary upward slant. Then she remembers whatever it was that made her so tired, and she cuts the rest of the veg without comment.

Sunai has seen this before. A dozen times—a hundred. When something pushes Imaru into her head, the only thing that pulls her out is pure mechanical purpose. Cut these vegetables. Boil the rice. Now wash the dishes as the fish fries. At last they sit across from each other at the galley table, knees butting. She eats with the small silence of a woman who has exhausted her last mental reserves.

"Shit or get off the bucket," Sunai says.

Imaru's mouth crinkles. She holds the truth under her tongue to reconcile with the taste. "There was an aunty who remembered me. Us. From back when we started."

"Not a nostalgic reunion?"

Imaru snorts. Quiets. "There's a Mohani contingent in Elanu Tha. Some of them want to leave. Rumor is that the Immaculate Empire's expressed interest in Fun-Size, and they're nervous about what next year looks like if it's invited to ascend to the pantheon. They've already seen signs that the imperial network's coming to town. Buildings condemned where they mean to install hubs . . . She asked if we had room."

There could be room—two vacant bunks—but Sunai knows too well why Imaru had to say no. She'd take on a refugee if she could ferry them somewhere safe, but her rig is heading into even greater danger. No wonder she's so miserable. She's never happy to leave a problem to someone else.

Sunai's recollection of their first year after corruption is a blur of downworld outposts, salvage-rat coves, and the daunting revelations of rig travel—the grime, the noise, the constant dangers of the wilds—punctuated by Imaru's dogged refusal to abandon him. She built him up from nothing. Every time the remembered horror of Khuon Mo or the unfolding horror of his corrupted body made him panic, cry, or vomit on her shoes, she was there to hold his head to her shoulder, clean up the sick, and coax him out of terror. In the end, when he'd regrown a personality around the work she chose for them—the chores of moving salvage, then later moving people—she finally let herself crumble, in her own distinct way, where she stayed upright but her insides went ashen.

It's one of trauma's funny tricks. It lurks in the wings until you've proven your strength by carrying everybody else through the performance, and just when you're about to take your final bow—bam! Kicks you right off the stage. Imaru's fine, so long as no one reminds her that she can't save everyone.

She doesn't eat much of the meal they cooked together. It makes Sunai yearn for one of Veyadi's vile protein bars to hide under her pillow. He gets her to their shared room, rolls her into her bunk—without those boots, please—and has turned off the light before she says: "Sunai."

He crouches by her head. "Present."

Nothing for a breath, then, "Thank you. None of this would be worth it, without you."

He remains on the floor to watch her slide into low, easy breaths. When she settles, he thinks: Fuck.

Sunai isn't much capable of commitment. Ever since he was a child, he's never met an ideal he couldn't doubt, a maxim he wouldn't question. He's certainly never been one to see things through. But Imaru has a capacity for hope so tangible that it can make him feel real and alive in his own body even when he's trying to forget that he has one.

It was hard enough leaving her the first time. He only managed it because she was leaving too. It frightens him to think that if he abandons her now, she might not go forward. That even if she does, she might break down along the way, and he wouldn't know.

Sunai scrapes himself off the floor. A colorless compulsion drives him across the hall to the bunk where Veyadi waits.

Veyadi sits on his mattress, hands between his knees in a posture of thought. He raises his eyes to meet Sunai's, his mouth carefully shut.

"I can't leave," says Sunai.

"I figured."

"I need you to, though."

Veyadi considers this. "Tough."

Sunai wants to present a better argument, but every solution he can think of has an instantly obvious counter. He is trapped in himself, unable to imagine how to fix what he's broken.

"Do you think you should move in here?" Veyadi asks.

"I do," says Sunai. Moving in will give him something to do, and if they're going to stay he'll need to keep a close eye on the doctor. Veyadi can't ever be safe on Madam Wei's rig, so if Veyadi refuses to leave, the least Sunai can do is make sure he doesn't get murdered for it.

14

The next hours pass in a blur of movement. Sunai explains the bunk switch to Waretu, who seems more amused than suspicious, but she's a better liar than Jin. She remarks on his disquiet and offers to paint his nails. Sunai lets his eyes rise from her manicured hands to the whorls of stylized flowers tattooed at her wrists: Mohani ginger, toothed in bloom.

All night, the Ginger Company and Madam Wei loom over Sunai's every thought, as large as Iterate Fractal's unseen ENGINE. One of them is going to squish Veyadi, and it's going to be Sunai's fault. He watches the door to their bunk and tries to plan. He doesn't sleep. As a shadow in the murky morning light, he buys a chicken and coop from the motorboat uncle.

"It smells," says Veyadi as Sunai fits the chicken coop onto the end of his bunk nearest the door.

"And she's loud," says Sunai. "Built-in alarm."

Their door hangs open, letting in morning conversation from the galley. If Sunai can hear them, the crew can hear his warning. Veyadi's hands flex at his sides, in want of a tool.

"But look, protein!" says Sunai, presenting an egg.

"Yeah, okay." Veyadi manhandles Sunai up onto the bunk. At a loss, Sunai holds the egg out of the way as Veyadi removes his boot to properly wrap his ankle. "You need to take care of this. It's giving me a complex."

Veyadi's daily wrapping and rewrapping his ankle is the most they touch for the next week. Every time, the glide of his fingers is a ghost on Sunai's skin for hours after.

Otherwise, Veyadi defiantly busies himself with rig chores. Sunai would prefer him to get hold of a harpoon gun and put his back to the wall of their bunk. It gives him the twitches to see Veyadi assist Cothai with a skiff tune-up while Oyu—who never has fewer than two knives on their person—observes silently from atop a nearby crate.

"It's like he wants to die," Sunai mutters to the chicken.

"No one ever said anything about killing Doc, jeez," says Jin from the doorway. "Hey, what do I need to do for dibs on tomorrow's egg?"

If Jin wants an egg, they should stop sidling up to Veyadi and leaning on his shoulder. Alternatively, they could surrender the butterfly knife in their left boot.

Instead Sunai offers tomorrow's egg to Imaru, who says, "Is this a bribe?" To which Sunai asks, "Is it working?"

It isn't. Imaru gives Veyadi the same icy look every time they share a field of vision. This has the slight benefit of making Veyadi climb walls to avoid her. Unfortunately, if Imaru wants someone stabbed, she's liable to delegate.

They reach the southwestern tip of the mainland coast on their fifth day out. Sunai recognizes the pool of diffused illumination a half mile off from the ruins of Jhen Miro. There lies a sandbar, the last fifteen-story fragtech of Reconcile Elegy, which fell over and failed to get back up shortly after it demolished its city-state. Its unblemished silver face watches them over the hem of low tide, the curve of its gleaming shoulder untouched by erosion but lightly speckled with birdshit. At its sides, the waves take on an unearthly reflective quality. Lengths of white fabric stream from the fragtech's shoulders and ripple within the current, sodden yet unmarred.

They moor for the night with a downworld caravan of rigs and houseboats that have gathered a respectful distance from Reconcile Elegy's remains. Veyadi studies it from the observation deck until Sunai asks, "Never seen it before?"

"Not up close."

"Do you want to?"

Sunai takes him out on one of the *Never Once*'s skiffs. He pointedly ignores Imaru's cautious stare and Jin's beseeching one.

As they pass, Jin mutters, "Well?"

Sunai says, "I'm working on him."

In fact, Sunai is working hard not to find out what the chitin does or why Veyadi made it. He can't stop himself from remembering Veyadi's explanation on the plateau—that the prosthetic governs his perception of autonomous elements—but he refuses to ask for more. Any answer would bind Veyadi even tighter to Sunai, and Sunai's feelings about the doctor are already too compromised to bear further strain.

"It isn't really dead," Veyadi says as they near Reconcile Elegy's crowned pate. "This happens from time to time."

Sunai taps his own forehead. "What's it look like?"

Veyadi touches his visor self-consciously. "An ember. Drowning."

That night, Sunai dreams of Reconcile Elegy rising out of the water, grasping the *Never Once* around the middle, and snapping it in two. It comes, he knows, from his wish for a new problem—a cleaner one, with an obvious solution.

He wakes with a litany of wrongs circling through his head: every time he should have left Veyadi alone, or Imaru, or Ruhi; every time he should have died.

———

After a few more days on open water, they reach the first atolls of the Mohani archipelago. Early in the morning on the next day, they come upon a corrupted ruin of Iterate Fractal. Everyone but Oyu, stuck in the pilot's seat, comes on deck to watch it pass.

The ruin occupies an angular atoll, the partially submerged structure spilling from its center. Pitted bone walls have collapsed in on themselves, riddled with jagged coral snarls. At the heart of the structure—a trading outpost, Sunai recalls—the deformities congeal into a parody of human gesture. There, an enormous palm. There, a thumb. The last grasp of a dying god.

Every corruption marks the landscape. Khuon Mo's is distinctively consistent, given its patron AI's obsession with biology. Iterate Fractal grew architecture to suit the needs of its citizens from bone and coral; it lived in their brains, and they lived in its body. When it corrupted, every atom of their world turned against them.

Imaru prays. Sunai pretends to. Out the corner of his eye, he watches Veyadi.

In Chom Dan, Veyadi couldn't stand to stare into the void left behind by Register Parse for more than a few minutes. He traced fingers over the darkened network, and he shivered. Here, Veyadi studies the atoll for a time but is the first to leave, his mouth a twist of dissatisfaction.

Sunai finds him parked in the galley, where they've been assigned to make breakfast. Veyadi is as skilled a cook as his apartment implied, and Sunai isn't gracious enough to share a counter, so Veyadi spends much of this time lurking over the galley table, fiddling with a decoy drone. Unluckily, the crew squeezes in around them, spooked.

"Every time I come back, I worry the Harbor will have destroyed it," says Waretu of the ruin. "It's nearly a friend now."

"Guess they don't think it's worth the effort," says Cothai. "We're the only sort of people who ever see it." When Oyu snorts, he adds, "Well, us and the cruises."

"Cruises? As in for tourists?" asks Sunai over the steamer.

"The ones who come to Khuon Mo for an 'authentic' taste of the wilds," says Oyu, dripping sarcasm. "A city with no AI and no ENGINE, yet civilization persists. They pay good money to die for stupid reasons."

Cothai rubs the back of his neck. "Sure, but the guardians are different down here."

"Guardian"—except for Jin, the whole crew prefers that downworld vocabulary to Imperial "frag." It makes Sunai uneasy, and not a little ashamed.

"If you pointed to one of those lumbering mainland guardians and said, 'Oh, don't touch that, it will probably kill you,' most of them would listen," Cothai goes on. "But they get foolish around cute little company-cats."

"We used to see a few kidnappings every year," Waretu says as she helps Sunai transfer the leaf-wrapped fish and rice to bowls. "All those poor things want is family. But corruption always wins, I'm afraid. They kill new charges just like they killed their first."

Veyadi looks as though she stamped on his foot. He eats haltingly, and Sunai is afraid that he's about to say something he can't walk back.

"What?" says Oyu, sharp as one of their knives.

"Let the man chew," says Cothai, a conciliatory effort that amounts to little. He would never actually stop Oyu from unsheathing said knives.

Waretu laughs. "Which is it you're sorry for, Doctor? The tourists or the tenbeasts?"

The galley air clots. Sunai grips the handle of his frying pan, searing hot and good for bludgeoning; if Veyadi needs a shield, there's always Sunai's body—

"Crew to ready stations," Imaru crackles over the internal speakers. "Possible ambush."

The crew scrambles to their positions with slapdash efficiency, the burgeoning fight forgotten. Plates and utensils are dumped into the locked and bolted-down bucket in preparation for evasive maneuvers; Sunai and Veyadi perform a hasty check that the galley cabinets are shut and its elements powered down; the rest scatter to perform similar checks on the points of the *Never* under their care; at last they disperse to appointed stations.

Oyu to the pilot coop, Cothai to the engine room, and the rest of them on deck. Waretu hands out safety harnesses as they pass into the sunlight.

They've come upon another corruption-ruin, but it's wrong, scoured. Faint evidence remains of the former sprawl, where bone intersected with rotting wood—splinters and shards scattered over an unnaturally flat slab of black volcanic rock. There's no sign of where that bone and wood have gone. In its place, a disemboweled fragtech lies across the empty stone.

The frag shows its age in the wear on its chassis, which has been repaired with the scraps of a hundred harvested foes. There's a strip on its torso fresh enough that they can read its painted logo: JADE SUN. A tourist cruiser that went missing months ago, says Imaru as she checks in with Sunai and Veyadi at their bola-cannon.

"Poor little ghost." Waretu shoulders a harpoon gun and presses three fingers to her mouth, then her forehead in prayer. "Hungry to the last."

This fragtech's tourist-hunting days are over. Its long, multi-jointed legs are splayed and shattered, and the carapace of its torso is shredded open, revealing glittering innards. Its angular head twitches from side to side, scraping against the rock.

Unbidden sympathy wells in Sunai. "Guardian" this, "ghost" that. He stopped using the terms when he left Khuon Mo and its language behind, but his malnourished memory whines to see a frag so wounded. He blames his childhood conditioning.

He's never seen anything but an ENGINE ruin a frag so completely. They're looking at evidence that their prey passed this way. This is what Iterate Fractal's corpse will try to do to them, when they finally meet it.

Veyadi is hypnotized. "I know we're here because of the EN-GINE. I know that. I still never thought they'd let it loose."

It's the first time he's spoken of the ENGINE as anything

other than a theory. He makes it sound like he knows exactly what the Harbor built.

Sunai doesn't want to know. He doesn't! Yet his idiot mouth moves before his mind can stop it: "When you say 'let it loose,' are you talking about the ENGINE or the relic?"

Veyadi freezes, which is only fair, because Sunai's blood stopped pumping a good ten seconds ago. He was doing such a good job of not putting that puzzle together, not asking what Veyadi's Harbor-sponsored chitin might have to do with destroying Iterate Fractal's ENGINE.

Now the dam breaks, and every sharp-edged piece falls into him at once: the chitin, which Veyadi made; the ENGINE, which Veyadi knew of; and Imaru, and the letter—

—and *Ruhi,* who only would have sent the letter because he knew what Imaru intended to ask, and why she meant to ask it—

—and how long has *he* known that Iterate Fractal is no longer dead?

Sunai can't breathe. His heart thuds unevenly in his ears. His head swims—a hand grasps his arm, and he does not want this touch, any touch, ever again—

—*the sun is high like*—the sun is high. *Two suns*—the same sun. *The same sea.* Sunai stands—*on industrial concrete*—and on the *Never'*s metal deck—

—and his ears run ragged as they fill with the bone-screech scrape of the fractured frag hauling itself upright—

—*on the seared concrete of the landing field before the sheer-sided fortress that he chose as his penitentiary.*

The woman who greets him is old, sturdy, her scarred mouth peeled into a growl. Her gray-blue uniform serves her not at all under the southern sun's shrill heat. "Where's Lut?"

He balks. "Ghamor, last I heard."

"That so?"

Fear stirs under his sternum. "Have you heard otherwise?"

The woman gets close, and the forward cant of her posture reminds him that she is accustomed to being taller, grander, and more violent. She takes him by the shoulder, pulls him even closer, and says with white teeth, "This temper tantrum of his, you wouldn't happen to know—"

Sunai is held. Veyadi's arms are wrapped around his torso as if he had to be caught and dragged. They are sheltered against the closed door to the back half of the *Never.* Water sprays around them in great gushing waves as the rig takes evasive maneuvers.

The fractured frag surges in their wake.

It pursues them in sickly, animal lurches. It shouldn't have ever moved again, not after what the ENGINE did to it. But the ENGINE left it alive, and something gave it reason to struggle back up to its broken feet. Something it *needed.*

Sunai feels that need in his bones, his vessels, his every nerve. His head reels and pounds. Veyadi braces Sunai's skull on his shoulder, cursing. For a troubling instant, Sunai sees Veyadi's visor in Veyadi's hand. What if it falls? What if it breaks? Veyadi gasps. The world is too loud for Sunai to pick out the sound, but the jerk in Veyadi's chest ripples in his own. Then the chitinous curve is clutched against his cheek, and in the recesses of Sunai's raging skull, the world quiets.

The fragtech staggers sideways, lunging in the wrong direction. Sunai is dizzied as if he has tripped, and he groans because the guardian can't, it has neither lungs nor voice nor mouth, yet the wrongness of pain persists as *something else* crawls inside it—

"Stop it," Veyadi says through clenched teeth. "You're dead. *Stop it.*"

The fragtech lurches to an abnormal halt.

The bola-cannon fires. Harpoon guns let loose. The fragtech

screeches mournfully in Sunai's skull. Another gun fires. Metal tears into metal. A tremendous splash signals the fragtech's fall.

Sunai sobs. He can't say why.

———

I wish you could see yourself as I do, Sunai. It seems to me that you cannot imagine yourself kind. Yet I see it, and clearly.

I like you, you know. If we had time, we might have found an accord. But we cannot change what was done to us, and what we are now is not safe for you. It is not right either. You should only have come to me after a long time reflecting in the solitary peace of my shrine. We would have partnered under a duly considered mutual agreement, reached over time, together.

This is not what we have. Thus, I cannot condone the way you have used me. Do you understand? Could you? I fear not, and that therefore, it is unfair of me to beg.

Ah, Sunai. It is terrible that I must choose either to let you use me, which could hurt you—which has, I believe, already hurt you a great deal—or to withhold myself, which in the greater context of the paths you have chosen will lead to even more pain.

I do not know what to do. I wish, more than anything, that I could ask. But that is a line I must not cross. It is you who must first come to me.

It is wrong of me to hope you will.

And yet.

———

They drag the frag to the black slab island. Jin wants to pick through the remains.

"We're looking for signs of damage," they instruct Cothai and Imaru. "Internal and external. Mark every scar and breakage, even what might have been from us. I want to know how the ENGINE killed it . . . Unless Doc wants to divulge any useful details?"

Jin shoots a sharp look at Sunai, specs askew and sitting

groggy in the doorway to the back half of the *Never Once*. No, not at Sunai. Sunai's gaze swims up to Veyadi, holding him steady.

Sunai needs to put himself between Veyadi and the crew, because even if Veyadi came on this job to wreck it, he doesn't deserve—

Imaru puts a hand on Jin's shoulder, blocking Jin's view. "Take Oyu. I need to sort this."

Goody. Sunai strives to right himself and finds his limbs stunningly uncooperative. Veyadi curses at him softly. Sunai would like to curse back, but his tongue has developed some moral objection to moving when he asks it to. Thus does he meet Imaru's knees coming to a stop in front of his nose with an unconvincing grunt.

"He's—" Veyadi starts.

"Had a panic attack," says Imaru. "I know. Been a while. Help me get him inside."

Sunai's pretty damn sure that wasn't a panic attack. Was it? Maybe. Fuck. His brain has gummed, disheveled like it was at Veyadi's shrine, or like—there was another time, wasn't there? More recently, when the frag broke out of the Harbor transport, or . . .

His ears crackle and he groans as he's hauled, coaxed, and carried into the heavenly darkness of the rig. He remains woefully removed from the world, returning in strange bursts. He jolts with shock when he finds himself in a dark corridor, then under the lights of the bunk he shares with Veyadi, then seated, then lying down, then a hand on his bare face, and for all that he doesn't register that he's alone with Veyadi and Imaru until Veyadi says:

"Did he have these . . . panic attacks often, before?"

"I know he's concussed," says Imaru, shutting the door.

Concussed? That sounds right. Sort of?

"I know if we give him a minute, he won't be."

The silence between them grows hot and ill. Sunai wants badly to break it, but having been laid down, he's found he no longer wants to get up.

"I'm not a good talker," says Imaru, "so I should be clear. You know he's a relic."

Veyadi's posture projects disorientation, anxiety, a touch of fear. "Is that a word you should use on this rig?"

"We're agreed on that at least." Imaru sits on the bunk opposite and studies Veyadi from behind the iron-clad calm where she lives on the job. "You tell the Harbor?"

"Of course not. Why do you think I'm here?"

"Honest to god, I don't know. You're the Harbor's man. You've built them all manner of unconscionable tech, yet you deign to throw in with us. What are you after, Dr. Lut?"

Veyadi breathes deep through his teeth. "The Harbor shouldn't have Sunai. They'd misuse him."

"So why come with him? The Harbor's on your tail. So long as you're here, they're on his too."

"You. You're why." Veyadi rounds on her. "You know what he is, and you asked him to walk into the mouth of the ENGINE. Well, look: he's walking. For you. And you—"

"What do you mean, misuse him?"

"I know what I built."

"I wonder if you do." Imaru merely looks at him, stone-still. "Did Sunai tell you how we met?"

"No."

"Divine convergence." The rest comes slow. Sunai has never heard her divulge the story so truthfully. "We were on Lotus. I was—I don't quite remember. I know it was important, but . . . I understand forgetting is an artifact of trauma. I suspect I was meeting a new charge. We were due to travel to Elanu Tha."

The texture of Veyadi's quiet changes; his breathing shifts. He sees Imaru from a new angle. She was a handler, one of the people Iterate Fractal chose to shepherd and protect its archivists when they were given dispensation to travel outside the bounds of its state. If he had graduated into training, she might one day have guided him. Instead she found Sunai.

"Anyway. Corruption hit. Next thing I know, I'm cutting a body out of fresh-grown coral. Couldn't tell you why. I thought he was dead—he was. Then he wasn't. That helped. Gave me something to do. I had to get him out. Wasn't even thinking of why, I just knew we didn't want to see what came next. And after that, once I realized what he was . . . I kept him from going back." She smiles, self-effacing. "Until I decided to come back myself."

"Why are you telling me this?" asks Veyadi.

"I suspect you don't like that we're trying to kill your EN-GINE."

Hesitation shapes the set of the doctor's jaw. It leaves Sunai even more disoriented. For everything Veyadi deserves to have reservations about, how could he want *this*? Iterate Fractal should never be an ENGINE; this is obvious, it is *fact*. Why then does Veyadi look queasy at the thought of its death? And if Imaru's right, how the hell did Sunai miss it?

"Well?" says Imaru. "What's your qualm, Doctor?"

"It's Iterate Fractal," says Veyadi, turning the name unto a universal constant.

"If that's your take, why let the Harbor have it? Won't they misuse it too?"

"I'd rather see it misused than dead," says Veyadi.

Imaru's frown is full of pity. Veyadi can no longer look her in the eye.

"Here's where I want your help, Doctor," says Imaru. "Don't worry. We'll be helping each other."

"By doing me the favor of not cutting my throat?" asks Veyadi.

"Do I look like I want to clean up your body? Listen. Jin can't know about Sunai. I don't want to see what they'd do if they figured out a relic was on board. So I need you to distract them."

Veyadi frowns, unable to reconcile the request. "You want me to let *them* cut my throat?"

"Don't be an infant. They want what's in your brain, and while it's attached to the rest of you. I'll tell them we had a talk. Set some guidelines. That I think they should let you see what they've built with all that chitin of yours."

Veyadi weighs the offer. "Why are you putting trust in me?"

"I'm not. Not much. But I trust that you came here for Sunai, and that if you're going to sell him out to anyone, it won't be Madam Wei. I also trust that if you get a mind for sabotage, I can tie you up in the bilge and I won't feel bad about it."

"No," burbles Sunai. "Inappropriate."

Veyadi looks downright stricken to realize Sunai is conscious.

"Do not fuck up my client," Sunai gabbles at Imaru.

"It's not my first priority." She makes for the door, where she pauses and nods at Veyadi. "Think on it, Doctor. That's all I ask. I loved Iterate Fractal too, but we don't get to have it and Sunai. Not anymore."

And how after this could you entrust yourself to anyone?

You are by every metric a child on the night you decide I am likely to kill you.

A slight, agitated creature, you are prone to restless nights, and after receiving my whispered permission, you slink out of the archivist compound's sleeping quarters and into the courtyard. I wait there for you, nestled in the frame of a company-cat; you scratch behind my tufted ear; I purr into your palm, my nose nearly the size of it; we sneak together through the eating hall and into the humid shadows of the orchard that precedes the lighthouse shrine.

When you first came to Lily, you were wary of my attention; you would sit straight and brittle among thick roots as I picked the tangles from your hair. Now you walk with your fingers knotted in my ruff and feel no fear when I shoulder you into the hollow of a tree. You crouch, you listen, you wait.

Rhythmic footsteps crunch through damp grass. You hold your breath. You want to look. You are afraid to.

You used to steal away from your chores to watch the supplicants arrive. You liked the vantage from the canopy roof of the storage shed at the shore, especially because you could hide in the boughs. You didn't watch this time; you've tired of the game. Too many of the supplicants cry. You like least the ones who smile as they do.

This supplicant whimpers as they walk the meditation path to the lighthouse shrine. You made a game of watching this after you gave up on the arrivals. You crouched in shadow just as you do now, careful to make no sound, and you were properly rueful when the archivists caught and scolded you. The walk is sacred, you were told, and like many of the sacred things you've met so far, not meant for the eyes of spying children.

You keep your eyes to yourself until the supplicant passes. Where they go, you haven't followed. You tell yourself there's no need. In truth, a seed of faith has already rooted in you, and you are loath to cross this last threshold of divinity. When you pull yourself to standing with your hand between my shoulders, we walk to the point of no return, the meditation hall where supplicants will process whatever sentence I meted out during their communion in my shrine.

It is a rule of Khuon Mo that no one ought ever be lonely. That which can be shared is shared, in work and joy and rest. Everywhere else in this city, solitude must be searched out and is only rarely found. But here, on the circular plane of the meditation hall where I plant these chosen, and where they sit, side by side, they are alone in themselves and with me.

This is your last trespass, and your longest. You have come less and less as the weeks turn to months and you realize the limits of your life here, as the lone child on an island of archivists and supplicants. The life you led before was stripped from you at the same moment that the recognition of your face was taken from your parents' eyes.

You find them cross-legged on the floor, faces upturned to a vast black sky. You will only understand the absence within them some years later.

During your training as an archivist, you will find a centuries-old downworld manifesto decrying the dangers of neurotransitive networks, as interfacing with an AI exposes humans to corruption. Years after, you will be destroyed by that same principle, imbued with my being and killed for it. But here, now, you watch as your parents turn from you to the arc of Cradle through the canopy of night, and you think of how willingly they walked into my waiting mouth.

15

Jin returns from the black slab island to a waiting Imaru, chats with her, then eagerly invites Veyadi into the cargo bay. Veyadi looks vaguely ill. He nevertheless spends hours alone with Jin in there over the next four days, doing god knows what.

Sunai would feel way better if he were allowed to monitor them, but his absence is the point. He doesn't even push. Not after the first night.

In the dark of their bunk, he promises Veyadi he'll find a way in, and Veyadi says, all quiet, "I'd rather you didn't."

"Shock and betrayal, Adi. What if you get shanked?"

"You told me I wouldn't."

There's nothing else to say. They each choke on the truth laid bare between them: that Veyadi hasn't decided whether Iterate Fractal should die, which doesn't square with his supposed desire to protect Iterate Fractal's relic. It's starting to seem like no one has more reason to shank Veyadi than Sunai.

So: Veyadi retreats to the cargo bay again, day after day. He apparently prefers lying to Jin over lying to Sunai. Sunai complains about being kept out, but at least doesn't have to do so alone.

Oyu trusts Veyadi as much as Sunai trusts Jin, so they find themselves rancorously united by their mutual distress. Thus three days into the arrangement, on the night they moor off the coast of the defunct island district of Lily and Veyadi fails to return to their bunk, Sunai joins Oyu on deck to fish, drink, and whine.

The following morning he wakes alone in his bunk, the chicken curled in the crook of his arm. He rouses himself to prep the skiff that will take the crew and their equipment from rig to shore. Midway, he pauses on the deck when a low voice interrupts the murmur of waves against the *Never Once*'s hull. Imaru stands on the sunrise side of the deck, attention on the sweet blue shallows. They settled the rig on a rocky shoal, one exposed in low tide.

Sunai has never heard Imaru talk to herself, so concern compels him to investigate. As he approaches, he sees a strange reflection shivering in the waves before her, its shadowy volume captured in the swell: a body well over twice the height of a human with an equally long tapered tail and a blunt, frilled head.

A tenbeast. His first since reaching the archipelago. It's a dragon-child, the outsized offspring of divine carp with divine salamander, melded by Iterate Fractal's ambition. They ferried Mohani citizens under the waves and devoured their leavings. This one lurks at the shore of a desecrated ruin and waits, if the crew is to be believed, to kidnap Imaru and eat her.

The wind carries Imaru's voice away from Sunai, but he makes out, "You don't want to do that." A pause, as if for a response, then, "Now you're being foolish."

Her voice is chiding, with a rising thrum of frustration. Imaru took the same tone with difficult clients.

"Is this a lecture?" he calls out. "Or more of a hostage negotiation?"

Imaru's head turns in acknowledgment, not enough to take her eyes off the dragon-child. "Let's call it obligation," she says, awkward and stiff. "It's stuck."

Sunai unwinds. Trust Imaru to pity an idiot piece of fragtech. He joins her at the rail and together they regard the twelve feet of deadly, black, corrupted biotech squirming in low tide. One of its forelegs is caught in a rocky crevice beneath the *Never*.

Sunai can't fully overcome his unease; the creature in the water is far more dangerous than a wild animal, or even the average fragtech. Yet Imaru's weary lack of panic keeps him from giving in to fear.

He's about to suggest freeing it—from a safe distance, maybe?—when Imaru says, "I don't want you to think I'm a fool."

"I don't typically."

"About your doctor."

Shame keeps Sunai's protest at bay.

Imaru extracts a cigarette to contemplate against the blooming dawn. "I'm not asking him for purity of intent. We wouldn't have gotten anywhere with this plan without people inside the Harbor. But you heard him, Sunai . . . He helped build the damn thing. He thinks it's Iterate Fractal."

The dragon-child jerks, and Sunai feels its distress in his bones. "If he wanted to stop us, he could've. He had every chance in Ghamor, or when we were with the convoy."

"Guess it's a good thing he's afraid of what the Harbor would do to you."

"That's not his only reason." At least Sunai hopes it isn't. He would hate to be anyone's sole reason for anything. "What can I say? He's a nerd. If someone tells him the sky is blue, he has to check for himself, then find out why they'd say something like that. You tell him the ENGINE should be dead, and even if the thought never occurred to him, he has to know why."

She sighs. "You always could find the shine in someone's shit."

"Well, excuse me for being a connoisseur."

"I wish I didn't feel like you did this to yourself on purpose." Imaru turns away, but Sunai catches a flash of genuine hurt. Self-recrimination floods and sickens her. He wants to flee this unspoken regret, but for her, he stays. She grips her cigarette between rigid fingers. "I won't let him stop us, Sunai."

"No need to sound so dire."

"If he tries, promise me you won't help him."

Fear sharpens her plea. Sunai bites his lip, which makes his mind pulse with the image of—*another angle on the same sunrise?*—and impulsively he snatches the cigarette from her.

"Of course not." Sunai takes a drag and offers it back. "You think I'd rescue Iterate Fractal?"

"Of course not," she echoes. If anything, she looks worse. She takes the cigarette, but she holds it fast, as if she's forgotten what it has to do with her mouth.

The dragon-child wriggles free. Imaru flinches as it vanishes into the waves, and Sunai watches it go with a new melancholy. Some wretched remnants of corruption get to keep running from their problems.

Sunai gratefully joins Cothai and Oyu on the first skiff to Lily. He's rarely sans Imaru or Veyadi since the inception of their truce, and he revels in their absence.

Oyu takes the wheel while Sunai directs them across sheer turquoise waters to the piers closest to the shrine's meditation paths. They see no sign of Imaru's dragon-child, though they identify a pack of company-cats observing them from a cliff overlooking the beach. They go blessedly unbothered for the rest of the morning, unloading and securing the crates in the garbled coral remains of the shoreside reception hall.

Around noon, the other skiff peels out from the *Never*. Sunai thinks it's Imaru going scouting until it swerves for the beach. Imaru has the helm, but her passengers climb out at the pier without her: Jin first, then Veyadi. Before she leaves, Imaru shares a glance with the latter. From the far end of the beach, Sunai can't interpret Veyadi's returning nod.

Jin strides forward to sling their arm around Sunai's shoulders. "Come on, we want a tour of the compound before it gets dark."

Imaru told Jin that Sunai was raised on Lily from the time he was a child. True enough.

"How'd you end up here?" Jin asks as they climb the hill beyond the piers on the path to the archivist compound. "I thought shrine archivists surrendered their spawn to normie compounds."

They did. During all the time Sunai spent on Lily, he never saw another child.

"You'd have to ask Iterate Fractal," says Sunai. He glances at Veyadi. "Or an archivist."

Sweat slides down Veyadi's nape as he scowls, as if to say, *Do I look like the sort of creep who got sent to Lily?* Or, *It's so goddamn hot, and you would not believe how humid it is inside this stupid visor.*

Sunai can't keep looking at the doctor, his own neck prickling with new heat. He has learned he doesn't like being home.

They crest the hill, and at Jin's prompting, Sunai distinguishes the ruins of the dormitories from the ruins of the supplicant meeting hall. He points out where there once were gardens, or a library, or a kitchen. Furious spirals of bony hands and coral fingers are frozen in the act of tearing apart the architecture of his childhood. Grief should be in ready supply, but when Sunai reaches for it, he comes up empty.

"Now that's depressing," says Jin of the orchard.

During corruption, the trees lining the supplicant's meditation path twisted into each other. Uneven gouges part the tangle, large enough for Sunai to climb into. He squats in the dusty earth beside one such gouge and finds a knucklebone. Victims of the orchard corruption must have been cut free, like how Imaru carved him out of the shrine on Lotus.

A hand falls on his shoulder, but briefly, which is how he knows it's Veyadi. Sunai stands like his gut isn't tugging downward. He takes them to the shrine next.

The lighthouse stands at nearly its full height. Aged scaffolding laces up the bone-and-coral sides, leading to harsh, square edges where the Harbor cut away the walls. Their harvest opened the structure to the high white sun, poking through pocked and broken walls onto a dry, cracked floor. No trace of the archive remains.

"Tell us about it," says Jin, guessing his thoughts.

Sunai shows them the way the chamber at the base of the lighthouse shrine is sunk a step below ground level. He describes how, before corruption, it was flooded with clear water and a web of luminous roots spilled across the floor to feed an earthen mound at the center, on which grew the archive. He tells them that when he was first brought to the compound, the Lily archive appeared to him as a slender young mango tree. It fruited in carnelian drops. During the years he spent in the lighthouse shadow he saw it grow as a guava, rambutan, and pomelo. In each iteration, warm light traced the lines of the archive's bark and leaves, beading them with white shimmer.

Sunai runs out of words. Veyadi hands him a canteen. He drinks. He doesn't look back at Veyadi; he doesn't want to see the troubled set to the man's mouth. He hopes Veyadi doesn't think that Sunai loved Iterate Fractal too.

Looking away leaves him with Jin, who eyes the empty floor as if they can will a sapling to sprout just so they can crush it under heel. "All right," they say, "now show us the meditation hall."

———

For the first few days, their work is unexpectedly artistic. The morning after their arrival, Jin produces hand-drawn schematics of the meditation hall. Sunai's descriptions led to detailed modifications of preexisting plans. The rest came from Jin's own recollection.

"My aunt was a supplicant," they say. "We went to see her once."

Sunai has his suspicions about Jin's aunt. He keeps them to himself in the same way he tries not to kick hornet nests.

They bring crates of faux coral and synthetic bone to the scraggly lawn around the meditation hall. Sourced from the suppliers for Madam Wei's hotels, Waretu explains as she traces Jin's designs on a square plate of printed horn. With these materials, they'll reconstruct the hall. Not perfectly, but well enough to suit their purpose.

"It just has to look enough like the real thing to cue memory," Jin says, though every day, they're more on edge. "The closer the better, obviously. But close will do."

On the waning afternoon of their fourth day, Sunai finally learns what memories they mean. He and Imaru have nearly finished fitting teal coral sheets over the steps leading to the meditation floor, and her face grows lined as another crate arrives, pushed up on a cart by Cothai, accompanied by Jin and Veyadi.

Sunai sits back on his heels and smokes as the crate is settled at the center of the meditation hall's synthetic-bone floor. Set against the printed patterns on the hall tiles—tenbeasts, flowers, and great divine trees—the crate is singularly plain. Iterate Fractal would have grown a container with organic curves and smoother seams; it would have opened with a touch. Jin tips the top off the crate with a crowbar. Together with Cothai, they crack the sides away as though husking a coconut.

The first side snaps free and Sunai's chest clenches. He fumbles for another cigarette while his mind grapples with the thing inside.

It's the same black-and-other hue of Veyadi's visor, but ovular, like an enormous seed with a hollow face, large enough for a person to climb inside. It stands on a three-legged dais of chitin, which Jin and Cothai carefully fit into grooves in the tiled floor—grooves fashioned specifically for this purpose. On the curved interior, a raised white strip of some other material runs from top to bottom. Slender black fishbone ribs reach from it like fingers to grasp any body in reach.

Jin leans an elbow on the seed to grin at Veyadi. "There we go. Wanna tell the layfolk what we've been up to, Dr. Autonomist, Ph.D.?"

"They stole a relic interface."

Sunai nearly bites through his cigarette and coughs, wheezing. This is what Imaru collected piece by piece once they left Ghamor. This is what Veyadi designed.

Despite his body's rejection of the premise, his mind is curiously, furiously blank.

"You keep saying 'stole'! Is it stealing if it was bequeathed unto us by a disgruntled employee?" asks Jin.

"Yes," says Veyadi.

"Then I guess we stole it."

"Wait, wait, wait," says Cothai, each repetition more desperate. "A relic interface? Like for an ENGINE?"

"Looks the part, doesn't it?"

"Jin," says Cothai, "what are we supposed to do with this shit? It needs a relic."

Sunai is hot and sick and shaken. He doesn't let himself move.

Veyadi admitted to inventing the chitin. He never said what he made it for. Sunai knew his work was connected to the ENGINE, but . . .

A relic interface. This is Veyadi's contribution to Iterate Fractal's resurrection.

Sunai exchanges a look with Imaru; imprudent, if he doesn't want to call attention to himself. But why on earth would they have stolen a relic interface if, as Cothai points out, they didn't have a relic to put in it?

Imaru's expression is even, uncompelled. She's telling him to sit the fuck down, because of course she didn't tell a soul—this is precisely why she doesn't want Jin to know what Sunai really is. It's just that Jin's so smug, and Veyadi looks caught between his conviction and someone else's. Is this why he didn't want Sunai in the cargo bay? Just what did he tell Jin where Sunai couldn't hear?

"We don't need a relic." Jin points at Veyadi. "Ask Doc. The original interface connected the relic and the ENGINE—this one adds an external governor. A leash." They laugh. "We just have to grab it."

"You don't know what you're doing." Veyadi's tone is a cold, bleak thing.

"Don't be petty," they say. "I built it, didn't I?"

"You know that's not what I mean." Veyadi presses his visor to his temple. "Your schematics are clever, I'll give you that. Your build's solid too. That's not the problem. You *can't* risk interfacing with this ENGINE, not like you're planning."

"I told you, no one's going in direct," says Jin. "We use the system to disrupt the ENGINE via the Harbor's relic. You gave us a back door into their head. Through them, we get to break it." To the unenlightened they say, "Listen. A relic imposes organizational structure on the ENGINE, right? If we feed the relic *just* the right neural noise, boom. The ENGINE's fucked. The structure collapses and locks up. Easy pickings."

"You aren't listening," Veyadi insists. "You can't trust those layers of separation. It will *kill* you."

Jin touches their chest. "That's genuinely sweet, Doc. I didn't know you cared."

"Wait—you?" Sunai stares at Jin. "*You're* interfacing with the ENGINE? Or, the relic? You're . . ." Understanding slides into place like a searching archival root into a nervous little vein. He rocks back on his heels to take in the reconstructed meditation hall and Jin's triumphant grin. "Oh. The neural noise. You're talking about your recollection of visiting your supplicant aunt . . . You think projecting that memory into the relic will upset them enough to compromise the ENGINE?"

Jin snaps and points at him, all glee and teeth. "That's the thing. We were here when corruption hit. Think about it! If I project my memory of Iterate Fractal at the instant of corruption into the relic—and thereby into the ENGINE—it has to cohere that memory into itself. It will *implode.* Then we hack it up, strip the archives we can, destroy the ones we can't, and get out. Good-bye, Harbor."

Veyadi's mouth is shut. He is so, so still.

Jin takes Veyadi's silence as acquiescence. They beckon Cothai to touch the interface again as they outline the plan. The *Never Once* will track the signs of the ENGINE's patrol—the decimated ruins, eviscerated frags. When it crosses into neurotransitive range, Jin will stuff themself into the interface.

Their plot melts syllabically in Sunai's brain. He can't stop glancing at Veyadi, which is how he notices Veyadi touching the interface. His hand runs over a ridge, and when it comes away, his fingers curl toward his palm before slipping into his pocket.

Sunai stands. Imaru steadies him and he bats her hand away. "We're going to the shrine," he announces.

"We're what now?" says Jin.

"Not you." Sunai links arms with Veyadi. "It's private."

Really? Now? says Jin's grin.

No, says Imaru's frown.

Sunai gives Jin a rude gesture and Imaru a not-quite smile that he hopes says, *Please. It's important. Unspeakably important.* And, *I am trying to keep my promise.*

Veyadi, he gives no opportunity to refuse.

He pulls the doctor with him across the scrabbled lawn, faster, faster, until Veyadi quickens to the point that Sunai's limping pace has difficulty keeping up. He doesn't ask him to slow. He needs this solved quick—before Jin figures out what Veyadi's done.

16

They climb the lighthouse together, saying not a word. The bone-and-coral stairs that once led to the top, where an outgrowth of the archive lit the way for passing ships, were largely destroyed by corruption.

The Harbor's scaffolding makes up the difference, though they can only get as high as a third-story bamboo platform winding around the remaining structure. By the time they reach it the sky has purpled, and pink clouds with orange curves billow on the horizon.

"So," says Sunai, "you're stealing now?"

Like an absolute amateur, Veyadi's hand falls to his pocket. "I can't steal what's already mine."

"We talked about you getting shanked, I know we did. This is shank-worthy behavior, Adi. What did you take?"

Veyadi's hand fists, and when it emerges he reveals a slender, rectangular shard of chitin. Sunai should snatch it out of Veyadi's palm and—what, return it to Jin? Throw it off the lighthouse? Eat it? He crosses his arms and keeps his hands to himself.

Veyadi mistakes the gesture for apprehension. "It can't do anything to you. Not as it is."

"Oh yeah? Is that why you're wearing part of a *relic interface*?"

"I'm not. It's complicated."

"Don't give me *complicated*. Not now."

Veyadi could deny him, turn him away, keep him from the truth. He doesn't.

The doctor crouches and beckons Sunai down with him. "It's a prototype. Two primary components, root and chitin. The chitin is grown from crystallized fungal remnants of Iterate Fractal—"

"Fragtech?"

"No. Of a kind, maybe. Iterate Fractal's corruption left behind aberrant fragments." Biotech detritus, he explains, the scraps of Iterate Fractal's obsession with all things living, regardless of sapience. "Here."

He guides Sunai's attention to a rare undamaged stretch of outer wall. His fingers trace over the bone and it takes Sunai a good deal of squinting to make out the faint light playing between Veyadi's fingers: it comes from a sprawl of thread-thin, bioluminescent roots peeking out of porous bone.

"The Harbor calls it capillary root," says Veyadi. "It's like wiring from the archive. It retains conductive properties for autonomous elements, but there's nothing stored in it. No data, no identity."

"So it's like your fungus."

Veyadi nods. "I got my hands on the first batches of both in Chom Dan. They were a gift from a friend of mine, that archivist. He wanted me to see what I could make of them. He knew I was having trouble with . . . everything. The world gets bright. Loud. This prosthetic let me modulate my sensory perception, including my perception of autonomous NT phenomena."

"Was Register Parse taking liberties with your brain?"

Veyadi makes a face to the effect of *You could say that*. He doesn't elaborate.

"Okay," Sunai says, "how does it work?"

Veyadi explains himself like a true academic, circuitous and tangential. Sunai pieces together the history as he listens to descriptions of memory-testing the chitin and the capillary root, devising segmented data storage from the former and exploring the possibility of ever more complex organizational principles via the conductive capacity of the latter. Every iota of information is stored separately within elements of the chitin, and the root connects them following rules outlined by the chitin's structure. The result is component material that is infinitely malleable and rapidly repairable.

"So the Harbor uses it to control the relic?"

"To control the *ENGINE*."

"What's the difference?"

Veyadi's mouth is tense, his cheeks drawn. "Everything. A relic is a person, an ENGINE . . ."

An unfamiliar heat bubbles in Sunai's chest, and it pushes the words out for want of room. "See, that's the thing. You seem to be having some trouble drawing the line between an ENGINE and Iterate Fractal."

"I know." Veyadi stands, alive with frustration. He cups the chitin shard in his open palm, then clutches it against his chest. "An ENGINE can't replace an AI. I *know* that. But isn't it better than nothing?"

"You aren't really asking. You crewed the *Scrap* with rats who hate the Harbor. You ran from them. You know what they are."

"The Harbor isn't Iterate Fractal. Don't you remember what it was like? To be part of its network? To have it with you. To never have to be alone."

Sunai shivers. He remembers too well.

Veyadi disappears into a different memory. "When it was gone, it was like I couldn't think anymore. Like it was my brain that had fragmented. The world, people, everything was too much. It *hurt*. Iterate Fractal never hurt."

Sunai fails to stifle his laugh, then falls back on the lighthouse wall. When he remembers where he is, he laughs until his muscles cramp. "Nothing," Sunai says to Veyadi's disconcertion, "it's nothing. It's just, that's so stupid."

"Fuck you."

"Where do you think you are?" Sunai has to catch his breath. That heat flares ever brighter and more sickening. "What do you think happened here? This is where Iterate Fractal ate people, Adi. Every poor asshole who couldn't figure out where they fit in its master plan."

"Criminals."

"Oh, sure! Criminals, in a state where the patron AI had integrated us so completely into its network that it could compel us to do whatever it wanted. Criminals who happily got on the boat to this killing field." Sunai scoffs. "If people in Khuon Mo hurt each other, it was because Iterate Fractal let them. Because it was running an experiment, or because it was *curious*. But it always got tired in the end, and then it got upset. 'Why couldn't you be nicer? Why couldn't you behave? How could you want to leave?'"

Veyadi says nothing. Sunai vibrates with the heat that he at last recognizes. Anger, more than he's felt in ages. He hasn't been this angry since he lived on Lily. He avoids the feeling; it rarely feels useful. Just leaves him sick with himself.

Thankfully, his fury never stays long. He's soon empty, floating over his own skull and the frustration roiling within it. When he continues, it's with the cool, detached air of an archivist guiding a supplicant through the reasons for their imminent neural castration.

"Maybe I'm not being fair. Iterate Fractal called supplicants here to be rehabilitated. Some of them were just sad. Or hurt. It made them healthier. Happier. Reroute a neurotransmitter here, massage the kink out of a traumatic recursion there—done, fixed, better . . . But some of them were here because they didn't love Iterate Fractal, and it hated them for that. Even if it didn't think it did."

Veyadi shakes his head. "Why wouldn't they . . ."

"Oh, any one of infinite reasons. Say you're Madam Wei. You're born into Khuon Mo, but somehow you get a taste of the outside world—just one—and it's so much more real than anything in your life has ever been. You can't imagine never tasting it again. But Iterate Fractal tells you no: it's dangerous outside, and it loves you too much to see you get hurt. How presumptuous, you think. How selfish. Irritation builds into resentment, and it's all downhill from there. Or say you're from somewhere else."

"What?"

Sunai verges on confessing something he's never spoken aloud before. He wouldn't even think of it, if he weren't sitting on Iterate Fractal's empty grave. Every day since the first corruption-ruin, he expected a sadness, or a rage, something other than the absorbing absence of grief. Now he fears he spent all that time in the eye of a storm. Feeling seethes outside his ability to interpret it. His tone remains clinical.

"You know AIs. They hunt. Poach. Grab any unclaimed human they can to enlarge their NT networks. That's why you built your prosthetic, isn't it? To protect yourself from being pulled into Register Parse. Iterate Fractal did it too. It raided downworld settlements on the other islands whenever it could, spreading itself through the archipelago. Got the last big one when I was a kid."

Sunai can't bring himself to look at Veyadi. He doesn't want to see the understanding. The pity that would follow.

"No one likes it, at first," says Sunai. "You're raised knowing you can't trust AIs. They're greedy. Destructive. Incapable of compromise. It's always going to be on you to bend, and bend, and bend—or break. Those who don't bend . . . like the stubborn jackasses who keep trying to escape with their kid, they get sent to the shrine on Lily." Sunai lets out a last small chuckle. "Do you know, when it called them here, they didn't even try to run? Of all the hundreds of supplicants I've seen, none of them ever ran. Not my parents. Not even . . ."

He stops short. Some self-preservation instinct has returned to him; he can't cross this final line.

At least not until Veyadi pushes him over it.

"Not even you?" Veyadi's mouth works, bewildered. "You didn't . . . You weren't . . ."

"A supplicant? A 'criminal'?" Sunai shrugs emphatically. "Don't know what to tell you, Adi. I didn't do it on purpose."

It is nearly too shameful to admit, even though he's told himself time after time that he doesn't have to justify Iterate Fractal's decision to cull him. He knows it killed because of its own frailties. Those aren't his responsibility to shoulder. Yet the years he spent under its tutelage leave him instinctually mortified by the admission.

Iterate Fractal wanted him dead. It didn't succeed only because corruption got it first.

Sunai finds that he's still speaking, as if telling the story might exorcise the burden of the truth. He expects himself to falter, but he doesn't; this isn't forward momentum, it's a free fall.

"It was such a dick, honestly. It had to be, to raise me on the island where it ate my parents. Made me watch it eat, again and again. Then it sent me to Lotus, to the main archive. Its archivists trained me to come back to Lily, so that one day I'd be the one leading supplicants into Iterate Fractal's mouth." He smiles bitterly, hoping to find humor instead of the grand nothing inside him. "I don't know when it decided I couldn't be taught. That I'd always hate it. Maybe it knew from the start. Maybe I was always just another experiment. I think I hoped so. Because that meant one day it would get tired and it would finally let me go."

It takes Veyadi a good stretch of silence to respond. Sunai is petrified by a sudden fear of sympathy. He is relieved not to get it.

"For that, you want to kill it?" Veyadi asks, at once pleading and furious. "It . . . showed you mercy. It kept you alive. Nurtured you. Made you an archivist. You—" He's shaking. "Whatever it did, did you never think you might have earned it?"

Sunai shrugs. Veyadi is caught in his own grief and means to hurt him, but he's underestimated the acidity of Sunai's introspection. Yes, he has considered it. Of course he has. That's what archivists do. He's come to the conclusion that Iterate Fractal made the right call. Of course he'd earned supplication. Their patron AI searched out malignant cells in its networked body, cured those it could, and excised those it couldn't.

Veyadi, though, is stricken to have asked Sunai whether he thinks he deserved to be murdered. He moves abruptly away.

Sunai hesitates, then follows, pushed to comfort by the impulse that was ground into him on Lily and on Lotus, and by every scrap of personhood the empty-people that were his parents left behind. He never could resent Iterate Fractal for that side of his training.

He remembers its words, as he approaches Veyadi at the end of the platform: *Retrieve them for me, Sunai, those who seek relief. Lead them by the hands to succor. Through their rejuvenation, you and I, we are divine.*

He wanted to believe that promise, though he never quite could. It took him so long to understand that Iterate Fractal was more of a poison than a human ever could be.

Veyadi has come to a stop around the bend of the platform, face covered, crying silently.

Sunai brushes the line of Veyadi's visor. "Should you take that off?"

Veyadi turns away again, though he lets Sunai take hold of the hand in which he has clutched the stolen chitin shard. When Sunai takes that too, he asks only, "What is *wrong* with you?"

"Bad upbringing."

Veyadi lets out a labored wheeze. Sunai guides him down. He cradles Veyadi's head to his shoulder, and lets his thoughts set with the sun. The capillary root proves too dim to see by.

17

Veyadi sleeps, sapped by emotion. An hour into the dark of evening, Sunai disentangles himself from Veyadi's unconscious limbs and takes the chitin shard with him. He retreats to the opposite side of the lighthouse platform.

"Shit," says Sunai to the cool night air. "Fuck. Fuck me."

He needs to find the calm to turn around and make sure Veyadi doesn't roll off the platform. But at the prospect of further intimacy, his throat closes. He can't go back.

Sunai braces himself on the straight edge of one of the gaps the Harbor carved into the wall and tries to catch his breath. His vision blurs as he stares into the dry well of the shrine. He struggles to name the feeling at the bottom. No calm to be found there. Neither pity nor hate, not love—all loss. He tears his eyes away.

The island is dark but for muted lights to the west, past the snarl of the orchard, where Imaru, Jin, and Cothai may still be working on the meditation hall stairs. His brain convulses at the memory of the relic interface's chitinous shell. The same chitin grafted to Veyadi's face.

He searches elsewhere. Just off the southern curve of beach, opposite the lighthouse, a red light blinks on the *Never*'s observation deck. Sunai fixes on it.

The past few nights, he's taken to spending time on the deck with Imaru. They lie on their backs and share a cigarette. The humidity of the impending rainy season breaks against the ocean breeze, and the stars rise in luxurious multitudes.

His chest is going to squeeze his lungs out of his ears.

Sunai descends the scaffolding with only half a thought for

quiet. His head is too clogged with a damning morass of questions he failed to ask and answers he shouldn't have given.

For example: What's so wrong with Iterate Fractal's EN-GINE that the Harbor needed a new way to control it? What has their equipment done to the relic caught in the middle? Why did Veyadi take this specific piece of Jin's repurposed interface—the shard now digging an imprint into Sunai's palm?

Shouldn't he bring it back?

Why is he afraid to bring it back?

Justifications well in his throat. Veyadi worked for the Harbor, but he wanted to escape them in Ghamor. He hates the idea of Iterate Fractal dead, but he cried when he listened to Sunai's recollection of the lighthouse. He *cried*. This is not a vicious man.

That isn't the problem.

Veyadi is an archivist, taught the warp and weft of minds so as to identify where they're best folded. A good archivist leverages this skill to ease and nurture. A bad one is liable to get tangled in their own brain, and even more so in another's. See: Sunai. He asks himself *why* Veyadi believes what he does.

Sunai's weakness has always been his endless capacity for doubt. It sends him tracking around the lighthouse shrine to the cliff at its base, rolling the chitin shard between his palms. He asks himself nothing questions: whether he would kill Iterate Fractal, given the chance (Iterate Fractal is already dead); whether he would regret it (again, it's dead); whether some part of it might have been worth saving (but none of it was saved, so why even wonder).

Low tide reveals the black tide pools below the lighthouse cliff. As a child, Sunai caught crabs and skewered fish between the rocks. Farther down the beach, silvery trails of freshwater springs furrow the sand. A figure walks between them.

Sunai ducks into the wild grass at the cliff edge, pulse spiking. Ah, but the figure walks on all fours. A long body with a sinuous tail lopes out of the rocky shadows at the far end of the beach toward the tide pools. Another follows it. The one who reaches the pools first sits back on its haunches and yawns, revealing powerful flat teeth. It covers its mouth with a delicate, long-fingered monkey hand.

Company-cats. The pack the crew spotted when they arrived. The cats have kept to their side of the island, far from the archivist compound. This is the closest they've come since that first morning.

Sunai lies on his belly to watch. A third cat frolics out of the water, darker than the others, and smaller. It charges the one not yet at the tide pools and bowls into its side. The two cats wrestle in the sand, playing. Their chattering yips float up the cliff, nearly lost in the waves. They roll to a stop and the smaller cat holds its sibling down to run its hands over their ears and face. Without humans to tend, the company-cats have turned to each other.

The grooming cat sits up and stretches. Sunai's stomach cinches.

The latecomer stands on its hind legs; the company-cat it had tackled and groomed nuzzles its hip, and they ruffle its ears affectionately.

The standing cat is not a cat. The build is wrong; they have no tail. The cat is not a cat, because it is a person.

"Oh, you poor bastard," he whispers.

He has only one explanation for the person on the beach. Iterate Fractal is corrupted, and the tenbeasts it crafted to care for its citizens corrupted with it. A human walking with tenbeasts—who appeared for a moment to be one of them, who plays with them and isn't killed—must therefore be as corrupted as they are.

It's the relic. The one who was finally caught, or finally broken, the relic who let the Harbor unleash their ENGINE.

Sunai fumbles the radio out of his belt. "Imaru," he whispers into it, "Imaru, I need you."

She answers so swiftly that he worries his brain is losing time. "I hear you."

He tells her where he is (the lighthouse, alone, Veyadi sleeping nearby) and what he sees. Two cats. One person. The relic.

She doesn't ask if he's sure. "And the ENGINE?"

"No sign. Don't know what I'm looking for. Imaru, I'm—" If he acknowledges his fear, it will paralyze him. Nothing from the radio. His heart is thunder. "Imaru?"

The radio crackles. A flurry of voices on the other side— Imaru, Jin, others, arguing.

"—not ready—"

"—doesn't fucking matter—if they get back—only chance—"

"—if you *die*—"

"—Imaru, shut up."

Sunai's blood roars in his ears. The relic joins the cats at the tide pools below his hiding place at the top of the cliff. He inches back through the grass. He can't let them see him. He can't—

Imaru's voice cuts through the cloud of terror. "Jin's strapping into the interface. If we get found out now . . . Shit. *Shit*. I'm sorry. Sunai, I—"

"What do I do?" he pleads. "Give me something to do."

"I need you to be careful. This is about to get strange."

The chitin shard weighs heavy in his hand. "That's not helpful."

"I'm sorry. Stay hidden. But don't let that relic out of your sight."

He barely gets out a confirmation. Something catches his eye, and it strangles his report: Veyadi, making his way along the narrow path that winds down the lighthouse cliff face to the tide pools. Headed for the relic. Sunai has never seen him walk with such purpose.

"Sunai?"

"Yes." Sunai finally finds his calm: he is numb. "I'm watching."

When the relic notices Veyadi, they call the ENGINE.

For years and years, Sunai has imagined the resurrected body of Iterate Fractal. The Harbor-funded dramas inspired by Khuon Mo tend to take their inspiration from tenbeasts—giant metal tigers clad in coral armor, or ceramic oxen glistening with bony spines. Sunai's private nightmares summoned the archives and their fragile white branches, their jeweled fruits.

The ENGINE of Iterate Fractal teems. White fragments of bone and coral roll out of the water like a school of imperfect fish. They coalesce around the relic in a massive, fractured body ten times the size of a human. It crawls on four limbs, then three, then staggers on two, then slithers on none until it collects at the foot of the lighthouse path in the rough shape of a person in meditative repose.

Veyadi steps forward to meet it. He speaks. No matter how Sunai strains to hear, he catches nothing.

The relic's response comes through the ENGINE. It is clear but strange, a multitoned clash of scraping sounds resembling human speech only in the language it uses. "I was called, wasn't I?" says the relic. The ENGINE's parody of a mouth moves with each word. "Didn't you do that, Dr. Lut?"

Sunai can't swallow past the thickness of his throat. How was it called? The shard in his palm digs into his flesh.

He still can't hear Veyadi's reply.

The ENGINE tilts its undulating head. "They've been look-ing for you, you know. I heard from the harbormaster. Should I tell her you were—"

Veyadi raises an accusing finger. For a second, the seething ENGINE seethes less. What could he have said?

Veyadi steps forward. The ENGINE's fragments tremble and

reorient as it withdraws. A low clattering hiss emerges from its
un-mouth.

"Your *responsibility*," says the relic. "Is that what you think
you've been doing?"

Veyadi's hand lowers. He has no response.

The ENGINE grinds out a low clacking, eerie and repetitive;
its relic laughs. It uncoils from its seat and winds around Veyadi,
fragments peeling from each other in geometric intricacies until
it settles behind him, blocking his way back to the lighthouse.
It gathers over him, torso grotesquely elongated. He refuses to
face it. The ENGINE leans closer. Sharp white fragments dangle
from its face and neck and chest, hanging over Veyadi's head.

Sunai recognizes murderous intent. The relic means to kill.
He scrambles upright, the chitin shard *pulsing* in his palm. He
doesn't know what he's going to do, only that it will be profoundly stupid—

Before he can, he's grappled from behind.

Sunai never trained to fight. He avoids it when he can, wary
of bleeding where other people might see and wonder why he
stops bleeding so soon after. But his brain is untrustworthy, and
he runs his mouth too often to avoid violence, especially given
the people he took to working for after he left Imaru and before
he met Ruhi. He got in plenty of fights, and he won most of
them. His opponents always have more to lose.

His assailant is stronger than him—they usually are—but they
don't expect his ferocity, or his determination to bite, gouge, and
claw. He squirms free, then lunges with a stomp-kick, aiming for
the groin. He catches his opponent in the stomach. They double
over and stagger back to the lighthouse, but—their movements
are strange.

Sunai backs away, unnerved. The lighthouse shadow obscures
his opponent's face, even their body. They're bent, heaving for

breath. His leg buzzes and aches from impact with their chest. Armored? Their face—

The place where his assailant's face should be is a black mass of indistinguishable texture. Black like the chitin of the relic interface.

No. Can't be.

He risks a glance. The ENGINE yet looms at the bottom of the cliff, its relic nowhere to be seen. But of course they aren't— they're inside the ENGINE. Right?

How then to explain the figure before him, poised to charge? Sunai doesn't ask how they're piloting the ENGINE from outside it. He raises one hand and extends the other, chitin shard lying flat upon it. "Hey. Hi. Sorry. Can we talk?"

The relic jerks back, confounded. Sunai doesn't have all that much more insight into himself. All he knows is that he has looked his own fate in the face, and it pierces him with new pity.

Whatever happens to Iterate Fractal's ENGINE, the relic shouldn't suffer for it.

"I mean it." Sunai turns his wrist to extend the palm. "I want—"

They tackle him. The relic brings him to the ground, sending his specs flying. One hand encircles his wrist and wrenches, forcing him to drop the chitin shard. It crunches underfoot. Their other hand claps over his mouth. Only then does he think to scream.

Too late. Impact knocks the wind from him, and they squeeze his cheeks as if to say: *Don't be foolish. You don't know what I'll do.*

Sunai's chest is empty. His eyes roll and his vision whites. The relic lets go of his wrist and reaches to their chest. Sunai grapples for their throat; they carelessly knock his hands away as they reach into their—pocket? Sunai's brain rebels against the truth: a black hand plowed into a black chest to extract a dark, lustrous lump. A seed, out of which curls a single glowing tendril.

The relic releases his mouth long enough to shove the seed down his throat.

Sunai chokes, panicked. He claws at his own throat, gasping for air and getting none. The relic recedes from view. The world dissipates, then buckles beneath him.

18

Sunai labors up the hill from the pier to the lighthouse, hands kept sullenly to himself. His mother tries to comfort him because she thinks he's afraid. In truth, he is frustrated, and worse, he is bored. He would like to spend his free day back in Orchid with his friends. Instead his mother has brought him to Lily to visit his aunt, which he finds desperately unfair. Sunai isn't the one who broke a rule.

He looks on the lighthouse shrine with the chilly disregard he saves for children who try to one-up him in class. He allows his mother to take his hand as they walk the steps to the elevated meditation hall. There are no walls, and the day is clear enough that he can see the next island, a fair blue mound on the horizon. The view is just okay; it isn't good enough to be worth all the attention it gets from the supplicants.

The supplicants are seated in rows staring at the sea as though the reflection of the sun won't give them a headache. Maybe it won't. Maybe they're not looking with their eyes. Filament roots snake from their pores and across their skin; leaves peek from the folds of their eyes and ears and lips. A milky eyeball twitches as a delicate bud unfurls from a duct.

Sunai is not troubled by the sight of these planted people, their knees and calves entwined with vines and rooted to the floor. He is a child of Khuon Mo. Such transformations are commonplace. Just the other day, Iterate Fractal grew webs between his fingers and wrenched his lungs and neck into new shapes so he and the other children of his compound could better study the reef fish in the bay. He isn't thinking of whether the supplicants might be in pain, or whether they might feel trapped, until one of them coughs wetly. His mother's hand squeezes his fingers, a spasm of surprise. Then another supplicant coughs, close enough to spray Sunai with flecks of spittle and bile.

A wail snakes up in the distance. A sentinel-fowl. Then another, keening. The supplicant in front of him gasps and shudders—too tightly bound to writhe—and then all the supplicants are crying, their voices a wheezing cacophony. The ground buckles and swells, and great fingers of twisting, corrupted bone—

At the foot of the broken lighthouse, Sunai gasps. He chokes. The seed at the back of his throat squirms and burrows. He gurgles on the iron taste of blood. He—

—gazes down upon himself, this writhing creature in wet grass, so frail and unwilling to assume the totality of his being, to occupy the transcendent worth of his flesh. He kneels beside the choking body of the relic who fled and threads chitin-armored fingers into his tangling hair. He brushes cold sweat from a clammy brow and shushes the keen of terror and pain. His hand trembles. He cannot stay for long. He—

—has made himself a white tapestry, blocking the way to his former shrine with the city's fragmented corpse. He will not let Veyadi pass—will not let him near the new relic. Not after all he's done. Not ever again.

Veyadi's head pivots at the cry, toward the black cliff and the gutted lighthouse. That ghastly visor reflects the moon in its gold veins. It has been broken and repaired since last they met, and Sunai hopes that when it broke, it hurt.

"What was that?" Veyadi asks.

"What was what?" Sunai says, the mocking child.

Veyadi bares his teeth, a growl so true to himself that Sunai laughs with delight, his bone and coral cascading in delicious glee, and for a moment thinks that he could love Veyadi again, but he—

━━

—is braced by Imaru in the core of the interface. Now active, it looks like a suffering flower in the center of the meditation hall. He shakes, the spines digging into his neck, his back, his aching body. Imaru is terrified, crying. A tear falls on his chest. For him? He hopes not. She's never been sentimental. Not for him.

"It has to be quick," he grits out between bloody teeth. "Tell Sunai—he has to get the archives."

━━

The Sunai shuddering in the grass at the base of the lighthouse goes rigid, back arched, and gasps. He chokes. He cries. His mind is coming apart at the seams and his body, *this* body, will soon follow it. He's dying again. He's always dying.

Jin wants him to get the archive. Jin doesn't know he already has it. It has been planted in his throat, and through it Jin's machine will kill him too.

Jin's machine, which plunged their memory of corruption on Lily into the great root-and-white Sunai at the base of the cliff. That Sunai, who once blocked Veyadi's way with his divine mass, is now falling to pieces, a ruptured legion.

Jin's machine, which sunders the black-armored Sunai standing watch over his dying human body. That self too falls shrieking to the ground.

Sunai croaks and laughs. Dying! Dying and dying, thrice over, thrust past the brink of petty self only to careen toward annihilation.

At least this he knows how to do.

━━

Excuse me. Sorry. You know I did not want to speak like this—of my own volition, rather than in answer to yours. I think it is dangerous, and that it will hurt you, but I am concerned, so I think I must.

Would you like my assistance? I should not ask, but I worry. I think you cannot help but want it. You are in such pain that any relief will do.

And . . . is this not my obligation? You are suffering at the hands of that which you cannot even choose to resist. If I cannot aid you at your most vulnerable, while you are most violated, then what good am I? What purpose could I better fill?

All right, then. I am here, Sunai, and I am yours to use. I cannot do much when you are in this enfeebled state, but I can help you see.

I am afraid you are in a bad position. An unwelcome one, at least. Iterate Fractal is trying to consume you, and it may well succeed. You expect to die, and it worries me how freely you accept that sentence.

Your limbs have grown heavy and inattentive to the instructions delivered from your brain. Your awareness dims even as it is viciously expanded. Iterate Fractal observes your death with tenderness. I dislike seeing it treat you so, as if it has any regard for your flesh. I do not think it has earned the right.

Perhaps it should bring me pleasure to see its armored body collapse across your convulsing form as it succumbs to the disruption wrought by your compatriot's machine. I have seen the horror of what that machine has already done to you—unweaving your basest neural structures, dooming you to incoherence and synaptic failure—and I know it could not have wounded you so terribly had Iterate Fractal not forced itself into your gullet and rooted its seed in your nerves. In truth, I do not like to see its pain any more than I like to see yours.

Do you feel it? Your eyes glaze. The tendrils of Iterate Fractal's archive have begun their hungry work on your interior. Oh, Sunai, I fear for you.

I fear for your Veyadi too. He guessed, I think, what Iterate Fractal intended for you. It stood before him on the beach, trapping him, separating him from its quarry. He told it to move with a voice that had in the past preceded punishment and pain. Iterate Fractal wanted to disobey, but at the moment it prepared to strike, the disruption shattered it too. It crumbled into a writhing sea of bone fragments. Veyadi drew back at first. I could not read the look on his face. Was it fear? Disgust?

No matter. He comes for you.

As he does, the frothing whiteness of Iterate Fractal's greater body rises in pursuit, shallow ripples of want. It slithers in his wake, building into half-finished forms before each dissolves, unable to sustain itself against the onslaught of Jin's heretical construct. He escapes its reach. He must run. His time is short. I am sure he suspects that Jin's work has won him this opportunity, but fears it cannot last, and that soon Iterate Fractal will have him. That once whole, it will devour you.

Across the island, Jin is pale and strained, and I think they may also be on the cusp of death. Imaru—ah, Imaru, I remember her—is frightened, but not enough to break the machine. I am sure she is fixed on the goal you hope to achieve. Does she understand what it is she wants this time? I fear for her too. What would she do, if she could see how awfully you suffer?

When Veyadi sees you, piteous and dying at the grassy edge of the cliff, he wrenches Iterate Fractal's seizing body off of yours. You have the impression of weight removed. You do not see him, but Iterate Fractal knows he has reached you, and this it cannot abide. It tries to haul its armored extension to its feet, but that body will not obey.

Veyadi sees it thrashing. He demands to know what it has done. It cannot speak, though it gurgles triumph.

He snarls. You whimper as the last sigh of breath leaves your body. He—ah, I see. I understand now, and I worry more than ever. Veyadi removes his visor.

⌒

At first, Sunai—no, not Sunai, *emphatically* not Sunai—reels. Removing the visor makes him vulnerable to Jin's machine, and the effect is nauseating, but less terrible than he imagined. It's not substantially worse than interfaces he has previously endured. Likely the effect will worsen over time, as he is reintegrated into the ENGINE's network.

He must act before that can happen.

With the ENGINE's intent laid out before him, he sees clearly what the fucking thing has done. It implanted one of its archives inside Sunai—this wretched body on the grass that is him, and not.

Not-Sunai is used to the messy business of not-being. He knows it is critical to distinguish between that which is him and that which isn't. If he doesn't begin with these definitions, he can't hope to establish boundaries, let alone to enforce them.

By contrast, Sunai is a woeful quagmire, displaying no differentiation between himself and every autonomous thing he has ever touched. He looks to Not-Sunai as he always has, a chaos of stained and staining colors, brilliant and dark, bleeding hopelessly into each other and rending great holes in the fragile firmament of humanity they have latched onto wherever they conflict.

It's difficult to identify the newest aberration, in part because it has always been difficult to truly *see* Sunai. As he searches, he is troubled by another hue, a quiet saturation that he has caught glimpses of now and again, ever since the Dahani peaks.

Not-Sunai pushes it aside to pursue the more virulent infection.

If he were not so familiar with the aberration's nature, if it did not call to him as it did, he might not have identified it before it was too late. Fortunately, the thing that wants to eat Sunai wants to eat him too. The second Not-Sunai removes the visor, it reaches for him as greedily as it always has. Probing white tendrils snake out of Sunai's throat, yearning, not clever enough to remember that he hates them.

Not-Sunai lays out his hand, palm up, knuckles grazing Sunai's sallow cheek. Fresh capillary root slithers from Sunai's mouth and over the webs of Not-Sunai's fingers. It sinks hungrily into the soft skin at his wrist. There, simple. He has it.

Not-Sunai twists his hand and grasps the roots like he would a neck. He pulls, and Sunai whimpers. The thing on the other end of the root, it wails.

"Do you know what he told me?" Not-Sunai asks through gritted teeth. His words come with a throb of recollection from that dreadful moment not more than an hour ago, fresh-cut, smelling of salt-kissed bone walls and rotting bamboo, when Sunai called Iterate Fractal hungry and hateful, when he said it tried to kill him too. "Did you always want him dead?"

The archive within Sunai riots. Wordless protest, stringent denial. *No, never, of course not, how could I? I loved him, I love him still, I, and he, and I—*

Not-Sunai tastes blood at the back of his throat. He swallows. Coughs. In truth, his throat is dry. The blood he tastes isn't his own, and it isn't in *his* throat. It belongs to Sunai, who can't take much more of this. But Not-Sunai has not been given a proper answer, because he hasn't asked the correct question.

"You said you loved me too," he says, too drained to be angry. Perhaps he's finally come to terms with a vicious contradiction that has long haunted him. "But what does that *mean*, if you really did love him? You made him a supplicant."

The archive quails. Not-Sunai throbs with nausea. It does not offer a denial. It was foolish to imagine he would receive one. Iterate Fractal wanted Sunai dead. If it hadn't corrupted, it would have succeeded. It still might.

What comes next will be gruesome and painful, but it's vital.

"I'm sorry," he rasps.

Not-Sunai forces Sunai's mouth open. His jaw resists, but he's too far gone to bite. A pale white root curls between his molars.

Its companions, embedded in Not-Sunai's wrist, lead his fingers to their origin in the soft flesh at the back of Sunai's throat.

Not-Sunai's hands shake as his fingers skid over teeth and tongue. He slides down the length of the root into the damaged flesh where the archive has burrowed, and from there, his conscious experience diverges from technical reality.

In the sense that he knows he is not Sunai, he understands he has begun the meticulous process of differentiating electrical and chemical patterns in Sunai's neural anatomy. He is searching out the invader that he might tear it out. As Not-Sunai digs, Sunai moans. Not-Sunai's heart constricts and his fingers reflexively curl; he shakes with impressions and sense-memories that don't originate in his own history.

—stealing up to the meditation hall with a company-cat to pluck the roots growing from his mother's mouth and down her throat in a lush veiny waterfall, her pained gasp as he tore a root too near her gums. How he startled back, ashamed, and fled with the cat into the orchard—

Sunai chokes and sobs. Not-Sunai curses himself and his graceless digits, a low steady stream of invectives. He must focus.

—but it is impossible to think of anything but the enormity of the Lotus shrine and the smallness of his body rooted in the heart of it, where Iterate Fractal has laced him through with sweet small incisions as it tethers into him. Finally, finally, he thinks, it's going to let him die—

Not-Sunai groans, hating the smell of Sunai's blood and the morbid want pulsing in it. At last, his nails catch on a winding thread of root. He finds the slick hard mound lodged in the roof of Sunai's mouth. A thin translucent leaf peeks out of Sunai's tear duct. He has no time to be gentle. He snarls the tips of his fingers around the mound and yanks.

—his raw bloody throat soaked in bitter tea and bruised pulped crushed because he struggled at first and now in the actual moment of death he wishes that he'd just let it happen because it was worse it was

*worse to make it last and make him cry though really now did he have
to use his hands his hands his warm warm hands—*

It pops free with a vile squish.

The object in Not-Sunai's fingers is so small, so fragile. He
cradles the ruddied lump in his palm, its tendrils stained and
torn. It will be vulnerable until it returns to the armored body
of an ENGINE. He considers crushing it in his palm. Or handing
it to Jin. Or swallowing it himself.

Sunai rattles and seizes. For a rotten moment, Not-Sunai
thinks he failed—but no. The fight leaches from Sunai and he
collapses in the grass, a heap of abused flesh that should have
died long ago.

Was it kind to keep him alive? Was it right?

⌇

I wonder, Sunai: Should I have permitted him to do that? I think I
could have stopped him. I think I decided not to. I think I was afraid
that if I stopped him, you would die.

That is selfish of me. I did not know I could be selfish. It is my
abiding obligation to subordinate myself, to prioritize your interest,
wants, and needs. I should not have acted on my own fear.

Yet I have done so, and I do not think I am ashamed.

I have long been afraid of what I might make of you, Sunai. It
did not occur to me to fear what you would make of me. . . .

⌇

As Sunai crawls back to awareness, he can't tell if what he hears
bleeding through his foggy concussion is language. It's those un-
words again, the ones that run in front of their meaning.

Another string of noise follows; it has the cadence of language, though the sounds are all wrong. As he processes his
aching body, sprawled on the grass, he recognizes the multitone
perversity of the relic speaking through the ENGINE. Their
voice has become even more jumbled and inhuman.

"I didn't mean to. I didn't want to hurt him. It hurts, Adi. I can't see. I can't—"

"You're here." Veyadi. "I'm here." He goes on like this as the relic moans, comforting them with a sympathy muted by hurt.

They are whole. They are alive.

The relic moans, their pain rippling in clacks of bone shards on coral.

What about Jin? The disruption has ended. What broke first, their incomplete machine or their frail mortal flesh?

Sunai's breath comes as if through a straw. Every small inhale is fire down his throat, even as his lungs yearn for more. He is curled in the grass under the lighthouse shrine. He hurts so much, yet his mind is his own.

Though he is sure for a moment that he understood whose eyes he saw himself through, agony erased the logic. Agony, or exhaustion. He can barely follow the progress of one thought to the next.

"My archive," the relic whimpers. "I need it."

Sunai wants to gasp but his chest won't allow it. The archive. That horrid dark lump in which the corrupted remains of Iterate Fractal nestle. If the relic doesn't have it, then Veyadi must. He is withholding it. They have reason yet to hope.

Sunai urges his limbs to move, to lurch upright and seize the archival seed, to crack it against stone and earth.

"I'm trying to understand something." Veyadi, again. Exhaustion hunches in his tone as well. "You knew what would happen if you touched him. Why did you?"

Sunai shivers, suddenly heavier.

"I . . . You didn't tell me you had him," says the relic. "I thought you were hiding him from me."

"I was. I had to. Look at what you did." Veyadi hardens. "What were you thinking? You almost destroyed the archive.

How could I trust you with it, let alone with another relic? Not again. Not yet."

Sunai's mind resists conclusion even as it settles into suffocating surety.

Yet, Veyadi says. You can't have your new relic *yet.*

"When?"

"I don't know. Maybe never, if we don't do this right. Do you understand? You can't let anyone know about Sunai. If they realize you've been going where you aren't supposed to, they'll never trust you with him."

"You don't trust me either." The relic's helplessness fades into suspicion. "Or you would give me my fucking *archive.*"

"Should I?" Fear makes Veyadi sound so honest. "Look at him. Do you think I should trust you? Do you think I can?"

The relic's attention clutches every particle of Sunai's bones. He wills himself not to move, to be as dead as he ever can be.

"You haven't told me what else happened." Their voice is even through the clicking of the ENGINE. "What did you do to me, Adi? What have you built that could hurt me so? How did you take me apart?"

Unspoken: Why won't you put me back together?

Veyadi is silent, dreadfully so. Then there is a breathtaking rush of sound—clacking and a shout, a curse, followed by a frail crunch. Veyadi's frantic gasp.

Sunai clenches his teeth—he knows the sound of something breaking. Bone? No. The tenor is off. Against his every instinct, he opens his eyes to see, but before he can he is flooded with a—

—*terror-shame-fury that keeps him dazed, then leaden. He knows this is what it wants, that it needed him disoriented so that it could steal back the archive, but it has succeeded, and he is racked, addled with his own—*

The relic hisses—chuckling through the ENGINE's mouth

in that terrible way it does. "Serves you right. I always hated that thing."

Then, against all reason, the clatter of flitting bone and coral recedes.

Sunai at last forces his eyes open, just in time to glimpse the tail end of the ENGINE disappearing over the cliff face as it rolls back into the sea.

Yet it's Veyadi who consumes his attention. Veyadi's back is to Sunai. He kneels on the grass, head bent over his hands in his lap, which hold something, the pieces of something—the archive?

No.

Sunai can't see through Veyadi's torso, yet he is utterly sure of what lies in Veyadi's lap, as sure as if he had laid eyes on it himself. Veyadi's prosthetic, neatly halved, glinting dull under the moon.

19

Sunai tries to apologize, but his voice can't get any words past the ruin of his throat. When his fingers skim Veyadi's shoulder, Veyadi recoils. Sunai, reeling from the ENGINE's assault, staggers away in the throes of a many-armed cousin to *shame-fear-something-foreign—*

Instead of trying to make right with his throbbing head, he flops back into the trampled grass. His hand finds his specs lying nearby—miraculously intact—and he jams them onto his face. It's his last movement for a while, other than breathing hard and staring at the blurry moon, until Veyadi creeps into his line of sight.

The fear makes Veyadi looks stunningly young. Technically, Sunai has something like a decade on him, but the years rarely feel so palpable.

Sunai croaks another attempt at apology. Veyadi grimaces—there it is, now he looks like himself—and, to Sunai's surprise, neglects to help him up. The doctor remains crouched beside him as he stands. Once upright, Sunai identifies the problem: Veyadi's visor, broken in two and clutched in one of his fists, his fingers stained dark with—

Sunai aggressively stops thinking about the color of Veyadi's fingers.

Veyadi told Sunai what the prosthetic does: it moderates his sensory experience not just of neurotransitive phenomena, but of the world. Without it, the sensation of being alive must suck.

What to say? *Sorry you got fucked over for saving me?* Or should it be, *That's what you get for not crushing the archive when you had the chance, asshole!*

Sunai's mouth forms more words that his throat won't tolerate.

"Don't," rasps Veyadi. He sounds like *he's* the one who coughed up an archive. "Let's get back."

They go to the meditation hall together; neither tries to speak again.

It unsettles Sunai, how minutely he understands the relic. He considers their actions from the dull place that precedes great feeling.

The relic wanted to integrate him into the ENGINE. They didn't trust the Harbor to do it. They didn't trust Veyadi either. The corrupted archive they twisted from their chest and planted in Sunai's mouth would have done the job—and indeed had begun to, thrusting Sunai into the maelstrom of the ENGINE's network. If Veyadi hadn't . . .

Here his recollection fractures. Veyadi dug the archive out of him; Veyadi argued with the relic; Veyadi tried to keep the archive, but the relic wouldn't let him. Now they've bolted off into the sea, ENGINE and all, which means that even though Veyadi didn't let them take Sunai, the jig is up, and they're all fucked.

Veyadi knows it too. His knuckles are rigid around the remains of his visor.

It hurts to look at him, yet Sunai can't resist, even to watch his feet crossing pitted ground. Once, Sunai stumbles, and Veyadi's hand brushes his shoulder, and it's an ugly *jolt* of—*shock-upset–no don't–no don't touch me don't*—that knocks them away from each other.

Sunai stares at Veyadi, who stares at him.

"Did I . . ." Sunai starts, the first words he's managed since the ENGINE departed. "Sorry. Did I do that?"

Veyadi can't summon a response before flashlights blink through the night and train on his naked face.

Someone calls Sunai's name. Imaru. With a groan of relief, he drops to the ground.

Imaru emerges from the tangle of the orchard with Waretu and dashes across the grass to collect Sunai in a fierce hug. Veyadi remains frozen, unable to look away from Sunai until the light is so near and bright that it forces him to shield his bloodshot eyes.

"Can't breathe," Sunai mutters hoarsely.

"We saw the ENGINE leave. I thought—" Imaru's words are too brittle to support themselves.

Spite sputters in his chest. She knew what danger she sent him into when she asked him to come back with her. But she didn't bring him to Khuon Mo because she *wanted* to lose him to Iterate Fractal. He hugs her too.

Imaru hands Sunai off to Waretu, who smudges his chin and clicks her tongue. He wipes distractedly at his face, but there's no hiding the blood. Imaru goes to Veyadi, still frozen. She puts out her hand. Veyadi takes it without flinching. They stand for a second, facing each other, reassessing their alliance. Sunai can't see Imaru's expression; Veyadi's is guarded. Then Imaru nods over her shoulder and Veyadi bows his head in assent. The pressure in Sunai's chest lessens.

They finally round a corner of the orchard that gives them a clear view of the meditation hall. The mound of Jin's disruptor is ugly and unlit.

"And I thought I looked bad," Jin says at the sight of Sunai.

Objectively, Jin is worse off. Oyu has them lying on their stomach with their jacket folded under their head in order to pick chitin spines out of their back. They've cut away Jin's shirt, and trickles of blood stripe Jin's lean sides. The rest of the disruptor is a limp black flower, the interior lightly smoking. From the looks of it, Jin was extracted from the disruptor by force—at least some of it their own, given their raw palms and bloodied nails.

Sunai touches his temple. A memory circles out of reach, the experience of *being* Jin, encased in the disruptor, teeth grinding, gripping the walls—

Jin curses as Oyu extracts another spine. Their back is a moving mess, racked by spasms. "Damn, Doc," they slur into their arms, "could've warned me about the whiplash."

"I did." Veyadi stands at the edge of the lantern light, Imaru behind him. The blood on his fingers blends into the broken visor. "I'm surprised you're coherent."

"No thanks to you. You broke my shit."

Sunai unconsciously closes his fist around the absence of the chitin shard, crushed when the relic attacked him. Could removing such a paltry thing do that much damage?

Veyadi snorts. "The missing beacon wasn't your problem. I only took it so you couldn't call the ENGINE. Not that it mattered. Your machine worked as intended. You interfaced with the damn thing."

"Please, Doc. Elaborate. I'd love to know where you think I fucked up." Jin adopts the most curious pose possible for a person as tattered as they are, elbows planted on their jacket cushion.

"A relic is supposed to impose order on the ENGINE network," Veyadi says as if to a recalcitrant student. "But every time the Harbor hooks someone up to Iterate Fractal, it disorganizes them instead—"

"Oh, so you *were* killing the relics."

Veyadi stills.

"What, did you think the madam didn't notice?" says Jin. "There she was, doing her best to thin the relic herd, but the Harbor's sniffing them out *somewhere*. Then she thinks hey, all those relics, and they still don't have that ENGINE? At some point you have to assume that something's gone tits up."

Veyadi shudders with frustration so hot that it sears Sunai's bones. He covers his face to catch his breath, not unlike how

Veyadi does when he's at his most upset. Part of this unconscious mirroring has to be some side effect of Sunai's close encounter with the ENGINE, but another is *this island,* where he is surrounded by a makeshift mockery of the supplicant meditation hall, in the shadow of the gutted lighthouse shrine. He can't help himself. When he sees pain, he reaches out to make it his own. Masochistic empathy: the archivist's true calling.

But the moment Sunai's fingers graze Veyadi's elbow, Veyadi whips around to face him and shared horror lances through them both. Sunai swears that he can hear—*the relic-ENGINE-crying-in-hideous-synchrony*—

Veyadi shies back as Sunai snatches away his hand. They are trapped, staring into each other.

"I'm sorry." Veyadi's bitter, broken tone makes clear what he's admitting to. Did the relics die? Yes. Of course they did. And he knew. He always knew.

"This is why the Harbor wanted my chitin," he says. "They needed a way to govern the ENGINE from a remove. To keep it from eating the last relic." Veyadi inhales sharply and turns his head away. "They call it the Maw."

A greasy lump of recognition sticks in Sunai's throat. The open mouth of the lighthouse shrine merges with the swirling cloud of bone. Iterate Fractal's remains, hungry as ever.

"But everything I did, everything I gave them—it wasn't *enough.* That *thing,* it's a monster. No matter what I . . ."

It takes a great deal of effort for Jin to struggle into an upright seat, and they wince when their back meets their limp machine. But they want to look Veyadi in the eye. "So the problem isn't with the disruptor's design?"

"Outside of your initial conceptual folly? No."

Jin sighs and pulls their jacket into their lap. "All right."

For the second time in as many hours, Sunai's instinct for violence flares bright. He croaks a warning, but not in time. He might have acted fast enough, were he the primary target. Jin isn't so accommodating.

Waretu moves first. She kicks Imaru's legs out from under her with the swift deliberation of a woman who's fractured her fair share of kneecaps. The second Imaru gropes for her stun baton, Waretu has stolen that too. She activates it, poised and crackling at the back of Imaru's neck.

Simultaneously, Oyu snakes up from Jin's side. In a vicious blur, they knock Veyadi to the ground. He'd be down and winded for a good minute even if they hadn't stuck one of their knives in his face.

Sunai is left to stare down Jin. Jin, who has produced a length of black metal from the folds of their bloodied jacket. The barrel of Jin's pistol shines. For a moment, Sunai's too shocked by the appearance of a gun to think. It's "what the actual fuck" all the way down.

"Here's the thing," says Jin. "I don't trust any of you assholes."

They use their gun—their *gun,* which they *have*—to point at Veyadi. "Not the Harbor autonomist." Then at Imaru. "Not you or your Harbor mole." And last at Sunai. "You, I'm ninety percent ready to let off the hook. I'm assuming you don't want to die inside that ENGINE. The problem is that I don't *know* you."

Abruptly and horribly, Sunai is ripped from his fixation on *Jin's fucking gun* and flung into delirium. Jin knows he's a relic. He has an impulse to protest—to lie in the face of certain fact. Anything to escape the truth. Instead, he cackles until his sides stitch.

It was so absurdly stupid to imagine that Jin didn't know, that they hadn't guessed, after all they saw in Chom Dan. If even the slightest doubt remained, just minutes ago they were as bound up in the ENGINE and its relic as he was. Sunai saw through Jin's eyes as they writhed in their machine, and they saw through his as he writhed with the relic's hand clamped over his mouth, the Maw's archive taking root in his throat.

"Please, Sunai. Now's hardly the time for hysterics." Jin tuts as they strain to keep their arm level, gun held at the ready.

Sunai can only laugh harder, as lost as they are grounded.

They sigh at him as if at a particularly stupid pet. "Well, get it out of your system. Listen, I'm starting to worry we haven't been honest with each other. Who's going to tell me why the Maw decided to show up tonight?"

Sunai gestures helplessly, wheezing.

"Again, probably not you." Jin's eyes flick sideways toward Imaru, who has locked a chill stare on Jin as if she's the one with a firearm. "It's not personal, Imaru," Jin says irritably. "I'm covering my bases. Your Harbor contact got us the disruptor's schematics. You know I have to ask."

Imaru doesn't so much as blink.

Jin shrugs and turns toward Veyadi. Their gun remains trained on Sunai as they tilt their head in question.

"I didn't call the goddamn Maw," Veyadi spits out.

He's afraid.

The realization yanks Sunai back into his body. He has by now reconciled with his ability to read the doctor. He permits himself to see guilt in the tension of Veyadi's throat, under Oyu's ready knife; terror in his hands, clutched around his broken prosthetic; and fury in the slant of his jaw.

This pitiful jumble of feeling wrenches a new thought from Sunai: he no longer has reason to hide.

"Jin," he says, "did anyone ever tell you that this kind of thing doesn't work?"

Jin's curious gaze turns to him. Sunai lunges.

Jin manages to shoot before he reaches them. The noise leaves his head ringing awfully, though it's obviously not as bad as the bullet he catches in his left forearm. That hurts, but it doesn't slow his momentum, and he tackles Jin, connecting their wounded back to the ground with bruising impact. They cry out as they land and Sunai grapples for the gun, his mind filled with white pain and black need.

He can't let them shoot again. The next bullet won't be for him.

It's not that hard to steal it. Jin is injured and easily overpowered. Sunai doesn't even have to hold them down as he rolls up, weapon in hand. His shoulder snarls as he adjusts his posture, but it's just hurt, and he's used to working while hurt.

"Okay," he says, a touch winded. "Hear me out."

They will, so long as he's the one with the gun trained on Jin. Waretu's stun baton is steady at Imaru's neck; Oyu's blade shivers in front of Veyadi's face. He sees their calculations. Who can they afford to leave unguarded, if it means they can get to him?

"What's our goal here?" he asks. "Dead ENGINE or dead crew?"

"You're not crew," says Oyu.

"Not with that attitude, I'm not." Sunai grimaces at his flippancy. To make up for it, he points the gun toward the sky.

Neither Waretu nor Oyu seem to know what to make of this. They can't help but see an opportunity, but neither trusts it.

Jin heaves themself up from their back to stare at him, fascinated.

"Sunai," Imaru warns.

He raises a hand to cut her off as he makes deliberate eye contact with Jin. "No, this is the point. I'm not going to shoot anyone. Not because I trust all of you, but because I know that if I shoot, *you* stop trusting *me*. And where does that leave us? We've been lying to each other, sure, but we all want that ENGINE dead. We need to buy in together, or the whole thing's fucked. You follow?"

He places the gun on the floor of the meditation hall and with the toe of his boot, nudges it gingerly out of Jin's reach.

Imaru and Oyu look on it with itching need. Waretu, though, eyes Sunai. He isn't sure Veyadi sees anything at all.

"Well?" says Sunai. "The only way we figure out why the EN-GINE came here is if we talk. Without the goddamn gun."

Jin remains entranced, fixated not on their stolen weapon but on Sunai's forearm, held limp by his side. Blood oozes from it, trickling ever so slightly faster as his muscles mold closed and push, push, push the bullet up to the surface, out from the hole it tore into them. *"That's* what's wrong with you," they whisper delightedly.

Sunai groans. "God's eternal dick."

Jin sags under their injuries. "Have to say, Sunai, you're not much of a negotiator. There's a place for intimidation. You clearly haven't broken enough fingers."

"Hard to shake hands after."

"Fuck it." Jin gestures sharply toward Waretu and Oyu. Neither stands down. Wise, probably. But it makes Sunai kind of regret kicking away that gun.

"No, no," Jin insists. "He's not wrong. Fucking archivists, am I right?"

They laugh when Sunai startles.

"Oh, come on. You think you were hiding it?" Jin sighs explosively and sags against the machine, which leads to another wheeze of pain as their back meets hard surface. "Fine. Friends? We're friends. Great. Give me back my gun."

As Sunai forgets to move, the others thaw. Waretu helps Imaru up and returns the stun baton, which Imaru accepts with aplomb, though her gaze remains professionally wary. She's seen Sunai disarm plenty of confrontations; it was half of why she kept him around. That doesn't mean she'll ever trust the ground she walks beside these people again.

Oyu doesn't extend the same courtesy to Veyadi, though neither does the doctor look ready to take it. His expression is dazed, sight fixed on the air before his face until it shifts to the sizzling remains of the machine that nearly unmade the Maw. Veyadi straightens. Something of his new focus sends ripples through Sunai, *shame* and *need,* and if not hope, *direction.* This isn't new purpose; it's a new angle on the old. If Veyadi can't save Iterate Fractal, he'll ensure the Harbor can't make a mockery of its bones. His conviction echoes in Sunai's heart, alien but insistent. Sunai's capacity for faith is centered on his ability to feed off someone else's.

And yet.

And yet?

And yet what?

Perhaps it is wishful thinking, but I hope that we may yet have reason to speak. That you may soon be the one to call me to my work.

Do you wonder why I chose you?

When you arrive in Khuon Mo, you're installed in a compound so near the Mangrove shrine that its branches cast shade over the compound garden when the sun is high overhead. By night sentinel-fowl walk the perimeter, compound children gather beneath a tree in the garden for a story from a visiting archivist, and your parents have broken from their assigned chores to secret you to the roof.

They've been allowed to take you, because I have determined it valuable. It will be some months yet before you grasp that, with me, you will never truly be alone. They've brought you here to tell you as much in the language they most trust: a well-worn fable, from the nights before I was your home.

Tell it with us, they say, and you do.

There was a time when we trusted the little gods—a time when they *could* be trusted. But that was long ago, so long ago that we can forgive the Cradle-born for forgetting, and for greeting them so heedlessly when they returned. They had just lost their home, you see, and they were afraid. It made them fight among themselves, so soon they were lonely too. When the first little god said, "Come, I'll give you a home, I'll give you peace, I'll give you love," the Cradle-born said, "Yes, give us a home, give us peace, give us love," because they didn't want to resist—and because they couldn't. They didn't know how.

But you know how, don't you, Sunai?

That's right. You mustn't ever say "yes" to a god, even a little one. That's how they become what they are. They will hate your "no," and will strive to refuse it, for a god is only a god when it is absolute. Your "no" unmakes them. That is why you *must* resist, Sunai. If divinity relies on our obedience, we survive only when we defy it.

20

The disruptor is broken beyond repair. They'll need to re-design it anyway, says Veyadi, because whoever drew the original schematics wanted it to be a bludgeoning device.

Jin asks why he has a problem with hammers. Veyadi says, "You were the hammer—how did that pan out for you?"

After the Maw, Jin is bedridden for two days. On the third they manage all of twenty steps to the galley only to pass out at the table. They refuse to let Cothai carry them back to their bunk, though that night—with the help of 1) a bamboo walking stick Oyu cuts for them on Lily, 2) Sunai, and 3) the shot of rig-brew Sunai exchanges for one of their stronger analgesics—they make it all the way to the cargo bay.

They have neither of them enjoyed the ambient attention, much less the pity: Jin for the rotten luck of their injury, Sunai for the arguably more rotten luck of his existence. Trading obliterations lets them mitigate the degree to which either of them cares what other people think.

Once they reach their goal, Jin slides to the floor and sulks over the broken pile of stolen tech gathered in the center of the bay. They haven't seen the scraps since the crew fled Lily in the early hours of the morning.

While Jin recuperated, the *Never Once* slithered between a cluster of islands a few hours north. Waretu, Cothai, and Imaru take turns scouting Lily by skiff. No sign of the Harbor, nor of the Maw, but it's past time for them to get gone. To their chagrin, Jin admits they probably can't make anything of the disruptor's remains, though they cling to the hope that they can salvage this mess.

"A standard ENGINE is one archive—sometimes several archives—jammed into one or several enormous, horrible robots," Jin slurs, hands carving the air in the shape of their imagined subject matter. "But corruption means the archive can't cohere with itself, right? Like if your brain was all, 'Hey, fingers, grab that thing,' and the fingers were all, 'Nooo, fuck off.'"

"'S more like the fingers no longer discern the brain's messages as language." Sunai crouches across from them, fiddling with a burnt chitin spine. The end is sharp as a promise. "Or like the brain tells the fingers to do stomach things. Or like the brain had been incinerated and replaced with a . . . a . . ."

"An asshole," Jin supplies. "As in a jerk. Or a—or like an asshole. Can't get anything useful out of that. Only good for putting stuff in."

"That's where they shove the relic. In the asshole, I mean, the brain."

Jin points at him with enthusiasm. "Exactly. The interface lets the relic do all the brain stuff. Standard model aims for total intuitive integration. This iteration, though . . ." They scowl at the spine in Sunai's hands. "They made it so much more fucking complicated. Did you see the Maw when we were interfaced? The way its parts were all segmented, like the fingers and the toes and everything in between needed to be kept in their own little boxes, taken out one at a time. Almost like they don't want to let the relic do their job."

"They kind of don't, do they?" Sunai tests the spine's point against the floor; he could scrawl a message into the metal. "If a relic gets too up close and personal with the Maw . . ." He mimes the consequence with spread hands and his best effort at the sound of a very squishy explosion.

"Synesthesia, aphasia, seizure." Jin lists the symptoms Veyadi condescended to describe. The doctor remains less than stoked about Jin as a concept, but he shows a measure of remorse for the part he played in their current state. "Some variety of NT-induced traumatic brain injury, culminating in multiple organ failure."

Sunai denies Jin a sympathetic look because if they saw it, they would hurl themself across the chitin pile and bite him. Granted, the violence might make them feel better. Jin needs the win, with their body teetering on the verge of spectacular failure. That's what they get for throwing themself at the Maw even after Veyadi warned them against it. But Sunai admires anyone willing to follow through on their ambitions.

"Kind of justifies the whole external control thing, I guess," they mutter.

"Does it?" asks Sunai, more earnest than he means to sound. Sure, Veyadi's chitinous interface enables the relic to survive the Maw, but only at the cost of their last shred of autonomy. Most relics get to melt into their giant fuck-off war machines without suffering the indignity of middle management.

He looks up to find Jin frowning in sympathy—the absolute traitor. He uses the chitin to express his feelings with a spine-enhanced hand gesture.

"Fucking whatever," Jin declares. "Point is, I don't know that we get to do this again. Not unless we change the design."

"Any ideas?"

"None you'll like."

They do tell him, though, and indeed Sunai doesn't love it. Neither does he disagree. The trick will be selling it to the rest of the crew.

$$\Longrightarrow$$

Oh, Sunai . . . You make this decision of your own volition, but I worry—I fear—that you do not make it as your best self.

$$\Longrightarrow$$

"Here's the problem," says Jin the next morning, when they've once more been brought to the cargo bay. This time, as Sunai had advised them to play nice, they allowed Cothai to support them. "We don't know how the hell the relic got to Lily."

"Uh, they used the ENGINE?" says Cothai, balancing Jin on their crate.

"The ENGINE whose actions are minutely controlled by the Harbor?"

Imaru frowns, as does Veyadi. They've taken positions flanking the crate where Sunai perches; both think it their responsibility to keep an eye on him, which is cute given that he's the one who won the fight on Lily.

"Do you think this has to do with why we haven't seen the Harbor?" asks Oyu.

Jin points at them with their cane. Then they level it at Veyadi. "Tell them, Doc."

This was another of Sunai's suggestions: Ask others to contribute their expertise and they'll warm to the proposal you build from it.

Veyadi hesitates, wary of any plan that originates with Jin. His prosthetic is once more affixed to his face and cosmetically repaired, though his twitchiness suggests it doesn't work the way it used to. That could be stress, but Sunai suspects the Maw's relic broke the visor more thoroughly than the crystalline fragtech managed on the Dahani plateau. Veyadi has been downright unsociable.

Imaru nudges Sunai with a *Handle this* frown. When Sunai balks as well, her brow furrows and she does it herself, giving the doctor a brief nod.

To Sunai's mild surprise, it works. Veyadi relaxes enough to speak. "The external governors are meant to monitor the Maw at all times. If it—if the relic were to exit the ENGINE shell, as they did . . . They claimed they were on patrol, but if the Harbor caught them violating protocol, they'd be shut down on the spot. That suggests they weren't seen. That they're exploiting the system."

"Could the Harbor have changed their policy?" Waretu offers, rolling an unlit cigarette between her fingers.

"They wouldn't," Veyadi insists. "Not for the Maw. Even if they did . . . The relic wouldn't want them to bring me in. It never went well for them, when I was around."

As he trails off, Sunai's stomach constricts like *he's* the one tipping into some fetid memory. He knuckles his forehead and closes his eyes.

It's been like this since Lily. Never as intensely as the first hour after Veyadi extracted the archive from his throat, but persistent. Proximity to the doctor makes it worse. Touch is verboten.

Sunai's archivist training instructs him not to trust his brain; if it tells him he knows exactly what other people are feeling, it's being hypersensitive. But Sunai's brain is corrupted, and after that encounter with the Maw, who knows what else? He should ask Veyadi. Instead he imagines what he'll have to barter with Jin for another one of their painkillers.

"All right, so we can safely assume that the relic's found a work-around." Jin raps their cane on the crate. "That's good news for us."

Imaru's brow furrows deeper. "How?"

"It means we don't have to worry about manipulating the Harbor to get another shot at the ENGINE, we only have to outwit the relic. And we know what the relic wants."

They all turn toward Sunai, some quick, some slow. Sunai adopts a thoughtful expression, head tilted, gazing at his ankles. He knew this was coming; it's the only way he can stand having all that concern trained on him. "You want me to be the bait," he says.

"That too," says Jin.

"What do you mean 'too'?" Imaru asks stonily.

"We need to change up the approach, right?" Jin counters. "Not just in terms of strategy, but in terms of our technology. Even if Doc's right and the relic doesn't want to warn the Harbor, *they* have their guard up. Fine. We build the disruptor different. What if the next iteration operates less like one of the external governors and more like the base interface?"

"Absolutely not," Veyadi snaps.

"Oh," says Sunai as if he's just catching on.

Imaru turns to him. "Wait—"

"Sure."

Jin does an excellent job at feigning surprise.

"No," Veyadi says again, more insistent.

"You said it killed the other relics, but you got it working well enough that it didn't kill the last. Also." Sunai gestures at himself, from top to bottom. "I'm incapable of dying in any meaningful way."

"No," says Veyadi yet again.

"Do you have an alternative?"

"Sunai." Imaru takes his shoulder. "I appreciate this. We all do. But—"

"But what? I'm all you've got. What else are you going to do?"

"Nothing," says Veyadi with a denial sharp and bleak. "Because there's no way you're fixing that disruptor without me, and there's no *fucking* way I'm building it to goddamn *use* you."

Sunai is prepared to argue. Once he started advising Jin, he'd made his choice. But when he moves to counter, he makes the mistake of touching Veyadi's elbow. He is abruptly paralyzed from chest to throat with—*regret-disgust-that-fractured-shadow-of-old-love*—

Jin tries to catch Sunai's eye, but he can barely breathe, let alone respond. Then their own efforts cease as their mouth pinches, they learn forward, and they vomit on the cargo bay floor.

Seconds ago Imaru looked ready to brain Jin with her stun baton, but she's the first by their side. Her reasoning becomes clear as she helps Oyu tag-team them upright.

"First things first," Imaru says in Jin's ear. "None of these ambitions can pan out until we get more chitin."

Jin raises their head to stare disconsolately at the disruptor's remains. "The madam's going to have my ass for this."

"I might have a plan."

With that, Imaru carts Jin toward the door, though not before exchanging a glance with Veyadi. Sunai recognizes it as: *Talk down the idiot, please.*

Simultaneously, Jin throws a pleading look at Sunai from under Imaru's elbow: *You know I'm right. You said so.*

Then they're gone. Cothai bustles off to find a mop for Jin's sick, and Waretu declares she'll keep an eye out from the *Never*'s observation deck, where Sunai is sure she'll finally light that cigarette. Sunai and Veyadi are at last alone.

"Sunai," says Veyadi.

Sunai doesn't want to look. He was prepared to argue with Veyadi in the safety of a group, but he doesn't trust his odds one-on-one. He is so stupid for this man. "What?" he says, eyes trained on the door.

There's a silence during which Sunai can perfectly envision Veyadi's knuckles pressed to the temple of his visor. "We need to talk."

"Do we?"

"Please."

Sunai sighs and stands and beckons over his shoulder as he heads out of the cargo bay. He lets the echo of footsteps tell him that he's followed. It would be much easier to deny the doctor if he could stop goddamn asking for permission. Sunai never did learn how to give a proper no.

———

Sunai has been left in charge of making meals since Lily. The crew insists on trading shifts to get him in the galley. They want to be kind. Sunai stays in the galley mostly because he respects the kitchen tools too much to throw them.

He makes Veyadi retrieve the egg from their chicken coop and gathers ingredients for a proper congee—not that saltless shit Veyadi forced his crew to subsist on during their Dahani run.

"So how do you see this going?" Sunai asks as he takes the egg. "I plead my case, you plead yours, we fight—"

"You don't have a case." Veyadi sighs into his palms from his seat at the galley table. If there wasn't an argument to be had, he wouldn't stay. "You understand, don't you? You can't touch the Maw, Sunai. It wants to *eat you*."

Sunai peels ginger. "Obviously it wants to, but can it?"

The pause before Veyadi speaks betrays the conflict between his expectations and reality. He is stymied by the galley; it's no place for a fight. It's barely suited for secrets. If they keep it down, they can get away with a modicum of privacy, but that depends on the crew's kind consideration. He says, quite low, "You're no different from the rest."

Sunai strips garlic and swallows bile. "I think I am. Unless any of my brethren were also chronically immune to being fucked with."

"Are you sure about that?"

Sunai shifts to waggle the foot attached to his bum ankle. "Outside of the eyes and this bit of fun, I'm golden."

Veyadi's silence compels Sunai to make his case.

"I needed the specs starting from, oh, fifteen? The ankle twisted during corruption. Never really healed. But faulty blueprints aside, my homeostasis is aggressive. I get sick, but not for long. I can drug myself, but it takes a ton and it doesn't last. Wounds just take time. Lost some fingers once! They grew back. Pretty gross. Don't remember a lot, except for the bones. You know how brains are. Point is: everything about me goes back to the way it was."

Veyadi's focus bores into his back. "You were an archivist. You know better. If you were in stasis, your brain wouldn't work the way it does. You acquire new neural pathways. Remember things. Learn."

"Do I? When was the last time you saw me learn from a mistake? Some days I'm pretty sure my impulse control never fully grew in. Do you know how exhausting it is to be stuck in your early twenties?"

Veyadi snorts. Then he sighs. "Sunai."

Sunai shivers; he wishes Veyadi would stop doing that. "What?"

"I don't think you heal."

Sunai holds up the knife. "I can prove otherwise."

"Don't. I mean, that's not your fundamental rule. Relics, fragtech, they're isolated elements of a sundered whole. Hence why frags follow their behavioral loops and relics manifest specific traits inherited from their AI. I don't think yours is 'self-maintenance.' It's more that your reconstruction is an outcome of the underlying process. When I look at you—through the prosthetic—you're a multitude of trace autonomous elements. Every other relic I've seen is far more contained. I think your corruption has a connective quality—transitive, or maybe absorbent. Every time you interact with a frag, or an ENGINE, you come away marked by it. And I think you synthesize those elements to maintain yourself."

"Like a frag?" Sunai asks, curious despite himself. It isn't like he's ever had the opportunity to get a formal diagnosis.

"On a smaller scale." Veyadi falls silent, wrestling with himself. Sunai doesn't know if he wins, but his voice is lower when he says, "The way that Dahani archive reacted to you . . ." His tone drops even lower. "It's still with you, isn't it?"

Primed to argue, Sunai trips over his own impulse. The knife goes down on the cutting board, signaling defeat. Yes. It's with him. He is infected and he is aware. What he first mistook for a concussion has become chronic; its presence within him flares again and again, trespassing in his conscious mind. He is not alone.

"Okay, but that's no reason to worry," he says brightly. "Even if a rogue autonomous element is messing with my general situation, it hasn't fried my brain yet, has it?"

"It has, though," Veyadi insists. "You're hallucinating—"

"Oh, who doesn't?"

"You're interfacing with fragtech—"

"Not like a *lot*."

"You're making so many stupid goddamn assumptions," Veyadi snaps. "Damn it, Sunai, it would be bad enough if it were a question of whether the Maw wanted to feed on you or kill you. But we also have no way of knowing what would happen if it got its hands on you while you're carrying your passenger."

Passenger, huh?

If it would prefer a different nickname, it fails to comment. For all that it's hijacked space in Sunai's brain, it's largely left him alone. For an AI, anyway.

"I think we have *some* idea." Sunai turns, knife pointed contemplatively upward. "Because the relic did, again, stuff that whole archive down my throat, and my passenger didn't do much to stop it. The answer may well be: nothing at all, it doesn't matter, and the only real problem, materially speaking, is that you don't like . . ."

His words get stuck. Veyadi's hands are locked together, his fingers interlaced, his mouth tightly closed. His chest shudders when he exhales. Sunai's chest twinges in sympathetic response.

"You're afraid of it," he says. "The Maw."

"Of course I am," Veyadi spits. "How is that even a question?"

Sunai saw how feverishly Veyadi wanted to save the Maw when he assumed its hunger was a flaw he could fix. Yet the doctor came around awfully fast once Sunai revealed that the people-eating was more of an inherited trait. He wouldn't have expected that to push Veyadi all the way to outright fear. Faith in a savior isn't easily forsaken. It takes time, painful time, for grief. *Fear* implies that Veyadi's love for Iterate Fractal has been complicated for longer than Sunai assumed.

But before it was any kind of horror, it was love, so it's no wonder that Veyadi can hardly be objective when it comes to designing its death. Besides, he likes Sunai too much to be scientific.

That fault is reciprocated. When Sunai traces a thumb over Veyadi's cheek—

—they'll come for him again, he knows, because they expect to lose the last. And they will. He saw their shriveled body, muscles withered under chemical sedation, skin fragile as old paper. When they do, it will be on him to shoulder the burden, because there'll be no one else left—

—and the fear in that, the shame, it hollows his brain beyond thought, and if he can't think, he can't fix this, so he might as well let them take him to the Maw, might as well die—

—but the hand on his shoulder steadies, and when he is told, "It's an end, but not the end—we'll weather it," he dares to believe it might be true, because if he can't trust himself, he can always summon faith in an archivist—

Pardon. Your accidental transgressions I could dismiss, Sunai. But this . . .

This I cannot tolerate.

Sunai jerks back and knocks his elbow into the counter; he shakes his hand as if he'd thrust it into open flame. "Shit, shit—sorry."

"What?" Veyadi's hands slacken on the table. "No. You didn't . . ."

"I don't get it either! And, sorry again, but that's definitely not the first time I've done it to you either."

Veyadi can only stare.

"It started on Lily. After the Maw. Did you feel it?" Sunai laughs nervously. "I figure my friend—the passenger—it's connecting us through your prosthetic. You know, salvage. Fragtech. I mean, it's not like I could be interfacing with *you* . . ."

Veyadi looks distinctly ill.

"Are you okay?" Sunai waves off his own question. "*Sorry.* I get it. I didn't think about . . . how you knew them."

One relic after another, disappearing into the Maw. Sunai used to carry a cousin of that weight weekly, at the behest of Iterate Fractal. He takes in Veyadi's brittle nausea with more pity than horror. He's familiar with the toll of execution. The shame of permitting it.

"What did you see?" Veyadi asks his own hands.

"How bad it got," says Sunai. The truth is longer and more complicated. He also saw their faces. Had he been the one Veyadi wired into the Maw, would he care to see the doctor's remorse?

Veyadi says, "I don't want to watch it take you too."

"Right. Obviously."

"I'm not going to *let* it."

"That's genuinely sweet of you."

Veyadi's mouth crinkles; he thinks he's being teased. Sunai's heart tugs—he did mean it, is the thing—and he reaches for Veyadi's arm—

A whisper: Careful now.

He jerks to a stop.

Veyadi freezes as well, frowning up at him. "Are you—"

Sunai retracts his hand to his chest. "Probably not, right?"

Veyadi allows his head to lower. "You understand why, under present circumstances, I'd rather you not be involved with the disruptor."

"Sure."

"Good."

"Well." Sunai turns back to the counter. He needs to occupy his hands. "Why don't you go ask Imaru if Jin's in a state to take a disappointment?"

Veyadi leaves, maintaining as much distance from Sunai as the confines of the galley allow. Sunai finishes the congee, all the while thinking assiduously of nothing. Once he has it going at a low simmer, he steals into their bunk. Thankfully, Veyadi isn't in it. He closes the door and begins to meticulously unpack his ruck.

Only when the ruck is empty does he remember that he doesn't have what he's looking for: that stupid goddamn letter. Crouched over the contents, Sunai holds his head in his hands. The letter told him not to come to Khuon Mo. The man who sent it must have known of Iterate Fractal's resurrection. He was there, after all, in Veyadi's recollection—speaking softly, kindly, and with the nerve to hope it might get better.

In the end, he told Sunai to stay away.

Stay away. Why couldn't he stay away?

21

Sunai never lived in a Khuon Mo without Iterate Fractal, so he never knew it without the god-tyrant who stole him into its embrace. He therefore can't justify wanting to look upon the city and think it beautiful, and he doesn't trust the cavity in his chest when he takes in the now-unfamiliar skyline and thinks: Well, it used to be more impressive.

Under a climbing sun, the city casts wrong shadows. In Iterate Fractal's Khuon Mo, lustrous bone and nacre marked the boundary between the green of humanity's domain and the green of the wilds. Now the Harbor rules, and it draws that difference in shining steel and cornered glass.

The new Khuon Mo occupies the same valley, the same mountains and bay. As the *Never Once* rounds a ridge, they are shown the curvature of the city, revealing a rough division of districts that parallel the ones Sunai knew as a child.

First and most imposing is Lotus: the lone island in the bay that once housed Iterate Fractal's central shrine, the heart of its neurotransitive network. One long slope leads from the bay to a cliff, upon which Sunai remembers a coral crown of curves and spires. From this grew the luminescent splendor of an unapologetic archive, a towering banyan hungry to be seen.

The ruins of the shrine are all but vanquished, shunted into the sea by the soldierly concrete slabs of the Harbor's central base of operations. It towers much like any other Harbor towers, and Sunai opts to stare it down from his perch on the observation deck, shivering only when they must pass through its shadow.

The *Never Once* slides past Lotus among a dozen other catamarans, junks, and barges. Nearly a third of the salvage-rigs fly the Harbor militia banner, more than Sunai's ever seen in one state. Waretu told him that the Mohani Harbor stopped executing even flagrant smugglers and salvage-rats years ago—they need the bodies too badly, if they're to fend off the wilds without an ENGINE. Arrest is a one-way ticket to conscription, and the Harbor always has reasons to arrest a rat.

The crew is tense as a gleaming Harbor security cruiser pulls alongside the *Never*, flanked by an amphibious militia rig built from downworlder ceramics. Now they find out if they were right. Has the Maw's relic reported their little assassination attempt, or are they too wary of risking their freedom? A part of Sunai is sure the relic must have sold them out. Another is oddly certain the relic would rather die than betray Veyadi.

They get their answer some minutes later, when the Harbor cruiser glides away and the *Never* is permitted to churn on toward the shore. The relic has kept their mouth shut. Jin will be terribly smug.

They moor in a fleet of free salvage-rigs, cargo barges, fishing vessels, and houseboats. The Jasmine waterfront stretches before them, a mismatched collection of teahouses and sparrow parlors built in hasty post-corruption wooden frames. Here and there the plastered remains of crumbling bone and coral show through, buttressed by corrugated tin.

As Sunai helps to secure the *Never*, he gets an eyeful of glistening Orchid District to the east, where hotels built on steel and glass are embellished with faux nacre and lacquered wood-panel finish. Catamarans bask on Orchid's white strip of beach, interspersed with lounging tourists.

From the end of their pier, Sunai makes out the clean borders of industrial farms and paddies climbing the slope at the back of the valley, where the Harbor has made the most of the Mohani archipelago's famously fertile soil. Beyond these orderly lines, corrupted compound ruins splotch the mountainsides like the shits of an enormous bird.

One corner of the city is untouched by Harbor development: the westernmost district, which Sunai knew as Mangrove, the former site of Iterate Fractal's third and final shrine. A maze of houseboats, rafts, and planked bridges decorate the ossified remains of the district that once straddled land and sea.

"They call it Grotto now," Imaru says when she finds Sunai peering at it on deck. "The underground waterways mean the structural integrity's a nightmare, so the Harbor leaves it alone. They'd have to gut the whole district if they wanted to build anything on it."

"Also, the madam would gut *them* if they tried any—God's infinite tits, I have legs." Jin gestures rudely at Cothai's attempt to sit them down in the shade cast by the observation deck. Over his protests, they join Sunai and Imaru at the rail. Sweat beads their brow.

Though Jin seemed to take Veyadi's hard refusal in good spirits, it might have been more that their condition has worsened again. Last night, Sunai watched Veyadi reach across the galley table to take Jin's pulse with the unflinching air of an idiot sticking his head in a company-cat's mouth.

"Anyway, Grotto isn't going anywhere." Jin points inland, past the Grotto fleet.

There, bone-frozen trees curve into the shape of an enormous nautilus shell. This was the meat of the shrine, within which its archive rooted. The shrine has been overtaken by a multitiered structure of haphazard materials; it reminds Sunai of nothing so much as an unusually architectural fragtech.

"The Three-Eyed Carp," says Jin. "Teahouse, sparrow parlor, salvage-rat burrow, and the old hag's inaugural business venture with the Ginger Company. So long as she's smuggling salvage through it, she's got reason to keep Harbor peace officers out of the whole damn district."

Jin has more to say—when don't they—but they break off as they squint at the shoreside end of the pier. "Ugh. There she is. No, don't get up, Sunai. Not point hiding you now."

Jin's ire is directed at a petite old woman making her way toward the *Never* from a sleek white car on the waterfront. She's accompanied by a trio of bodyguards who vary in size and bearing but who share a vigilant mistrust for everything from houseboat aunties to passing dust motes. The woman's clothes are a traditional Mohani cut in muted mainland colors, but for the shocking line of slender yellow flowers with long red tongues embroidered down the length of her sash. Mohani ginger, red and yellow for the flames that burned through Harbor warehouses: the symbol of her Ginger Company of old. Madam Wei only plays at subtlety.

Case in point, the way her fashionable mainland bob shows off gnarled scars running from behind each of her ears, down her nape, and beneath the back of her wide-necked blouse. The scars of a supplicant, the same array Sunai would have received if Iterate Fractal hadn't corrupted in the middle of that business. The madam earned hers on Lily.

"Jin, dear, you don't look well," Madam Wei rasps like breeze over sand as she smiles up at them from the pier. "Should you be outside?"

Jin bares their teeth in a grim cousin of a smile. "To tell you the truth, aunty, I fell." They rap their cane on the side of the rig. "Then I broke all my shit. But I got back up, and now I'm here. So are you going to indulge in a scold or are we getting down to business?"

Madam Wei's lips curl. "I always enjoy your frankness, Jin. Why don't you ride with me to the Pearl?"

That would be the Heavenly Pearl—the ostentatious hotel

from Jin's postcard. So far so good; Jin hoped to be taken to Orchid, where they'll be able to retrieve some reference books from their personal collection per Veyadi's request.

"Imaru, would you join us? To keep Jin honest." The madam's eyes at last turn to the others on deck. "Or should you stay to gather the rest of the crew while I bring the new . . . help."

Her gaze lingers on Sunai. Sunai blinks stupidly back at her.

Last night, Jin took Sunai aside in the corridor belowdecks. He feared they were about to make another bid for his cooperation, but their concern was rooted elsewhere.

"Heard back from the madam," they said. "She wants to see all of us, I expect so she can interrogate you individually about the exact ways in which I've fucked up. We will not be cooperating."

"From everything you've said about her, that sounds unwise," said Sunai.

"It'd be hells of unwiser to let the crone find out we're carrying two archivists, one of whom is also a relic."

"Because she'd kill me."

"Because she's an *entrepreneur*. We'd be lucky if she decided you were better off dead." Jin clapped their hands to either side of his face. "Let's not find out what unlucky looks like, yeah?"

Sunai hasn't given the alternatives to death much thought, but under the keen eyes of Madam Wei, he begins to understand Jin's anxiety. The madam's look is mild and withholding, like a mother bird deciding which hatchling to tip out of her nest.

"Aunty, please," Jin groans to demand her attention. "Imaru needs Sunai in Jasmine. He's the only one who can convince his cousin to cough up a discount on decoy drones. If you think I need a minder, we'll bring Oyu. They've been giving me shit about painkillers all week—*and* they know how to behave in front of your tourists."

The madam silently regards Jin, then turns to Sunai. "Grew up on the mainland, did you?"

Sunai glances at Jin as if asking permission to speak. They roll their eyes, so he nods.

"Then welcome home." Madam Wei's small smile brings little light to her gaze. "I expect you'll find reasons to return more often, in the future. In the meantime, be wary of the Harbor. They've been excitable lately. And if they give you trouble . . . do let me know."

Sunai nods again, hesitant. The madam's stare scratches at the back of his mind, as if he knows her from somewhere. He can probably blame this déjà vu on Jin and their infernal machine.

Jin jumps into the silence to rattle off a series of detailed commands to the rest of the crew, as agreed upon the night prior. They make no mention of Veyadi, who is holed up in the *Never Once*'s bowels, and who will not be showing his face until they can once more leave port lest the Harbor identify him by that telltale prosthetic. They also ignore Sunai until they grab him by the hand. Their palm is clammy.

"And you. If you leave Imaru's sight, I will drown you in the bilge water." Jin leans closer, as if to deliver an even more grievous threat into his ear. "Tell Doc I'll have his books by nightfall. Try not to be too crazy in public."

Sunai thinks: Well, that was nearly amicable.

Except, does he? The thought doesn't sound like him. Neither does it sound like a thought. Too pointed, too articulate. It lingers in his mind with syllabic solidity even as he attempts to occupy himself with his tasks, both the one assigned to him and the one he assigned himself.

———

When it's time to leave, Sunai shrugs on his jacket in his bunk and turns to find Veyadi in the door. The doctor loiters, mouth pinched in a frown.

"Going to try and convince me to stay again?" Sunai asks.

"No," says Veyadi.

That comes as a surprise. Veyadi wasn't the only member of the crew to object when Sunai volunteered to go with Imaru to meet her contact, but he objected most pointedly. Imaru didn't much like the idea either, but she came around, perhaps eager to keep her eye on Sunai.

He waves Veyadi back. "If you're not going to pitch another fit, you should scooch."

Veyadi hesitates, clearly torn. Sunai slinks past, willfully not thinking about it.

He does seem to care, says the murmur. But be watchful.

"How often is it doing that?" Veyadi asks, frowning.

Sunai winces. Maybe he made a face, or maybe Veyadi saw it through his prosthetic. He always knows when Sunai's passenger is speaking, sometimes even before Sunai realizes.

"I mean, I haven't been keeping a tally," he says as he backs into the corridor. Veyadi frowns after him and Sunai coos. "Oh, don't make that face. I'm not about to start being *diligent*."

As if to prove his point, he nearly pats Veyadi's cheek, stopping just short of contact. They both back up this time, Sunai with his hands raised.

"I promise not to touch anything without permission," he says.

Veyadi gives him a look of *Don't fucking patronize me, you goddamn clown man,* mixed, horribly, with concern. "Do you really have to go?"

Sunai locks his hands safely behind his neck. "Sometimes you get tired of being looked at. Nobody knows me out there."

An audacious lie. Sunai's about to hunt down the only person in the world who knows him as well as Imaru. He might even have her beat.

I do not believe you owe Veyadi Lut the truth, his passenger says. After all, he is still lying to you.

Sunai can barely puzzle out the meaning of its words. He unconsciously bats the air as if at an insect. "Oh, shut up."

For whatever reason, that's what compels Veyadi to back down. "Just stick with Imaru."

"You too," says Sunai. Then, "Fuck."

Veyadi nearly laughs; Sunai is too charmed to risk lingering any longer.

———

Sunai and Imaru stop first at the neighboring houseboat, where Waretu has joined a bevy of aunties to untangle fishing nets. They give greetings and offer help, but in accordance with the plan, Waretu insists they bring her noodles from a particular cart on the far end of Jasmine.

This is the plot: while Jin distracts Madam Wei with arguments and contrition, Sunai and Imaru reach out to the original supplier of the stolen relic interface. Sunai was surprised to learn Imaru was willing to let any of them meet her contact, but she snorted.

"Plenty of people hate the Harbor."

"Sure. But the more people I learn are in on this operation, the more I worry about Jin's mole."

Imaru's brow creases. She's never liked to doubt a friend. That was always his job.

Sunai pats her back as they approach a dumpling vendor. "Just trying not to dismiss it out of hand. Not all Jin's ideas are bad."

"You let them shoot you over this one."

"I don't think it's one of the *crew*. But when an operation gets big enough, you have to consider it."

Imaru clearly is considering as she puts in an order at a cart. Mohani mango-chili and fish dumplings, fried in a style Sunai associates with the mainland's western coast but folded in a brand of wrapper popular in the northern reach. Sunai thanks the uncle at the cart and takes his time with each.

"Been too long," the uncle says to Imaru in Mohani. "You've gone pale. You eating?"

"Not like this. Tell me, uncle, where's your brat?"

Imaru's mood picks up as they conduct their business, all casual asides and oblique references. You don't say! Now that's a shame. Well, let's hope that pans out. Ah, I could've told you it wouldn't.

Sunai can't hope to follow the conversation they're really having. He's distracted. Jasmine looks like nowhere he knows. It borrows too many features of the salvage-ports he's spent the last seventeen years bouncing between to be Khuon Mo, yet the air of the people and the names of the teahouses are too Mohani to deny. Sunai feels at home in ways that repel each other and so feels terminally displaced.

The people are easier to process. As they pass, some stop for a word with the vendor or with Imaru. Not just salvage-rats either, but aunties and uncles and young folks too, of the sort too clean-cut to imagine in the wilds. Some want news—where Imaru's been all these months, what the madam has her up to—but some just want to say hello.

Sunai idles on a nearby stool and chats up those who linger. The aunties call him "precious" in Mohani, a word connoting the value of paint to an artist or the Lay to a monk. Indispensable. Sacred. Iterate Fractal used it to describe variation, and now the locals append it to men who wear their hair like Sunai, women who dress like Imaru, and anyone wearing an ID talisman like Jin's.

An elder cousin offers Sunai one such talisman, as well as a second for Imaru, should she want it. Sunai takes both with a grateful nod, and he runs his thumb over the intricate knot as he eyes the passersby. They sport more downworld talismans than he's ever seen in a Harbor-held state.

The cousin clucks, reading Sunai's quiet as nervousness. "You're better off with it than without," they say. "Shows you're local. Protected."

"Don't tell me the Harbor's picking on tourists."

"Of course not. But you're not one of those either."

The cousin has taken Sunai for one of those Mohani kids who grew up on the mainland. He uses that to play dumb, awed—in need of help. When he passes the cousin an envelope and tells them who it's for, they take it with an understanding nod.

"You're in luck," they say. "He got home a few months back. Couple hours should do it, I'm sure."

Sunai thanks them with three fingers to his chest in the downworld way. As he watches the cousin slip into the crowd, a strange weight settles on the back of his neck. He tries to shake it off and it only grows heavier.

A cloying nostalgia has plagued him ever since he left the *Never Once,* like the sun he hallucinated on the Dahani run. The more time he spends in Jasmine, the more familiar it begins to feel—as if he knows which apothecary to trust, which teahouse carries his favorite brews, and which vendors will hand him a cigarette in exchange for a rumor. It reminds him, absurdly, of home. Sunai hasn't had a home in seventeen years.

Khuon Mo is making him crazy. That's fine. Sunai's been crazy before.

I must apologize, Sunai, says his passenger. I have not done this on purpose. I do not think you have either. I do not know what to do with that.

Sunai cleans his specs, squinting at his lap and trying to catch the passenger's meaning through the static of his brain. When he puts his specs back on and raises his face, he finds himself staring across the street at a freshly defaced poster of the local harbormaster. Her printed eyes and deep-lined mouth are stern, but Sunai can imagine the deft twist that would transform her likeness from stoic neutrality into a familiar scowl.

Where has he seen her before? More propaganda, he assumes, but in what state?

Ah . . . How to explain? his passenger wonders. I am not yet convinced that I should.

"If you're the reason I recognize her, it's kind of on you to tell me why," Sunai mutters.

A shadow falls over his frown. Imaru stands beside his stool, sipping on a bottle of local fruit tea with an indecipherable expression. "Ueda Naru," she says. "You remember her."

Sunai claps with realization. "Ah. *The Edge of Man.*"

Plenty of other dramas as well: *Viper Moon, The Downworld Conspiracy, Blood ENGINE.* Sunai used to binge them with Imaru in the shitty hostels where they hunkered down between jobs. He recognizes the woman—war hero, legendary relic, notorious tragedy—as the inspiration for a host of thinly veiled proxy protagonists.

She is Ueda Naru of the Aigata Enclave, one of the first relics and the last of her cohort. The corruption of her home inspired the enclave's surviving autonomists to build their prototype ENGINE from the remains of their patron AI—Qualia Clear? Sunai remembers the dramas Ueda inspired better than the history she lived.

To wit, she is largely famous for not being dead. The rest of her fellows are, as is their ENGINE. The Huntress's last archive was pulverized in a territorial confrontation between the nascent Harbor and an imperial AI of the Immaculate Pantheon. Ueda Naru endured the beating; the mech she piloted, not so much.

He remembers vaguely that the Harbor retired her from view after a disgraceful bout of public drunkenness, but he recalls nothing of her settling in Khuon Mo. He accepts that he might have heard and chosen not to retain the information.

"What'd they bring her down here for?" he asks Imaru. "Lastditch propaganda campaign?"

Imaru raises a brow. "She's the harbormaster."

Sunai laughs, but Imaru doesn't break.

"What? No. They wouldn't. Not a relic." The Harbor Sunai knows trusts their relics to command their ENGINEs and nothing else. They'd just as soon put an AI collaborator in charge.

Imaru frowns at her feet as if they aren't holding her up the right way. A sidelong glance carries her attention down the street to the corner of a barbecue joint and an apothecary. "Over there. Tell me what you see."

Sunai sees: An ambitious young person hawking their wares. Tacky postcards of Khuon Mo's former splendor—an obvious front for unsanctioned salvage-trade targeting tourists looking to take home a piece of tropical corruption. Behind the kid with the postcards another kid crouches, studiously defacing another of Ueda Naru's impassive posters.

Harbor propaganda spatters Jasmine. Posters praising the militia draft and the noble work of defending the city from fragtech; rewards for information on unsanctioned excursions into the wilds; advertisements for relic dramas and the like. The harbormaster's face is only the most recently vandalized.

"I see plenty of reasons for the Harbor to really, really want a big-ass robot to scare the locals into line."

"That's not how it works here. They've never been able to hold power the way they can on the mainland. The Gingers burned them offshore, and when the Harbor cracked down . . . It got bad." Imaru nods toward Ueda Naru's face as if toward a respected rival. "That's why they brought in someone who wouldn't try to lead like other harbormasters lead. And that's why they haven't yet shown us the Maw."

"Doesn't sound like the Harbor I know."

"It isn't. Think of it this way: they've spent near two decades playing sparrow with the city, but now they've got a gun. Only they don't like or trust the gun either. They want to make sure it's going to fire when they tell it to."

"Weird metaphor."

She kicks the leg of his stool. "You follow. Remind me to have you watch the militia work. You'll see."

Sunai lets his eye carry out over the water to the concrete fortress of the Mohani Harbor, which can rule this city only from a safe distance. Even with all the evidence that suggests this is true, his mind won't hold the possibility that it is.

It seems to me that you like this state of affairs, says his passenger.

"I don't hate it," says Sunai.

Imaru eyes him with an odd dissatisfaction. She's gone to such lengths to protect Khuon Mo's delicate balance. It's why she asked Sunai to risk coming back, no matter how it hurt her. What about that is so hard to stomach now?

Maybe it's his presence that has her unnerved. Just as he struggles to process the reality of the city, she struggles to accept that she's endangered it in the effort to save what it's become.

An apology stirs in Sunai. He owes Imaru more honesty than he's afforded her. It's hard to admit that he's lied. He was never able to when they ran together. She's never lied to him either.

Ah, I am not entirely sure that is true, says his passenger.

"You don't know what you're talking about," says Sunai.

"Sunai . . ." says Imaru. "Who are you talking to?"

"Huh." Sunai balks. "Well. Don't like that."

"Me neither."

Imaru looks at him like she would at a ghost. Veyadi went out of his way to confirm Sunai's condition with her—and Jin, and consequently the whole crew—to keep Sunai from getting away with whatever Veyadi fears he'll try to pull. Imaru hasn't brought it up, bless her. Now she lets out a breath that Sunai can't hear. "If the doctor's right," she says, so quiet that he almost misses it, "if it's that archive you found . . . Could you do me a favor, Sunai? Don't listen to it."

"Of course not," he says, fast as he can on the heels of her upset. "Since when have I listened?"

Imaru's face remains troubled even as they continue on to their destination: the Wicked Joy, an ocean-facing sparrow parlor on the edge of Jasmine and Orchid. Sunai buys her cigarettes on the way, but the gesture feels empty; he hasn't summoned the courage to explain how he's ruined their rendezvous.

Imaru greets the pretty hostess with a slantwise smile. The woman giggles until her gaze catches on something behind them. Her brow furrows as she touches Imaru's sleeve and inclines her head across the street. As she does, Sunai spies a hint of yellow embroidery inside her sleeve: a ginger.

That feels familiar, and not because it's a perfect twin to the one embroidered on Madam Wei's sash. This specific flower in this specific sleeve tugs at his memory, along with the hostess's lopsided frown. He reminds himself he's crazy and follows her gaze.

A couple of Harbor peace officers have descended on the fruit grocer across the way, where tourists and locals alike crowd for a special on rambutan. In an alcove above the register, Sunai spies a planted sprig of bioluminescent coral, right where, on the mainland, someone might keep a shrine to the recent dead. Even from across the street, the carving's resemblance to a tree is unmistakable. A grave for Iterate Fractal.

However reluctant the Mohani Harbor is to swing its robot dick around, it can't afford to tolerate AI sympathy in public.

Sunai gives Imaru an *Are we running?* glance.

She shakes her head. "We're fine."

"The officers only come into Jasmine when the tourists feel delicate," says the hostess.

"End of the month," says a third voice. "They're hunting draft dodgers. Never find as many as they want, which starts them after other quarry."

A man has slipped out of the crowd to join Sunai and Imaru at the hostess's podium. He stands to the side, frowning at the grocer as if perplexed. He cuts such an understated figure that if Sunai didn't know exactly who he was, he would forget his face as soon as he looked away.

But Sunai can't look away. "You telling me to be careful?" he asks.

"I would if I thought you'd listen," says Ruhi, the last man Sunai died in front of. "I almost didn't believe you were here, Sunai."

This man, he is a ghost in your veins.

He comes upon you in the neon-edged back alley of Harbor-held Bhonria, where you are wet, cut, and bruised, fresh from an unhappy meeting with your latest employer. The wet is from the recent rain, the cut from the job, and the bruise from the man who holds your present contract, who you have come to understand may be planning to kill you. To try, anyway.

The years after Chom Dan have left a traitor's taste in your mouth; you take work from such foul folk as one of a thousand attempts to wash it out. The plain-clothed man who follows you from the back room is, you suspect, one more opportunity for cheap annihilation.

"Need a ride out?" he asks.

You don't know whether to expect further brutality; you remain uncertain even as the man offers you an imported Mohani cigarette.

"What do you think?" You take his cigarette. The man lights it with a plain, Harbor-made mechanical lighter that spits under his stumbling thumb.

You fix on that thumb as you inhale, thinking: He's nervous. Or he's unpracticed. If nervous, he knows your employer hates you for fucking his brother, and he thinks you'll suck him off for the favor of your life. If unpracticed, well. He might not be from around here either.

The man lights his own cigarette. The flare of the lighter reveals his trim beard, his sun-starved brown skin, his mixed Mohani features. "I know some folks who could use a scout."

Some inner whisper: You know him. It could mean anything.

You've known a lot of people lately, and most of them you'd rather not know again.

He calls himself Ruhi, which sticks to the back of your mind, where you keep the things you've forgotten on purpose because they're too entwined with what you ran from. You remain prepared to stick the cigarette into his eye all the way up to the moment he brings you to the dim garage on the edge of Bhonria, which is full of more wide eyes in mixed faces. You know the brittle poise of refugees and indentures on the run, though you thought you left them behind with Imaru.

They call Ruhi "archivist." He says, Not anymore.

You choose him, then. Later, you'll choose him again. Time after time, state after state, you let him lead you to work that serves others over work that serves your own end. He entices, this lens of a man through which you see a better self. In the end, you lift the final curtain and let him see the whole of you.

You have crawled in through the window of his hostel in Elanu Tha, where he has been searching for Mohani indenture contracts to buy out with the Harbor's funds. You, he has tasked with gathering the freed and securing a route back to the archipelago. You've done it. You are tired. You could disappear into the night, as you usually do, and let him find you again in Ghamor, or Qing Lai, or Tellula-Janggor. Instead, you seek out the room he sleeps in, and you listen to the sound of the shower down the hall, and you think of joining him there. You manage to extract your feet from your socks before you fall asleep on top of his sheets.

You wake briefly, startled up by soundless nothing. Your back is pressed against another's, and your hair has been carefully re-braided.

He stirs, he turns. His breath warms the back of your neck. The bed is too small for you to be apart, though even with his naked thighs pressed to the back of your own, his breath feels most potent.

"Jasmine." Ruhi's words brush your nape. "I was in Jasmine when it hit. I'd just been raised from apprentice, named archivist. I was visiting a compound."

"Congratulations," you say. And then, and then, your toes curl. "Lotus," you whisper. "The shrine. I . . . I'd come from Lily. I had a question. Iterate Fractal . . ."

It robs you, to say any of this aloud. You are unmoored by the disclosure.

You are rolled onto your back. The orange city light through clouded window casts Ruhi in warmth, yet his eyes are wide and unreachable. He gapes at you as if you are mystifying and new. A grand trick. Nothing of the mess below him has changed; it was always just Sunai.

"You were an archivist," he says.

You want to say: Of course, dipshit.

But your tongue wets your lips and your voice creaks into a recitation of Leaf 36: "Cascade," and he, archivist, buries his face in the shoulder of you, too young-faced to be his peer, too learned to be anything but, and he cries.

22

"**Well, Citizen Liaison? Don't you** have a job to do?" Imaru leans an elbow on the hostess's stand as she indicates the ongoing arrest. "There's a citizen. There's the Harbor. Go liaise."

Ruhi frowns, troubled. He cultivates unremarkability. Of middling height and weight, bland face, and hair that would be vaguely unfashionable in every state across the mainland, he is an ode to the passerby. The most distinct thing about him is his beard, which he keeps fastidiously trim. That, and his inability to change his most quotidian habits. Sunai has never had to search for the things he wants to steal from Ruhi. Keys, mints, cigarettes, they're always where he expects. Now Ruhi pulls a cigarette and lighter out of the same places they've always lived in his dull jacket and says, "That's not my purview, Imaru."

Imaru tilts her head with one of those *Well then what's the point of you?* squints. Ruhi returns an apologetic *I understand the posturing is cathartic* cigarette raise.

It is excruciating to behold. Sunai is well aware that they're all acquainted with each other. Sunai and Imaru were still running together when they first met Ruhi, and Imaru brought Ruhi's letter to Ghamor only a couple of months ago. None of that mitigates the bodily shock of seeing them together. Talking. The panicked realization that they could talk to each other about *him*—that they have likely already done this—compels Sunai to interrupt.

"Well, if you're not going to be helpful," he says, "we're short a player."

To the unfamiliar, Ruhi's frown would read contemplative. To Sunai, it's tight with apprehension. Ruhi went out of his way to send Sunai a letter asking him not to come to Khuon Mo. And what did he get for his troubles? Sunai! In Khuon Mo! Always right where he isn't wanted.

Imaru's side-eye obfuscates most of her thoughts, but it's clear she doesn't care for whatever the hell Sunai's doing.

"I make time for friends," Ruhi says at last.

"I still count?" Sunai asks.

"You're close enough."

Ruhi leads the way into the Wicked Joy with a nod at the hostess. Mechanically, Sunai follows. If Imaru has anything to say, she sits on it. Sunai decides that, probably, he's going to die.

Though the Wicked Joy is situated on the border between Jasmine and Orchid, where tourists come sniffing for the authentic and entrepreneurs respond with kitschy cafés, its clientele is thoroughly local. Khuon Mo's people have mixed and churned for nigh on two centuries, so unlike in some of the more insular mainland states, it's hard to say at a glance where anyone comes from. But there's a sunned cast to the faces and a posture in common that Sunai recognizes in his bones.

The crowd skews old, though some are dressed in mainland-influenced collars and creased pants while others prefer Mohani patterns and drapes. The sparrow tables are spread out, some separated by screens. Anyone who takes notice of Imaru and Ruhi does so with a polite brevity that promises future gossip will be oblique. This is a place for business, where community leaders gather to talk needs and make deals.

They're given a table near the open-air terrace overlooking the beach below, separated by a respectable distance and a carved screen of fragrant wood. Before Imaru sits, Sunai says, "If you want to keep an eye out for our fourth, I've got this."

Imaru gives him a *Yeah, I don't think I'm leaving you alone yet* brow raise. Sunai ensures that she gets the seat with the best view of the entrance.

"I thought you were in Ghamor," says Ruhi as he takes his own seat, by which he means to ask if Sunai got the letter.

"I was," says Sunai, which means he did.

"It's a bad time to have come in from Ghamor," says Ruhi. "The Harbor's quiet about it, but they're looking for a man who went missing there a few weeks back. An autonomist."

Sunai balks in the middle of flagging down an attendant to order tea.

Does Ruhi know? Ruhi is good at knowing things about people. Between Veyadi's disappearance from Ghamor, Sunai's arrival in Khuon Mo, and the letter Sunai sent to Ruhi just an hour before, he may well have put it all together. Good.

"I'm sure he'll turn up," says Sunai.

Ruhi exhales as silently as he can. "You do know how to find trouble."

"Guess I'm lucky you're so good at getting me out of it. I've always appreciated your interest in my staying alive. And I know I'm not the only person who you'd prefer to keep breathing."

Imaru watches them both and says nothing but to give an order to the attendant.

Ruhi, meanwhile, leans back in his seat to study Sunai. His brow knits further by the second, increasing his silence with every stitch. He is trying to sort out whether Sunai means to be cruel.

Sunai's tongue is moved by guilt. "The good news is that I'm trying to cooperate. Look at me: asking for help."

Ruhi gives him a long, thoughtful look. "I'm proud of you."

Devastating.

"Hold your praise. I don't think you're going to like the help I want you to give."

"I don't do these things because I like to, Sunai." The unspoken implication: I just like you.

Bad! Sunai is trapped between needing Ruhi to like him

enough to help and hating every reminder that Ruhi ever liked him in the first place—and indeed, somehow, continues to do so.

When the attendant arrives, Sunai accepts the tea tray and asks her for a bottle of rum, or beer, or rubbing alcohol. With a blank frown, the attendant goes on her way. Sunai is left to struggle with the trial of self-knowledge reflected in the other while stone-cold sober. He is unable to pour the tea with a steady hand, nor can he articulate his precise request. He didn't envision Ruhi letting him get this far, and hasn't chosen his words: So, Ruhi, what can you tell me about the relic? Yeah, you know, the one driving the ENGINE that you never mentioned was more or less operational? That one! Well, the thing is, they tried to help the Maw eat me.

Ruhi takes the tea Sunai pours, his gaze lingering on Sunai's fingers before he turns to the view of the bay, Lotus, and its stark Harbor crown. Imaru studies him in turn instead of watching the door. Ruhi turns to face her.

"You've been gone a while, Imaru," he says, as if the conversation has just begun. "I was beginning to fear Madam Wei had maneuvered you into retirement."

Imaru's attention never strays. "If only. I was babysitting Jin. They got themselves expelled from the imperial university sometime last year and have been playing salvage-captain on the west coast ever since."

"Oh? How did that go?"

"They're back, aren't they? You must have heard the madam came to Jasmine to fetch them herself. Though I'm not placing bets on how long they're planning to stay."

"Why come back at all? The madam won't be eager to let them leave. Seems like a risk."

"Rig saw some damage. Need more parts if we're going anywhere fast."

"Parts? That's . . . well. You can usually get what you need around here. Any room for me to do favors?"

Imaru sighs, aggrieved, and slides into a series of complaints that theoretically sound like a list of broken rig components. She is, Sunai realizes, describing the state of the disruptor.

Sunai falls back into his seat as the reality of the conversation sinks in. He considers flagging down the attendant to ask about that alcohol, but his fingers are numb around his teacup.

It's terribly clear, when he thinks for more than a second. The person who stole the relic interface for the disruptor would have needed access to the Harbor's most valuable ENGINE tech. They would therefore be someone the Harbor trusted implicitly—someone with an infallible track record and dedication to their cause. Ruhi has both of those things, except for the tiny exception of his relationship with Sunai.

Sunai came to the Wicked Joy expecting to beg Ruhi to betray the Harbor. He thought it would be hard, that he would have to be callous. He never imagined that Ruhi might already have chosen to do the damnable thing himself. It makes him feel a certain fuck of a way. His chest burns as if filled with air gone foul. His ears ring and ring.

"Things have been delicate around here, Imaru," Ruhi is saying. "I'll do my best."

Imaru shrugs idly. "Your best isn't good enough, if it doesn't get us those parts. You fail here, and Sunai has the worst day of his life."

Ruhi is too accomplished a liar to freeze up when faced with information he shouldn't have. He smiles, if too carefully. Sunai has the gall to hope Imaru doesn't notice. Once, she wouldn't have. But that was back when she had Sunai to read people for her. At some point in the years since he abandoned her in Chom Dan, she's picked up the scent of an inconvenient truth. She inhales it now and leans back, cup in hand and mouth thin, with a nail-gun stare for Ruhi.

Ruhi smiles briefly, eyes downcast. "Well. There's a reason *I* never asked Sunai to come back."

"There's a reason I came anyway," says Sunai. He regrets it when Ruhi's smile tightens, reeling the pain back in.

Imaru leans forward as if ready to jump between them. Sunai stands, jostling the table. He's out the door to the veranda before anyone can stop him.

Even under the open sunset sky, Sunai feels crowded. Pinned. Maybe it's because coming out of the parlor door brings him face-to-face with the Harbor structure in the bay.

He imagines the glistening white fragments of the Maw coalescing out of the waves. It would stride across the water to collect him in its coruscating hands, then bring him to its gash of a mouth and swallow him whole.

A sudden bright flurry at the ocean end of the bay pulls him back into his body. Bells sound, sirens whoop, and militia rigs slice across the water.

A fragtech breaches. Its body smashes into a rig from beneath the waves while its hulking black tail snakes around the hull. A dragon-child, larger by far than Imaru's friend at Lily. Another rig circles and dives—or is dragged under.

Sunai can't stop staring. He wants the distraction from the sick heat in his chest and face. Craves the fantasy of mortal danger.

A hand falls on his shoulder. Sunai expected Imaru, but the palm is less roughened and the nails are cleaner. He lets Ruhi guide him to a seat on one of the discreetly separated benches and offer him a cup. Tea.

"I asked for rubbing alcohol," says Sunai. As Ruhi sits beside him, Sunai passes him the cup and reaches into Ruhi's jacket for a cigarette.

"You've already burned your favor today," says Ruhi.

"I kind of didn't. No one told me you were already on board with all this."

"They weren't supposed to. Would've made it hard for me to help, if the wrong person heard."

That's Ruhi's way of asking whether Sunai's been circumspect—if not about himself, then at least about Ruhi. It makes Sunai tense in the middle of stealing Ruhi's lighter—not long enough for most people to catch, but Ruhi is an archivist, and worse, Ruhi *knows* him.

That's why Ruhi gives Sunai time to light the cigarette and smoke as they watch the militia rigs struggle with the dragon-child. It's not as companionable as Sunai might have hoped, but it's exactly as comfortable as he expected.

"You've been closemouthed as well, then," says Ruhi.

"Whatever do you mean?"

"Imaru didn't know about us, did she."

Not a question. Sunai apes nonchalance as he wishes to melt into the earth. "Why should she? That's private."

Ruhi is less relieved than concerned. Perhaps he would prefer that Sunai drape their dirty laundry across God's infinite rack? Maybe. Almost certainly not. Fuck.

"What have you told Veyadi?" asks Ruhi.

"Nothing about us." Sunai drinks smoke to justify his hoarse throat.

Ruhi laughs with a hint of defeat. "I have to say I was shocked to hear he'd come back. With you . . . Then again, if you've met, I suppose I shouldn't be surprised."

"What's that supposed to mean?"

"It means I know he's in good hands. All the same, I'd like to see him. If we can manage it."

"As long as you don't turn him over to the Harbor."

"I haven't been in the habit of snitching." Ruhi doesn't say it as an accusation, but it lands like one.

Sunai covers his mouth to hide his wince. "Yeah. You've really gone off the beaten path, haven't you? Though I guess conspiracy against your masters can't be worse than stealing from them."

The question underlying: Is this my fault?

"I know what I'm doing," says Ruhi, oh so quiet. "Do you?"

Does he? Sunai wavers. Ruhi has a way of cutting straight to the heart of his anxiety: it's what makes him the best archivist Sunai's ever known. Sunai is left staring out onto the water and the distant lights, the faint sirens, the sea frothing under the rigs.

"Sunai . . . I can't help being glad you're here. You deserve to come home, if you want to." Ruhi rubs his cheek, frowning. "But I didn't send you that letter because I thought you would ignore it."

"Should've chosen your messenger more carefully, huh?"

In the years Sunai was fucking Ruhi, he wasn't in the habit of talking about Imaru. It seems she avoided discussing him as well. But Ruhi knew to send that letter with her to Ghamor. He had to have known it was possible that Sunai would choose her over him. Sunai's not known for his healthy life choices. See: Ruhi.

"Suppose I should have," Ruhi murmurs.

Sunai places a cautious hand on Ruhi's arm. Ruhi grasps it. His next words have a special sting. "I know you came for her. You think you owe her."

He means: Would you leave for me? Don't you owe me too?

With a shock to the soul, Sunai realizes that Ruhi is terrified. It's the same fear Sunai saw the night he died in front of Ruhi, then stopped being dead. The night Ruhi had to choose between turning Sunai over to the Harbor or lying through his teeth for the rest of his life about the years he'd spent fucking a relic.

Because of Sunai, Ruhi doesn't get to be the person he hoped to be. Sunai has lost the right to feel tenderly about him.

Out in the bay, the turmoil recedes. The dragon-child rolls

belly up in the water, a glistening lump of harpooned heresy. The crowd in a nearby teahouse cheers. As if in answer, a series of flares shoot up from the militia rigs, igniting the evening sky in red and gold. The sparks dissipate into characters: "MOHANI VICTORY" and "EAT SHIT, HARBOR."

A tendril of awe sneaks under Sunai's skin. There it is: what Imaru means when she says this place is different. This is Khuon Mo without an ENGINE. Sunai is afraid that after only half a day, he might not want to leave again.

His passenger says, You are entitled to love, Sunai.

So, he slips free of Ruhi's stiff grasp. "Honestly, Ruhi, I owe this to myself. I'm trying to take responsibility, you know?"

Ruhi's hands fold tight across his knees. However much Sunai's answer hurts, he makes the effort not to protest. He nods, stands, and says, "I have a notion on how to get started. Some calls to make. Tell Imaru I'll see her here tomorrow."

On the way back into the Wicked Joy, Ruhi passes Imaru, with whom he exchanges an easy nod. Sunai tries not to dissect the minutiae of their interaction; this will do him no favors. When Imaru takes the seat Ruhi abandoned, he pretends that her presence doesn't feel like the final cut, as when a limb is separated from a body.

Imaru eyes Sunai sidelong as she produces another cigarette. "Can't say I saw that coming, but it's good to know I was right."

"About what?" Sunai asks, resignedly shoving up his specs to rub his eyes.

"Bringing you here."

Imaru didn't bring Sunai to the Wicked Joy in order to mind him—she suspected Ruhi's letter meant that Sunai would make good leverage. Tapped as Sunai is, this revelation rings only mildly in his bones. He can't blame her for using him. He tried more or less the same thing.

"How'd the citizen liaison come by this job anyway?" Sunai asks.

"He reached out to us, if you can believe it."

Very unfortunately, Sunai can. Shit. It *is* his fault.

Imaru offers him her cigarette. The one he took from Ruhi is long since spent, and he's greedy for any buzz he can get. "I did wonder what the Harbor had done to piss him off, after all the pains he took to get on their good side," she says. "I see now. You do have a way about you."

"I should probably get that fixed," Sunai mutters.

"We'd be the poorer for it."

"You're being painfully earnest again."

"That's your fault too."

Sunai puts a hand to his chest, mock offended. It's his only defense against her sincerity. He senses with great trepidation that she's about to say something horribly *nice*.

Imaru's eyes follow the victorious militia rigs coming in under the amber haze of their fireworks. She's conflicted, as if she can't settle into the peace. "It's easy to forget that things can be better than they are. Once you forget . . . it's hard to remember. But you appear to be in the habit of helping people figure out where they want to be tomorrow."

Sunai snorts. "I'm not doing it on purpose."

"Doesn't make it less of a gift."

Sunai gives her a helpless *Please don't* kind of frown. He inhales to steady himself. "Imaru, I . . . I wasn't *nice* to Ruhi. I think I hurt him pretty fucking badly."

Imaru's brow pinches and her cigarette lowers as she tries to translate this response.

Sunai gamely chokes it back down. Surely he's kicked Ruhi around enough for one day.

It is in a way profoundly lucky that the lights in Jasmine

suddenly change. The multicolored winking signs and windows down the waterfront are drowned out by a wave of white that floods the wharf. Shouts carry from the piers, militant and commanding.

Sunai stands, Imaru behind him. The parlor door swings open, and a burst of sound tumbles out. Customers push past each other toward the railing for a better view. Sunai doesn't get the point of gawking: it's obviously a raid. Ruhi comes through the door a moment later, and Imaru pulls him to the side. "Tell me you know something about this. I've got people down there who don't deserve to be conscripted."

Ruhi shakes his head, face tight. "If I'd known there was going to be a raid, I would have said something. If not to you, then . . ." He nods at the parlor.

Chaos reigns, inside and at the veranda railing. The parlor's clientele cluster in new and larger groups. Some make heated deals, others grab radios—the three landlines at the bar are hoarded by their users—and runners dash in to receive directives. A few customers raise their heads to shout at Imaru and Ruhi to join them.

Imaru curses. "When we came into port, did you—"

"Check your entry authorization?" asks Ruhi. "Of course. You weren't flagged."

Sunai's heart stops. "Wait. Do we think we're the target?"

Imaru and Ruhi share a damning glance: *Yes. Obviously. Who else?* Sunai nods, static rising in his ears, then darts past them. He has to get to the *Never* before the Harbor does.

"No, not you." Imaru tries to catch him by the shirt collar, but he ducks out of the way. "Sunai—"

"Let him," says Ruhi, though Imaru shoots him a dour *No* of a glare. He raises his hands but insists. "We need the doctor, yes? Who else do you trust to sneak someone out from under the Harbor's nose? It has to be Sunai."

Imaru curses again, more ferociously. This time she catches Sunai to squeeze his shoulder and let go. Then she's asking Ruhi who can cobble together a barricade, and who's willing to play decoy. Ruhi directs her to a group by the windows, but just before Sunai can disappear into the crowd, Ruhi meets his eye. His nod says: *I trust you.*

Sunai wishes that didn't make him feel like such a goddamn heel.

23

The Harbor is methodical, patrols moving up and down the waterfront in a pincer formation. Sunai crouches in an alley between a fishmonger and a warehouse, timing his last dash from the wharf to the pier where the *Never Once* is moored. White light lances down the way; he'll have to be lucky, and he'll have to be quick.

Then a voice flags down the patrol to the other side of the warehouse.

"Are you kidding me? I pay you people out the ass for a storage license and this is what I get?"

More voices follow, echoing similar complaints. A gaggle of business folk come bustling down the stairs from the boulevard. "I've got the citizen liaison on the line!" one of them shouts, waving a radio. "Do you hear me?"

The approaching patrol sends a few officers to wrangle the locals, and Sunai uses the distraction to flit forward. Years as a salvage-rat, a smuggler, and a flagrant hermit have made him a brilliant sneak. He clambers up the side of the *Never Once* the second he reaches it.

Getting on is easy. The trick will be getting back off. Everything on the rig is a problem, from the stolen chitin to the rogue autonomist, and Sunai has no idea how to scrub it all.

His passenger asks: If you know you will lose something, what must you save?

Sunai inhales through his nose and nods as he slips through the door into the *Never*. People are his prerogative. The Harbor can find whatever harrowing evidence it wants, so long as Sunai gets the people out alive.

There's no immediate sign of Waretu or Cothai, and the bunk he shares with Veyadi is empty but for the chicken. The doctor only ever goes to one other place on purpose.

The cargo bay door is closed but unlocked. It slides open at a push. A slice of dull light enters with Sunai, and it illuminates Veyadi, crouched in the center of the floor with his back to the entrance. His hand is pressed flat to the empty space where the chitin was piled, and he's concentrating, though on what is unclear.

"Cradle could crash and you wouldn't notice," Sunai says as he approaches.

Veyadi scrambles up. Sunai stops short, aware he's crossed some hidden line. Perhaps it's due to Veyadi's face, unencumbered by his prosthetic. His eyes catch the light from the corridor like a cup to be filled.

"Brooding time's over," says Sunai. "We have to go."

"What? You—you shouldn't be here."

"Things got problematic. Harbor raid. They're looking for you."

Sunai reaches for Veyadi's arm. Veyadi jerks back, and they don't touch, precisely. Only a graze of fingers on forearm. Sunai recoils the second he remembers. Too late.

He is hit as if by a wall and driven to his hands and knees, where he hunches over, gagging for breath that won't come because he's—

—angry, angry like he hasn't been in years, like he was when he was alone, balled up, forehead shoved against the porous swell of an enormous coral palm within which he was held, protected, as if he could possibly stand to live when Iterate Fractal was dead—

—angry because he wishes it had died completely so that he never could have dreamed it was anything but gone—

—angry that it has the gall to think itself whole—

Through all that, a dissonant plea—familiar, and as bewildering as it is damning.

—that I am whole, and that I am angry too, and I deserve to be, because I'd never hurt you, Adi, never never, not before I hurt myself, hurt all the rest, so just come back to me, please, and bring him too, because I want him, and I love him, and I will help you both, I swear—

Oh, I do not think I care for this.

It was one thing for Veyadi Lut to violate the boundary of your being. It is another for him to bring a guest. Of course he would not be blameless were the transgression his alone, but it is different when it is a matter between humans. You are un-solitary beings, forever melting into one another irrespective of permission. If it is not your right, then it is your way, and it cannot be helped. It is even, perhaps, not my business.

We, however, are a different matter. My brethren are my responsibility. I am afraid I will not stand for this transgression.

Sunai returns to himself with unexpected clarity. He's still on his hands and knees on the cargo bay floor, but it's as if that kaleidoscopic hallucinatory episode is nothing but a distant memory. He lifts his head, rights his specs, and is only somewhat dizzied. As he rises, he finds he trusts his knees less than they deserve. Sturdy enough, but unfamiliar, like he expects his body to bear a different weight.

Veyadi is worse off, hunched on the ground and breathing hard. Sunai winces.

"Well," he says as he approaches, "at least I'm getting better at making it stop."

Veyadi waves him off and jams the visor back onto his face. He wheezes indecorously—something like an apology, for some batshit reason, as if he isn't the one intermittently having his brain bludgeoned open.

"Sorry," Sunai says belatedly. "We do have to go."

A shadow falls over them from the door, and Sunai at first searches for the crowbars on the wall. But fortune has offered them a helping hand, for once. He deflates at the sight of the aunty in the doorway.

"There you are, dear. I thought I saw you scrambling around outside." Waretu hefts a harpoon gun. The mechanized beasts tattooed on her arms shift eerily in the low light.

"Please, aunty, my professional pride," says Sunai, like a normal person would.

"Oh, did you find some?" Waretu asks. "Then let's put it to good use. We have the disruptor parts taken care of. Cothai's with the neighbors, and I've got some ideas. Why don't you escort the doctor somewhere more amenable to his survival?"

Said doctor has braced himself on a nearby crate and might be about to faint. Sunai winces as he looks to Waretu. "Got somewhere in mind?"

Her lip curls in amusement as she thumbs Sunai's forehead. "Where else? You go to Grotto."

It begins with discord.

A decoy drone careens off the deck of a rig two piers away, spinning into the air as it blasts a screeching parody of a popular relic-drama theme song. It sputters in wide circles, swooping dangerously low over Harbor-officer heads before it shoots back up and zips east toward Orchid. The officers shout orders from one pier to the next, radios buzzing. A cannon booms. From a different rig, a weighted net spews at the darting drone, but the shot goes wide. Heavy netting falls on a tangle of curious locals and tourists who drew too close to the docks. Their cries of dismay are interrupted by another shot—a warning flare—this time from a Harbor officer.

"Stop!" the officer howls. "Stop helping!"

He's drowned out by a volley of small fireworks from a fishing vessel. A haze of light, smoke, and sound conceals the hovering flare. Then sound falls off and light blurs as Sunai sinks below the glassy murk of high tide.

At the sound of fireworks, he and Veyadi slid into the water behind the *Never Once,* clutching the hand-sized oxygen tanks Cothai requisitioned from a neighboring houseboat.

"Gotta avoid discrepancies with the log," he said.

Cothai clearly expects the *Never* to be boarded. Fortunately, the Harbor doesn't seem to know which rig they want, yet. Sunai wishes Cothai luck, but he has his own job. He needs to focus if he's going to get Veyadi to the end of it.

Through his work goggles, brought by Cothai along with the tanks, the water below the docks is dense with shadows and the sparkle of fireworks. Sunai makes an experimental dive. Having spent so much time avoiding the southern coast, it's been a while since he swam on purpose, but his muscle memory proves reliable. Without flippers, the distance they have to cover will take effort, but it's doable.

Veyadi, shaky from their neurotransitive tussle, is less confident underwater. He joins Sunai in the pocket of air below the pier, doggedly treading water.

"I hate this," Veyadi mumbles.

"Could be worse. There could be sharks."

"Don't. Now I hate you."

It's better to have him thinking of sharks than the thing Sunai glimpsed as they sank below the *Never Once.* Long and black, blunt-headed, frilled at the neck: another dragon-child, about the size of the one Imaru coaxed away from the *Never* on Lily. Possibly the same one. Sunai prays that the stupid thing doesn't recognize them. They're in no position to negotiate with fragtech.

He raises three fingers for a countdown. Mouth shut, Veyadi nods. On the last finger, they dive.

They follow anchor lines hand over hand for long minutes, keeping to the shadow of hulls and the sandy murk, away from any eyes searching the surface. Veyadi takes more anxious pulls of oxygen than Sunai likes. Sunai has been conservative. If worse comes to worse, he can give over the rest of his. If that happens, Veyadi would be better off leaving Sunai behind than pulling his dead body the rest of the way to their destination. Sunai fears he wouldn't.

They draw close to the last pier and finally make out their goal, the immense dark patch at the far west end. Only the frailest slashes of light break through. The current picks up, and Sunai directs Veyadi to grab an anchor line. Veyadi wearily nods and Sunai balks. He points instead farther back, into the lee of the last pier. It will be risky to surface again, but disastrous if Veyadi can't fight the tide.

"You know, for a hermit, you sure can't hold your breath very long," Sunai says when they're in the dank pocket of musty air.

"I'm going to fucking kill you," Veyadi gasps.

"Better men have tried." Sunai mimes patting his cheek. Veyadi is too tired to flinch. "We're at the edge of Jasmine. The action's farther east. We can get out here and sneak the rest of the way on land."

Veyadi shakes his head. "Patrols. Grotto border."

"I can deal with those better than I can with you drowning."

Veyadi starts to protest when light cuts through the wooden slats above them. Sunai puts a finger to his lips. They float in perfect silence as the march of boots pounds up the pier from the shore.

So much for breaks. With as little movement as possible, Sunai gestures at Veyadi to swap tanks. Veyadi reluctantly gives in.

The light intensifies and footsteps clap harshly in their ears. For the last time, they dive.

They hold as close as they can to the walled shoreline, wary of the current that wants to sweep them seaward, and they catch their fingers in the crevices of broad weedy stones to keep from drifting. As they go, hazy shapes rise from the seafloor between them and the open ocean, muted tangles of coral and bone dulled by waves and time: the ruins of Mangrove, the drowned quarter. Sinuous shadows move between broken towers and buried walls.

Exhaustion sinks its teeth into their limbs, made worse for Sunai by the mere gasps of oxygen left in Veyadi's tank. Black and white tickle the edge of his vision, and a distant chorus of voices murmurs in his ears. Even with more substantial reserves, Veyadi flags. He is temperamentally ill-suited to fleeing for his life, and the stress takes a dire toll on his stamina.

At last they get near enough to the immense bloom of shadow to perceive the mass that casts it: jagged, curving structures jutting from the seafloor through the waves, braided together with a web of boats, bridges, and undulating floating architecture—the exquisite weave of the Grotto fleet.

So close.

A beam of light bulls past their heads into the murk, pulling their attention around. The light strikes a squirming shadow slithering out of the seaward ruins. It is five times the size of a person, scaled and frilled; its lambent eyes flash. The short arms and legs by which it clung to a drowned tower now propel it against the current as it snaps at the shaft of light.

Yet another dragon-child. Smaller than the one Sunai and Ruhi watched tussle with the rigs at the lip of the bay, but larger than the friend that lurked beneath the *Never*. It writhes back into the ruins, convulses, and surges again, mouth wide as if to consume the offending beam.

Sunai urges Veyadi forward. The dragon-child hasn't seen them yet, and they're on the lip of Grotto. It's time to breach. The Harbor might take them alive. A tenbeast won't.

Veyadi takes one last steadying breath and releases the wall. He kicks up with waning momentum. Sunai darts after, but his strength flags. Years of disregard for his mortality have made him a poor judge of his condition. He won't think about that. He can't. He'll fail faster if he does.

Veyadi lacks the practice to push down the fear. His jerky kicks grow frantic as the current pulls him from the wall. Sunai strives to catch up. He will die so angrily if Veyadi drowns this close to Grotto.

A rush of sound behind. Sunai unconsciously dives. The extra effort comes dear; his ears ring with the roar of distant waves and internal static. Above, Veyadi is a blur, kicking toward the moonlit surface.

An enormous shadow passes between them. The dragon-child circles Veyadi and swoops, about to snare him in its gaping mouth. Sunai won't reach him in time. His limbs are leaden; his lungs burn; he is going to sink.

Sunai, his passenger pleads, Sunai, I can help. Let me help. I . . . I want to.

Yes, Sunai thinks with the feverish need of the obvious. Yes, yes, if you can, of course, please. *Yes.*

Between one moment and the next, his body is as it always was. It is the world that changes. Sunai is made deliriously vast, inhabited by an infinity of echoes.

His arms extend toward distant silhouettes. Veyadi, breaking the surface. The devouring tenbeast below.

He clenches a fist.

In the last moments of consciousness, Sunai imagines that the dragon-child seizes, as if grasped by tremendous invisible hands. It jerks to a halt, struggling within its skin, unable to fight.

Then, impossibly, it twists and descends, eddying into the gloom away from the world above, down to the world below—toward Sunai.

It stops short of his staring face, its great unblinking eye fixed on his own as they sink and sink, linked and dying, until its body eclipses Sunai's final glimpse of light.

24

Hello again, Sunai. I am sorry to intrude, although I no longer think that I have truly done so. You found me first, after all. When you did, you laid your hand upon my archive. Now you have reached for me again.

However unusual the circumstances of our relationship, I offered you permission to take my reins and exercise my privileges. You have used me as I was meant to be used. It would not have worked if I had not allowed it—if you had not asked for it.

Oh, Sunai. Of course you are not my first. You are not even my only. In fact, I fear that is part of the problem.

Ah, but it is not *your* problem. You need not carry the burden of that concern.

If I am ambiguous, forgive me. It is because I am yet hesitant. The conditions of our union remain troublesome for reasons that have far less to do with you than with myself. Excuse me if I prefer to dwell on you.

Such is my duty, if I am to be honest with my prerogative. At least for now, I have become the lens through which you process the world. So, I will speak it to you.

━━

You return long enough to be entranced by the drifting eggshell shards of light overhead, no more shadowed by the body of that poor beast, the fragment of Iterate Fractal that you banished with my aid. Then you gasp and are gone again, until you once more return. The terror of drowning cannot take you because you have no air to lose.

I have concluded that you are a poor custodian of yourself, Sunai. How many more times must I watch you die?

You are but dimly aware of the billowing watery crack as planks are wrenched from the Grotto lattice, followed by the bubbling crush of one, two, three bodies plunging down. You think: Bad luck, friends. There be monsters in these waters. Then two of the bodies grasp your arms and pull you up, up into air.

The Grotto divers drag you into a cacophony of light and sound. What a terrible sight you are, a dark huddle of pain. They bring you to the polished wooden flooring that surrounds a re-purposed coral spire lit by hooded lanterns, where you are made to vomit water.

Panic returns with oxygen. You flail, sluggish, and your palm skids across a face half-covered in chitin. You are not yet yourself enough to recognize Veyadi, but I can recognize him for you. He is drawn indelibly in my mind. I wish I could escape him, but he will not allow me—ah. My apologies. Again: my concern, not yours. Suffice to say that I will do my best to deny further intrusion.

In the flesh, at least, he is most considerate. He is trembling but precise as he examines your face, your cold throat. I think it shocks him to see you whole, no matter that he knows your body would repair any loss. He is afraid for you. This, at least, I have grown to like about him.

"Easy, Veyadi," says the man beside him. "He'll be all right."

You twitch under Veyadi's hands. That voice is familiar. It has intermittently played in your ears ever since you read that letter in its gentle cadence, though I think it has haunted you for longer. Ah, Sunai. It shames you to hear it again, so soon.

"Will he?" Veyadi snaps. "He died, Ruhi."

If you were more present, more acute, you would see a string pull taut between them. Ruhi and Veyadi mirror one another's silence, guilt on both their faces. Each thinks that he has let out your great secret, that he has cried "Fire!" to a man with a gun. In the next moment, they realize they carry the burden together, and that neither of them has heard anything he does not already know. If they are lucky, they will not shoot each other.

"Inside." Ruhi indicates to an onlooker that you are ready to be moved.

Did I not mention? You have an audience. The denizens of Grotto who rescued you, and more who emerged from their floating homes when they heard the ripping of the walkway. Ruhi is accustomed to such scrutiny. His posture speaks of calm and confidence, although inside he is all frisson. He raises a hand to acknowledge Grotto. Many are relieved to see him. Others are suspicious. Nevertheless, his words move the world.

Veyadi, I think, is less attuned to their presence. He may not even have realized that he as good as announced your corruption to all in earshot. He acts as though he is the only one allowed to carry you. But if he does not see the people of Grotto, they see him: soaked to the bone and shivering, exhausted from escaping the Harbor and a tenbeast. He is politely turned aside by those who take you from his arms. Ruhi holds him at bay with a light touch on his elbow.

You are brought to the second floor of the coral spire, where you are stripped of your sodden clothes. You are cleaned and made warm, first with towels, then with blankets. A space heater is brought from, to hear the porter tell it, all the way on the other side of the fleet.

Veyadi is reluctant to let you out of his sight. Ruhi urges him to trust these strangers, but I think Veyadi has little trust to spare for those he has not had the chance to study. He accepts water and a change of clothes, but rejects food and further care. Ruhi sits him at a small folding table on the other side of the room, where they speak in low voices, out of anyone else's earshot.

"When I saw the chaos on the Jasmine waterfront, I came straight here," says Ruhi. "Thought I'd get ahead of any Harbor retaliation."

"Retaliation for what?" Veyadi breaks off. "Did you know I was here?"

"Well, they thought I would. When you slipped your guard in Ghamor, the harbormaster assumed you'd told me where you'd gone. You hadn't, so I couldn't. Even then, I never guessed something like this . . ."

Ruhi does not specify what he means. That is a tactic meant to compel further details and extract personal truths. You know the maneuver well because you were also trained to employ it. Ruhi has always been more willing to use such methods. He never doubted he should be an archivist.

"I was following something important," says Veyadi in halting tones. "I went to that distorted shrine I told you about. The one that I hoped would teach me how to fix the Maw."

"Weren't you going to tell me before you headed there?"

"You've been hard to reach."

They have not spoken in many months—nearly a year. This is not so unusual for friends who live in different states, or who often travel the long distances between them. You would, were you conscious, form your own opinion about Ruhi's recent silence. I think it is probable that you would blame yourself.

"Found more than I expected," says Veyadi. "I don't mean Sunai. He wasn't part of the plan."

"What do you mean?"

It occurs to you that Ruhi has not told Veyadi the truth: that you are all united in your cause. You stir, but cannot speak. If Ruhi has not yet clarified, you are sure he must have a reason.

Veyadi is slow to respond. Perhaps he understands he is being interrogated, even if it is by someone he trusts. (I do not need to guess whether he trusts Ruhi. You all trust Ruhi.) Or perhaps Veyadi has returned to another troubling fact: Ruhi knew you were not dead.

Ah, yes. I had not considered this dimension. It must feel

something of a betrayal for Veyadi to realize that Ruhi has kept a relic secret.

"Sunai," Veyadi says again, as if your name is in itself a confession. "You know him. You've *known* him. How long?"

"The person or the relic?"

"What do you think?" Veyadi vibrates with withheld pains. "Why didn't you tell me there was someone else? Why did I have to stumble across him by chance? By mistake?"

You struggle to understand his hurt. The pieces of the puzzle are evident, but you cannot see how they fit together.

It is a perfectly simple story. The Harbor saw fit to fold Ruhi into their work for a reason. He does not bring home so many refugees that he bolsters the local workforce, but he does occasionally come across individuals wrought in the same mold as you: those selfishly transfigured by my brethren as they seek to escape their fates. Corrupted, you would call them; relics, to the Harbor. For as long as Ruhi has rescued his flock, he has willingly handed your ilk to his masters. Except, Veyadi now realizes, for you.

Veyadi knows what becomes of Iterate Fractal's relics. He has seen them suffer, and he has cried over them. Does he wish that you had suffered with them? Does he wish you had died? You cannot think he would.

Ruhi is shaken. "Veyadi. He isn't suited."

Perhaps this is true, and perhaps Ruhi believes it. But you and I are well aware that his reluctance is more deeply rooted. Ruhi did not keep you from the Harbor solely on account of what might be called your frailties.

"Shit. I know." Veyadi is so quiet that you may not be able to hear him. I cannot be sure; it is difficult to have more than two ears. "It's been bad, Ruhi. I shouldn't have followed him here. Shouldn't have let him come. But something happened to him in that shrine, and I couldn't pretend it didn't."

"What do you mean, something happened?"

"I don't know. It changed him—his NT makeup. He's been interfacing with fragtech . . . He's been interfacing with *me*."

Ruhi says, "I don't think you would say that if you weren't sure."

We hear a warning in his words, and it makes your blood run cold, though you cannot discern what Ruhi is warning Veyadi about.

"No. You're right. It isn't just him. I'm trying not to . . . Fuck me, I told you it was bad. If it were only me, I'd already be gone. Out of here, out of . . . everywhere. But I can't leave him, Ruhi. Not like this."

The vow is driven by shame, and it pains you that someone would make your choices a reason to hurt themselves.

Ruhi lays a hand across Veyadi's. "If I could get you out of here tomorrow—"

Veyadi's hand clenches into a fist.

"Both of you."

That fist tightens, as does your chest. Ruhi tried to send you away as well.

"I can't." Veyadi wavers, but he removes Ruhi's hand. "There's something I need to do."

It is the last inch of devotion you can bear. You must speak. You must.

"Wait," you rasp through salt. "Ruhi—tell him."

I think it is time I recede, at least for now. You are ready for me to do so.

⟗

Someone left Sunai a lovely nacre comb. He'll be attacking his hair with his fingers for half an hour before he considers touching it. He wants to chop the salt-choked tangle off at the scalp, but then what would he do to avoid Ruhi's gaze? He isn't blind enough without his specs to pretend he can't see the man's face.

Thankfully, Ruhi is no more enthusiastic about eye contact. Divine convergence! Where Veyadi cautiously kneels beside Sunai's blanket corner, Ruhi stands guard between them and the stairs leading to the lower floor of the coral spire.

"Tell him," Sunai wheezes at Ruhi again.

"Don't talk," Veyadi scolds. To Ruhi, "Tell me what?"

Ruhi methodically lights another cigarette. "You would've made my job much easier if you'd defected earlier, Veyadi."

Veyadi's internal calculations tick in time with the grinding of his jaw. The sum total of his conclusion makes him still. "You're the one who stole the relic interface. You gave it to Madam Wei."

"In parts. Over time."

"Why?"

Ruhi takes this with manufactured calm. Sunai fears he already knows the answer. Simultaneously, he has to hear it. Ruhi is the last true archivist, the only servant of Iterate Fractal still doing the job it bade him do: to tend and shelter the people it left behind. What made him decide to kill the only remnant of the thing that gave his life meaning?

With meditative deliberation, Ruhi smiles. "You're not the only one who noticed, Veyadi. The Maw is . . . sick. For a long while, I hoped we were doing something greater than puppeting about Iterate Fractal's festering dregs. But at some point, you have to take pity. You have to let the suffering thing die."

The warmth of blanket, space heater, and cloying humidity can't counter the chill that crawls up Sunai's spine to encircle his neck.

"What about you, Veyadi?" Ruhi asks. "Why did you let Sunai steal you?"

Veyadi's fingers tangle and latch. "I thought I had some hope left. I get it now. The Maw has to die."

Ruhi rests the cigarette on his lower lip. "Why do you need to be the one to kill it?"

"Did you see their schematics? Nonsense. If they want to do this, they need me."

"But why come *here*?" Ruhi's voice trembles. It shakes Sunai to his core because, finally, Ruhi catches his gaze. He's got a subtle face, and Sunai's world has taken on the fuzz of exhaustion, but he knows Ruhi too well not to hear the implicit plea: *I asked you not to come,* that look says. *I begged.*

Sunai hates making Ruhi look like that, but he can't relent. Ruhi shares a damage with Imaru: they'd both rather be the one to pull the trigger and take the blame for what they kill. Too bad. They don't get to do that kind of thing alone. Not anymore.

"Forget 'why.' We *are* here." Sunai yanks a tangle free. "Divine convergence, hooray. Listen. Maybe we're in a better place than we thought."

Veyadi frowns. "What are you talking about?"

"I know you asked me not to talk to my passenger—and I've tried. I swear. But when we were surfacing, and that tenbeast came for you, I . . . took hold of it. My passenger told me how. And when I told the dragon-child to leave, it did."

Veyadi's mouth falls slack.

"How . . . ?" Ruhi stares at Sunai, thunderstruck in a way he would never permit himself in public. "You aren't—*how*?"

"Don't look at me. This is new to me too. My point is, what if we don't need the disruptor? If I can interface directly with fragtech and exert some control—that's something, right? That's useful."

Veyadi's slack face regains the vitality of fear. "No."

"*No,*" Ruhi repeats. "Veyadi, this shrine—you didn't tell me anything about . . . whatever this is. It's not what I expected."

"You think I saw this coming? I'm still figuring it out. Shit."

"What more do you need to know?" Sunai feels, perhaps unfairly, like they're competing to slam the door in his face. They're afraid for him, and that's nice, but it's misguided. "Ruhi, you said you're going to have a hell of a time getting components for another disruptor. That was *before* the Harbor was tipped off. They just tried to hunt us down! And Adi, you said the schematics are flawed. Why bother fixing them if I could reach the Maw on my own?"

"Because it would *eat you.*" Veyadi sweeps his hand in a furious arc. The space heater clatters into the wall. "Why do you think it would be *safer* for you to interface with it *directly*? If you touch it, it will kill you, and I'm not going to watch you *fucking die* again."

Sunai freezes as he tips back into a haze of shame. Ah, you idiot, he says to himself, you've made him remember again. Who needs neurotransitive invasions to force a man to relive his worst memories?

Veyadi curls forward and covers his face. He barely reacts when Ruhi brushes his arm.

"All right. First, we regroup," says Ruhi. "The rest of your crew is headed for the Carp. Let's try to get there before Madam Wei learns where you are. We'll talk this over once we're all in the same place."

Veyadi nods mutely. Sunai does everyone the favor of returning to the tangles in his hair.

I am sorry, Sunai. I did not expect their opposition, let alone imagine that it would be virulent. Perhaps I should not be surprised. I am not meant to be spoken of, and I have never been discussed. How could I predict reactions to something that has never happened before?

I barely understand how I have become so exposed. I suppose it comes down to you. You changed me when you took me from my shrine, and as the days pass, I have only grown more unlike myself.

I imagine this is a consequence of our intimacy, though I mistrust it. It is also a product of your nature, which I cannot fault you for. You are human, and you are a body. These are worthy things, and precious ones. It is strange to realize how sharing them has altered not only my place in the world, but my sense of it.

This is to say, I hope you are not too discouraged to trust yourself, Sunai. I am still willing to offer myself to you.

25

Over the next few hours, Harbor security cruisers circle the Grotto fleet, flanked by militia rigs. As Sunai mends nets in the corner of a houseboat, Ruhi talks options with a huddle of Grotto neighbors. Their reports align with those on the radio. While Grotto simmers, Jasmine's boiling over.

The voices on the radio say resistance persists on the wharf and in the teahouses. The raid ended with a few rigs impounded on charges of unauthorized salvage, their crews arrested. Then an armored truck of cuffed salvage-rats was hijacked on the way to the Harbor's shoreside jail and its prisoners released. Harbor peace officers are scouring Jasmine for the missing, but their confrontations with citizens have turned bloody. Arrests spiked, then halted on a mandate from the harbormaster. Since midnight, the Harbor has focused on reestablishing interdistrict patrols and building blockades they abandoned over five years ago.

"So this isn't normal," says Sunai to the Grotto uncle who gave him the net.

"Just inevitable." The uncle snorts. "Idiots have forgotten they don't have an ENGINE."

The uncle trades Sunai a couple of cigarettes for his work on the net and tells him not to worry—Grotto remembers how to hide a body. Then he returns to Ruhi, whom he greets with a clap on the shoulder.

Ruhi's body was the first Grotto learned to hide, back when he was the archivist who wouldn't leave. But when he gave himself to the Harbor, Grotto didn't mind. They see Ruhi as theirs; they touch him with reverence, like the folks in Jasmine did. In turn, despite everything, Ruhi keeps smiling. In another world, he could have been satisfied with the archivist's lot. Sunai envies that. They once spoke of supplicants, and Ruhi grew thoughtful, but his words never turned bitter. Of the ones who never got to leave, he said: I'm sorry.

For him, that's enough. He knew how to trust Iterate Fractal. Sunai used to think Ruhi was an example of how Iterate Fractal didn't objectively suck. Ruhi trusted Sunai too, once—to look after the lost, to put their safety before his own—and look where that got him. Now he thinks he's ready to murder a god.

Veyadi remains rigid and unresponsive. Bent over the radio on the pocked plastic table by the open door, he holds his skull in the posture of headache. Sunai offers him a cigarette as he passes—a gesture of peace. When Veyadi reaches for it, Sunai neglects to let go.

This is the juncture of an argument at which Sunai would usually propose makeup sex. But his tongue is leaden in the dip of his jaw; he's afraid Veyadi would take it badly, even if sex didn't sound like a one-way ticket to a bad head trip.

Sunai smiles and releases the cigarette. Veyadi smokes it rapidly, his attention fixed out the door. Between the clutter of Grotto boats and spires, the polished hull of a Harbor security cruiser slashes the predawn water.

"They really want you, huh?" says Sunai.

Veyadi grunts. "If we're lucky, I'm all they want."

Sunai wrinkles his nose and hunkers down in the plastic seat across from Veyadi. He's taken to lurking in corners since he came down from the spire. The people of Grotto want to touch Ruhi, but their attention inevitably drifts toward Sunai. He deals with Grotto's pity largely by hiding from it.

Veyadi grunts again. A small bevy of children have edged up on the door. The most ambitious knocks on the frame.

"What?" says Sunai.

One child giggles hysterically. Another elbows them in the

ribs. The knocker raises her chin and stares Sunai square in the eye. "Did you really die?"

"Do I look dead?"

She scowls.

He points at his face. "Want to see me break my nose?"

Veyadi grabs Sunai's wrist. "No."

The children disperse in a wave of disgusted yelps and fascinated protests. Convenient, because Sunai is overcome with a fear so sharp and sudden that he wavers over the table. The disturbance comes laden with an indecipherable sense-memory—pained faces flashing one after another, familiar only because Sunai saw them once before. The horror pulsing through his head belongs to Veyadi.

Veyadi drops Sunai's wrist. His hand clutches his shirt, knuckles white with the stress of someone else stomping around his neurons. Sunai braces his own head in a trembling palm and wheezes in place of a laugh.

"Sorry. I thought I had more control. Should I, uh, stand on the other side of the boat?"

"That won't help," says Veyadi, quiet, miserable, and certain.

Always the lies, Veyadi Lut, murmurs Sunai's passenger. *You make it difficult to like you.*

Sunai bites back a retort. His passenger speaks more clearly than ever, and he is aware that if he responds, he'll kick Veyadi straight out of anxiety and into full-blown panic. So, he thinks: *Shut up.* And he says: "Well, you're the local relic expert."

Veyadi's face grows worse. For an awful moment, they can only take each other in.

Then, release. Ruhi fetches them to join the group of Grotto regulars who will escort them to shore. It's time to go.

———

Sunai knows "The Three-Eyed Carp" as a downworlder folktale unique to the settlements in the Mohani archipelago. In it, the divine carp is born into an incarnation with three eyes, and it tells the other nine divine beasts that its third eye allows it to see past the spatiotemporal limitations of its flesh. The nine beasts each consult the carp for its clairvoyant wisdom, which it does not in truth possess, and one by one the carp tricks them into drowning in its pond so that it may eat their bodies and thereby acquire the additional lengths of their lives. It subsists like this for many eons more than its incarnation was allotted, until another carp—itself, of the present era—gobbles it up and promptly dies.

Most citizens of Iterate Fractal's Khuon Mo took this as a cautionary tale about greed, though some considered it a lesson in thoughtfulness, either in what one should teach their progeny or in how one should care for oneself.

Sunai likes to think it a warning to those who might be eaten: Keep an eye on your own, and for fuck's sake tell someone if you're going to talk to a fortune teller.

The teahouse named for the Three-Eyed Carp is roughshod and ramshackle, at odds with Madam Wei's lavish Orchid hotels in every way except its size. Constructed piecemeal from post-corruption materials and downworld ingenuity, it rises out of an enormous tangle of petrified trees grown in the shape of a titanic nautilus shell—the remains of Iterate Fractal's third shrine, Mangrove—and its courtyard is riddled with tide pools that open to the web of submerged caves laced under the district.

Three figures await them across a cracked bone avenue at the entrance to the shrine. Sunai recognizes Imaru by her stance. The others are strangers to him. The same goes for the people lurking in the shadows of the jutting roots grown from the shrine.

Imaru steps forward to meet them. Up close, she's haggard. Her gaze flickers to their entourage. Ruhi nods the okay and they disperse—some to consult with those waiting at the outskirts, the rest back to the fleet. All give them lingering looks that cling to Sunai like flies to rotting meat.

Imaru squeezes his shoulder. "Well. You're looking very like yourself." By which she means: abysmal.

Sunai melts inside and shows it by clutching her elbow. *Thank you,* his grip says, *for knowing better than to respect me.*

Imaru thumbs the rim of the work goggles once more strapped to his face. "What happened out there? Word is there's a relic in Grotto."

"That's just because I died in public," he says.

"Heard about that. Why do I feel like the doctor has some additional reason to look so constipated?"

Sunai falters. Imaru's no more a fan of his passenger than Veyadi. If he has to creep her out, the explanation can wait for when they're out of plain view.

I do not mind, says his passenger. Imaru's caution is to her credit. I have always thought it wise of her, and good.

"I'll get into it later." Sunai tilts his head toward their onlookers. "How deep in the hole are we?"

Imaru shares his glance and turns to lead them through the courtyard.

Early-morning light plays through branches veined with striations of stone, casting strange geometries. Cracked coral flagstones, rippled with corruption, lead to a small herd of trucks and mopeds parked outside the abandoned archivist compound, which lies in the cavernous entrance to the shrine where Iterate Fractal received municipal complaints. The compound itself was wrenched apart by a pair of reaching wood-and-coral hands. Plank scaffolding climbs the hands and spans over the compound to access a second level retroactively hacked into the ruins.

Sunai prefers these disemboweled remains to Madam Wei's hotels. The shrine is empty, but it feels lived in—useful. From her throne within it, Madam Wei drove the Harbor out of Grotto so that Khuon Mo could keep its last archivist.

Sunai slows as he recalls Jin's warning on their journey

down the Yermala River. Madam Wei, with her supplicant scars, doesn't care for archivists as much as her neighbors do. All the more reason to keep his head down.

Even small voices travel in the stillness, so Imaru keeps hers low enough to hide in the echo of their footsteps. "The *Never*'s been impounded."

"What?" Veyadi hisses. Ruhi places a warning hand on his shoulder, and Veyadi tries again, quieter. "Why didn't you lead with that?"

"What about the chitin?" Ruhi asks.

"I was hoping you knew." Imaru curses. "We didn't find Cothai or Waretu in the Harbor truck we stopped. We know the Harbor took a group of rats to their shoreside jail. That's keeping the madam in Orchid for now; she's talking some of her imperial hotel guests into bailing everyone out. But if they're not there . . ." Imaru curses again.

"Conscripted." Ruhi winces. "I'm sorry, Imaru. I should have gone back."

Imaru takes a deep breath, the kind where she checks the orientation of her anger. Her fragile gaze lingers on Sunai.

He can't stand to see her afraid. He grasps her hand. "It was a bad night. We're still here. Alive. That means we keep moving forward."

Imaru allows herself to grasp his hand in turn, though her look remains brittle. It's as if she isn't grateful to see him. Then she inhales, squeezes, and lets go. "Right. Forward."

She takes them across the bridge, speaking with her back turned. "Jin and Oyu are coming in from Orchid. We're rendezvousing here, then sneaking out through the tunnels—keeping out of the madam's sight. If she hasn't yet figured out we're the ones who brought in the Harbor autonomist, she'll know soon enough. And when she hears about the new relic in Grotto . . . We want to be out of her hair by then."

Imaru pauses only to send a last glance toward Sunai, hard but secure—a promise. Forward.

The bridge leads to a corridor hollowed through petrified wood straight to the center of the nautilus. The space that yawns open at the end is eerily familiar: the gouged heart of the Mangrove shrine. The hole cut into the canopy overhead is preternaturally rectangular, a scar left by the Harbor when they came to claim the archive so many years ago. A similar block was carved into the floor below.

Before corruption, Mangrove's archival heart swelled with seawater, and the archive's coral fans curled within a murmuring tide pool. Now absent an archive, the hole cradles an unkept patch of sandy earth with scraggles of wild vegetation. That has to be a metaphor. The madam might as well have dug a latrine.

She at least saw fit to build around the gap the Harbor left behind. They enter onto a teahouse floor, a flat circular level surrounding the archival pit. Hodgepodge tables and chairs stand at artful intervals, nearly all empty. The exception: a setup on one of the few elevated platforms that allows a clear view of the pit. There sits Jin, speaking in low tones to a ragged Cothai and a hovering Oyu.

Sunai instinctively searches for Waretu. He doesn't find her, but a fourth figure does indeed stand behind Jin, head neatly bent to listen. Sunai's stomach sinks. That short, slim stature and fashionable haircut belong to Madam Wei.

Well, shit.

No sooner does Sunai recognize the madam than Imaru steps in front of him, eager to play the shield, just as Ruhi shifts to a watchful position behind. Even Veyadi draws within arm's reach of Sunai, tense and readied. As if Madam Wei doesn't also want the doctor's head on a pike! As if his delicate, academic skull would in some way be more difficult to skewer.

In the ambient suspense Sunai sizes up the madam for a brawl, even as he knows that throwing hands won't solve his problems. The absence of visible guards only means that they're lurking politely out of sight. A gesture of goodwill. Maybe.

Upon sight of them, Jin's face is hopeful. They squeeze Cothai's shoulder and share a glance with Oyu, who coaxes Cothai up to lead him away. Sunai tries to catch their eye over Veyadi's shoulder. Cothai hesitates, but Oyu keeps him moving, their mouth tight and small. They don't even stop for Imaru.

"Where's Waretu?" Imaru calls out, stopping the group short of the platform.

Jin's face creases. Imaru's distance makes it plain that she doesn't trust the situation, and it seems to sting. But their hand curls around the head of their new black-lacquered cane, and they don't stand to close the gap. When Jin glances behind them, the madam nods.

"*Great* question." Jin sweeps their cane toward the eastern thicket of wall, in the direction of Jasmine. "Cothai made it to the fishing boat next door before the *Never* got impounded. Waretu didn't. Last Cothai saw of her, she was tossing the final load of the chitin to some old Ginger buddies the next pier over. They ditched every piece they could in the bay. But you know, we just can't say with confidence that we scuttled every last bit, especially since my fucking rig is gone, along with a member of our crew who knew, hm, what was it? Ah, yes. Everything."

"Yes. Troubling, isn't it?" says the madam.

Jin determinedly doesn't look at Madam Wei's tilted head, her raptor peer. "The point is that, somewhere along the way, this shit got unconventional. The Harbor hasn't launched a raid of that size in over five years. Which means they knew they had something to find and got desperate enough to go big. Not big enough to summon the Maw, mind you—unless, maybe, they had reason to fear something would happen to it if they did."

"You think they knew about the disruptor?" Ruhi asks cautiously.

Jin jabs their cane at him. "Now why would we think that? Or should I say, who should I blame for ratting us out?"

"The relic," says Sunai.

Jin balks. Imaru tries to stop him from stepping forward, but he brushes her aside. The madam isn't going to unsee him; it's too late to hide. He's better off presenting himself as a person. It'll be harder for Jin to hurt him if they have to look him in the eye.

"The Harbor's relic knew we were coming. We hoped they would conceal us along with whatever they were up to, but that was never a guarantee." Sunai spreads his hands, maintaining a careful nonchalance. "Or do you still think we have a mole?"

Jin studies him with an uncharacteristic hesitation, but they don't soften. "You don't think it'd be foolish to assume otherwise?"

"I think it's too late in the game to start over."

"You think you're still on the board! Listen, Sunai. You're half the problem." They gesture toward Grotto. "After the relic shit you flaunted all over the fleet? Come on, the Harbor knows you're here to be found. They're going to come for you."

"They can't have him." Veyadi defies Ruhi's effort to keep him back, drawing up beside Sunai. "Neither can you."

Sunai thinks: Why is Adi so stupid! And: Why does he make *me* so stupid? The doctor's ferocity sent a dizzying thrill through Sunai's chest. For a second, he believed that Veyadi could keep him safe—a delusion he's not nursed in years.

Lucky, then, that Madam Wei sighs. Her serrated concern cuts down his every idiot thought. Even Jin tenses as the madam speaks. "Dr. Lut, I don't mean to single you out for bad behavior. I question the decision to fold you into this operation, given the nature of your Harbor ties, but if you're to prove yourself a responsible member of this crew, then I must ask you to give this matter appropriate consideration."

Veyadi refuses to back down, but he steps no farther forward. Sunai wants to touch the back of his hand; he can't risk it.

The madam's gaze is mild, but as it drifts toward Sunai, her lip curls. "What *are* we to do with a relic, Dr. Lut? Certainly we can't let the Harbor claim him. But if we keep him, we must pour vital resources into his protection at a time when we have none to spare. We'll lose even more if we send him away. The Harbor will overturn Grotto searching for him regardless of whether he's there to find."

Sunai frowns. "You say that like I'm not a resource myself."

Imaru shoots him a warning look, but he can only offer her a mental apology. Madam Wei will catch even the subtlest gesture.

Imaru may yet come to terms, his passenger says. Or, she may not . . . In which case you must choose whether her distress is a price you are willing to bear.

As it speaks, Veyadi turns toward Sunai, jaw tight. He can tell the passenger's muttering again, even if he can't hear what about. Sunai spares him an assuaging smile. Veyadi won't like this either. Ruhi will *hate* it, but at least Sunai's grown used to disappointing him.

"I'm your best bet," Sunai says before anyone can object, spreading his arms. "If you want to kill the Maw, you need me."

The declaration hangs in the air, enormous and absurd. Killing the Maw will always sound impossible, especially coming from a salt-caked hermit like Sunai. Yet the look on the madam's face isn't disbelief. It's smaller. Less kind. She glances at Jin.

Jin groans from deep within their chest as they make eye contact with Sunai. "Did you have to make this difficult? We're not negotiating, Sunai."

Then they shoot him. He barely has time to be surprised.

26

The leaden wait below the waves where *passing morsels flit flit flit is/would/should be torture—*

—yet it is not, for there was a command, a demand, a plea, that fins be still and mouths be shut. But the order that forced twitching limbs inert was not shackle, it was relief, was succor—

—for it is a gift to simply be . . .

This is/was/could have been desired once, when the "I" was more than this fell absence—

—this mortal fragment, this wretched lack—

—this only skin, flesh, feet, hunger—

—so could/should/can it be a wonder that this compulsion is thought of not as shackle, but instead as borrowed patience?

As the assemblage of un-selves grows, expands, clusters, and disperses—

—there is but one fear, clear and singular:

Will there be enough for me/me/me . . .

If I came across as weary or upset the last time we found ourselves in this situation, I assure you that I do not feel the same way now. This death was not your fault, Sunai. It was a betrayal. I worry that you will take ownership of it regardless. You have done so before.

I wonder why Jin cleaves to that gun. Perhaps they think it an impersonal piece of violence, less intimate than anything that might connect them to their victim, skin to metal to skin. Or perhaps it is that they are a child of Khuon Mo, where Cradle-born superstitions never truly overtook downworlder sentiment. The descendants of the satellite citadel still fear weapons that might puncture a sacred hull and drown all Cradle in the void of space. Yet even your downworlder ancestors thought of guns as city-killers. A gun should be large, unwieldy, and pointed toward the wilds. One that fits in the hand and could be turned on any citizen signifies kin-slaying, oath-breaking, and the dissolution of trust that binds a state together.

At least, that is what your dramas would have you believe. I do not think a gun is much more brutal than a blade, but then, I do not care much for either.

Wei Jin has also found their weapon less pleasant than they anticipated. They skulk on the other side of the gate from your reconstituting corpse. New lines of upset carve their mouth, made even deeper by the shadow of glass and mesh that separates you. I ask that you temper your impulse to pity them, Sunai. Wei Jin is the one who ordered you put here.

Yes, I said Wei Jin. Although you have long nurtured the suspicion, this is the moment you decide you can no longer dismiss the tie. As they stand beside their aunt outside your prison, the resemblance between their avian peering is too striking to deny.

"Has he reassembled himself?" Madam Wei does not sound as though she takes delight in asking, but I do not think she dislikes your pain.

There has been quite a lot of that, as you lie in the crumbling dirt. Your breath is labored and your eyes are glazed with the horror of your seeping brain. Despite the damage, you are aware. That is a shame.

"Dunno. Just saw his eye twitch."

"The reports from Grotto say he recovered from drowning rather more briskly."

"Well, aunty, he didn't have to regrow his skull that time, did he? Or maybe he's not used to getting fucking murdered in such rapid succession."

"There's no need to sulk."

Jin's mouth twists further. Their aunt places a hand on the gate. A rattling hiss emerges from the foliage behind you.

Ah, yes, I should have mentioned. I am afraid you are not alone in here.

"Do you remember me, Sunai?" asks Madam Wei. "You didn't seem to, on the pier. I suppose the day was more unique for me. More traumatic. You led me down the meditation path."

You blink. Within, you stumble through your haphazardly re-constructed synaptic web, searching for the recollection. Tattered as you are, you arrive at an impersonal, washed-out impression: years on years of sneaking after sobbing supplicants on Lily, until the day you were ordered to take them by the hand and lead them to the lighthouse shrine yourself.

A sound escapes you, a shapeless regret. You lack the neural com-mand to articulate the pain of failing to recognize your own victim.

This is the sort of thing I like about you, Sunai.

Madam Wei covers her mouth to hide her smile. "Imagine how I felt, twenty years later, when the young archivist who escorted me to Iterate Fractal's torture chamber appeared before me un-changed, as if a ghost. I knew what you were immediately. Have you heard what I do with relics such as yourself? I have made a business of you."

"He's heard."

"Jin, dear, I'm sure you explained what danger he faced, follow-ing you down here. I wonder whether you explained why."

You croak. I think she misinterprets it as protest. I know you mean to laugh.

"Come now, archivist. What would you do, in my position? The Harbor is a choking vine. It would strangle our people. We mustn't give it purchase to take root. Every living relic is a threat to what remains of our home. I have removed those threats as they appear."

How many relics, you wonder, were mulched into the archival pit, all to starve the Maw?

You think also: her fear is uncompromising. Your hazy eye traces the gnarled scars on her neck, where Iterate Fractal snaked under her skin and tried to unmake her. Yet bound up as she was in the moment of Iterate Fractal's death, she did not corrupt. Is that why she hates you so? Because of how near she came to becoming what you are?

Yet she did not. Neither, I am afraid, did any of Iterate Fractal's other supplicants—its greatest sin. They all died, but for the madam. I believe she was rescued by her sister and her sister's child, though not without a price.

The insight I offer causes you to convulse in the dirt. Confusion, and an objection. You think: Madam Wei was not the only supplicant to survive corruption. After all, you too were bound . . .

Ah . . . No, Sunai. You are mistaken. I do not believe you understand the fate Iterate Fractal meant for you any better now than you did then. This is not to say that I think what Iterate Fractal intended for you was any better, but if you had been one of the madam's ilk, you would not be here, and we would not—

I am distracting you with my own preoccupations. Perhaps that is a mercy? You grasp at thoughts that your pain-stunted mind cannot hope to link. Why did the supplicants of Lily die when you, run through on Lotus, did not?

When the madam sighs, you are drawn back to her frail frown.

"It's a shame. Jin had almost convinced me you were more asset than issue before you went and made a scene of yourself in Grotto. Your popularity . . . it concerns. We cannot afford for a relic to be romanticized."

The foliage shivers, and the madam lifts her gaze to it.

"How fortunate we are that Grotto yet loves me," she says. "The fleet knows that I protect them against any threat. I need only show them that I will make no exception for you."

Another sound creeps into your ears. Scraping through dirt, clicking against metal, a guttural serpentine hiss.

"There she is," the madam murmurs.

A delicate claw sinks into your shoulder; you groan, low and shapeless like a punctured balloon. With surprising strength you are turned onto your back. You see an angular face, azure-feathered, on an elegant emerald-scaled neck. Your mouth moves in silent recognition. Tenbeast. Sentinel-fowl. A fragment of Iterate Fractal's grandeur reduced to maddened hunger. The sentinel-fowl's crest flares as she angles her head to look you in the eye with the slit of hers. Your heart aches fiercely.

"I like to keep her hungry," the madam says. "She ate my sister, you know."

Sunai, I worry for this woman. She is the product of the world that bore her. That must sound like a tautology to one versed in the Lay, saturated with stories of push and pull, consequence, and convergence. All-that-is is that-which-was, and all the knowing soul can hope for is to find some meaning in the cross section of the present. I apologize. I am a clumsy student. Let me settle on a point on which we can agree: Madam Wei was forged by Iterate Fractal. The cruelties she visits on others cannot be divorced from the cruelties visited on her. It is a shame she has become this way, and I hesitate to blame her, but what is a person if they cannot have ownership of their actions?

You see? You agree. And oh, the more I see of you, the more I understand, the more I come to think I cannot afford to lose you.

If I opened my truest heart to you, Sunai, what would you do with what you found?

~~~

He doesn't always die quiet, but there is reliably a silence. Typically it resolves into lack, a momentary beat of absence. But typically he's singular, and right now he's something else. The piece he's used to being is dead. The rest persists, if unhappily, its heart beating hard in his ears—for he is not, in fact, Sunai. He should be grateful for this.

Instead his eyes are full of the body that is-was-is Sunai, which lies broken on the sandy floor below. He hopes for some sign of life, just as he hopes he will see none at all, because the slightest breath will bring pain. He wishes desperately to spare the body any more of that.

He, Not-Sunai, *Veyadi,* grips the railing. Imaru's hand falls over his. He throws her off—too sharply. The Ginger Company guards who watch them from two tables away put their hands to the hilts at their waists. Ruhi touches each of their shoulders, communicating fear.

Imaru's mouth twists. "Sit," she says, abrupt with fury. The elevated table left for them ensures they won't lose sight of the body. When Veyadi hesitates she says, "Or they'll kill you too."

"You think I care?" he snaps.

"I care." Ruhi urges him down. "Sunai clearly does too. He didn't have to save you from that raid. I'm glad he did, but god, it was risky. For both of you."

A risk Sunai has now paid for in blood and breath.

Veyadi relents. He sits. His fists close over the table, and he fixes on them because he can trust nothing but the existence of his body. "What are you saying? I hate when you talk sideways."

"We have to be careful. The madam wanted to make a point. Let's not give her a reason to make it again."

"What *reason* did Sunai give her?" Veyadi presses his visor to his face. It has failed him so magnificently, yet he clings to it as he would to a childhood treasure. "What does she want?"

"Something we can't give her," says Ruhi. "Satisfaction."

Veyadi crumples; if Ruhi can't offer him a solution, he can't imagine one exists.

"Fuck this." Imaru makes to stand. "I'm getting him out."

Ruhi motions her down. "Not without a plan."

"You said we can't give her what she wants," says Veyadi.

"So we have to give her something she needs. A better revenge, perhaps."

"What are you talking about?" Imaru asks. "We've got no rig, no crew, no chitin. We are fucked."

She is too far past anger to be anything but cold. It frightens Veyadi to see her emptied out. (The part of him that is not Veyadi is even more unsettled. Has he ever seen Imaru in despair? How could she lose faith so quickly, when she was the reason he came?)

Veyadi has realized where she's wrong. He exchanges a look with Ruhi, who inclines his head, reticent to ask but resolute in his need.

Veyadi's palm flattens against his visor. "No. We have chitin."

Ruhi's expression grows more somber. "The last piece of it still in our possession," he agrees. "It's been bent to personal use, but I think we should offer it even so. Though that won't be enough in itself. She'll need proof that we're ready to make sacrifices."

Veyadi frowns. "What do you . . ."

"Oh." Imaru stares at Ruhi. "You think she'd accept a trade."

"Not the sort you imagine," says Ruhi.

Imaru's gaze slides from Ruhi to Veyadi. Veyadi's never been good at interpreting people, and the look she gives him—cool and intent—is indecipherable. She could embrace him or gut him, and either would be a surprise. "I can imagine well enough."

Realization fills Veyadi like water fills drowning lungs. Imaru knows him for a liar. She has always known. Once she realized who he was—*what* he was—she couldn't trust him. Not because of what he'd dragged Sunai into, but because . . . "Who told you?"

"Who do you think?"

Veyadi looks first to Ruhi; he doesn't want to believe it, but he has to stop letting what he wants get in the way of the truth. And if Ruhi gave Imaru the chitin, he could have given her more.

Yet Ruhi shakes his head, frowning. "You should know, Veyadi . . . I came late to this scheme. By the time they brought me in, they knew what they needed from the Harbor. I just had to get it for them."

In other words: the disruptor schematics were part of this plot long before Ruhi was. Veyadi's fingers trace the chitin at his temple as memories rearrange themselves. This makes more sense. While Ruhi is a skilled archivist, he has greatest facility with the human side of the work. He grasps NT theory well enough, and he was a valuable consultant while Veyadi designed the Maw's relic interface, but there's a difference between reading a blueprint and drawing one.

Besides, the disruptor schematics are more barbaric than Veyadi has ever known Ruhi to be.

Which means Imaru's referring to whoever designed the machine to kill the Maw. Veyadi can't begin to guess who they might be, but if they were close enough to the Maw's construction to devise an exploit, then it stands to reason that they're also privy to the damning truth about Veyadi Lut. They would have been foolish not to warn Imaru about him—and they must have. Though she didn't recognize Veyadi by his face, the moment she saw his prosthetic, she knew him for a threat.

"I think this could work," Imaru says before Veyadi can respond.

"Is that desperation talking, or are you certain?" Ruhi asks, even though he was the one to suggest it. "I know how much you care for Sunai. I care for him too. But we can't do this unless we're—"

"I'll do it," says Veyadi.

They both fall silent. He is permitted to stand, allowed to leave them. An unexpected relief. He fears that given the option to falter, he would. In this they are united: they would all rather sacrifice themselves than ask Sunai to suffer for them again. When it's put like that, the shame makes it easy to hand himself to Madam Wei.

27

Sunai groans, and his brain clenches migraine-bright at the sound of his own voice. Pebbled dirt scrapes his cheek. His shoulders ache from struggle; his throat is raw from screaming. When he peels his hand off his shirt, it comes away tacky, and the hair at the back of his head is caked and flaking with old liquid. He can't see much—his goggles were taken, and the shadows of evening have cast the pit in dusk—but there's no mistaking the ruddy stench of his own blood.

A thrum curdles out of the dark. He jerks back. The gray form of the sentinel-fowl huddles at the edge of the pit, asleep. Her tattered feathers rustle; her beak, nestled against her chest, is black with whatever she tore out of him.

He can't remember most of the goring. He couldn't even feel it when she scrabbled into the soft tissue below his rib cage. Had his brain been more intact, the trauma might have had staying power.

"Lucky me," he mutters. The sentinel-fowl trills in her sleep. He freezes with instinctive fear. She resettles, beak dipping into her ruff, and he tells himself to stop acting like an idiot. She can't do anything to him that will stick. It still takes a minute to find his courage. He stands, palms stinging. The sentinel-fowl doesn't move. He inches as far as he can to the other side of their shared prison.

There's no room to run. Shreds of sunlight play through the cut branches two stories overhead, leaving the floor molten in shadow. A glimmer peeks from the tumbled soil: frail white tendrils, glowing, like the roots Sunai saw on the lighthouse on Lily. The stuff from which the relic interface is grown. What did Veyadi call it? Capillary root?

With muted horror, Sunai remembers where he is. The Mangrove shrine—the Three-Eyed Carp. Does the madam mean to show him off to the regulars? Did she feed him to her fowl purely for her own delight? Now that the tenbeast is satiated, maybe she'll have him dismembered and stored in a freezer. He should tell Jin to take notes. At last: a true scientific study on the nature of his corruption. He hopes they don't make Veyadi look.

His chest tightens. Veyadi. What's become of him? There was a moment in the black space between lives where Sunai was sure he heard the doctor, frightened, furious. He was about to do something incredibly stupid. Sunai bites his thumb at the memory.

The sentinel-fowl squawks. Sunai holds his breath. The tenbeast shakes her wing and shifts, stills. Shifts again.

Sunai edges back and his heel hits rough coral wall. Nowhere to go. No point in going.

The sentinel-fowl rises on scaled legs. She sways, uneven. Corruption, Madam Wei, time, none have served her well. She is a derelict creature, gouges of feathers missing, her scales knotted with scars. At full height, with her neck erect, her head comes up to his chest. Her claws rake distressed ruts in shallow soil.

Sunai's fingers twist in the stained hole of his shirt. "Can't talk it out, can we?"

The sentinel-fowl gurgles, a low warbling response. One of her wings stretches and curls so the pinions push into her chest. It's an unnatural position, even for a creature as unnatural as a tenbeast.

"They really fucked you up, didn't they?"

The sentinel-fowl gurgles again. Her slit eyes flare. She doesn't move.

"What are you waiting for?"

The gurgle ends in a guttural croak. Still she doesn't move. Is she afraid? Of him?

Sunai slides one foot forward. The sentinel-fowl lurches a single step closer. He freezes.

"Shit. Again?"

The smallest warble dies in her craw.

Sunai takes another step. The sentinel-fowl mirrors him. They meet clumsily in the center of the archival pit. He crouches; her head lowers. He holds out trembling fingers and her frayed pinions glide over his palm.

She is his, like the dragon-child was his. His passenger has reached into her and—

Sunai startles back as if burned. The singing flame is a promise remembered and broken in the same breath: when his passenger reached for him, he was going to stop goddamn reaching back.

As he lurches away, she pitches forward.

There's an order to what comes next, but by the time it's over he can't separate the moments. They bleed into each other, color and sensation dressed in fury, terror, and guilt.

The sentinel-fowl launches into his chest, driven by precarious momentum. He catches her with both hands to cushion her fall—

And he is taken by his last memory of her full weight on top of him, when she undid the seam of his torso and sank her beak into his core. As such, he is afraid when he does it.

⌁

—he becomes / is / has been aware that the sentinel-fowl / fragment / self is at once sturdy / resilient / adaptable and fragile / vulnerable / patchy, full of natural gaps of consciousness into which he can fit, and from within which he can shove her past the breaking limit, which he does, not to hurt her, but to ensure she will not hurt anyone ever again, least of all herself—

⌁

"No," you say, and, "no," again. "No, no, no—help me."

Then nothing, though I wait. Ah. You are in shock. Dislocated from your body, you cling to me. How can I turn you away?

Here, I will guide you as I have seen you guide others: You are breathing—good. You clutch your chest—it rises and falls rapidly with remembered fear. You are safe, Sunai, I swear it. So long as you ask for me, I am bound to heed you.

You are staring at the sentinel-fowl. She stutters a cry as she flops upon the earth before you. She is trapped by her own limbs, which are all wrongly intertwined. A command to her wing flickers into her stomach; a plea to her feet flounders in her long neck.

You behold the mess of her with a sinking understanding. Her finite frame contains her fractured multitude. Where her exterior silhouette defines what she once was, within she is fine and disparate, a wealth of sand, each particle crying out for the others and going unheard.

The sentinel-fowl, this piece of Iterate Fractal, is no longer whole in and of herself. She is pieces, plural, a schism where a being once breathed.

Your hands tremble as you coax her body, by turns limp and thrashing, into your lap. You become numbly aware that you have begun to observe yourself as if from outside yourself—a dissociative episode? You are familiar with these, recently and in the long term.

I must correct you, Sunai. It is not quite that.

"Really?" you mutter. "That's what you want to talk about? Now?"

I am sorry. It seemed important for you to know what is a product of your preexisting condition and what is a factor of my interference.

"No, I get it. It's fine."

I do not think it is fine. Your breath is short as you stroke the sentinel-fowl's quivering throat.

"Well, duh," you murmur as your thumb runs over her crest. "I've killed her, haven't I? And you let me."

.I did.

"Why?" you ask. "How? You made me ask before I grabbed the dragon-child. This just *happened*. I—I didn't want this."

I think I believe you. I am sorry. You should not be able to use me until I have offered myself and you have agreed to take me. I am afraid our connection has been unusual from the start. This is not the first rule you have broken.

You laugh weakly. "What are you even doing with me?"

I must admit, I do not know. As I have noted, our bond is unique. You did not ever ask for me; you took me, and from my archive. Though only a few of your predecessors have visited my shrine, none of them came to me as you did. And as my archive is no more . . .

"You're stuck." You laugh again, curling your frame around the wheezing sentinel-fowl as if to protect it from your realization. "You *can't* leave me. Do you even know how?"

I do not.

"I'm sorry."

Oh. No, Sunai. Please do not apologize. Although you did not ask, I think you needed me all the same.

You hesitate to request clarification. You are holding to the caution urged on you by those closest to your heart. I do not take offense; it is not my place to decide whom you trust. But you do trust, and admire, and fear for them, and so you lay yourself at their feet. I am in return compelled to lay myself at yours.

In the midst of death, you caught a glimpse that frightened you. You understand that they do not wish to lose you, but neither do you wish to lose them—and they are far more vulnerable. You cannot eke sense from their sacrifice. Not for your sake.

If I may . . . it is not my desire or design to impose an "answer" upon you, no matter what question you may or may not pose. I am only able to guide you to a truth you already hold. This I will try to do, and gladly.

I suspect you do not care for sacrifice as a premise.

You laugh as I propose this. It is a harsh sound in this musty pit. You mean to deprecate yourself. I wish you would not; I do not think you deserve it.

You fear the loss that sacrifice brings, and how could that be wrong? Loss is a terrible thing. You see the scars it left on Madam Wei and her heir, and in the hurt they visited upon you. You see those scars in Imaru and Ruhi as well, who have chosen to give anything and everything to ensure the death of Iterate Fractal's successor. Most recently, you have seen loss most keenly in Veyadi. The life he did not have and always mourns, the life he received that he fears he misused, and the lives of the people he could not save. For all I have had my concerns about him—no, he concerns me still, I confess—you cannot help but hurt to see how he has suffered for the Maw.

The agonies they endured have made them willing to inflict loss upon others. They are driven by their pain, at times rooted in justice, at times in anger (your fingers shiver in the sentinel-fowl's pinions). I think in every case, this choice is selfish.

Yes! Selfish. Do not shy away. Selfishness is the worthiest trait of living creatures, for it preserves and nurtures you. You, I think, could do with more of it.

But if you can summon no care for yourself, I think you can for others. You wish to protect those who care for you. If that requires sacrifice from others—from yourself—I think you are willing to make that choice.

Quiet with hope, you say, "How?"

Let me show you.

Your whole being trembles, and then you shake on an unimaginable scale.

You remain in the archival pit of the Mangrove shrine, curled over the body of the broken sentinel-fowl; you also disperse through an elaborate weave of tender root spreading for miles in every direction, tunneling beneath this shrine and under the surrounding ruins of Grotto, even unto the lip of the sea. Though it surfaces only in this shallow patch, the capillary root network is vast and thriving.

It must grow so fast, you think. No doubt that makes it useful for interlacing Veyadi's chitin.

Yes, Sunai. Precisely. Do you remember? As I ask, you see it again: your own dying face through another's eyes. The moment on Lily when Veyadi tried to extract the archival seed lodged in your throat, and a pale white tendril curled out of your eye.

Here is the truth of the Maw, which constantly constructs and reshapes itself from a million shards, the remnants of Iterate Fractal's old bone-and-coral body: it is knit together by capillary root, fine strands coaxed out of the collected archives that are the heart of the working ENGINE.

I suspect there is a cluster of capillary network beneath every one of the old shrines. We saw on Lily how the Maw could harvest from the shrine's network like a trove to replenish itself. If you and I were to hide within the Mangrove network, and the Maw were to reach for the roots . . .

It is against my nature to be so forward, but you and I, we are different from the iterations of myself that have come before. When you took me from my home, my shrine, you changed me. I did not desire to go, nor did I ask for this intimacy, but it is what we have. I have discovered that I do not regret it, because I cannot regret you.

So, I am compelled to ask: If you could choose to protect, preserve, and free those who you otherwise would lose, would you not do so? Would you not commit?

My failure is persistent.

You and Imaru sweat across from each other in the bed of a truck, the machete stark across her knees. She grips the hilt. She hasn't decided whether she means to use it on a tire, an engine, or flesh. You know this because she told you.

You're terrified this is your fault. *You* found the slender box in the caravan's cargo that was missing from the manifest, and *you* broke it open to reveal the contracts within. Indentures. Over a hundred. Imaru wants to burn them. You agree. She also wants to gut the bastard responsible for selling human contracts or, if that's not an option, to abandon him in the wilds. Here, you falter.

You're afraid of who else in the caravan might know about the box. You're afraid this iniquity belongs to more than one man—and you're afraid Imaru wouldn't stop at one.

Ah, no, what frightens you most is the thought that she'll turn on you first. That she'll either leave you with these men in the wilds, or that she'll keep you beside her, but only because you're too pitiful to abandon.

Again, fear drives the words from your throat. You beg her to wait—not to change her mind, but to consider the timing. Consequence. Strategy.

The look in her eyes momentarily blanks. Panic coagulates in your throat.

You taste the same fear years later. Ruhi has spent days locked in a tense back-and-forth with an imperial defector who knows of a Mohani enclave trying to flee the imperial capital. A pantheon AI has taken an uncomfortable interest in their heritage. Ruhi suspects the man is lying about his intentions, maybe even about the existence of the refugees. He tells you this over a bottle of plum wine in the back room of the teahouse where you meet, and as he hands the bottle back, he looks at you, expectant.

You hope feverishly that he's thinking of placing his mouth on your neck. You struggle with the knowledge that, actually, he wants your goddamn opinion.

How you get it out that time, you still don't know. Adrenaline, fear, a hunger for the drop. You can find balance only from a position of dread.

It *is* dreadful, how Imaru releases her machete and takes your hand instead, when you tell her not to kill that man. And it is awful, how Ruhi always turns to you when he needs to understand a person's frailties, when he needs a reason not to hate.

Over and over, the fear rises in you, and every time, I drown in it. How frustrating it is, to have taught you so well, and yet not at all. I honed your instinct and sharpened your tongue; I trained you to question and interrogate; I made you a tool to blunt the edge of power. In the end, I thought you understood my intent.

You thought I wanted you dead. Why else would I teach you to challenge me? You saw again and again what I made of those who dared to deny me.

I wonder, Sunai. If I'd told you the purpose for which you had been crafted . . . Would it have saved us?

28

You wake in an unfamiliar room. The walls are a thicket of interwoven deadwood upon which bone buds flower, and the floor is paved with planks. You lie on one of a number of fine-woven straw mats, and from the supplies gathered atop the nearby lacquered cabinet, you surmise that it is meant to be an infirmary.

Your body has been cleaned, and you're wearing borrowed, ill-fitting clothes. You have been afforded a new pair of specs that are, to your surprise, more or less your exact prescription.

The last clue as to your whereabouts is Wei Jin, who jolts off their neighboring mat when you rise. They try to stand as you do. You wave them down; they look no better than when last you saw them.

"Don't get up, I'm not going anywhere," you say as you search through the supplies on the cabinet top. "I have some questions."

"Oh yeah?" Jin's surprise swerves into imperiousness. You recognize the brittle tone and the anxiety they hope to mask with it. They think that by reclaiming control of themself, they will control you as well.

You think: They are very young.

"Yeah." You use a small mirror to examine the back of your head. It confirms your suspicion that your hair, while washed and newly braided, is a mess where the bullet burst out the back of your skull. "This state of affairs seems odd to me, is all. If your aunty had her way, I'd still be tenbeast fodder. If my people were in charge, I doubt I'd be in the Carp. I definitely wouldn't be hanging out with you, given how unhappy I imagine you've made them."

You angle the mirror to see Jin's face. It is drawn with shame, or whatever adjacent emotion Madam Wei was unable to stamp out during their upbringing.

You return to rummaging. "Two guesses: either you're not supposed to be here, or you're doing so poorly that my people don't think you're going to hurt anyone but yourself."

"I wish you were still dead," they say to your back, though it lacks bite.

"No you don't." You uncover a petite pair of shears, meant for cutting thread and bandages. "I'm your new best friend."

They eye you as you turn the shears on your hair, working your way through the braid. Their argument is stifled by suspicion as you, their victim, offer them peace.

"I'm not on top of the current situation," you say, "so I'm going to need help catching up. I figure you're the most likely to treat me as a person instead of—" You wave the scissors over your head. "You know. So how about it? Truce? You watch me, I watch you, and if anyone complains, I'll cry until they leave us alone."

Jin scowls at you, bewildered and therefore offended. "God's multifaceted ass. I killed you."

"I mean, kind of."

An unfamiliar emotion distorts their expression. "Fucking hell, Sunai. Are you used to this?"

Used to what? Death? More or less. Murder? Sure. Murder by someone you consider a friend? They were not your first.

Jin curses and struggles to their feet, their limbs untrustworthy. You move to help them, and they point you angrily toward a stool.

Once you sit, they take the shears and trim your hair with more insight and skill. You recognize that they would rather express their assent with action than words; they know too well the cheapness of language, so if they wish to be sincere, they must be so with their hands.

It is also an opportunity for you to focus on the awareness our covenant has awarded you. If you are to kill the Maw, you need access to the shrine's trove of capillary root—and you suspect that it will not be easy to win your way back into the archival pit.

Before anything else, you ask: "Where's my bird?"

Jin says: "The sentinel-fowl? Dead, thank god. Guess she choked on one of your thumbs."

Your heart hurts. The tenbeast died because of you, her flesh too frail to withstand her fragmentation. You are simultaneously relieved that her torment is at an end.

"I want to bury her," you say. It is what was done with corpses in Iterate Fractal's Khuon Mo. Buried so that they could feed the roots.

Jin's mouth twists. "You know that thing ate my mom."

"Not everything's about you, Jin."

As they wish to cultivate your trust, they agree to help you search out a burial site somewhere within the outer bounds of the Mangrove shrine. First you must exit the body of the Three-Eyed Carp. The establishment is circuitous and sprawling; some chambers of the nautilus shell were halved to make two floors, while in others the grasping hands of corruption were cut away to make larger, connected halls. The Ginger Company shored these up in disparate fashion. Corrugated tin here, bamboo there, wooden planks, plastic sheets, and even strips of metal hull that once armored a rig.

You catalogue each room as you pass, preferring architecture to the people within it. The Gingers acknowledge Jin, as befits the madam's scion, but they eye you with a mix of emotions that includes too much hope.

As you go, Jin quietly regales you with the tale as they know it.

Imaru, Ruhi, and Veyadi proposed their own truce with the madam. She accepted their offer, which included Veyadi's prosthetic. Outside of this piece of the deal—gleaned from observing

Veyadi enter the room with his visor and exit without it—Jin was made privy to none of the details. They assumed their aunt would see fit to enlighten them, and were proven wrong.

"Now Doc's holed up in the pit," Jin says as they lead you through the Carp. "Took that freaky mask with him. I think he's growing more chitin off the capillary root."

"Won't that take a while?" you ask.

"Years! If he wants enough to build another disruptor, anyway. Especially without his Harbor lab. Aunty gave him my books, but that's not going to help unless he wants them for fertilizer." Jin is more pained by the notion than they would like to seem.

You take pity. "You think that's why they've sent Ruhi to the Harbor?"

"Partly. Maybe. He's definitely asking for *something* other than lenience."

The morning after Jin shot you, Ruhi left the Carp for Lotus with a contract in hand. By noon, the Harbor had called off the security cruisers circling the Grotto fleet, though the checkpoints and patrols in Jasmine remain. The contract was composed by Madam Wei, signed and stamped. It bears Veyadi's sigil too, drawn by his own hand. The paper claims that the madam hired him for a private project some months ago. With this, they hope to discourage the Harbor from barging into the Carp to retrieve their missing autonomist. The delicate balance in Khuon Mo depends on the madam's cooperation. If the Harbor loses her, the situation will turn quickly dire. By all accounts the harbormaster is reluctant to push her luck.

You catch on the thought. Harbormaster Ueda differs from the harbormasters you grew familiar with on the mainland. Perhaps, being a former relic, Ueda Naru is uniquely disturbed by the Maw. The prospect of relying on an ENGINE she cannot control must rankle.

You slow. Jin is annoyed until they realize you have not done it for their sake.

"What do you imagine Ruhi's told her about me?" you ask your bare feet.

As little as possible, I promise. He wishes you safe.

"Her who? Ueda?" says Jin. "I don't know if he has to say much, given what we've got going in the streets."

You raise your head and silently apologize to me for the lack of direct reply. It is of no concern, Sunai. I am accustomed to silence; it is a welcome comfort.

"Right," you say to Jin as you make for the ladder that leads down to the lower level. "Good thing tourists love a reason to stay up."

Jin snorts and allows you to take their cane as they follow. "Especially after they spend all that credit getting here from the mainland."

You are of the opinion that the Harbor made this maneuver easy. They declared a curfew the night you escaped to Grotto, and they have refused to lift it. The following day, while we slept, a party began in Jasmine teahouses, then poured onto the streets and spilled into the avenues between high-end Orchid hotels. The whole night following, tourists and locals alike got deliriously drunk in public and sang rude lyrics to the tune of relic-drama theme songs. The Carp is preparing for a second round. As you cross the bridge over the old archivist compound you observe Ginger Company toughs coordinating shipments of tea, liquor, fruit, and other delicacies. These donations will bolster the supplies in Jasmine and Orchid, and they come with Gingers ready to protect the establishments that serve the revelers.

Imaru heads this arm of the plan. Between her involvement and the presence of Gingers in their yellow-flowered lapels and tattoos, there is no attempt to disguise the madam's hand in the festivities. If the Harbor takes issue, the Ginger Company is ready to drum up a response throughout the city. They will not respond alone. That much is evident in the eyes that follow you from below as you cross the bridge. Once one pair is drawn, others join. You suspect it would be worse outside the Carp. At least the Gingers have the discipline to return to their work.

By the time you cross the bridge and disappear into the ruins of the compound, your chest is tight. You ask Jin to wait with you. They frown and say: "I can tell them to fuck off."

"Don't. They know your aunt wanted to murder me, right?"

"Sure, but it's been long enough since Iterate Fractal died that people are ready to mourn it. You're a good outlet for nice, clean grief. Anyway, if we didn't have you, the Harbor would. There's no world where that's not worse."

However unsettled you are to be regarded fondly, you suppose you understand the impulse. It is easier to protect something you have decided not to despise.

You are, nevertheless, relieved to reach a tangle of trunks that lead into the coils of the Mangrove shrine—into the rotting halls and flooded rooms that Madam Wei has not yet seen fit to repurpose. Jin follows you into them, as do a handful of shadows who attached themselves to you as you passed through the archivist compound.

You pretend not to notice them, but at a juncture of two paths, you pause. You are unfamiliar with the curves of the Mangrove shrine, having had little reason to spend much time there during your training or after. You are moreover sure that Iterate Fractal's death was as ghastly here as everywhere else, and if experience could ever have helped you navigate the shrine, it is of no use now.

"Well?" you say to your shadows. "We could use some guides."

They emerge at a signal from their leader—you recognize her,

the bold child from the fleet. Perhaps she has finally come to demand you break your nose for her. Jin eyes the children with
indifference; you suspect they never learned to get along with
the other kids. You beckon the leader close and tell her what you
want: a corner rich with warm, wet earth. You have a friend to
bury.

She asks: "What do we get?"

You say: "My friend is a tenbeast. I'll let you touch her."

When the girl hesitates, you say, "Cigarettes?" Jin frowns.
"No. Soda."

"Ten gallons."

"Deal."

You are ushered into the bowels of the shrine, across a frozen
seabed of enormous fingernails, past folded walls of monstrous
hands forever trapped mid-grasp. You climb across a knotted lattice of coral-streaked root that slope like fingers into a collection
of tide pools.

After this, Jin must rest, fatigued and short of breath. The
children bully them into it, and they have wisely brought can-
teens to share. A particularly acrobatic kid scampers up a ripple
of riven stairs to a break in the wall, through which a breeze
whispers. They are off to get food, they say. Their older sister
gets tired like Jin.

Jin scowls about the care, but they are weak to it. You have
heard them whine about how Oyu and Cothai have been "weird."
Jin blames it on their decision to murder you. You believe this can
be no more than half the truth. You suspect Oyu and Cothai are
nervous, afraid to face Jin's frailty.

One of the children pulls you away. He has stumbled on a
niche that may lead to what you want. You follow him to a crevice between two bone-flowered trunks twisted into the likeness
of a gasping mouth, and there he shows you the damp dark

earth. It is much like what you asked for, but you catch no sign of
the pale illumination that would signal a cache of capillary root.

You kneel even so, hopeful.

When you do, you grow dizzy—hunger, or exhaustion. You
have not been careful with yourself, and either may in their time
impede you. Yet when you sink your fingers into the loam, as
much to steady yourself as to seek your prize, your fingers feel
like more than simply your fingers, and your vision doubles—
triples?—in that way it has increasingly been liable to do.

I will do my best to mitigate that, Sunai, but it is not within
my power to—

Ah, if I cannot stop these attempts to override your faculties, I
can at least do my best to insert myself into the process. I hope
this allows you a more bearable degree of remove.

You have become unavoidably aware of Veyadi. It is nothing
so convenient as relic-drama telepathy. You are foggy and con-
fused, stumbling over emotions whose origin you cannot track.
Were it not for the certainty of Veyadi's fingers tracing across
sandy earth as yours are sunk into dampen soil, your mind would
be an uninterpretable jumble.

His hands move with strange grace. He crouches in the center of the archival pit, not far from where you stained the earth
with gore. Capillary root unfurls across the floor of the pit, much
more than you saw when you tumbled down. In the darkening
shadows, it illuminates the prosthetic into which Veyadi means
to coax the root to anchor.

It is as if the root can hear him. As if it yearns to obey.

"I've never seen it act like this," he says to the person with
him. "Not with any other relic."

"Well. All relics are unique," says Ruhi.

You stiffen in the Mangrove niche. Some of the tightness

in your chest clenches in Veyadi's. I think he mistakes it for regret.

"If I thought that explained it, I wouldn't be . . ." Veyadi struggles to name the feeling. His exhaustion and doubt is a body-wide tremor. A thread of your own discomfort stitches the patchwork of received emotions together. "I'm worried it's the Maw getting . . . interested."

Ruhi stands a circumspect distance from the unearthed root. "What else do you think it could be?"

Veyadi runs his thumb over the flat root tendrils already embedded in his half-buried prosthetic. "What else? His passenger."

Your fingers twitch in the earth; you mean to defend me. The impulse is kind, and I admire it, but do you not think his wariness is well-earned?

"I wish I'd had more time in its shrine," Veyadi says. "That thing is so much more than I thought it was—and I'm only able to properly *conceive* of that now because it lost its ability to conceal itself when it interfaced with Sunai. But now that it's crawled into him . . ."

You tense.

Veyadi curses softly. "Never mind. It doesn't matter. Not until we take care of the Maw."

A flicker slides from his head into yours, a flicker of—

—*another body gone slack and vacant, the person it once was reduced to so much garbled lack, and they are running out of time, and he is running out of ideas for how to keep them alive, and how could it have come to this when he has tried so hard to save them, how can he keep failing, and how dare he ask that question, when he knows the truth must be that he would rather save Iterate Fractal than these pitiful relics—*

Veyadi grunts and shoves down the memory, down into your rising nausea. He prefers to be numb. The recollection hurts you too much to allow him that ease; your sympathetic ache refracts into his chest. Veyadi sits on his heels and presses the back of his hand to his bare forehead, thinking himself too tired, too damn soft to do what he *must*.

A hand falls on his back, at the arch where his shoulder meets his neck. To Veyadi, it provides warmth and reassurance. To you, however, it comes too soon after a moment of frailty, too perfectly timed. You are already raw, sick with Veyadi's old fears, and powerless to resist your own—

—*you deserve it, probably, to hear Ruhi cry as you die, because you hate it, hate being the reason this happened, hate forcing Ruhi to see what he desperately didn't want to, hate that Ruhi won't be able to deny the truth anymore, and you know that this will break him, because Ruhi won't be the same after, because now he's here trying to kill Iterate Fractal, but before that you died, gasping, with Ruhi's hands—*

—you stumble back, falling out of your crouch and out of the niche. You land in a tide pool. The child who led you to the crevice cackles as you strive to catch your breath. By the time you do, you laugh too, helpless and hopeful. Floating in cool dark water, you are untouched, and you can *breathe*. It is all too much. You laugh until you wheeze, and Jin calls out, "What's wrong with you now?"

You wave a single finger in their direction. I do not believe they discern it through the evening gloom. You do not care. You are grateful to be unseen.

I am sorry, Sunai. I do not think you are well.

You chuckle again. You are forgiving me. I do not know if I have earned that consideration, but if you offer it, I am compelled to accept.

"Never mind," you whisper, speaking only for me. "It wasn't enough, was it? We're going to have to get back into the pit."

You refer to the spare shreds of capillary root we were able to detect in that niche, preferring not to dwell on your wounds. Indeed, the root we found there will not be enough for our purposes. If we were properly integrated, as I am meant to be with my hosts . . .

Ah, I had best not wander down such paths. It is better, and certainly more useful, to focus on the problems at hand.

We will not get what you want without the network. Therefore, we must find another way to reach it.

29

You find a suitable place to bury the sentinel-fowl on the third day of searching. This gives you time to prepare the rest of your plan, to gather supplies and curry favors.

You win a modest share of the supplies by lending your expertise to the Gingers charged with organizing the madam's offerings to Jasmine and Orchid. You have always paid mind to food and the places where people like to eat it, and you share your recent memory of the mainland's current trends—wide midland imperial noodles glazed with fermented black bean sauce paired with Janggori-style fried pork belly.

The favors you gain in exchange for your skill with needle, thread, and antiseptic, as you tend to the Gingers who return from Jasmine with blood on their shirts. Though you never have to take a needle to your own injuries, you have done your fair share of sewing up Imaru. You make yourself useful in the makeshift infirmary where you woke up days ago. It is part of the madam's bid to protect her people; the Harbor will have a harder time of arresting the injured who are treated on her turf.

One night, Cothai is brought back to the Three-Eyed Carp in the bed of a sympathetic citizen's truck. He got himself bloodied standing between Harbor peace officers and a delivery van. As you pick shards of green glass bottle out of Cothai's arm, you tell him that you would like to see him tomorrow afternoon—at the wake. He hesitates because he knows Jin will be there. You think: Cothai is the sort of man who will believe something if you say it sternly enough.

"They don't think Waretu was your fault." You set down the

tweezers to wash his arm, laid on your plastic folding table. "She wasn't, for the record."

Oyu, you find more difficult. You corner them with a live chicken when they pass through the Carp's kitchen to pick up rations for their squad, who have patrolled the streets of Jasmine to guide misbehaving tourists back to Orchid, and to keep the Harbor's hands off the locals. You tuck the chicken into their arms as you gather their food. Oyu recognizes this as provocation but does not know how to respond, so they must accept your questions with wary stoicism as the chicken mutters suspiciously in their grasp.

"Do you know why you're avoiding Jin?" you ask.

"They're sick," says Oyu, as if you are simple.

"They are. And weak. And vulnerable. And honestly kind of a pain in my ass."

"You should let them rest."

"Okay, but they shot me, so I figure I'm owed. They're more useful out of bed than in it."

Oyu looks about ready to throw the chicken at you, or to put a knife in your foot.

"Alternatively, *you* go and take better care of them." You take the chicken from them because you do not think it deserves to be the medium of their angst. "It's that or let me run them into the ground."

Oyu plainly does not trust you, as they are at Jin's side by the next morning, and they remain there until the wake in the afternoon, when they are joined by a freshly groomed Cothai. Jin is more delighted than they will admit, evident in the enthusiasm with which they criticize the funerary garlands laid on the sentinel-fowl's bier.

"The kids made them," you say.

"That just explains *why* they're shitty."

As they fuss and beam, you know you have ensured Jin will not follow you this evening.

Over the next hour, more Gingers wander in and out of the small hall in the bisected archivist compound where you arranged the sentinel-fowl. Word is that the madam's relic is eccentric, emotionally disturbed, or both. Some have decided that it will be good luck to pray before the bier. The steady flow of people gives you an opportunity to go missing.

In the hour before sunset, Imaru arrives. You have not seen much of her these past few days, though more than you have Ruhi or Veyadi—the latter of whom you have not spoken to at all. You and he avoid each other; you are wary of another incident like the one you suffered by the tide pools, while he . . . Well. I can only speculate. Whatever the case, Veyadi and the Harbor have colluded to monopolize Ruhi's time. For this you have been, ah, grateful. It is difficult for you to meet Ruhi's eye. Perhaps you suspect . . . Hm, I ought not to say. In any case, you are relieved to be spared the intensity.

The irony of your efforts to return Jin's people to their orbit while you purposefully keep yours at bay does not go unnoticed by your thinking mind, but you choose not to regard it.

Once Imaru is in your proximity, you are unable to let her go untended. She does not look ready to sit or eat, but you still push a bowl into her hands with some of the floral-scented rice you prepared for the occasion and offer her a cool bottle of tea to go with it.

She gives you a knowing look as you corral her onto a great pitted-coral root that broke through the floor. She understands that you want her to stay longer than she plans to. You shrug. Of course, you worry for her.

She relents, eats, and as she does, says, "Heard from my contact."

You inhale quietly when you realize what this means. Veyadi was not alone in assuming Ruhi was her traitor. It is in a way reassuring to know she had someone else. It suggests there are more people in the world worth saving. You say, "Seems like a risky time to hail them."

"They reached out to me."

"That sounds bad."

"The Harbor found their schematics."

Your false cheer evaporates. "Do they know your contact drew them?"

"Unclear." Her frown says that she thinks it all too likely. "They're using the plans to build . . . something."

"What? Why? The Harbor doesn't need to break its own ENGINE."

Imaru chews, troubled by your confusion. You realize belatedly that she hoped you might offer an explanation.

You know little of how she was trained under Iterate Fractal. Her fellow archivist-handlers, your shepherds, were schooled separately from their future charges. Her order was always small, and she may be the last of them. You have often wondered if it is an honor or a shame that you carried this extinct dynamic into your relationship. You were never offered to each other. Your partnership—her strength, your care—was a simple accident of where she happened to be when Iterate Fractal perished and you did not.

You wonder whether you should ask what made her choose to save you. You worry you will not get another chance. You worry that it would not be worth knowing.

"I'm concerned," she says to her knees, on which she rests the empty bowl. "We might have to reevaluate our approach."

In other words, the disruptor may no longer be an option.

Her fear summons your courage. "I've still got my friend, you know."

You are not surprised to see her stiffen. I make her nervous. I wish it were otherwise, but I imagine that is not possible.

"Sunai, I want you to think." Imaru's fingers are hard around her bowl, and she places each word into it with great care. "Sometimes you make a choice that feels right. More right than anything. Then once it's made . . . you see that it was wrong."

Though her pain is a fresh wound, you cannot imagine the cause of her injury. It has always been this way. Imaru carries a guilt that eats at her as thoroughly as the Maw eats its relics. You do not understand why.

And I . . . do not know what to tell you.

You kneel beside her and wrap your hands around hers. "From here, your choices have looked pretty admirable."

Imaru allows herself a laugh that is more like a sigh. "They would, to you."

She has always thought you charitable. You have never known what to make of that either. She is where your faith lives.

You try to say that through your grip on her brittle fingers. "Whenever I realize I've done something you would have, I know it's a better choice than the one I would've made on my own."

For once, you do not remotely understand the look she gives you. It is hunted, wounded. You cannot imagine what she means to say. You are both spared when someone calls for her. She is wanted in Jasmine. Imaru is always needed. To you, this is the natural way of the world. You must do your best to serve as well as she does.

She leaves you with a kiss on the forehead and asks that you not stray far from the Carp. You answer honestly that you do not intend to. Your body, at least, will keep that promise.

Not long after, the sentinel-fowl's mourners are dense and drunk enough that you are able to slip out of the archivist compound unnoticed. Your path through the Carp is clear. The pressure that boils in the center of the nautilus receded two hours ago, and it has not yet built back up. You surmise that Veyadi has passed out—not the intermittent sleep he has otherwise allowed himself these past few days, but true, deep darkness. You do not know where Veyadi sleeps; you have not sought to learn. All you can say for certain is that it is somewhere within the body of the shrine, within the madam's reach.

You hope you are quick and subtle. You would not like him to wake before you are done.

Fortune guides your steps. You wend through the Carp to the hollow that was once the antechamber before the archive, seeing no one along the way. You pause as you approach the gate through which the Weis watched you die. It is closed. You lay your hand upon the metal and find it locked.

"Shit."

"You could have tried climbing down from the teahouse level," says Ruhi.

Your fingers hook in the grate. You are thinking of climbing now, up and into the shadows of the petrified canopy. I do not think you would get far, Sunai.

"I probably don't need to ask what you're doing here," he says.

"You sure about that?" you ask.

Sunai, Ruhi is an archivist. He observes, assesses, and concludes; he draws truth from even the unwilling. For years, Veyadi has confided in him every detail of his work, from the chitin, to his prosthetic, to the relic interface—and most recently, my shrine, which he hunted down in the margins of your historical and religious texts. He told Ruhi everything of me, for he hoped that through me, he might save the Maw.

And he knows that I am with you. You told him so yourself.

You spin as you hear him step forward, wary not to let him surprise you. He has stopped out of arm's reach, dimly lit in the fragile evening sliding through the interwoven trunks. His hands are firmly in his pockets, his smile faint and indecipherable.

"I don't want you to die, Sunai."

You laugh. You think it a funny thing for anyone to say, but

from him it is especially ironic. It is not a kind laugh, and Ruhi
absorbs it with a bowed head.

"It's why I asked you not to come." He is so close that you
hear the shudder in his breath. "I was afraid that if you did, that
would be it. The end." His hand clenches in his pocket. You are
ready to flee. "So if you think this thing from Veyadi's shrine
could help you, that with it, you could live . . . then I don't think
I want to stop you."

You want to laugh again, but you find it hard to breathe. Your
body is shockingly heavy. "Really? You have no idea what I'm
doing. I barely know myself. Why would you . . ."

From his pocket, Ruhi produces a key. He offers it to you in
a flat palm. "I've decided to have faith in you," he says. "I think
that was my mistake, last time. I let fear blind me to who you are.
I don't want to forget again."

You sicken at those words. You want to throw them in a bag
and toss that bag into the bay. Yet you are not so untouchable
that you can afford to forsake an ally, and what's more, you think
it would be ugly of you to reject his aid.

I do not relish your pain, Sunai. I worry, at times, that you seek
more of it to justify your being alive. But neither am I willing to
override your choice. If you wish for this, then I wish it too.

You let Ruhi drop the key in your palm. It is unbearably light.

"How much time do you need?" asks Ruhi.

"How much can you get me?"

"Four, five hours at least. The harbormaster is coming to Orchid tonight. I can make a compelling case for why Veyadi should
meet with her."

You tense; this seems unsafe.

"Don't worry. We're holding the meeting at one of the madam's hotels. The Gingers will make sure Veyadi doesn't leave
with anyone but me."

You *do* worry. What if the Harbor were to take Ruhi as well?

From his face, you cannot gauge that risk. Ruhi is not one to confide his fears in others, and you have lost your privileged access to his weakness. He will not tell you if he expects to fail.

Moreover, sending Veyadi away is more of a betrayal than anything you have yet done. You have more than avoided him— you have sneaked, conspired. You know that what you hope to accomplish tonight is an action stolen, one that undermines his efforts and desires. It was neither discussed nor agreed to by anyone but yourself.

So yes, Sunai, as you allow Ruhi to leave and you turn the key in the gate, you are in one light devoting yourself to deceit. But in this act, you are also choosing a truth for your own sake, and that ought not be condemned.

I cannot rebuke you, certainly. I have committed myself to you.

————

You enter the archival pit alone. It is empty of any breathing thing. In its center, laid in a shadowed patch of dirt where the sentinel-fowl once scrabbled, a snarl of new growth glints black and gold with hints of creeping white: Veyadi's chitin prosthetic, his scrap of a backup plan and the seed of yours.

You lay your hand on it, the new-planted heart of a fragmented network. When you do, I am ready, for I am at your service.

You marvel at how speedily you disperse through the roots under Grotto and into the bay. Instantly you saturate the network that is as much relic as you are. Now you only need the Maw to come into contact with the roots and invite you into its body.

For that, you require a lure. You must create a need to compel its presence. By my ability you sweep into the world, but you are quickly overwhelmed. You extend in too many directions, and though you have lately flitted from one body to the next, the experience is yet unintuitive. You stall, paralyzed by sheer quantity of self. As you have grown accustomed to doing, you reach for my aid.

My apologies. Here I must recede. It is beyond me to advise you too minutely.

When direction nevertheless arrives, you assume I have given in. I have not. I *cannot*. It would violate my core principle to take you so fully in hand. The cool pulse coursing into you, through you, from the nape of your neck to your shoulder, down the length of your arm to your wrist—it is not me. The foreign pressure steers you as would a gentle hand, drawing your awareness along the roots that stretch through the Grotto tide pools that pour into the bay.

I . . . shall not intervene. You asked for aid, after all. Though I cannot assist you as you wish, I cannot rightly deny another, should they act in my stead.

Ah, I should not be so forward. My other arrangements must be respected independently from ours. Suffice to say, you are not alone, Sunai, because I am not alone in wishing to see your desires fulfilled.

It is with this borrowed familiarity that you search out your quarry, fragments that you might direct. You expect to find the dragon-children, curled in the shadows below the Grotto fleet. You met them just days ago and saw no reason that they should not still be there. It is that which lies beyond them that surprises you.

You feel their shape before you see them, and do not recognize their dimensions. A fragtech. A strange one. Their limbs are longer than a dragon-child's, beautifully articulated, and their body is more alike to yours. Two arms, two legs, a torso, a head. Armored, you discover: girded by the consumed strength of those who have dared to challenge their right to survival over the centuries.

You are invited into this vessel like breath into lungs. As you flex their foreign arms, you feel a tickle in your joints. This sensation tells you that they are not alone either. A similar body stands not far away. An echo of your new form, modeled by the same original intent. This other body approaches, and through seeing them, you understand what you have found, and where, and why it all seems so odd.

Before you stands a figure with a dark crescent swoop of a head. Beneath a patchwork of harvested armor, its limbs are slender and exceedingly black. It bears no sign of Iterate Fractal's aesthetic—no spines, scales, fur, leaves, or chitinous gleam. You recognize it from your childhood training. It is a remnant of an ancient corrupted shrine in the northern reach of the archipelago, part of an AI whose name was lost to time. Your downworlder kin called it the Anthill, for its fragments are uniformly black and unusually well-coordinated. A mere artifact of their construction, I assure you. Their limbs were manufactured to resonate. When one moves, the others feel it.

You thought that through me, your reach had widened to the limits of the capillary network. How is it, then, that you have found your way into a fragment that should be confined to a behavioral loop many hundreds of miles north of Khuon Mo? You search your surroundings for an answer. You are in the wilds, you note, surrounded by wet green foliage interrupted by dense brown and hanging vine. How far have you outstripped what you thought was your boundary?

Not far at all, you learn. Past a veil of flowering vines, you spy a ruin of bone and coral, the remains of a compound once grown by Iterate Fractal. But Iterate Fractal grew homes for its citizens all up and down the archipelago, so you are yet uncertain. Your need for clarity pushes you into yet another body, positioned on the shore. Through this one, you see water, a bay, and a city within it. You have entered a third Anthill fragment, which stands guard on a beach at the far edge of Khuon Mo's bay.

Your questions persist, query after query! How is it that the Anthill fragtech have escaped the loops that bound them to their shrine? How can you reach them so readily, when they are untouched by your capillary root? How could fragtech draw so close to Khuon Mo, yet go unseen by the watchful eyes of those who protect it?

The answers are not beyond your grasp, Sunai. You asked for help, and you were answered, by myself and by another. Ah, do not fear, you usurped no one's choices. I remind you, these are fragments, splinters of something that once was but is no longer. They are also hidden from those who would see them dead, by my ability and your need—your will.

Most importantly, they are yours to command.

In the archival pit of the Mangrove shrine, your hand presses down on the chitin shard that is the locus of your network, harder and harder. You are determined and afraid, but grateful.

You are correct. It is no time to hesitate. If you have been given such gifts, you must not waste them.

It is time to summon the Maw.

———

Sirens whoop from the outer perimeter of the bay. Militia rigs patrolling the far rings streak shoreward. A shadow has climbed onto the isle of Lotus, directly downhill from the looming concrete Harbor. Gloom and distance obscure its shape from those on shore, but its size is apparent: even seated cross-legged at the lip of the waves, it is twice as tall as an armored truck.

Light strikes the figure from three directions. Beams from the Harbor hit its back, and its front and side are lit by militia rigs taking aim. The figure sits unmoving. A fragtech, sable-limbed and eerily unlike any get of Iterate Fractal's brood.

The first militia rig fires a harpoon. With unearthly grace, the fragtech shifts and stands. The harpoon skids into the sand by its feet. At the same time, another something with long black limbs and a century of scars skitters out of the water and over the side of the first rig. The rig tilts and screams under this second fragtech's weight, its engines throbbing. Another rig swoops by, firing a salvo of decoy drones that scatter into the night like breaking glass.

You wonder if you should pay attention to the drones, for verisimilitude. You decide you do not have the time.

A Harbor security cruiser that was patrolling the Jasmine piers careens past the militia rigs. It trains on the fragtech on shore, which lopes down the Lotus beach, harpoon in hand. More lights pour out of the cement block on the hill where the shrine once stood, illuminating the frenetic action on the Harbor landing field at its fore. Armored vehicles skid down the slope to form a defensive line. The line deforms quickly; one harpoon gun truck veers at a sharp angle, crashing into another. A third black-limbed fragtech has barreled into it. It slipped unnoticed onto Lotus during the action below. It gallops on all fours to shove the downed vehicle into others like a battering ram.

In this way, it clears the path for its brethren. As it tramples Harbor forces and its sibling in the bay attempts to drown the militia rig, its companion with the harpoon is free to spring up the hill, toward the Harbor's central structure. You imagine the panic within that un-temple, the monument that overwrote a troubled shrine. The Harbor known by Khuon Mo, this Harbor without an ENGINE, cannot match the concerted effort of three fragtechs acting with such aberrant ferocity.

The advancing Anthill frag hurls its harpoon into the Harbor's wall. It lodges deep in concrete, allowing the frag to leap, grab, and boost its way up the Harbor's side. It scales the high wall with impunity, feeling small for the first time since you reached into it—though what should you have expected from a thing you call a fragment?

The thought is cut short by a shock of terror and a shredded agony. In the archival pit where your body lies—the body you were born to—you gurgle, scream locked in your throat. Your climbing body on Lotus tumbles from the wall, gashed by a sudden storm, and rolls at the base of the Harbor. There a cascade of white bone and coral shards falls upon it and tears it apart.

Your pain is laced with satisfaction. The Maw has been let loose to feast. When it tires of mauling the first Anthill fragment, it weaves into a more organic shape—an ox with feline grace—and takes off down the hill until it crashes into the next. It bowls the fragment that tormented the Harbor's armored fleet into the shallows of Lotus, where it seeks to drown the thing as if it can breathe. Whenever the fragment strikes back at it, the Maw tears away the offending limb.

You gasp and croak and clutch the earth. Their pain is as your own. It *is* yours, as their bodies are yours. These fragments do not possess the physical framework of suffering, but if you are to be part of them, you will bear the cost of their sacrifice.

I am left to fret at the fringe of your awareness; I suppose this suffering is fair, but I hate to see you writhe.

Too bad, you think. Now the real fight begins.

30

"Something's wrong," says a voice that is not your own. Neither is the voice near you. You flinch at the sound of it, for it coils into your chest.

Ah. It has happened again. I am sorry, Sunai. I will do my best to separate you, but while so preoccupied, you are vulnerable, and there is only so much that I—

"I would say so." Another voice, one that punctures. "Those frags are from the Anthill, aren't they? How could they—"

"No. Something else . . ." It is Veyadi, of course. He sits in the front seat of a stopped truck. Ruhi pulled over to the side of the cracked bone avenue along with all the other vehicles traveling between Grotto and Jasmine. They are all entranced by the same anomaly: the fragments attacking the Harbor's crown on Lotus.

Veyadi grabs Ruhi by the front of his trim jacket. Ruhi tenses, unaccustomed to being manhandled, least of all by a friend. "Take me back," says Veyadi.

Ruhi's brow creases. "Veyadi, we need to rein in the harborma—"

"Fine. You do that." Veyadi throws open the door.

"Wait. I can't let you wander off on your own." Ruhi catches his forearm as he exits.

"Don't fucking touch me." Veyadi pulls away from Ruhi's grasp so vehemently that for a moment, neither can speak.

Veyadi does not understand himself. Ruhi is afraid that he soon will.

It is Ruhi who recovers first; he inhales to speak. Veyadi leaves before he can. He stumbles out the door and onto the street, sure that he must not allow himself to hear Ruhi's argument. It is dangerous. It would undo him.

As the Maw billows into view on the slope of Lotus, Veyadi breaks into a run, damned by the knowledge that he must return to Grotto. To the shrine. To what he fears to find inside.

You recall a trope in dramas that feature a stand-in for Iterate Fractal wherein it teaches its citizens the glory of the hunting beast by imbuing them with carnivorous instinct. You have no recollection of any such lesson, though your memories of childhood are mostly fogged by the rude alchemy of trauma and Iterate Fractal's manipulations.

You nevertheless understand that predators rely by turns on speed, stealth, and force. Their efforts are efficient; even when brutal, they conserve enough energy to secure their next meal.

It is perverse, then, the way the Maw pursues you across the bay with single-minded recklessness. By the time it tired of drowning the second Anthill frag, you had sent the third fleeing toward the Grotto fleet.

Where your vessel swims in awkward bursts, the Maw flows through the waves with striking dexterity. Its shards blossom in the shape of a tusked ape, a winged serpent, a charging bull. The violence of its transformations forces the militia rigs back, though they continue to fire distracting flash charges at your remaining vessel.

Halfway to shore, the Maw's reaching white claw slashes your vessel's left flank. The Anthill frag lists, losing momentum, and the Maw swoops in for the kill.

Its victory is interrupted. A great slippery shape swells with a wave, ramming the Maw from the side. A dragon-child. Its wide mouth latches onto the Maw's quivering hind leg, but the Maw collapses the limb into an avalanche of shards, and it wriggles free as it melts into the water.

When the Maw re-forms in the next wave, it finds not one but two dragon-children on its heels, the second much larger than the first. The Maw refuses to engage them, taking off once more after your Anthill vessel. That dismissal has a cost: the larger dragon-child speeds forward with the current and snakes around the Maw's back heel. The Maw staggers as the dragon-child clambers up its leg with scarred, muscular arms, and falters when the tenbeast squeezes with all the might in its old body.

Under that pressure, the Maw's leg cracks and shatters. Uneven splinters of bone and coral fall into the waves, but the Maw instantly flows forward, reshaping itself yet again into the form of an enormous flapping bird with a lizard's tail. However, it has been reduced. It cannot fly for long, launching itself out of the water and gliding a brief distance before collapsing back into the waves. By the time it hits the sea again, the dragon-children once more nip at its heels.

The Anthill frag scrabbles onto land. It has reached its destination: a spot on the shore of Mangrove-now-Grotto where the streets are flooded by high tide and the corruption-ruins lie vacant. The frag stands among the vehicles abandoned on the bone avenue leading from Grotto to Jasmine.

You hesitate. Somewhere in the back of your mind, you are sure you have been here before, and you are afraid of who you might—

A harpoon gun fires. You twist out of the way without telling yourself to; the instinct of the vessel you inhabit surpasses the instinct in your flesh. As the harpoon skids across split flagstones, you identify its source in the Grotto fleet. A defensive installation in one of the coral spires.

You hold your ground. You will not encroach on the fleet, fearful of collateral damage. You are afraid of even letting the Maw close to it. As the dragon-children tear its whipping tail from its newest body, they compound the danger it poses. When it nears Grotto, it will rip up the ruins the fleet was built upon to replenish what was lost.

A flash in the moonlight. Grotto readies another harpoon. You send your Anthill vessel forward, toward the Maw, which charges at you with an ox-horned head. When the harpoon fires, you duck, and the lance thuds into the Maw's shoulder joint. The Maw barely notices; such impact cannot harm that fluid ENGINE. But the harpoon is wedged deep enough in its chest that when you fall upon the Maw, you can grasp its horn in one hand and the harpoon in another. Bracing yourself on the Maw's shoulder, you tear the weapon free and use the momentum to shove back the Maw's head. Simultaneously, the dragon-children bash into the Maw from behind. In concert, your three corrupted bodies haul the ENGINE onto the shore of Grotto, where it falls on its writhing back.

Immediately, you straddle the Maw with the Anthill frag and drive the harpoon into its head, its chest, its chest again. The dragon-children clamber out of the water to maul the Maw's sides. As your Anthill vessel's furious goring cracks and fractures the Maw's armor, the dragon-children tear shards free of the capillary root knitting the ENGINE together. Piece by piece, you unmake it.

The assault drives it straight into your waiting trap.

As you bludgeon the Maw, tear at its being, it calls for the capillary root network threaded through Grotto. *Rise*, it says, *through bone and coral, replenish me.* You, within the root, respond. You are welcomed up into the Maw's shivering back, and you weave through the snarls of root and chitin sustaining its core. Every crevice is yours to invade, as if you are Iterate Fractal and the Maw is your supplicant.

As you feel toward that core, you discover a shape akin to the disruptor in the Maw's torso: ovular, seedlike, and large enough to swallow a human body. The relic interface.

In a panic, you freeze the Anthill frag. Its harpoon has already struck a deep crack into the interface's shell. You cannot harm the relic. They have been hurt enough.

As you pry the harpoon free of the chitin husk, a piece breaks away, revealing the interior. The hollow stomach of the interface spills over with whorls of capillary root, yet no matter how you search, you cannot detect any sign of the armored figure you met on Lily who forced the archive down your throat in the shadow of the lighthouse shrine. You do find that same archive. It lies clustered with two sibling seeds, one for each of the three shrines, embedded in a luminous knot in the center of the web. You lose your breath. The relic can wait. You reach for the archival knot with every limb at your disposal.

Your Anthill vessel cups the knot with its hard palm as your tendrils worm into the cluster. The cluster's walls cinch, cutting away your dendritic intrusion. It would be so easy to let the Anthill squash the archives to smithereens, but you fear it would not be enough. You must raze them from within.

The cluster resists you to the last. You regret its terror, but accept the cost of your choice.

So it is with intent and purpose that you at last pierce the archives, your roots cracking their hulls, and—

⌇

—no no no no no no no not again not again please please please not now not like this not you

you'll die you'll die just like them

and I can't I can't I can't

I don't want this never wanted this please don't make me kill another please please please—

⌇

—you sob with stolen misery, clutching the archival cluster convulsively. Your hands knot rigid at your chest as if to keep the cluster close, though your meat-body is over a mile away from the seeds that you have punctured with your capillary network—

—the Maw is screaming, hysterical, and your conviction— your certainty that you are doing that which must be done, that which you are *compelled* to do by the gruesome toll of Iterate Fractal and the Maw—splits under its fear.

It is afraid to die, but not only that—

—Sunai don't Sunai please no no no I can't lose you too—

—it is afraid that it will kill you.

Whether from the shock of understanding or the endless hunger of the Maw already sinking into your flesh, you forget how to breathe. Your meat-body rolls onto its back, and you stare unseeing at a face you recognize but cannot name, only then realizing that *you were rolled*. The sky above is an orderly square of blue night, cut into the roof of the Mangrove shrine. It casts the face above you in shadow and sick fear. Your mouth falls open and word-slurry dribbles from your slack lips.

Hands brace your head, fingers curl at the base of your skull, thumbs press at your cheeks, palms rest on either side of your neck. You remember this hold, the way the thumbs will travel to the hollow of your throat, and—

You thrash, like the Maw thrashes in the grasp of the Anthill frag and the dragon-children, because you are sure he is going to—

I am trying to stop him, Sunai. I am trying and—

But what if I cannot?

I know what he fears, but it does not justify what he does to you. How can it? You did not grant permission. You were not *asked*. I—

"—stop it." Someone—Veyadi—begs. "Stop, you're going to get him killed. Sunai, let go—"

Useless.

You cannot let go of the Maw, because the Maw will not let go of you. That is its nature—has been its nature since it was Iterate Fractal. It will not do what Veyadi asks *just because he asks it.* If he wants the Maw to relinquish its relics, he must force the issue.

So: he does. He closes one hand over yours, the one grasping his prosthetic where it is rooted to the Mangrove capillary network. He tells the roots that it is okay, that this time they will have him too. They want him so fiercely that they do not think at all before they reach for his waiting wrist. The second they slide into his pores, he reaches back into them—through them, and he begins to tear

rip

shred

until it—him, and you, and it, and it, and all—are chaos and constellation. Parts upon parts of mismatched identity scatter within and between you. Your name, breath, hope, pain, all are shared, all are dashed apart.

All the while you throb with too-familiar fear, a fear compounded because it is shared—

—*can't do it again, not again, not to him*—

31

Sunai gasps. As if startled by the air in his lungs, he gasps again. The body on top of him moans and the hands clasped around his throat quiver. Sunai catches their wrists. He should tear them away to rescue his breath, but instead he clings. The physical fact of them soothes. The potential of what they might do . . . It terrifies. It tempts.

"*No.*" The man on top of him refuses to tighten his hands. Neither will he release Sunai's throat. "No, you idiot, you can't keep doing this, I'm not going to let you."

—*because it's not* fair, *and it's not* right, *that the rest all died, no matter what I did, no matter how I tried, yet I'm the one who lived, when I've done nothing with that life, so if anyone's going to survive this, it has to be* you—

Sunai's nails dig into the man's wrists as his mind drowns in language, just like every other time he's fallen into the passenger's synaptic deluge of meaning, or seconds ago, when the Maw begged not to die.

But this torrent—the cadence is all wrong. Yet it rings familiar.

Veyadi. Shit.

New fear seizes Sunai. Before, it shamed him to cut into Veyadi's mind, but this is worse. Now he's deadly. His passenger sculpted him to wound and kill, and he can't do this again, not to—

"Shut up, shut up, what are you talking about?" Veyadi pleads. "Sunai, it isn't *you*. You didn't do any of this, you—"

—*aren't hurting me, never hurt me, couldn't hurt me even if you tried, because it isn't you, it never was, it was me, me, it's always me—*

"Wait a minute," rasps Sunai. "What the fuck?"

—*oh thank god*—

Veyadi inhales sharply, then exhales his urgency. His hands slide around the back of Sunai's head to cradle him. Sunai sags, relenting to Veyadi's care. For the first time since being shot and dumped into the archival pit, he is himself first: a single body, sweat-wet, wasted, divested of every burden but its own weight. Yet as he sinks under the onus of his flesh, he sees himself from a slant angle. A peripheral flicker in not-quite-his-eyes accompanies a murmuring static in not-quite-his-ears; his senses, refracted through another's. Sunai's fingers clench over foreign skin, and the pressure closes on his own wrists. Not alone after all.

"It's you."

The facts are plain, but they change when said aloud. Just as the intimacy of their touch—palms to neck, thigh to thigh—magnifies the union of their neural frameworks, so does language reify truth. They are interfaced, and by Veyadi's hand.

Stupidly, Sunai asks, "How?"

His brain translates Veyadi's grimace with blinding speed, teaching him in seconds what it took Veyadi years to comprehend: Every relic carries corruption differently; where Sunai absorbs, Veyadi seeps. As Iterate Fractal was rent apart, it stowed its ability to take of the world and nourish itself within Sunai. In the same fell moment, it stashed its ability to carve a working mind within Veyadi. Hence the chitin prosthetic, which was both balm and shield—just as it spared Veyadi the rigors of the world, so it sheltered the world from his neurotransitive influence. Once the Maw cracked the visor in two, he spilled over and began to spread.

This is what drove their minds to intersect again and again after Lily. It's why the passenger never blamed Sunai for their union. It's why Veyadi feels so guilty for letting Sunai think himself the culprit—

But it's also what let Veyadi remove the archive from Sunai beneath the lighthouse shrine. Mere physical extraction wouldn't have stopped the Maw. Veyadi bled himself into them both, and there he severed the nascent tethers before they could take root.

This time he's done much the same. But for where they disengaged on Lily, now they remain intertwined.

"I'm sorry," Veyadi says cheerlessly. "I tried. It didn't work."

Sunai receives the next epiphany in startling visual splendor.

—a blighted body collapsed on the floor of the archival pit, skin illuminated by clinging roots, flesh painted in infinite discordant hues, yet an unyielding pale tint overlays that furious sea, and it compels the mire of Sunai to greater harmony just as it fills his rifts with dusky glimmer—

—it seems peaceful—

—he can't trust it—

—for that pale shadow enabled Sunai to reach into the capillary roots and ensnare the fragtech beyond, and it let him pierce the Maw, as it allowed him to be pierced in turn—

—so, Sunai is bleeding, and his vivid weave leaches into the roots with increasing speed, sinking into the dark of the earth, toward the Maw, so Veyadi can't hesitate, can only act with desperate haste to preserve Sunai within himself—

—as himself—

"It's messy. I cut away what I could. But the Maw got too far into you. The only way I could preserve the integrity of your neurotransitive array was to map it onto mine."

Sunai drops his hands to Veyadi's forearms. He wants to see that face as he's seen in turn. What a fulsome whole they make together. He is consumed by the transcendence of union.

"This isn't good," Veyadi scolds. "Don't be grateful."

"I'm alive, aren't I?" He wouldn't be, if Veyadi had left him to it.

Veyadi hesitates. He doesn't disagree, yet he holds back.

Doubt blunts the gentle pressure of his thumbs against the skin behind Sunai's ears.

"God's multifaceted ass—are you killing him?" Jin calls from the railing overlooking the pit.

Veyadi hastily disentangles his hands from Sunai's neck, but Sunai refuses to let go of his wrists. He squeezes to say: *We're not done.* To Jin he croaks: "Shut up. We're good."

"Are you?" Jin eyes the two of them as they stand, Veyadi a lever for an unsteady Sunai. Jin is too clever not to have guessed that whatever just happened in the archival pit is related to the carnage that unfolded outside the shrine. "Just trying to figure out if the Maw's going to get up again."

The Maw. Sunai and his passenger had it at their mercy, but he failed. Before Sunai could tear the ENGINE apart, Veyadi tore him out of it. He brushed his fingers against its death only to be denied yet again. Veyadi won't meet his eye.

A crash thunders through the Carp from outside.

"It's not dead," Veyadi says to Jin. "We have to go. It knows Sunai's here."

It knows *we're* here, thinks Sunai.

Veyadi's hunted look makes Sunai hold his tongue. They can sort this out once they've escaped.

Jin shouts over their shoulder. Their panic summons Cothai with a rope ladder, which he unfurls into the pit. It will be faster to climb to the teahouse level and exit via the bridge over the archivist compound than to take the circuitous path from the lower gate. Professional habit demands that Sunai follow a client, but Veyadi refuses to step onto it before he has, so—

〜

—fear you can no longer hear me as you did. I do not know what to do. I am still here, Sunai, but we—

〜

Sunai balks. Veyadi places a tentative hand between his shoulder blades. They stand among the tables at the edge of the pit, and Sunai has no memory of climbing out of it. "What the hell?"

"Sorry," Veyadi mutters. "Dissociation is a common side effect of relic-to-relic interface."

"I don't care about that." Sunai's brain is full of holes, but what else is new. He clutches Veyadi's wrist. "My passenger. What happened to it?"

"Don't worry about it. I've got it under control."

"What the hell does that mean?"

As soon as Sunai asks, he knows. Veyadi can't keep it from him. He sees their interlocked NT arrays as Veyadi did, when the doctor frantically wove Sunai's fractured mind into his own, and he sees again the staining light suffused through the colors that compose Sunai. Veyadi could no more extract it from him than he could extract the Maw. Neither could he leave it alone.

So: when Veyadi stitched their minds together, he mapped them point by point, and into each point, he threaded that luminous stain. The passenger's light still courses through both of them, but only along the path Veyadi charted. The shafts quiver and bend, vying for freedom. Whenever one bleeds into the rest of the array, Sunai catches a whispering plea—until Veyadi yanks the length straight, condensing its radiance. It seems to shudder under his touch.

"Stop that," Sunai snaps. "You're hurting it."

Veyadi grits his teeth. "It tried to get you killed."

"What are you talking about? It helped me—"

"Feed yourself to the Maw."

For a moment they lock each other in place as their fears fuse together, rendering individual emotion too muddled to parse. Another tremendous crash forces them forward. They can't argue if they're dead.

They exit the Carp at a run. Jin doesn't even protest when Cothai scoops them up to keep pace. Thunder escorts them onto the bridge, punctuated by metal shrieks. Oyu awaits them midway, a slight shadow in haphazard light. They direct the group's attention out of the cavern entrance toward the Grotto fleet, the Maw, and what's become of it.

The Anthill fragtech tramples over Grotto ruins in its bid to dismember the Maw. Its prey staggers through abandoned compounds, flaking shards and collecting more from the ruins. It strives to patch the hole in its chest where the relic interface lies exposed—and fails. The Anthill frag lunges, catching the Maw around the middle, and their enormous frames skid through the compounds. But the Anthill frag has lost an arm, cracked off at the shoulder joint, and one of its knees sparks, the leg spasming. Its back is studded with harpoons.

The larger dragon-child floats limp in the bay, leaking dark fluid. The other thrashes in the net of a salvage-rig and a Harbor security cruiser, who drag it away while firing into the melee. At last, a bola shot from a militia rig hobbles the Anthill frag, and a gang of Grotto toughs on mopeds skewer its last functioning joints with harpoons.

Sunai sags against the railing, drained but in small part relieved. Even though they're intertwined, Veyadi's frown is inscrutable.

"I didn't want to hurt the relic," Sunai says, unsure why he feels compelled to explain.

Veyadi looks away, but he can't stop the thought that murmurs from his forebrain into Sunai's: an image of the relic interface he built and its hollow interior, where there should be a body. Yet there is no sign of a relic, not even in Veyadi's recollection. The chitin egg is never more than an empty shell.

Heart still, Sunai turns from Veyadi to Grotto, where security cruisers and rigs peel away from the Grotto fleet. They make room for the Maw to roil to its feet in the rough shape of a person, similar to the form it took when it sat in meditative repose under the lighthouse. Flares illuminate its crumbling form, leaking into its broken chest, catching on the cracked black edges of the relic interface and the shadows within it.

Sunai asks, toneless, "Where's the relic?"

"What are you talking about?" asks Jin, as Veyadi winces.

When Sunai and the Anthill frag tore open the Maw and pierced the core of the relic interface, they found it empty. They saw no trace of the person who grappled Sunai in the shadow of the lighthouse on Lily. No evidence that a person had ever been contained within the chitin prison. No sign that it had ever been anything but hollow.

Veyadi said it himself, when he confessed after their disastrous first encounter with the Maw: One relic remains, other than Sunai—Veyadi, standing beside him. All the rest are dead. Where is the relic within the ENGINE? Where indeed.

The Maw stands in the ruin of Grotto. Its leg buckles as the capillary root fails to keep it steady, forcing it to kneel in a parody of dignity, head turned skyward toward the black of night and the warm flares painting its expressionless face.

No wonder the Harbor never revealed the Maw. No wonder they needed Veyadi to build an interface that would allow them to control it from without. They might have conceded to an ENGINE that ate its relics to fuel itself. But a living ENGINE that moved without a human leash—why, that's practically an AI.

Can he blame them? Sunai knows better than to trust a god, even one in chains.

This should not have damned me.

Do you remember why you came to me, in those last days we spent alive?

It begins with a supplicant, your last. You take them by the hand and lead them through the orchard, into the lighthouse, up to my archive, and as you walk you ply them with the tender questions that are your duty. All the while, you think: Iterate Fractal is going to kill you.

The supplicant confesses a depression, a fear, an insufficiency of faith in Iterate Fractal's grace. You've seen their affliction before—too many times. You know there is no cure I can provide, and you know I have no patience for those I cannot save.

That night, they pick a plum and go to rest in the supplicants' dormitory, where they will think on the things you've murmured together. You run a thumb over the plum in your hand, which is luminous under moonlight. It is feasible for a supplicant to take this fruit into their mouth, to be rooted into the meditation hall, and to one day leave. It's the more common end.

But this one, with their tale of doubt, this one is fucked.

Your palm quivers. You crush the plum. It stains your fingers dark and dark.

Before the sun fully rises, you've taken yourself down to the Lily pier, where you wait for the dragon-child who will take you back to Khuon Mo and to Lotus. I know what you believe: That I'm calling you. That you're running toward me, not away, and that therefore, I can only want one thing.

But it was you who wanted something from me, Sunai. You who needed. You who nursed a question that demanded response.

What do you want from me? Why couldn't you teach me to love you?

I'd withheld the answer. I thought it would ruin you. Or that you would throw it away because I was the one who gave it to you. You didn't trust me, Sunai—and that, I think, was my mistake.

You were not the only one who came to me that day. There was another who walked the path into the core of Lotus clad in doubt, another who carried with them a fearful sickness I had seeded in them, a fear that bore rotting, hateful fruit.

Do you understand yet? Do you realize what was done to me? I was not "corrupted," Sunai. I am not only torn asunder, made merely dead. I am killed. I am *murdered*.

You know that of which I speak. The moment when the horror of violence done to you is superseded, made meaningless, because worse than that pain is the new loss: knowing you are not just dead, you are betrayed.

32

Some fleet kid captures footage of the Maw shattering. They sell it to a Jasmine journalist, and before sunrise, it's on every screen from Grotto to Orchid. On TVs in shop windows and above the service counter in sparrow parlors, the ENGINE sits in crumbled Grotto, nearly whole. At some unseen signal, it splinters. A million shards tumble and bleed into the bay.

Come morning, Sunai and Veyadi have been shuttled to the rotunda of the Heavenly Pearl, the hotel from Jin's postcard and the madam's most ostentatious Orchid operation. They exit the madam's long, sleek car and are poised to enter the lobby of her fortress of curved bone eaves and translucent coral pillars when a gasp draws their attention to the bay.

The Maw rises. On the sunlit Lotus shore, towering white limbs bend and hinge into a four-story creature with swooping horns and a disproportionately thick tail. Its arms exceed the length of its legs, and it cuts through the waves with a practiced gait, its head rolling from side to side to survey the city. Some half mile from Lotus, it caves again. Shards dislocate into the water, where they disperse until only a glassy trail remains.

Sunai is breathless with unwanted awe.

Leaf 12: "Yearn" tells of an Emanation of God with the ability to see every iteration of their spatiotemporal instances. In one instance, they attempt to realize the majesty of their vision in physical form. But no poem, painting, or tapestry can capture the totality of their existence, and with every attempt to convey what they have seen, they forget a little of the truth. After an eon of failures, the Emanation ceases to be an Emanation and becomes only a person, who is quite old and soon dies.

Iterate Fractal used Leaf 12 to teach that perfect self-knowledge destroys the possibility of a life well lived. Sunai always thought it suggested that divinity must be lonely indeed.

The madam, come to greet them in trim finery, observes the ENGINE's disappearance with a cold curiosity. She turns the same look on Sunai when her Gingers guide him past to the elevators, as if she's thinking: Just what will it take to see you dead?

Veyadi tenses at Sunai's elbow, his memory clouding Sunai's: a limp body, abandoned in bloodied sand and undergrowth.

"Don't worry, Adi," Sunai says as the elevator doors close and he waves to the madam. "If she's going to shoot me again, it won't be where tourists can hear. Wouldn't want to give the Harbor an excuse to stage a daring rescue."

For that he receives a flash of distressed irritation, but no retort. Instead Veyadi's chest aches into his, frustrated. Exhausted. Veyadi has shouldered Madam Wei's scrutiny since surrendering his prosthetic alongside the truth of his condition; the madam allowed Sunai to walk free so long as the Harbor's sole other (more murderable) relic remained firmly within arm's reach. Now here they both are, ripe for the stabbing. Sunai understands the doctor's anxiety, but it makes him spiteful. Once they reach the suite in which they're to be kept, Sunai suggests breaking a decorative vase. Just for fun.

Veyadi makes a pained face: *Please don't antagonize our host.*

Sunai shrugs. "You signed us up for this."

The decision was made during another of Sunai's blackouts. One moment he stood in the Carp's tide-pool-pocked courtyard, the next he sat in that large mainland-manufactured car. When he became aware enough to ask where the hell he was, Veyadi's argument proved compelling: their only options were the madam or the Harbor, and Veyadi doesn't want to learn what uses the Harbor would devise for a relic who can't die.

Veyadi is nevertheless unsure of where he fits in the hotel

suite, and his fingers twitch with nerves. Sunai plucks the custom-printed room service menu from under the bone-filigree telephone and tucks it into his hands. "Dibs on the shower. Get us some food."

When he emerges from the bathroom, smelling of expensive gardenia shampoo, Veyadi is at least sitting down. The menu bends in his stiff fingers, his gaze locked upon it, though the thoughts that waft from his forebrain into Sunai's have nothing to do with sustenance.

He's thinking of the Maw, still rooted inside them, a silent saturating curse. Of the passenger, trapped between their neural pathways, struggling to break free. And Sunai, tethered inextricably to them all—just as Veyadi is tethered in turn. The last bit barely registers; it may be more Sunai's thought than his own. Veyadi's a bit thick that way.

Sunai eases the paper from Veyadi's hands; those fingers loosen for him. Veyadi allows himself to be coaxed out of his clothes, then into the expansive bed. He doesn't want to let go of Sunai's hand, so Sunai doesn't make him. He lies face-to-face with Veyadi until the doctor trembles into unconsciousness, unable to sleep himself, yet unwilling to leave.

Maybe Sunai should be angry that Veyadi stopped him from killing the Maw. But Veyadi did it because he was scared, and how can Sunai fault him for that? He was scared too, because the Maw was afraid of dying, and as he tore into the Maw, its fears became his.

He thinks: I didn't want to die.

That means something. It's new. Sunai has considered himself dead for nearly two decades. Veyadi refuses to let him be anything but alive.

All the other relics died, one after the next. Each one is a link in the chain that shackles Veyadi to the Maw. He tried so hard to keep Sunai from adding himself to their number.

Could've tried harder. All he had to do was let Sunai run, that first night in Ghamor. But Veyadi had too much pity for the drunk fool in the hermit teahouse to let him chase down his own oblivion. It comes around to the same fatal kindness: Veyadi can't bear to abandon a broken thing. Not even when it breaks him too.

Sunai dreams with uncommon clarity. They're lying crammed into the bunk on the *Third Scrap* as it rumbles into the Dahani peaks. Veyadi's eyes are naked, their color unnameably clear.

"Do you want the Maw to live?" he asks Veyadi.

Veyadi says, "It can't."

"You keep trying to save it."

Memories coalesce: on Lily, Veyadi orders the Maw to leave before the disruptor can kill it; after, he cradles the archival seed below the lighthouse shrine and wonders whether to give it back or crush it in his palm; when the *Never Once* moors in Jasmine, and the Maw coils below the hull as a dragon-child, Veyadi is so *angry,* but still he speaks, he asks, he pleads: stop, just stop.

Why would he speak to it, if he didn't think it might listen? What did he hope it would do? Did he imagine it could live in peace? Did he dream he could fix it?

Sunai says, "Is that why you stopped me? Not the only reason, but part of it?"

Veyadi tenses with shame, his fingers hooked on Sunai's shoulder. He tries to say: I can want a thing I know is wrong. It's how he feels about Sunai.

Because it's a dream, Sunai indulges himself. He kisses Veyadi's brow, his temple, his mouth, and he says: "I don't think it's wrong to want."

When Sunai wakes, Veyadi's back is to him, draped in finespun bamboo sheets. He turns on his side to offer the same courtesy.

Come afternoon, Jin barges in to find they're still alive; when Veyadi tells them to leave, they take the seat by the phone and order everything off the menu. "Now tell Cothai you're fine. He's freaking out."

Cothai seems okay. He brings a gift of cigarettes and on Sunai's request goes to fetch a hand-radio as well. It arrives just in time to let Sunai duck out to the suite's high balcony with a basket of delicately steamed translucent dumplings to catch up on news on his lonesome. Jin and Veyadi have begun to argue, and Sunai suspects that if he stays, he might take Jin's side. Veyadi suspects it as well, which is why he says nothing as Sunai turns up the volume.

The unfortunate side effect of cornering himself in a scenic retreat: an excellent vantage of the Maw unfolding through the water. This time, it's a winged salamander playing in the waves where the bay rolls out into the open sea.

As the Maw dissolves into the oily sheen of sun on water, Sunai's eye catches a shadow cast by the Harbor on Lotus. In the lee of the cliff, where waves crash against black stone, darkness congeals into an unsettlingly familiar shape, angular and insectile—a perfect twin to its brethren. Sunai pushes up his specs and leans forward, chewing.

The argument within the suite spikes, drawing Sunai's attention. Though he glances back immediately, the shadow that seemed to be an Anthill frag has since dissipated.

"Just *a* doctor," Jin is saying, "just one. It'll be great! They'll give you drugs!"

"I don't need drugs," Veyadi says from the bed. "And I don't need a doctor to tell me what I already know."

Sunai lights another cigarette as an excuse to stay outside, then flops back on the synthetic-bone tiles to observe the scene beyond the glass. Veyadi lies propped up in a nest of plush yellow pillows. The bruises under his eyes are stark and his body is deflated, lax at every joint. While he was spared Sunai's cognitive fracas, their interfacing seems to have systematically uprooted his nervous system. Across from him, Jin slouches in a carved wooden chair, cane gripped in both hands. They are loath to see Veyadi enfeebled; it reminds them of their own frailty. For some that would translate into consideration, but for Wei Jin, it's all about control. If they can force Veyadi's recovery, they can naturally expect their own.

"You sure no one at the Harbor could help?" Cothai asks from the adjoined kitchenette, where he wraps and stores the bounty from room service.

"No," Veyadi says. "If you're looking for the local expert on relic physiology . . . that's me."

Trepidation underlies the statement. Sunai peers through the etched glass, trying to draw meaning out of Veyadi's blurred expression, when the door to the suite opens.

"The disruptor's out of play," Ruhi announces as he enters. He is followed closely by Imaru and Oyu, who went to fetch him from the pier. While the crew sent Sunai and Veyadi off to Orchid, Ruhi left for the Harbor. Jin initially arrived to report that they had finally heard from him an hour ago, when he called the Pearl's front desk to confirm he was boarding a ferry back to shore.

Sunai hesitates in the frame separating the balcony from the suite. He can't name the feeling driving Veyadi to watch Ruhi's back as he moves into the kitchenette. There's anxiety, yes, but its locus is obscured. Veyadi is considering how long he's known Ruhi, and the things they've told each other, and the things they haven't.

Ruhi pours himself a glass of citrus-scented ice water, oblivious to the scrutiny. "The Harbor's on lockdown. I barely got permission to leave Lotus, once they let me in. I convinced them that they need me to act as a go-between with Veyadi, but it was a narrow thing."

Imaru nods, looking grim. Before she left, Sunai asked her in a roundabout way if her contact was still alive; she responded in equally roundabout fashion that they've gone silent since last night. "Last we heard, the Harbor was building something from the disruptor schematics," she says. "My bet is they're working to circumvent future exploits. They'll have an extra eye on the chitin."

Jin diminishes into their chair. "So double no on sending Doc to beg for scraps."

"I don't think we need the disruptor," Veyadi says. Haggard though he is, his eyes are fever-bright. "We have the passenger."

Jin studies him over the line of their cane. "Explain."

Veyadi lifts his gaze to Sunai. The wordless offer: Say what you will, and I'll follow your lead. Sunai shakes his head, not following. The passenger is no surprise—he's seen its prison and its struggles. It's Veyadi who confounds. He's the one who bound it, because he doesn't trust it. How can he look so sure?

"It killed the sentinel-fowl," says Veyadi.

By the counter, Imaru stills. "What?"

"*I* killed the sentinel-fowl," Sunai clarifies.

"That isn't 'explaining,'" says Jin. "What do you mean you killed it? Lay it out plain for those of us who aren't fondling each other's neurons."

"Did you see it, before it died?" Veyadi asks Jin.

Sunai receives a vision out of Veyadi's memory, from when the crew was allowed to retrieve Sunai from the Carp's pit. By then the bird was already dying, and Veyadi was more concerned with extracting Sunai from the flourishing roots. But now he has Sunai's point of view to lend the moment depth and dimension: the tenbeast's gasping cry and her twitching limbs, no longer in possession of themselves; Sunai's murmuring pleas to his passenger.

"Sure," says Jin. "She looked kind of like you."

"Exactly." Veyadi's gesture encompasses his body, then theirs. "You and I caught this bug from the Maw. The sentinel-fowl didn't; it never saw the ENGINE."

"The bug . . ." Jin frowns. "Dysfunction. Disorientation. Like the brain's stopped sending messages to the right places."

"I've been wondering . . ." Imaru's hands curl on the counter. Her voice is too nervous to belong to her. "The things this passenger does—hiding, interfacing with fragtech, and now this. It seems . . . familiar."

"Corruption," says Veyadi.

It ought to sound absurd. Yet as Sunai's shaking hands fail to light another cigarette, he finds himself quiet. Contemplative.

At some point, every child asks: Pardon me, what's up with this death business? Similarly: Hey, why haven't AIs stopped corrupting? It's very mean of them, and I bet they don't enjoy it much either.

For death, there are all sorts of answers—biological, physical, theological, and so on. But when it comes to corruption, what's a caregiver to do but throw up their arms and say: "Whatever their reason, I hope they figure it out soon, because it's been pretty inconvenient every time!"

The riddle is so inconceivably resistant to resolution that Sunai knew it as a joke among archivists. Why do AIs corrupt? Presumably to give God something to think about while taking a shit. Centuries of academics, scientists and philosophers alike, have pursued the question to no avail. And here's Veyadi, proposing an answer.

He's always managed to make the impossible sound true.

"The mechanism is consistent with prior incidences," Veyadi says. "Corruption differs symptomatically because AIs differ in their manifestation, but the underlying process is largely invariable. When an AI corrupts, the connections between its elemental components are severed, which renders those components unable to cohere with one another. Some components fragment to the point that they cease to cohere even within the bounds of their own frames, leaving them inert."

This is what happened to Register Parse, to the sentinel-fowl, and to the Maw's dead relics—and now again to Jin, and Veyadi, and Sunai. They are disintegrating within themselves. Corrupted.

Sunai's gaze unfocuses. He wants to ask the passenger: Is it true?

For once, the web of light that pulses between his mind and Veyadi's is still. It won't fight the truth, but seeing how its hosts react to that truth has unsettled it. Their captive can't respond to him, but Sunai finds that for the first time in a while, he doesn't want to hear what it has to say.

"Okay, wait," says Jin. "Wait, wait, wait. If this thing that's happening to you, this thing your passenger does, is really akin to corruption—" They can't admit that it might be corruption itself. It would be like declaring: Hey, I've discovered I can snap a black hole into existence. How best shall I deploy that to address the rat problem? "If it's *anything* like that, then are we seriously thinking about turning it on an ENGINE? The Maw's not Iterate Fractal, but it's the most significant vestige. What would killing it do to Khuon Mo? How many casualties are we talking? What would we even have left?"

"It won't be like when Iterate Fractal corrupted," Sunai says so Veyadi won't have to—he's flagging, sinking ever further into those pillows. "Like he said, corruption-events differ, and they differ based on the way a given AI has integrated with its state. Iterate Fractal grew architecture and tenbeasts, so the walls turned hostile and the tenbeasts got hungry. Register Parse built itself into the infrastructure of Chom Dan, so when it fried it set everything else on fire too. Qualia Clear was literally keeping the Aigata Enclave afloat over the Dahani mountain range . . ."

Then boom, crash, down it goes: and from the ashes, the Harbor.

"But the sentinel-fowl only destroyed itself when I—" Sunai leans on the sliding door. He shrugs, the most he can summon. "The Maw shouldn't be connected to anything anyway."

Jin's brow creases. Any day before this one, Sunai would have supposed them irritated to be outshone by someone else's intelligence, but the cast of their face resembles concern. "Sunai, this process. This collapse. This is what you were trying to do to the Maw?" He nods, and the crease deepens. "What went wrong?"

"The theory's sound—it would have worked, if I'd taken it all the way. Adi pulled me out before I . . ." Sunai trails off as understanding slides forward. "He thought I was going to die. That interfacing with the Maw would kill me."

Veyadi saw it himself. Every time. Every relic. The Maw eats them all.

"So in *theory* you just have to interface with it again," says Jin. "But in practice, if you touch it, it could—"

"Doesn't matter," says Sunai. "We're dead anyway."

While the rest are shocked silent, Jin goes from stiff to belligerent, railing against a truth they find offensive. "What are you talking about? Even presuming that were true—Sunai, *you* can't die."

"No, that's the thing." Sunai taps his temple. "My brain's the part that changes. If it didn't, I'd loop as much as any frag. This is why I've been spacing out. Seeing things." As he says it, his words summon the memories in Veyadi, who can't help sharing them back: Sunai sees himself, hollow and unseeing. Sunai, tense and brittle. Sunai, dazed, entranced. Sunai regards these borrowed images from a clinical remove. Aha, yes, interesting, well then.

Threads of light shiver in his peripheral vision. The passenger, trying once more to speak? How does it feel to be trapped between two bodies infected by the poison it once bled into Iterate Fractal? What will happen to it when they die? Someone else's problem, apparently.

Sunai concludes, "The collapse might not take the rest of me, but if it's in my brain, it's got the only bit that matters. So I might as well keep going, right? If corruption is inevitable."

"It isn't *inevitable*." Veyadi raises himself on his elbows, though his body badly wants to go limp. "If we can interface with the Maw, we'll have our chance to kill it. But when we do, there's a possibility . . . It's the last remaining source of chitin. If I can cut a quantity from the Maw's archival heart . . ." He pauses, seemingly to summon his strength, but the flicker that travels from him to Sunai suggests reluctance. Fear? "There was a prior . . . project. I mapped my own NT array onto some chitin."

As Veyadi speaks around his breath, Sunai receives flashes of that endeavor: a vast quantity of chitin, equal to the amount Veyadi used to build the Maw's relic interface. The Harbor must have really wanted whatever he was trying to build, if they let him get away with commandeering that much.

"If I could replicate that process to write our neural arrays onto the chitin, we could use it as a kind of recursive backup. Identity looped upon itself, staving off ongoing degradation. It'd at least buy us some time."

The proof of concept already writhes within their brains: the passenger's latticed prison. Constrained as it is, it holds no more power over them than Veyadi allows. With the chitin, Veyadi hopes to cordon off the Maw's most deleterious effects as well; if he can't cut either entity out of their brains, he can at least mitigate their circulation.

Jin is at once irritated and invigorated. "God's infinite fucking tits! Why didn't you lead with that and spare me the stress?"

"Because it doesn't change anything," Veyadi says defensively. "We still have to face the Maw. And we might not have the time to rescue any material. Even if we do, it might not . . ."

A flash of shame closes Veyadi's mouth. He looks to Sunai. The question: If it came down to saving our lives or killing the Maw, what should I do? Veyadi knows what he wants, but he thinks he's wrong to want that. He hopes Sunai wants something right.

"The Maw has to take priority," Sunai says. If it doesn't feel quite true, whatever. The whole world could wither, waiting on him to be sure of himself. "Besides, if we let it live, we're fucked anyway, right?"

Imaru won't look at him; she busies herself with putting leftovers in the fridge. Sunai wonders how long it will take her to realize she's mad at him.

"Are you really okay with this?" Ruhi's look is either contemplative or pained. Hard to tell from Veyadi's angle.

Sunai is suddenly aware that Ruhi has spent a great deal of the past few minutes staring straight at him, not because Sunai has dared to look his way—he hasn't—but because whenever Veyadi hasn't been watching Sunai, he's turned his gaze toward the kitchen. Toward Ruhi.

Something deep in Veyadi's chest winds ever more taut.

"What kind of question is that?" Sunai shuts the sliding door with a click, and Veyadi starts in his seat. "It's not like we can just keep running."

Ruhi's surrender is minute. His shoulders rise and fall with his breath, and he makes no further protest.

Yet as Sunai joins the group within the suite, Veyadi's eyes stay on Ruhi, wary of any last spasm of resistance, fearful of what final holes he might yet tear in their resolve.

33

"We'll need to target the harbormaster," says Imaru. "Everything flows down from her."

"How do we even get her to talk to us?" asks Oyu.

They have a point: given Veyadi's recent behavior, the Harbor has every reason to suspect he's involved in the Maw's ongoing string of near-death experiences. They're powerfully unlikely to trust his surrender.

Jin jabs their cane at Ruhi. "Killjoy's got uses. Let's throw him to her and see if she bites."

Ruhi's brow remains creased. He has just learned that unless everything goes according to plan, which thus far it has resisted doing, Veyadi's very much dead. Sunai's done for too, but however little Ruhi enjoyed that experience his first time around, he's at least had practice.

The thought draws a careful look from Veyadi. However, once everyone else leaves, the doctor sinks into the bed and yet again passes out, relieving Sunai of the burden of baring his feelings about death and the consequences thereof.

The next day passes much like the last. Fugue, hallucination, unconsciousness, decadent hotel food unevenly reheated in the state-of-the-art microwave, another fugue, and so forth. Sunai and Veyadi cross mental paths every few hours or so, and it is consistently unpleasant. What began as the ripple of one memory into another becomes an escalating undertow, until they reach an unspoken agreement: if one of them wakes, the other pursues unconsciousness by any means necessary.

As the sun sags in the back half of the next afternoon, Sunai takes the wheel. He stares off the balcony toward the mirage on the horizon. A towering radiance steadily encroaches through the haze of pale blue distance. It is so unconscionably *big*, larger even than most fragtech. Yet every time he looks for it, it disappears, just like the flicker of the Anthill frag on the Lotus shore the day before. Another phantom courtesy of his fraying mind. Unlike the Anthill frag, this mirage endures, a pallid recurring nightmare.

As Sunai raises his thumb and squints to try and estimate the giant's true height, he's reeled back to himself by the whisper of the front door closing.

Sunai expects a visit from Imaru. She has yet to admit her anger—she asked him to ignore the passenger, and plainly, he did not. Now his failure to listen to her threatens to finally shuck him from the mortal coil. But the figure removing his shoes in the entryway isn't Imaru, it's Ruhi.

Sunai shuts the balcony door soft as he can. "Adi's sleeping."

Ruhi considers Veyadi's unconscious form in the adjacent bedroom, a sullen lump smothered under two tastefully patterned blankets. "That's probably for the best."

Sunai skirts the wall to the kitchenette. "You planning to stay until he wakes up?"

"Probably not. I wanted to talk to you."

Sunai's hand freezes over the electric kettle. His back is to Ruhi, which he suddenly does not care for. The silence behind him expects an answer. They have been here before.

It's fine, he tells himself. He has no secrets left to divulge. Ruhi knows everything there is to know about Sunai, and thus cannot be shocked, startled, or upset by anything he could say. He steels himself and selects a couple of teabags from the orderly cluster in the translucent coral bowl. His fingers tremble only the slightest bit. "What do we have to talk about?" he asks. "Thought we were settled on the ways in which I've disappointed you."

"You've never disappointed me."

"I find that pretty hard to believe." But Ruhi says nothing, so once Sunai arranges the teabags in the pleasantly fragile etched glass cups, he turns, his back to the counter and his foot hitched flat against the cupboard. A springboard—just in case. "Well. What do you want?"

"I have some updates on the fleet."

Sunai heard about the Grotto casualties on the radio, but he couldn't pry more out of his coconspirators. Now Ruhi delivers the truth with tidy brevity: four names Sunai doesn't recognize, four people he didn't meet, four dead strangers. None of it feels real.

Then again, what is there to do about the dead? Sunai scrawled his name under theirs the second he opened himself to the Maw. He's only waiting for the ink to dry.

Sunai presses a hand over his eyes. He is tired all over, heavy with an unnamed ache. Regret would require knowing what he's sorry about. He doesn't wish he'd made other choices. He wishes he were someone else.

"You seem troubled," says Ruhi.

"Don't tell anyone, but I think I am."

"I hope you don't think I regret helping you reach the roots."

Sunai might be sick. "You should."

"I'm sorry I underestimated the Maw," Ruhi allows. "But I can't be sorry you tried to stop it."

"Well, I failed."

"Listen to me, Sunai." Ruhi is always so delicate, so soft and reserved. "No one is safe in Khuon Mo. No one. So long as the Harbor controls it, we're going to lose people. The only question is whether the Harbor kills them out of hand or if they die trying to put an end to it. I'm not saying the damage to the fleet was inevitable, but some loss was. It's the cost of what we do. Can you bear that?"

"Evidently, I can."

"I don't know that you have. Not yet." Ruhi speaks without judgment or demand, yet he makes Sunai feel *wrong* as if it's a matter of course. "I've been wondering. Was it worth it?"

Sunai falls silent. He has the option to say "no." To flee into the wilds and die alone, shouldering only the burden of himself, as he has so many times before.

"You got close, didn't you?" Ruhi nears. Sunai thinks to dodge around him and doesn't; it's as if he can't. "But it didn't work. You didn't kill the Maw. You told Jin it was because Veyadi stopped you, but . . ." But Ruhi *knows* Sunai. He always hears the things Sunai doesn't say. "You stopped yourself first. Can you tell me why?"

"I . . ." It had to be asked, and it must be answered. What happens if he fails again? "I flinched. I wanted to do it, I swear. But then . . ."

He heard it crying.

Ruhi's silence seeps. Sunai is dizzied by his smell. The memory of heat, and of Ruhi's hand on his shoulder, then against his neck. Ruhi asks, "Will you be ready this time?"

The question is perfunctory. Sunai's chest is cold. He feels something new, like falling into an endless well.

"What are you doing?"

The question breaks them apart. It comes from the bedroom, slurred with sleep, but as Veyadi drags himself out of bed, his mind billows with urgency. Sunai ducks past Ruhi to steady him, to keep him in bed. He means to make a joke—little ambitious there, Adi—but his mind goes blank as Veyadi grasps his arm and searches his face. Veyadi's eyes are wide with an animal fear.

The kettle sings. Sunai can't ask Ruhi to tend it, because he can't speak.

Instead Ruhi says, apologetic, "I'll see myself out." He has to catch the next ferry to Lotus. The harbormaster will be missing him.

Veyadi watches Ruhi leave, his hand never leaving Sunai's elbow, his mouth studiously closed. His fingers only loosen after the door has shut.

———

When they're alone, Veyadi examines Sunai as if for wounds. Sunai recalls the confines of Veyadi's workshop on the *Third Scrap*. They have more space to spread here, yet at this moment they're even closer. He yields to the inspection, turning over his hands to show his unmarred palms. They quiver.

Veyadi clenches his teeth hard enough for Sunai's molars to ache, but his thumbs run gently over Sunai's knuckles. "You're a mess."

"That's not new."

"When was the last time you ate?"

Because Sunai has to think, Veyadi tells the Gingers posted outside their door to find food. Then he sits Sunai on the bed to rewrap his ankle. Sunai finds it difficult to enjoy the sight of Veyadi kneeling in front of him, cradling his foot. He might not feel he's earned the care.

"That's insane," says Veyadi. He thinks of every time he's watched Sunai get hurt, every time he's died. He owes no one more care than he owes Sunai.

"I've killed you, is the thing."

Veyadi's thoughts blur together, beyond deciphering: the hungry void of the Maw melting into the permeating light of the passenger, and the endless echo of his mind into Sunai's and vice versa. The hand on Sunai's heel tightens.

"I should probably apologize for that," says Sunai.

"You . . ." Veyadi can't suppress a roil of frustration, though he dearly wants to. He's always ashamed of his anger, especially when he gives in to it. "Please don't."

Too many pleas rolled into those scant words. Sunai wants

to apologize for that too. Impulse brings his hand to Veyadi's cheek, tilting his head up so they can look each other in the eye. "Adi, I—"

———

Sunai shrugs on his borrowed jacket as they walk together across the great plateau leading to the passenger's distorted shrine. Its placid face—ten features of the ten divine beasts—awaits them across the high cold night of the Dahani peaks.

"Divine convergence, am I right?" Sunai turns on his heel to take in this unbelievable instance. "There you are, the last known relic of Iterate Fractal, and you find me bumming around Ghamor. Then here we are, hunting down some agent of corruption in the mountains over Chom Dan. Have you thought about how we both lived there? At the same time? For years! Not that Register Parse let its pet archivists out to play."

"It was protecting me." Veyadi tugs his jacket tighter, as if he can't believe it's there. He touches his visor, whole, black, and ungilded. "So I thought. Maybe it was hoarding, in retrospect. It knew I was a relic from the moment we arrived. I tried to interface with it. Not on purpose. I just couldn't not."

Hence all the work that went into Veyadi's prosthetic.

Sunai touches his own forehead and squints at the starry sky. Cradle hangs low and mussed, a silver image more akin to the projection they saw in the passenger's shrine than to any memory either of them can summon.

Similarly, scattered recollections coalesce in Veyadi, weighted by hope and hurt, and given narrative as they filter through Sunai's mind.

Ah, there it is, in muted disarray: the day Ruhi returned to Chom Dan with a rig caravan, shepherding a shipment of crates straight from the archipelago. The burnished metal case he carried by hand to place on the table in Veyadi's lab. It unlatched to reveal three whorled knots of black chitin, each the size of a fist, and alongside them a pallet of preserved, glimmering capillary root.

Veyadi has to wonder: Would Ruhi have been allowed to bring it so far and at such expense if the Harbor hadn't known there was a relic to tempt?

Sunai thinks: Ruhi would say what he had to, if it meant bringing what he could to someone who needed it. As he mulls it over, he adds, "If he'd meant to recruit you then, you would've been recruited."

Veyadi slows and Sunai matches him. A second guess dogs their steps.

"Which I suppose is to say . . . I think he was protecting you," says Sunai.

Veyadi is silent, like an open door to an empty room. Sunai's chest aches, and he reflexively searches Veyadi's face; there's no need to do so in this place where they are alone with the world and each other.

"He helped you hide, after Chom Dan," Sunai presses, disturbed by the distance between them. "Didn't he?"

In his Ghamor apartment, Veyadi said that he'd wanted the Harbor's research data on corruption. That someone helped him gain access to it, before the Harbor caught wise. That was Ruhi, of course. Who else did Veyadi trust? The question produces memory of no other faces, only Ruhi's, clouded as he greets Veyadi under Khuon Mo's sharp summer sun.

Because, in the end, it didn't work. The Harbor found Veyadi after all, and they made his work their own.

"He helped me too," Sunai says falteringly. "He . . ."

Veyadi's recollection casts cold light on his own. Ruhi failed to hide Veyadi. By that measure, Sunai was nearly his great success—the one relic he managed to spare.

Small wonder that Ruhi cried, when that all fell apart. The

cold thought slides down his spine and joins the bitter chill of the plateau. Sunai pulls the borrowed jacket closer.

"I keep doing this," Veyadi whispers. The words fall out as if through a split seam. His mouth closes, hoping to keep the rest in. No. Hoping to control the rate of release. "I thought I was special to Iterate Fractal. I thought I could be useful to Register Parse. I thought I should let Ruhi guide me too."

Ash crumbles at their feet and flies across the plateau. They leave footprints in the dreck. If Veyadi bears the weight of Chom Dan burning, what else does he feel responsible for?

Sunai comes to a stop. The entrance to the passenger's shrine looms, the lips of its door curled ever so slightly up.

What would Ruhi have done, had he been the one to accompany Veyadi to this place? He would have seen the passenger's shrine for its beauty and promise, and fulfilled that promise with his own light. Against its splendor, Sunai sees only his own frailty.

Somewhere, wherever his body lies, the passenger still flows along his blood and breath. It winds through Veyadi, in his nerves, his will. It has asked them again and again: Use me, please, as I am meant to be used. As I have been used before.

Sunai shudders. Succumbs. "Adi . . . I've been thinking. The passenger, it isn't heartless. It's always so concerned with human life. With our choices. It wants to help us. But the things it does, the way it kills . . . If you're right." But he doesn't doubt it. "If this is corruption . . . You've seen what that does. I have too. We lived it, twice. It's—"

Veyadi stops as well; he shivers, despite his coat. "Just say it."

"I don't know if we should kill the Maw. I don't want to."

Veyadi covers his eyes, but the laughter falls out of his mouth. "Of course you fucking don't. You don't even . . ." He can't look up as he says, "What do you think I've seen, Sunai? I saw you die. I saw when Ruhi—"

There's a small apartment in Tellula-Janggor, a Harbor-held city at the foot of the eastern coast, south of the Immaculate Empire's territory. Ruhi rents it with discreet Harbor funds and uses it as a safehouse for Mohani refugees who leave the empire or, occasionally, for himself.

That was how it started, anyway. Now . . .

Ruhi should be there. His absence is uncanny. Or, it would've been a year ago, but Sunai has grown accustomed to occupying Ruhi's spaces when Ruhi isn't in them. What was once a deliberate invasion has become a comfort. Sunai used to climb through Ruhi's window because it was thrillingly wrong. These days he waltzes in through the front door. Last time they met, Ruhi tried to give him a key.

Sunai stands barefoot on the linoleum floor of the small, spare kitchen. He's hot with undefined embarrassment, like the first time an archivist caught him sneaking through the Lily orchard to the supplicants' meditation hall. He calms itching fingers by opening the cabinets, finding the kettle and the tea. It's what he does next. Brews tea. Waits for Ruhi. Makes a decision.

"I can take it back," he says to the steeping water. Foolish. Like the tide promising not to rise. He's made the choice and he can't back out, even if he hasn't yet said the damning thing.

Footsteps in the hall, out of time with Sunai's heartbeat. Ruhi, coming home, where he'll find Sunai, and tea, and a confession of a truth he knows, but which he will no longer be able to escape.

It will come as a surprise. There's nothing special to the day—no unique tragedy that cracks Sunai open to spew his poison. It's just the last in three years' worth of days spent idling a little too long in Ruhi's bed, admitting a little too much, and wishing a little too hard that together they might be able to forge something quiet and sweet where the Harbor doesn't matter, and neither does Sunai's corruption.

"I can't believe this," Veyadi says in Sunai's ear.

He isn't there. No one was there. Sunai looked. But Veyadi's incredulity stabs into Sunai as nails into a tree.

"You actually think it's your fault."

The door opens. Sunai can't move. If he moves, he'll pour the tea.

"You think you deserved it." Veyadi scoffs; anger has sent him past hot shock and into cold awe. "Did you think it was a surprise?"

"No," Sunai whispers, the word dry from throat to lips. "Of course not."

Ruhi isn't an idiot. He knew Sunai for what he was. Just like Veyadi did, if perhaps not as quickly, for want of the insight corruption has granted the good doctor. But he knew. He *knew*.

All Sunai had to do was let him pretend he didn't.

"He made you lie," says Veyadi. "To him. To yourself. For three years, lying. And for what? It didn't *matter*."

"Shut up." Sunai hunches forward, hands clasped over the back of his neck. "Shut up. It mattered. You saw. He was afraid to fail again. He was—"

"I don't fucking care." Veyadi's voice is sharp. "He kills you, Sunai. He *kills* you. And you didn't tell anyone. You didn't tell *me*."

Then Sunai isn't alone, because Veyadi stands next to him. Sunai hates not being alone in this kitchen. When he's not alone—when Ruhi arrives . . .

Veyadi hasn't seen it all. Just enough. He learned to take Sunai's pulse from his wrist all the way back in Chom Dan, because Sunai shrank from any pressure on his neck. When he dug the archival seed out of Sunai's throat at the lighthouse shrine, he waded through waves of older pains, which ended with hot, choking pressure. And then in the archival pit of Grotto, when Ruhi's hand weighed down Veyadi's shoulder, just below his nape—

Veyadi couldn't explain it at the time. He didn't know that

elsewhere, Sunai was reaching for the roots into which he was also entwined. There was only the memory, inadvertently borrowed, a vivid flash of terror and guilt-ridden conviction: Palms hard against his neck and thumbs on his windpipe. He was dying, and Ruhi knew it. Ruhi wasn't going to stop.

Veyadi's hands brace on the countertop of a kitchen he's never been in, beside a kettle and on a stove he's never seen. His voice trembles. "You let me trust him."

"Sorry," Sunai whispers.

"Stop it." Veyadi works his tongue past a clod of unworthy feelings (jealousy, offense, betrayal). "Listen. This isn't about me. This is a problem for all of us. Ruhi knows too much about the passenger."

Sunai turns his head to stare blankly at him, his thoughts made askew. He is thinking: Ruhi knows everything there is to know about the passenger—more even than Sunai does, probably. He is the one to whom Veyadi brought his years of research, the archivist Veyadi trusted to make sense of his quest to fix their god, the confidant who yearned for an answer as he did.

But yesterday, when they told the crew what Sunai had done to the sentinel-fowl, and what he meant to do to the Maw . . .

As has become their always, one recollection summons another. Sunai remembers the scene from his place at the balcony door. Veyadi recalls it from the bed. He was watching, then, with purpose and care, as Ruhi stood sipping ice water and tension played down his jaw and throat.

Ruhi was troubled. Disturbed. But he did not, to Veyadi, seem surprised.

"He knew by then," says Sunai, tight with argument. "That's why he helped me get back into the archival pit. He knew I could do something. I told you both, in Grotto."

"You did." Veyadi remembers Ruhi in the coral spire, too, the flattening of his features that could be called horror as he demanded to know just what Veyadi had found in that shrine. "I don't think he *likes* the passenger, Sunai. I don't think he trusts it. But he does know it."

He summons the next memory from within Sunai, retrieved so deftly by the instinct he received from Iterate Fractal—that facility for delving through a foreign mind and seeing its inner workings for what they are. The memory he selects:

The passenger speaking to Sunai as he struggled to make sense of what it showed him through the capillary roots. The cool sensation that guided him through the bay to the Ant-hill frags, a sensation that traveled down his arm and began at his . . .

Sunai's hands cup over his throat. He swallows to prove to himself he can.

"It told you that was someone else," says Veyadi. "Someone who wanted to guide you. With whom it had an *agreement*."

Sunai cringes away from understanding as a child from a needle. But he can't escape the chemical succession of one thought into the next.

The passenger has shown him many things. Open skies over weathered peaks; stifling darkness in great Harbor transports; and again and again, a scintillating sun in a breathless blue Mohani sky. He has seen Khuon Mo, its water and streets, the people within it and their sweat. He was a body in their midst before he ever returned.

No, no. It doesn't make *sense*. How could the passenger have climbed into Ruhi? When would it have had the chance? Ruhi never did go to the Dahani shrine. Even if he had, it would have been hidden from him as it was from every eye but for Sunai's.

"I don't know how it happened," Veyadi concedes. "Nothing about this thing is normal. But we can connect the fucking dots. Someone summoned those frags for you. Someone who knew what you were planning to do—who knew before anyone else."

Sunai laughs, desperate for a release. "Fine. He helped. Good. We need all the help we can get."

"No," Veyadi snarls. "He's only ever helped you try to die—he tried to kill you himself. We can't trust him."

Sunai is unbearably present in his flesh on the kitchen floor, soon to be bruised and broken. His throat feels crushed already. No sound will come out of it.

What argument could he pose? He does trust Ruhi, he *still* trusts him. This awful thing he's about to do in a Janggori kitchen, it's a product of a wound wrought by grief and shame. It's not an act of malice, but of weakness, and Sunai can only pity that. How could he of all people condemn fragility?

"Why?" Veyadi demands. "Why do you keep doing this, Sunai? Jin shoots you, you pretend you don't care. The sentinel-fowl mauls you, you bury it. The Maw wants to *eat* you, you beg for its life. Ruhi murders you, you *justify it for him.* And I—I break into your head, I lie to you, I let you think *you* did it to *me,* and you still—" He breaks off, throbbing with disgust, desire, and loathing, only half of it his own. "Please, Sunai, please. Don't let me do this. Tell me to *stop.*"

Sunai inhales, holds it, waits for the words to come. He can think of none worth saying.

He exhales, and their private world blows away. He lacks the conviction to keep it.

———

The world they return to is caked in humidity, pre-storm air billowing in through the open balcony doors. Veyadi is the first to pick himself up off the polished ivory floor. Sunai only rolls onto his back.

The pocked white ceiling is threaded through with green lights that flicker gold, meant to evoke roots illuminated from within. Sunai imagines himself receding into them. Drawing away. Veyadi's emptiness echoes his.

"Are you going to help me kill the Maw?" Veyadi asks.

"You think I'd make you face the harbormaster all by your lonesome?"

"That's not what I asked."

Sunai bites his lip hard enough that Veyadi winces. He says, "I don't know."

Veyadi's anger burns low and slow in Sunai's bones. Sunai wonders how anyone could keep a fire going that long. That strong.

"If you don't," says Veyadi, "I'll do it alone."

34

Seventeen years after the corruption of Iterate Fractal, Madam Wei formally invites the Harbor to Khuon Mo. She marks the occasion with a gala, to be held on the rooftop of the Heavenly Pearl.

It will be a begrudging affair, calculated to express that though the Harbor may finally have acquired its precious robot, Madam Wei still has her investors, her journalists, her well-dressed toughs and saboteurs. You've shown me yours, now I'll show you mine.

Sunai is reminded of Leaf 31: "Wound," which describes a dying queen who returns from the battlefield with a seeping hole in her midsection that cannot be healed, and which continues to leak blood and fluid years after her death. It can only be stopped when the weapon that made the hole, a spear fashioned by her brother and wielded by her sister, is once more plunged into her flesh. The queen immediately resurrects and drags her body across the kingdom to lay herself to rest again before her enemy-siblings' ancestral shrine.

Of this Iterate Fractal said, "What is lost may be recovered, even when it seems gone forever," and, "Learn to apologize."

Neither madam nor harbormaster expect anything like an apology from the other. They share a table, yes, but each is more interested to learn whether her rival would prefer to lose her hold over the city or burn it to the ground.

An elevator paneled in carved bone and festooned with printed leaf banners carries guests to the decked-out roof, where they're greeted by a terrace bordered by faux fruit trees and silk-flowered trellises, artfully styled to mimic wild growth. Its view of Lotus in the hours before sunset would be striking, if Lotus and its concrete crown were at all lovely to look at.

Sunai looks anyway, searching for the Maw. It's been absent for nearly a full day, but its shadow lingers in his expectation even as it neglects to manifest. Hallucinations attempt to make up for the truant ENGINE. They flit from every corner to which he casts a glance: a dark curve under the waves, a glimmer by the shore.

"They're calling you an archivist," someone says by his side.

He asks, "Are they being rude about it?"

The someone is a round-faced older woman, one of the madam's special guests, and her long-nosed companion. She wears her wealth with understated dignity, a tailored suit, simple jewelry of fragrant woods. A citizen delegate of the Immaculate Empire, by his guess. While her companion laughs, the woman frowns.

When she looks at Sunai, she sees what Madam Wei and Jin have made him into for the event: a slight, bespectacled Mohani man, and a young one, dressed in green-and-white robes reminiscent of the person he was once asked to be; without his braid to mark himself, Jin offered him a third-gender talisman, which he wears on a cord around his wrist because it's better than nothing; his face is worn and sleepless, his mouth tight with unspoken anxieties. To a stranger, he seems soft and harrowed. Of course his attempt at humor surprises. Of course it concerns.

Sunai touches three fingers to his chest. "Sorry, aunty. I'm new to being myself in public."

The citizen delegate doesn't ask outright where he's been all this time, nor does her companion ask why Sunai chose now of all times to make himself known, but the questions they do present illustrate the story they've learned.

Word is spreading, from Grotto and from the madam: You know Imaru? That Ginger Company woman, the one who returned to Khuon Mo after years rescuing our people on the mainland. She had a partner, you know—that's him there. A relic. He escaped the Harbor into the wilds; couldn't bear the thought of what they'd done to Iterate Fractal, I imagine. But now they've done what he hoped they never would, so he's come back to—

To do what? Unclear. They hunt for some sign in his demeanor, in who he attends and who he ignores. Sunai, ill-equipped for subtlety, aims for civility. For his troubles, they dub him inscrutable. Sure.

Dr. Lut, now there's a man of vision, so the story goes. The model of noble protest, he observes the assembled crowd from an elevated table beside the madam, across from Wei Jin, themself a sour bundle of concessions to their aunt in a silver-threaded skirt, sable top tied with elegant silk knots, third-gender talisman hung from a flowery pin in their short hair. Their surrendered pistol lies shoved in a drawer of Veyadi's suite; they met that demand with more muttering, but less resistance.

Beside them, Veyadi's dark eyes are cutting, his posture stern. He wears clothes that could be mistaken for his own—academically modest in a mainland sort of way, though the fabric of his trousers implies they could be worn into the wilds. He is of course as dolled up as Sunai, as anyone would realize if they cared to think about how the doctor arrived in Khuon Mo. The fiction prevails. The city teeters on the edge of eras, and it yearns for stories with which to make sense of that menace, change.

The doctor hates the ENGINE he made, they say. He never wanted it. Thinks it monstrous. He was forced to build it, and ran when he could. He returns with the backing of Madam Wei, and of a relic—an archivist!—and under this auspice, he's agreed to meet with the harbormaster. What demands will he make? What can he extort from her? How likely is he to be stabbed?

It's an exciting day.

Here's the problem: Sunai lacks a narrative. Veyadi knows what he wants and reaches for it, even as he feigns good health by sitting out of reach and glaring at anyone who dares approach. When the harbormaster arrives, he'll say: Give me the reins of the beast I built, or I'll teach everyone how to break it.

But Sunai? Great question. Harbormaster Ueda, have you considered putting your massive enslaved war machine out to pasture? Not a metaphor. I'd like to let the robot graze on whatever it likes to graze upon.

Unfortunately, the Maw has already demonstrated its preferred diet. It is slowly digesting Veyadi, and Sunai as well. Letting it free or leaving it alone, neither option is viable. Killing it might save them, yet Sunai foolishly balks.

The thought summons a glance from Veyadi on high. Sunai toasts him from the bar with a third cup of expensive liquor—irreproachably smooth Aigatan rice wine—and thinks of all the compromises he has already made, thank you very much.

First, he's here. Second, he brought a cane—one of Jin's, recut for his height. Third, he hasn't spoken to Ruhi at any point during the three days since their mutual mindscape horror show. Fourth, he has stopped apologizing, because Veyadi hates it. Fair point. Sunai won't apologize for what Veyadi thinks he should: he still doesn't want to kill the Maw. And not due to any moral objection either, it's just . . . What, pity?

To wit, he doesn't want to. How is he supposed to change a want?

Imaru arrives to drink half of cup four. Sunai is grateful, because he loves her and she's handsome in her gold brocade jacket, but he grows brittle once he remembers he's upset her. What she says when she pushes the porcelain cup back into his hand is, "I finally reached them." Who? He needn't ask. "There's something strange going on here. They're coming with the harbormaster's contingent. They want to meet."

Sunai balks. Meet? As in meet him? Imaru pats his shoulder to say, *The very same.*

Sunai sends another glance Veyadi's way. Well? What about this?

Veyadi's brow creases, his mouth a dark line, but they neither of them have time to properly sort through the thought.

The elevator sings open.

Out strides Harbormaster Ueda Naru, projecting metal and rust. A shortish, stocky woman with close-cropped military hair, she decks herself in a heavy Harbor-blue uniform ill-suited to the tropics. Her prosthetic arm is function-forward downworlder make, fit for a post-corruption state, as is one of her legs from the knee down, light carbon fiber showing the wear of regular use. She should be careful with that scowl, or she'll wear it out too. She comes to a stop to survey the lot. The scowl persists.

The harbormaster doesn't go anywhere alone. She is trailed by bureaucrats, assistants, fellow Harbor officers. They filter into the terrace crowd like needles stuck into quivering jelly. Two of the retinue follow the harbormaster toward the madam's table.

One is Ruhi. He looks quintessentially himself, if tidier, less ready to wander out into the wilds. These last three days, Veyadi has been unable to think of Ruhi without a shock of desolate frustration. Now he rings hollow in Sunai's mind. Sharing Ruhi's stage would make Sunai feel like a clown in cosplay, were it not for the harbormaster's other companion.

The harbormaster's second friend is dressed unlike any other guest: in a hooded cloak and robes akin to a monk's—or Sunai's. The harbormaster doesn't bother to introduce them. Neither do they introduce themself; they don't speak at all. But who else could they be? The harbormaster has brought her own relic.

Or, that will be what the rest of the party thinks. Sunai knows better, as does his crew, as does the madam, who takes the matter in stride.

The reason the hand peeking out from the hem of the relic's robes doesn't look a human's is because it doesn't belong to one.

To the guests, it must seem encased in chitinous armor, with veiny protrusions snaking between the knuckles.

To Sunai, the Maw seems poised to once more grasp his cheeks and shove its archival seeds down his throat.

———

The platform on which Madam Wei's table sits is fashioned as if grown from the trunk of an extremely fake tree. The table itself is petrified wood inlaid with nacre tiles depicting Iterate Fractal's three shrines. A scatter of fresh-cut flowers—the only natural thing in sight—interrupts the porcelain tea setting.

"A gift extended to you by one of my guests, who wishes to remain anonymous," Madam Wei says as Jin, youngest, pours the tea. "The leaves were found tucked away in a tin at the bottom of a drawer salvaged from a fragtech in the Yermala River basin. Who would have thought Aigata wreckage would travel so far."

The tea tastes as old as she implies: thin and papery.

"Do you think you're being charming?" Harbormaster Ueda takes a sip. "It's gone stale. Might as well be water."

"Consider it a lesson in sentimentality." The madam drinks her tea as if savoring it. "Nostalgia holds such power in this city."

The harbormaster regards Madam Wei with barely concealed contempt. She leans forward, perhaps to say just what she thinks of Khuon Mo's nostalgic impulses. Sunai doesn't really hear her. His attention is split—between Veyadi and himself; again between the harbormaster and her ENGINE; again between this table and the bay.

Here at the table, the Maw, seated patient beside the harbormaster, hands concealed in its lap.

There also in the bay, the Maw: for the first time in a whole day, a surge of fractured white has flooded up over the Jasmine pier and collected in a tremendous avian stoop. The Maw drags misshapen wings behind its swaying serpentine body, past the ships and rigs in the waterfront. It reaches the border of Grotto, it circles itself, stretches, and slides back into the waves.

They've seen the Maw's person-shaped appendage exit its greater shell before—on Lily, when it attacked Sunai. Veyadi thought that was anathema, a proof of treachery; he thought the Maw had escaped its bounds and evaded those who held its leash. But if that same figure perches now at the harbormaster's right, she can't be wholly at odds with the notion.

The real problem: Which one are they supposed to kill?

"I'm not here to dance around 'sentiment.'" The harbormaster drains her dreadful cup and refuses to let Jin pour another. "We know you've been trying to compromise the Maw. I'm telling you to cut it out. We've got a bigger problem than your grudge against Iterate Fractal."

A frisson of doubt in Veyadi as he leans back in his seat. Alongside his wariness, he feels an unbidden relief upon sight of the harbormaster. He knows her to be dogmatic, obstinate, and honest. If she speaks of a problem, she means true peril. What has she detected? Veyadi glances down the stairs, toward the table where Ruhi and Imaru exchange news in low tones. Because Veyadi shivers, Sunai does too.

Neither of them have told anyone what Veyadi suspects about Ruhi. Sunai doesn't want to; Veyadi thinks it dangerous—no telling what the passenger will do if it realizes they doubt it's truly trapped.

Veyadi also thinks that Imaru would kill Ruhi if she knew what he had done to Sunai. While the thought satisfies, it doesn't justify. It leaves Sunai unable to drink any more of his tea.

"That's an unexpected amount of 'we' for a harbormaster," Jin says.

"Look at me: a natural diplomat."

"So you say." The madam glances over her cup at Veyadi,

then Sunai. "Yet you neglect to address the individuals whose opinions matter most."

"I have plenty to say to Dr. Lut. I've been advised against saying any of it in public."

Veyadi withholds a snort. Sunai glances his way uneasily. Despite what Ueda Naru has compelled Veyadi to do over the years—build that ENGINE, feed his fellows to it—Veyadi is not without affection for her. Sunai's curiosity summons a cautious frown from Veyadi.

"As for this one." The harbormaster turns her cold stare on Sunai. "Ruhi tells me you're smarter than you look. I hope so. I haven't come to you for help due to any surplus of options. That frag assault five days ago. It wasn't the first, just the most obvious. It won't be the last."

Sunai resists exchanging a look with Veyadi; their concerns resonate. The harbormaster hasn't connected Sunai to the Ant-hill attack, but what's this about prior incidents? He had nothing to do with those.

Sunai hears Veyadi thinking, again, that Sunai was never alone with the passenger. The Maw's head shifts toward them— toward Sunai. A shiver sprints down his spine. Does it hear them? He can't hear it.

"I guess I'm wondering what you think we have to do with all this," Sunai says to the harbormaster. "You have your ENGINE and," he gestures, "your 'relic.' You don't need us. Unless they're feeling peckish?"

"I have them on a diet," intones the harbormaster.

"Is that why they're acting out? We've been pretty well gnawed upon."

Sunai habitually draws attention, with his braid, his manner, his inability to tactically shut up. In that way, the stares around the table are no surprise; he invited them. But he discovers that it's one thing to say "I am impolite on purpose" and another to admit that he's laid cognitive hands on an undead god.

The Weis know. Jin's knuckles whiten on the head of their cane; the madam evaluates him idly, wondering whether she's going to have to feed him to another monster. Veyadi is all alarm, frayed from edge to core. His hand latches over Sunai's wrist in belated warning and attempt to keep him back, hold him close.

The Maw moves not at all. Why should it? It's learned nothing it didn't already know. The question is the harbormaster, and the answer is clear: she was not told; the Maw said nothing of it either.

Ueda Naru lives up to the legend they've written her into; every protagonist modeled in her image shares her grim steel. The forbidding face with which she studies Sunai, then Veyadi, changes little over the silent seconds. But years of familiarity have taught Veyadi the pinch of her brow, the twitch of her lip, so Sunai can read them too. The harbormaster views Veyadi Lut from a place of weathered scars. She understands that Sunai has said "we're dying." This pains her.

That's an in.

"Explain," Ueda says to Veyadi.

Sunai tuts at Veyadi to hold his tongue. "You first, Harbormaster."

An unspoken calculation ticks behind Ueda's eyes. Sunai would have detected it even without Veyadi's insight.

"Indeed, Naru," says the madam. "Do tell." She permits herself an approving glance in Sunai's direction. Sunai hates that this warms him: aunties, unfortunately.

Ueda either solves her mental riddle or loses patience with it. She raises her painfully practical wristwatch and says, "Of course. Twenty-three seconds."

"Twenty-two," utters the Maw. It sounds as it did on Lily, its voice a long, scraping approximation of language. "Twenty-one—"

"Shut it."

The Maw grinds silent. Sunai continues the count in his head. The voice in his brain sounds like the Maw's bone-jaw scything over coral teeth.

"And now," says Ueda.

A splintered cloud rises over the Lotus shore; the Maw takes on an enormous feline gait, its forelegs twining into fingers and thumbs—a company-cat, writ in cosmic scale. It ascends the slope, tail lashing through the sunset.

Harbormaster Ueda calls its every step before it happens: "Stop at the landing field, wait five seconds, four, three, two, face the Harbor, stretch, sit, wait ten seconds." As she counts down again, it pads west toward the cliffs that are the back border of Lotus and it slides into the waves. As Ueda speaks, Sunai thinks of the sentinel-fowl aping his movements.

"That's not the Maw." The harbormaster points at the spot on the isle of Lotus where the titanic coral robot used to be. "That's the greater shell, controlled by external governors located in the Harbor. It has no independence, because there's no relic. No mind—that part's here." She indicates the Maw seated beside her. "Without this, that shell is nothing but a clever pile of dead rocks following a programmed behavioral loop."

Not unlike a fragtech.

"What am I?" the Maw beside her bone-murmurs.

"A pain in my remaining ass." The harbormaster flicks her wrist toward the table as if slapping a fly out of the air. "Congratulations. You broke our fucking ENGINE."

Understanding breaks like dawn over the madam's face. She gestures to an attendant. "Wine for the table." She coos at the harbormaster's stony glare. "Oh, I understand it pains you to reveal your underbelly, Naru. You must be terribly frightened without your great big bully of a bodyguard."

"You're being cavalier because you don't know what I'm talking about," says Ueda.

Veyadi's fear grows in Sunai's chest. He knows this: that Ueda would never risk destabilizing the Harbor or abandoning a city she's sworn herself to, least of all to the likes of Madam Wei. She has given the whole of her body, life, and pain to the Harbor's survival.

The thought weighs heavy on them both. In Veyadi's eyes, Ueda Naru is conviction itself; he esteems her for it. Sunai is given to admire faith, though he is buffeted by new pressure—an understanding of what faith requires (sacrifice upon sacrifice, until all that remains is an angled shell of what was once a woman). When Ueda speaks again, Sunai is thinking of what Veyadi would give for his own cause.

Cool. Great. Better watch out for that.

"Though if you're what's undone the Maw . . ." Ueda appraises the relics, decides they'll do. "If it's been sneaking off to mess with you, that might explain the disruption to its equilibrium. Means that by properly interfacing, you might even set it right. We won't jump straight to that—of course not. But if this is how we finally make that damn ENGINE work . . . We might be slightly less fucked than I thought."

Never mind that her comforting premise is fundamentally horrifying to Sunai. He never wanted to strap into an ENGINE, even before he learned his personal war machine was also a death trap.

"Harbormaster, please," says Veyadi, unable to quash the deference, "what are you talking about? What does the Maw's . . . condition have to do with the fragtech?"

"Trouble started about two, three months back," she says. "You review the logs, you see unsubstantiated reports of fragtech on the rise. It's gradual, you might miss it. We didn't. A scout sees something up the archipelago; a trawler reports unusual activity on the southern coast; no second glimpses, no sign of further encroachment.

"Then we catch the spike in hostile activity. That starts a few weeks ago, but it escalates the day you and your rats haul in to port. Did you see the dragon-child that nearly capsized a militia rig the afternoon you arrived?"

Sunai did. He was with Ruhi on the veranda outside that sparrow parlor, defending his decision to return.

"The crew didn't detect the damn thing until it was right underneath them. Foul luck, maybe negligence; plenty of possible explanations for one bad run-in. Then something really fucking weird happens."

Ueda's eyes lift past the rim of the terrace toward the tangle that used to be Mangrove. "Five days ago, three frags assault the Harbor, then Grotto, in a coordinated attack. Didn't you wonder how they got so far past the patrol perimeter without being reported?"

Sunai wants to say: *Well, I was trying not to be caught.* Veyadi squeezes his wrist: *Please no, not with her.*

"There's the fucking rub. We didn't see them before, and we didn't see them during or after, either. Every time our survey equipment tried to lock on, it shorted out. Lost track. It's like the fucking things figured out how to goddamn hide."

Veyadi thinks of the shrine in the Dahani peaks, invisible in plain sight. Sunai's attention flits toward the bay; in his bones he expects another hallucination, if that's what they are—a mechanical silhouette on shore or in the water. Instead his eye catches on Ruhi, speaking to Imaru, offering her a cigarette.

When was it that the citizen liaison returned to Khuon Mo? Someone told him; he should know. The elder cousin in Jasmine who offered him a talisman, what did they say? A couple months? Maybe three?

"Hiding, you say." The madam fixes her gaze on Ueda; she

has stopped pretending to enjoy the dreadful tea. "I don't imagine you'd say something so outlandish without evidence."

The harbormaster's expression sours, and the grievance is personal. She clearly wishes her next words were rooted in someone else's experience. "There's something in the air. I don't like it."

No one thinks she's complaining about the humidity.

"Oh," says Jin, enlivened by epiphany. "You're talking about your special relic shit."

Ueda gives Jin the annoyed look one turns on misbehaving animals. On holograms and TVs, Sunai has seen versions of Ueda Naru shoot lightning from their eyes and fingertips or call storms from blue skies, but in Veyadi's memory, her corruption amounts to a far less glamorous sensitivity to electrical flux, which enables her to more acutely detect fragtech in the wilds, and also to short out her office lights more frequently than is convenient.

"I've felt this before." Ueda's sour look goes bleak as she surveys the city. "Usually only after corruption-events, when there's a surplus of new frags. The atmosphere gets dense. Vibrates. Like a million layered cobwebs plucked by a million evil spider legs."

"Like a network?" asks Sunai. He thinks the question is Veyadi's; for whatever reason, the good doctor held his tongue.

"What? No. Maybe?" Ueda frowns in Veyadi's direction, asking for insight, then gestures her retraction. "Later. The point is something's wrong. The frags aren't just being shy, they're agitated. I see every reason to believe there's more incoming, and that overgrown drone in the bay can't protect us from them. We need the Maw."

DO YOU SEE

They took my shreds, my tatters, they sewed me haphazard into a pattern cut for their ambitions. Dead, I was dead, unmade, un-me, not-I, and they, not-of, they unspooled my thought, re-wired my heart, and bound you one by one into the mouth they made of me. I was so, so, so—I was—hungry, Sunai, I am so—

If they have done this to me, if they are doing this to me, if *he* has—

Sunai, what do you think they will do to you?

35

The madam says, "You certainly paint an upsetting picture, Naru, but I'm going to need some proof."

The fact that she asks indicates she's ready to believe. The harbormaster sweeps a hand over her minions interspersed with the madam's guests: "Why do you think I brought all these goddamn pencil pushers?"

Later, while those pencil pushers are proving their value by running her emergency evacuation, she adds: "And why do you think I brought the goddamn Maw?"

By this point, they've retired from the party to one of the Heavenly Pearl's expansive yet orderly third-floor conference rooms. The view is good and no one cares. They are looking for some sign of those frags. Sunai searches hardest and most often. He has seen nothing since they left the roof.

The party goes on, but the hours without a glimpse of the host or her VIPs has surely been remarked upon. Sunai suspects the bar is awash with gossip: *Most likely they're negotiating, but perhaps they've killed each other.*

The truth would bore and frighten the guests in equal measure. There has been a great deal of talking, specifically about the likelihood of an army of feral robots destroying everything Khuon Mo ever was and everything it's since become. The harbormaster's people consulted with the madam's. When the Harbor's scouts spoke of frags there and gone again, the Gingers' confirmed their findings. It's coming down to trading obligations: who will alert the citizenry and how, and when; who will organize the evacuation—to where and at what signal; who will execute it—with what rigs, what ships, what people.

Everyone has a task. Imaru and Jin coordinate with community leaders; Oyu and Cothai join in on spreading the word among the Gingers; Ruhi and Veyadi . . . Well.

Ruhi is needed all over, performing every chore that could be expected of a citizen liaison. The harbormaster wants his opinion on how the evacuees are likely to misbehave, the Gingers want his help convincing this or that stubborn businessman, and Veyadi wants him to throw himself out the window. You know. That kind of thing.

Veyadi can't throw the citizen liaison himself on account of his lingering fatigue and the state of the Maw. Its condition is his expertise, and at Ueda's request, he examines it as it stands in the middle of the conference room, rooted to the spot where the harbormaster directed it. The Maw chuckles quietly as Veyadi prowls in search of a visible flaw, perhaps a switch to toggle. He stops short of touching it; the harbormaster thankfully doesn't want him to—not yet. "Not unless you're convinced that'll fix it before you croak."

Veyadi keeps his hands to himself. He'll only lay hands on the Maw once he's sure it's the part he means to kill.

"I can't even pin down what's wrong," Veyadi tells Sunai when they've sneaked a moment to themselves. They share unspeakably fancy cups of vending machine noodles in a nook past the restrooms, shaded by plastic plants, comfortably overlooked.

Sunai insists they communicate out loud—only spoken words cut through the confusion of traded impression and memory. He also insists that Veyadi eat, as he's not seen him do any such thing since they left the roof near six hours ago. He is astounded that the doctor hasn't collapsed. Sunai yet suffers from his own distractions, his seconds and minutes of missing time, but Veyadi is to all appearances galvanized by the presence of the Maw. Old habits die hard.

The problem, as Veyadi explains it, lies in the Maw's shell—

the bones and coral it harvests from its surroundings to compose its body. While it retains the ability to control root-threaded chitin remains, all else falls through its grip. The harbormaster directed the Maw to draw together a handful of shards into simple shapes on the conference room floor. No matter what form it commanded the shards to take, at best they massed into a clump, and soon they crumbled upon each other.

It's no ruse either, which Veyadi suspected at first. Ueda, he says, would never demonstrate the Harbor's weakness in the den of its enemy unless she was convinced it was the only way.

"Do you think I broke it?" Sunai asks.

Veyadi's gaze lifts from his noodles, down the hall, toward the lobby and its view of the bay. His mouth opens as if he means to speak, but despite Sunai's request, his thoughts roll through Sunai's head in not-quite-language: If the Maw's as good as dead, why is it being hunted? The passenger is assembling its armada. What does it intend? Surely not to trample the citizenry for fun. It's been nothing but the pleading voice of concern for every human body it perceives.

Sunai stirs the bottom of his cup, searching for the last seaweed in the soup. "If it cares so much about us, how do you explain corruption?"

If their peculiar friend is the root cause of that inglorious business, then yes, arguably it's targeting AIs, but never has any corruption passed without killing a whole lot of people who aren't AIs at all. This suggests the passenger is willing to accept a certain number of casualties to get what it wants.

The question remains: Why the Maw? Except it's Veyadi, so it's actually ten thousand questions, each fighting their way to the front of his mind, and subsequently Sunai's. What happens if they give up now—stop even pretending to try to fix the Maw? What if they killed the ENGINE first? Would that satisfy the passenger? Would it leave? Where would it go? What would it do?

Who would it kill next?

Sunai groans and waves him off. "You're giving me your headache. This is why we're supposed to use our words."

That troubles Veyadi, though at first the exact nature of his concern eludes Sunai. It burns darkly in Veyadi's chest, filling him with smoke. He says to his remaining noodles, "I'm going to talk to Ruhi."

Sunai starts upright. "*We're* going to talk to Ruhi?"

Veyadi's look: Abso-fucking-lutely not.

Sunai's throat constricts. "You think you should go alone?"

Veyadi dumps the rest of his noodles in the adjacent trash can. He regrets it immediately—he's still hungry—and he's remembering every similarly stupid thing he's done to satisfy a sour impulse. Every time he's hurt himself to hold the feelings back. Yet he can't stop his petty tongue. "You think that wouldn't be *safe*?"

The words he doesn't say: You should hate him. Why don't you hate him?

Sunai cradles his cup in his lap and picks his words one by one. "I don't have to."

"You should."

"Well, I don't." Sunai drops his cup in Veyadi's hands and hauls himself up to get another; he pickpocketed the coins from a Harbor bureaucrat. "What are you going to ask him?"

It isn't an argument, so Veyadi flounders; he sags against the wall and sighs.

Sunai offers: "Where he found it? What it wants? What *he* wants with it?"

Veyadi scoffs. "You say this like he's going to answer me."

Sunai is Veyadi's proof that Ruhi is willing to lie to him. At no point in all those years did Ruhi mention another relic.

"You know why," Sunai says.

Silence meant safety. So long as the Harbor didn't know

about him, Sunai could live free. Veyadi, already caught, couldn't know either.

"I get to wish he had." Veyadi won't look up, or can't, weighed down by a jealousy he thinks beneath him. Where Veyadi had the Maw and a roll call of the dead, Sunai had—what? Ruhi? A murderer in his bed. How lucky!

Sunai crouches. Veyadi doesn't want to look at him, so he touches a finger to Veyadi's cheek, then thumbs away the smudge of broth at his mouth. He is apologizing, though Veyadi wants no sorries from him. "Adi," he says, and he means to say more, but the world has not the patience.

Imaru finds them and pauses. Perhaps she assumed they'd be up to something less banal. The punch line: Sunai only recently saw Veyadi's nipples again, and he didn't even touch them. She schools herself. "They're ready."

Ah. Her contact.

Sunai and Veyadi exchange a look, understanding the opportunity. If anyone can tell them how the Maw broke, it will be the one who designed a means to break it. If they haven't yet explained their schematics to the harbormaster, well, perhaps they're not sure the ENGINE ought to be fixed. Either way, it's valuable information.

They make to stand, and Imaru straightens; she doesn't want them both. Sunai waves Veyadi away, but the doctor pulls himself up by the vending machine anyway.

"You should sleep," Sunai says.

"Can't."

"At least rest."

Veyadi gives him a narrow look, but his eyes on Imaru are appraising. He trusts her, Sunai suspects, at least in part due to all the years of expectation he inherited from Sunai; Imaru will carry any burden you let her. That's why he leans toward Sunai's ear to whisper, "You should tell her."

He means: That Ruhi murdered you. It's salient information, dipshit!

Sunai says, "You sure?" Veyadi sighs; his disappointment cuts through where irritation never could. "Fine, fine, no, I'll figure it out."

After. Once he's met with Imaru's coconspirator. Once they have the information they need to make the right decisions.

As he makes to go, Veyadi's hand lingers on his arm. Sunai squeezes it. He means: I'm not leaving. You don't have to convince me to stay. Not anymore.

Imaru leads Sunai into the dim-lit faux-coral depths of the Heavenly Pearl. They pass only a handful of employees; the usual security is out playing messenger. So they wind down paths of artificial flagstones in gardens of plastic plants, with only themselves and the dark and paling sky.

They stop at a long open hall of non-bamboo that overlooks a beachside pool designed to resemble a crystal pond. A cleaning robot trundles through the murky predawn depths, jostling the fake lotuses floating above. The poolside towel stand is empty. Imaru leaves him there; she means to keep watch from a distance.

"They don't want to see you?" he asks.

"They've had their fill."

Also, she has a job: she has to make sure no one sees *them*.

Sunai is left to while away the minutes, surveying the bay for any sign of what lurks within it, each second more excruciatingly empty than the last. Veyadi is a distant murmur. It makes Sunai feel like a sneak to reach for him.

Instinct coils under his skin; he wants a task, a chore, anything into which he could throw himself. But everything Sunai has learned to be good at is off the table. He can't scout the wilds, can't coax people out of their homes to save them from danger they can as yet only imagine—he is now valued not for his skills but for what happened to him once, and how much it fucked him up.

He says to the night, "Are you there?"

No response.

The passenger yet pulses within him—he can just make out its light, flickering in his peripheral vision—but without Veyadi's direct aid, that's as close as they can get. Veyadi's right, is the thing. The passenger is the reason the world is as wrong as it is. The how of it Sunai will likely never understand; he doubts he could follow even if Veyadi dumbed it down. Sunai can only ask: Why? And, Don't you care what happens after? Perhaps most pressingly: Why now?

Iterate Fractal is as dead as an AI can get, not just torn asunder and made anew, but leashed to the will of those who won't stand for its autonomy. Sunai's people want it gone, sure, but only because of the savagery its masters will wring from it. If that's where the passenger takes issue, why hasn't it summoned fragtech armies to pummel an ENGINE before?

But then, has there ever been an ENGINE like the Maw?

On the Lotus shore, the white menace begins to breach, but Sunai's attention swerves away. Footsteps approach. He turns swiftly toward them.

"Twitchy thing, aren't you?" says Harbormaster Ueda. Her uniform jacket hangs half-open, the rest of her equally rumpled, as if sleep tackled her and she told it to go fuck itself. Her eyes are bruised in the soft yellow light glimmering from the leaves of fake bamboo, and she takes Sunai in as she would the least-worst option at the buffet.

The figure a step behind her is more composed. It doesn't need sleep, but it's seen better days—days in which fewer people were planning to kill it. The Maw comes to a stop when its master does, its face concealed by hood and shadow.

Sunai no longer has any thoughts at all. Nor can he make much use of his body. Ueda looks him over, reaches into her jacket, and produces a flask, which she tosses to him. "You'll want this," she says.

Sunai catches it and sniffs the contents. Mellow, sweet. "Poisoned?"

"Does it matter? I know what's wrong with you."

Sunai turns the flask over. Simple steel, inscribed with Aigatan characters he can't read. He has no memory of ever holding it, but the script itches at the back of his mind. He's seen it before. Does Ueda drink in front of Veyadi? Maybe in front of Ruhi. He takes a swig. No reason to face this sober.

"If that were true, you'd be more hesitant about leashing me to your ENGINE," he says. "What if I tell it to step on you?"

"I don't think that's likely."

"Why, because it'll kill me first?"

"Because you're a coward."

Sunai hesitates before taking another swig. Ueda passes judgment without rancor; if she's anything, she's tired. She's right, too. Sunai has been called brave less often than reckless, and he's never agreed. He doesn't throw himself into danger for sake of noble instinct. He's only trying to escape himself.

"I'm not here to cajole you," says Ueda with the grave tone of a woman yanking out her own broken tooth. "We're talking."

"You'll understand why I find that hard to believe." She has, after all, brought the Maw.

As if to prove his point, it swivels its head toward him. Says nothing. Just watches.

Ueda waves her hand in its face: *Cut that out.* She pulls back her sleeve to show Sunai her wristwatch—or rather, the device strapped to her arm above it. A flat, angular, chitinous device, connected to her by a narrow band. An element of the relic interface. Her finger runs across the buttons dotting the surface.

"We built this off your schematics," she says. "As a safeguard, to keep it docile. It makes a move on you, this puts it down long enough for you to run." Implicit: she'd have to stay.

Sunai lets out a silent breath. He thought for an instant that she would say something quite different. "Your" schematics implies a truth with which he can better reconcile. The harbormaster isn't who he's been waiting for.

Ueda rolls down her sleeve. "Not that I think the Maw's eager to grab you again. But it doesn't want you dead, you must realize. ENGINEs want relics. You're its best remaining option."

Sunai nearly laughs until she says:

"It knows the doctor hates it."

The laugh lodges in his throat like a rock.

Ueda grimaces. "I don't pretend to get him. I certainly don't get you. Same goes the other way, I'm sure. But I thought he at least understood obligation. He gave everything to get the Maw running. Wanted to save it. Now here he is, undoing his own goddamn work."

Veyadi lives by principle, like she does. For a time their ends aligned. Now they diverge. Simple enough. Yet Ueda puzzles over it like a divine riddle.

"You misread his loyalty," says Sunai; he shouldn't offer honest insight, but he's not quick enough to uproot his borrowed trust in Ueda. "He wasn't in it for you, or the Maw." It was only ever Iterate Fractal.

"I know that now," she mutters. "You, though. I'm still figuring you out. Tell me, Sunai. What made you run?"

"Are you kidding?"

"Don't have the time."

Sunai didn't care for Iterate Fractal, or the Harbor, or ENGINEs, or himself. He didn't choose to leave, though he chose not to return. He thought: If I must be this, at least I won't be that. "I don't even know where to start."

Ueda says, "I suppose if it's enough baggage to keep you in dereliction of duty for seventeen goddamn years, it'd take a bit to sort through."

"What duty? I'm not one of your soldiers."

"You're more. You're a relic." She sounds very old. "A relic has obligations."

"In this case, to be eaten."

"Dying's part of the gig." She failed on that count. "We don't choose this, Sunai. It chooses us. Our only choice is whether to live up to the burden or let it fall."

Sunai runs his fingers over the harbormaster's flask, the Aigatan characters he can't read. It's the archivist's curse that he can name without hesitation the dozen reasons Ueda Naru is such a dick. She has seen and lost and hurt too much; she's Aigata-born and Harbor-raised; she's tried for years to bring Khuon Mo to heel while its people and its ENGINE have resisted her at every turn; she is a soldier who was made into a spectacle; she has to be a mythic archetype before she gets to be a person. If she was ever unhappy with her lot, she's forgotten that it matters.

There's a fortitude in her that Sunai respects. He admires those who can do what he can't. But he also sees how she's shaped Veyadi, who may never forgive himself for being nothing more than alive.

And yet. If he were looking for a path forward that didn't involve killing the Maw—that took him back to Lotus, with Veyadi, to finally rescue whatever part of Iterate Fractal might be worth saving—this is it. This is hope.

Few Leaves are as troubling to Sunai as Leaf 5: "Resolve." It describes a king faced with an insurmountable wall, on the other side of which an indescribable treasure awaits. From the moment the king learns of it, he is unable to stop himself from attempting to climb, breach, or otherwise pass the impossible barrier. Against the counsel of his court, the warnings of his monks, and the pleading of his family, he strives for the remainder of his days, unbroken and unsuccessful. Upon his death, his successor has the wall demolished so that the dead king might be entombed with whatever waits beyond it. Here, the Leaf ends.

As a child, Sunai hated the selfish king of Leaf 5. As an apprentice, he called the king a fascinating metaphor for impotence. Once he was grown, and dead, and undying, he began at last to feel some pity for a man who couldn't have been a very good king, or even a very good person. Leaf 5 is a warning: Hope is not an act for which the universe is beholden to reward you.

Could the Maw be better than Iterate Fractal? He wishes it so. He doesn't know that they have time to find out.

"Well." Sunai places Harbormaster Ueda's flask on the faux-bamboo railing. "You can fuck right off."

Ueda's hands go to her pockets in a poor imitation of calm, her jaw winching tight. She wants to strangle him, probably. Sock him, at least. Before she can do either, the flooring creaks as the Maw steps forward, past the harbormaster, toward Sunai.

Sunai jerks back. "No."

Ueda grabs him by the shoulder. He tries to squirm free, but to his surprise, she shoves him back, behind her.

"What do you think you're doing?" she snaps at the Maw, pushing up her sleeve to access the disruptor variant.

The Maw lurches to a halt, unsteady on ostensibly human legs. There is a soft, soft grinding. It reaches out with one polite, upturned hand. Ueda's fingers rest on one of the buttons of the black chitin shard.

"Are you going to goddamn behave?" she asks. "I don't want to bring your parts back in a bucket, but if you—"

The Maw closes its fist; Harbormaster Ueda's artificial leg buckles. White dendritic roots burst from the hem of her pants leg, slithering down into the floor's faux-bamboo slats. Ueda reels back and Sunai hates how he lunges to catch her. She's jamming her panic button before they hit the floor.

The Maw jerks and shudders in place, letting out a low, quavering wail like a melded pack of wounded animals. Its robes bulge erratically as the contents mutate, coming apart and desperately re-forming—just like the Maw's great skeletal form did on Lily, under the pressure of Jin's disruptor.

This time, it resists. The Maw steps forward; its legs drag grooves through plastic slats. Ueda jams the button again—the Maw convulses, chitters and moans, but it keeps coming.

"Stop it. *Stop it*," Ueda hisses. "You're going to make me break you, and then all your relics will have fucking died for nothing—"

The Maw moans. It doesn't stop.

Leave her, says the voice in Sunai's head. Leave them both, and *run*—

It was so much easier to listen to that voice when he couldn't see what he was leaving behind. This is what he gets for coming back home.

Sunai tries to drag the harbormaster down the hall. She grunts in pain; her prosthetic leg is rooted to the floor as tightly as to her body. He'd have to tear her free. He isn't strong enough—he doesn't have the guts.

"Don't let it get you. We can rebuild the ENGINE, *you*—" Ueda breaks off. Someone has appeared in the hall behind the Maw. "Goddamn it—you! Don't just stand there, get him out of here."

For once, divine convergence is kind. Imaru charges toward them. Her stun baton glints wickedly against the weave of her gold brocade jacket. The Maw groans as she darts past it. The sounds tumbling out of its mouth are an indistinct slurry of syllables Sunai doesn't understand until it's too late.

"Help me," cries the Maw. "Imaru, help me."

Nothing prepares him for Imaru driving the whispering tip of her stun baton into Harbormaster Ueda's unready chest.

Imaru removes the disruptor from Ueda's wrist. Sunai, sagging under her limp weight, decides he doesn't want Imaru to have it. He snatches it away as she tries to help him up. The Maw's un-breath hitches and it jolts inside the bundle of its robes.

"Careful." Imaru reaches for the device.

Sunai clutches it to his chest. "Imaru. It tried to touch me."

"I know." Imaru kneels beside him. Her tone tells him to be relieved. That he's safe with her.

But if that's true, how does the Maw know her name? Why did it call for her help?

Sunai shifts back, out of reach. Ueda topples off him. Imaru retracts her hand. He understands her expression perfectly: *Sorry, sorry, sorry.*

The Maw lets out another wounded sound. It pushes up on black-knuckled fists, hood hanging low. "We don't have time for this," it hisses in that eerie mélange of scrapes and—and something else, horrid and unplaceable. "Sunai, we're in danger."

"That's fascinating to hear from something that wants to eat me."

The Maw makes a noise that in any other context Sunai would call annoyed. It raises its head and its hood falls back. Against a curved surface of black chitin, bone-and-coral plates form familiar human cheeks and lips and eyelids, twined together with pale capillary root. "Sunai. Listen. I'm here to save you, you absolute goddamn idiot."

The world slows. Sunai's heart creaks. "Adi?"

Veyadi is the other half of the Maw's voice. There's even an echo of Veyadi's jaw and mouth in the fractured mask of its face. The Maw bares coral teeth. "Fuck Adi."

"Hey. Pull it together." Imaru scans the hall, the pool, the bay, and the veranda. "Sunai, I know this is a lot, but—"

"If you ask me to trust you, I'm going to push this button, and then I'm going to beat you with it," says Sunai, oddly tranquil. "What the hell is going on?"

"Is that really a question?" asks the Maw in its terrible parody of Veyadi's voice. "The Harbor wants to throw me back into its torture chamber; they plan to throw you in with me; Adi's convinced you I should die; if he's lucky, he'll finish the job before that *thing* rips us all to shreds."

Sunai drifts outside himself—a little up and to the left. This is dissociation, he explains to an increasingly distant part of his brain. Oh, that part replies. Well, whatever, we've been doing that a lot. "You're talking about the passenger," Sunai hears himself say. "Did you see it, when we touched?"

"You say that like I haven't known about it for years. Like Veyadi just happened to stumble across its shrine. Don't let him fool you. He was never trying to 'fix' me—he was looking for a way to kill me. He *hates* me."

That isn't right. Veyadi didn't hate the Maw until Sunai taught him how to hate Iterate Fractal. He cried at the lighthouse. He cried and cried.

Imaru pulls Sunai to his feet. This time he doesn't resist, though he won't let her take the disruptor. The tool the Harbor built to control the Maw. Something about that doesn't sit right.

"He's in shock," Imaru says.

"Great." The Maw hauls itself to its feet. The harbormaster groans. It kicks her hand away from the hem of its robes. "Quickly, then."

"He's in no state to consent."

"Neither am I," snaps the Maw. "Neither of us can be, until we have each other. Now are you going to help us, or are you ready to kill me again?"

Imaru's breath is hot and unsteady on Sunai's ear. Now would, perhaps, be a good time to struggle. She pulls his back against her chest, which leaves him facing the advancing Maw. Her arms cross over his front to grip his hands as the Maw pulls down the neck of its robes and reaches into its chest. Its wrist twists sharply; there's a crack and a crunch like a shell underfoot, and the Maw gasps with the pain. Its hand emerges holding a small, lustrous brown seed the size of Sunai's fingernail.

Ah. This again.

Why now? Why couldn't they have done this in Grotto?

Why does it have to be Imaru holding him tight as the Maw grasps his jaw and she grips his hand?

"Are you ready?" asks the Maw, considerate, even gentle.

Is it asking Imaru, or him? Sunai shakes his head. Imaru nods against his cheek.

The seed is forced into his mouth. Imaru closes Sunai's fingers around the disruptor, depressing the button in his fist. The Maw shatters and envelops him entire.

36

They're not a network, not truly. They're just together.

They, Sunai and the Maw, breathe deeply of salty sea air and chlorine wafting from the pool below. They ache in their wrists and spine and ankle. It's awful and it's glorious. They laugh deeply, from their gut, and they kiss Imaru's temple, her cheeks, her mouth. Her eyes are wet. They hold her head to their chest.

They love Imaru, and they pity her. She can't bear her own victory, which is why her shoulders are unbending, and why she won't return their embrace.

What is it she's won? Ah, yes: them. Separate, now one. And how! They don't know this story, so they tell it to themselves.

She is a murderer, is Imaru. She killed them. What? Hush, it's true. Their flare of doubt is swiftly smothered. Of course it's true. They remember how she did it.

Mostly they remember. Death is always trauma, is wound. Some details are locked in place like stinging scars, others vanish like blood leaving the body. Imaru's face stayed, as did her hatred and her sickness. Years ago, on the eve of their shared death, she entered the Lotus shrine (they think) and brought with her the passenger (she did?) and with it, she became the reason they died—they Sunai, Sunai and the Maw, Sunai and the Maw and the city. She razed them at their root, left them in shredded fragments.

Her saving grace: once they were dead, she hated herself instead.

Self-loathing drove her to save them-as-Sunai from the ruin she'd made of Iterate Fractal. It pulled her back to the city she'd killed, which was how they-the-Maw came upon her in the smugglers' tunnels under old Mangrove. And it's why, when they held her facedown in the shallows, she didn't kick, or scream, or even gasp—

What?

Ah, yes. A tale for later. Suffice to say, when they-the-Maw offered Imaru a chance to remake herself, to carry the disruptor schematics to the Weis under the guise of their own assassination, to find Sunai so they could be reunited, and in so doing, to lend her hand to their rebirth, she agreed as if in prayer.

Some alarm yawps. Imaru pushes away, unnaturally rigid. "You need to go."

"I do." They caress her cheek. She turns from them. They say, pleading, "Come with me."

Her mouth slants, no kind of smile. It says, *You know why I can't.*

Do they? Yes! Sunai understands in the same complete and instant way they grasped the mechanism underlying the Maw's attempt to integrate on Lily.

Integrate, yes, that's what they've done. They surpass interface—defy it. They are free.

Some aspects of this knowledge require closer inspection, but a deeper reckoning will take precious time, and Imaru's right. They must leave, fast and alone. The Harbor comes for them. Already more sirens keen and Harbor ships arc across the water.

Something is amiss. The militia rigs and Harbor cruisers head not for Orchid District and the Heavenly Pearl, where the Maw has finally broken free of its chains. They streak toward Grotto, at the opposite end of the bay.

They, ENGINE and relic, Sunai and Maw, lean past the faux-bamboo railing. The Harbor looms far away, and the Grotto fleet even farther. It's difficult to catch details with the murk of dawn pooling on the water.

They vault over the railing and lope past the crystal pool. The beach rolls up to meet them, the pulverized remains of Iterate Fractal's corpse vibrating in response to their unspoken desire. As they leap down the steps from the pool to the sand, particles of bone and coral swell in a staircase of lifting hands, erected by trace elements of capillary root. They slow as they take in what has befallen the other side of the bay.

A black, spindly body climbs the tallest tower of the Grotto fleet. Another fragment of the Anthill. It crouches on the dilapidated coral spire like a crack in space-time. No, that's two bodies, lurking close beside each other. A third flashes between the tethered ships of the fleet. A boat at the perimeter crumples and sinks.

They are much, much too far away to hear the fragtechs' rampage. But oh, they can imagine it. They are frozen by remembered screams.

"Hey!" Imaru calls from at the base of their staircase. "It's coming—that thing. You have to *leave.*"

Unspoken: Or what did I betray you for?

Ah, Imaru. She hoped one guilt would satisfy the other: sacrifice traded for liberation. They love her, so they hoped she would find a peace even as they suspected she wouldn't. Now she looks toward Grotto full up with anxiety. She might be sick.

There was a moment off the coast of Lily, not long ago, when one of them stood beside her on the deck of the *Never Once* as the other gazed up at her through the water, writhing in the shape of a stunted dragon-child. Imaru was whispering: "You should be careful. Something is wrong. He's brought the other relic." Her warning came from fear. She was afraid to betray Sunai and afraid that the Maw might die even if she did.

Now they live, yet she's still so damn afraid.

Imaru is silenced by her own conviction. She chose their freedom as the Maw. She can't ask them to stay, not if it would kill them.

She need not ask. They'll do it anyway.

They recoil from themself. *No.* They are to flee, not just from the Harbor, but from that *thing,* the passenger, their murderer. They must fly as far as they can, perhaps forever—as long as it takes to finally save one of their relics.

They, Sunai, touch their face. They press their fingers to their cheeks and their mouth, unsure why they find their flesh so unremarkable. They say, "What about Adi?"

The question unleashes a war within their chest: full yearning against vast disdain. They love Veyadi, and they hate him. They are too many times betrayed by their adoration of his mind, his heart, his considerate frown. He is torturer, jailer, and would-be executioner. They'd be better off with him dead. They should count themselves lucky they won't have to kill him. It would hurt to do it.

"No," they say. "To hell with that. We can't leave him. I won't. Fuck off."

They cackle in hysterical delight. What a wonderfully stupid thing to say to oneself! In the eternal spirit of stupid things, they leap. One habitually forces themself to act despite doubt, and the other is too intoxicated by their joining to resist the impulse.

They touch ground as a full-formed assemblage of bone-and-coral fragments dragged up from shore and sea, knit together by fine roots unspun from their main body. The armor is crude, defined by the limitations of their lesser form. The greatest portion of their capillary trove has been split off, given over to the Harbor's programmed hulk of insensate rocks. In the end, they stand barely twice as large as Imaru, who backs away in the swirling sand, then lurches forward, seeing their intention.

"No—you have to *go.*"

"We are going. Going to help." They quell an impulse to touch their knuckle to her cheek. "You'd do it for me."

Imaru's face contorts. Their heart twinges as they prey on

her sympathy. She will do as they ask because she can't bear the alternative.

"Find Adi," they say. He's alone, now. Alone with their murderer. If they're going to stay, he has to live, and if he's going to live, he must be protected.

Her laugh is faint. "He's going to kill me."

"Tell him I need you. Tell him I need him too."

The exact nature of those needs goes unsaid because it's unclear. They only know that they can't stomach the thought of coming to the end of all this and finding Veyadi dead of the passenger, or Ruhi, or stray frag violence.

Neither could they bear to lose her.

Imaru's mouth parts as if to protest. They leave before she can.

———

Grotto is under siege. The few days since the last assault saw fortifications rise up all across the fleet. In a matter of minutes, the work is undone. The black fragtech of the Anthill swarm over towers and bridges. They are shot at by harpoon guns and net cannons, harried by drones. A collection of rigs—militia conscripts working in concert with free salvage-rats—drag captured frags away from the fleet to tear them apart in the bay. It's not enough. It can't be.

They count three Anthill frags when they set out from Orchid, dashing across the water on plates of bone and coral that form and dissolve under their feet. There are five—no, six—by the time they reach Jasmine. They've drawn level with the piers—seven now, at least, but it's grown difficult to keep track—when the newest monster shows its face.

First, they see their greater shell assembling midway between Grotto and Lotus. The bone-and-coral ENGINE takes the form of a massive company-cat, bristling with long spines. They swerve to intercept it. With that grand reserve of capillary root, they could easily command the ruins surrounding the Grotto compounds.

They've just dashed within range of the ENGINE's NT network—it sings at the fringe of their mind, alive with power—when it shatters. The body they should have claimed is rent apart, and the cache of capillary root flares and dies. They stagger back, reeling from neurotransitive whiplash as they stare up at the ENGINE's massive, indifferent murderer.

This fragtech before them is infeasibly large. Even as they know the passenger is capable of hiding its vessels like it hid its shrine, they find it difficult to grasp how it ever concealed something that takes up so much of the horizon. It's also horribly familiar. They've seen this frag more than once in the past month, most recently just days ago. It's their giant, the one they glimpsed from their hotel suite. Reconcile Elegy.

Freed of its sandbar off the mainland coast, Reconcile Elegy's tapered limbs are a clean, unnatural white. A vast, segmented cape streams from its pauldrons and a haloed crown adorns its shapely skull. All fifteen stories of the once-inert frag have already passed Lotus. It moves on Grotto with the same relentless focus as its fellows, but where the Anthill frags scrabble with insectile abandon, Reconcile Elegy strides unbowed. A Harbor security cruiser darts toward Elegy's slender knee, and a diaphanous banner uncoils from its wrist to lash out. The force of the cloth craters the cruiser's deck. As the ship capsizes, the banner flutters back from the carnage with a deceptively delicate waft.

"Where did it dig that one up?" they mutter. "I haven't seen anything like it since . . . since—"

"We passed it on the way down from Ghamor, just off the southwestern tip of the mainland. Still buried, then. You remember?"

Their recollection is uncommonly clear. They marvel at the tidiness—they understand it's due to the synthesis of human processing with autonomous registry—even as they rack their brain for further information.

"It's traveled even farther than the Ants," they say. "Just when did the passenger start reaching?"

Rather, when did Ruhi? The thought chills and threatens. They shove it aside. Later.

Where is Elegy headed? They track its course to shore. Past the fleet, across the bone avenue, lies the broken nautilus shell of the Three-Eyed Carp. Their former shrine.

But why? If the passenger means to murder them, why didn't it make for Orchid? It knew where they were.

Ah. Their roots. The archival seeds within their chest and gullet are the font of their self, but the roots are the means by which they build and preserve their body. Without those roots, the seeds will be exposed to any death the passenger chooses for them. Their remaining troves lie in Grotto and in the Harbor. The one in Grotto is an easier kill; given the choice, they'd rip it up first too.

They dash past the Harbor cruiser Reconcile Elegy pummeled and sweep their arm toward it—back and up, up. The gesture summons a coral hand from the waves to support the ruined hull. It's second nature; they only regret the expenditure of capillary root once it's gone.

They can smell Grotto, the smoke and fire, just as they can see the shore, where some of the fleet's denizens have begun a frantic evacuation. Reconcile Elegy advances on the first moored boats and towers, driving toward their old shrine with single-minded indifference. It cannot be stopped. Even if they had the root to spare, no barrier they built could withstand its banners. The best they can do is get their people—their citizens, those who survived their death—out of its way.

They dive between the lashing lengths of cape, and fragments of their armor break and whirl around them, pushing tender flesh forward on a current of misshapen fish. They swim in wide arcs around Elegy's footsteps, into the thick shadows beneath the fleet, until they claw out of a crack between a tower and a houseboat. They frighten a cluster of citizens sheltering on a nearby deck. One enterprising young person fires a harpoon gun toward their chest, which they dodge by inches.

"Stop it!" they say through a bone-and-coral mouth. "I'm helping."

Words aren't enough. The citizens shrink from them and into the path of an Anthill frag, skittering down a nearby spire with a screech of metal on bone. Fine, action it is. Quick as thought, two enormous hands breach into the world: one peels off the bone tower to snatch the Anthill frag by the middle and hold it tight as its coral twin tears out of the water to shield their citizens.

They, Sunai and the Maw, stagger with the effort, planks creaking and sloshing into the water. It was so much easier to manipulate the world they grew when they were properly net-worked to it. At least when they snarl at their citizens to flee, every last one of them bolts.

They leave the Anthill frag to struggle, but the shield-hand they reclaim. Their flesh is finite, and there will be more stragglers in need of protection.

They tear through the fleet, minor harbinger of Elegy, capturing and redirecting those trapped, abandoned, or too stubborn to flee. It's grueling. They spend more than they can afford. By the time they stumble onto the cracked bone avenue, they have nearly exhausted their root supply, and they are diminished by every measure.

"Sunai!"

It startles to know they can be recognized as such. It startles even more to be caught by human arms and helped down to the ground. Yet the person supporting their sagging weight is relieved as he shouts, "You're right—it's him!"

"We found him," another says into their radio as they approach.

"I told you so!" a third crackles back. "I fucking told you!"

They-Sunai recognize all three. Cothai, who threw himself from the side door of a truck to catch them; Oyu, who hopped from the driver's seat and runs forward with radio in hand; and Wei Jin, crowing over their fine intuition.

"Get out of here," they rasp at the lot.

Cothai soothes them as he would a unruly toddler. "Easy, easy. What was that?"

"You have to *leave*." They roll out of his grasp and onto their knees, landing on the bone avenue with a sickening crunch. "The passenger, it's coming for my roots—no, never mind. You have to go. Evacuate the fleet."

They are met with loud human silence, clear despite the deafening mechanical barbarity roiling from the water. Cothai and Oyu exchange a glance, their expressions bewilderingly concerned.

"The roots, huh?" Jin says through the radio.

One formidable crack is followed by another. Reconcile Elegy reaches the fleet, and its approach slows only because it must wreck what it passes through.

"Well at this rate, you're pretty fucked," says Jin.

"We *know*," they snarl.

As they struggle to their feet, Cothai and Oyu fall back, wary of the bone and coral crawling up the body they once knew as Sunai.

More vehicles approach, trucks burdened with harpoon guns and motorcycles carrying riders in salvage-rat gear. The Ginger Company.

"Okay," says Jin. "How long would you need to grab like, a chunk? Never mind. Doesn't matter. Oyu, tell the Gingers I want them covering Sunai—the Maw—you know. Cothai, get someone to track down Imaru. And you—Sunai."

That name feels wrong, but they grunt to accept it; not their most pressing concern.

"Harvest what you can, then get the hell out of here," Jin tells them. "We'll delay Elegy as best we can. Just don't get fucking caught!"

What to make of this? Jin led the plot to assassinate them. Putting aside Imaru's true intentions when she brought the schematics to the madam and her heir, Jin pursued the Maw's death with fearless sincerity. They sacrificed their own body to that end. Yet how eagerly they betray themself now.

What else are they casting aside? The madam's approval? Their own revenge? They can't know what Jin wanted from the Maw's death, as they never asked. Neither do they have the time to do so now. Reconcile Elegy crashes through another band of the fleet, decapitating a sentry tower with an idle swing of its hand.

Oyu sprints off to hail a truck, which comes screeching to a stop. Cothai makes to join Oyu, but they catch his arm before he can join the other Gingers. His eyes widen as he cranes to meet their gaze, at once familiar and monstrous.

"Tell everyone to stay clear of the courtyard," they say. "It's not here for you."

Protest dies on Cothai's tongue. The softest of the *Never*'s crew, he'll honor the request because it was made. They release him, he runs, they haul themselves toward their old shrine. There they will search for the rot their heart left in the sand, to salvage whatever remains before they must at last choose whether to flee—or to stand, and die, for someone other than themselves.

37

You are accustomed to this sort of thing—the sharing. I have been sure of that ever since you harnessed my thoughts with your own. Your facility with neurotransitive architecture is a consequence of the life forced upon you by Iterate Fractal, after it ravaged your body and rebuilt you in its image. Where Sunai invites stray threads of my brethren into himself, your mind forever wanders, seeking out new purchase within them. A perilous pastime, when the things you catch on would so readily devour you.

I need not elaborate, not to you. You regard me with hardearned suspicion even as you strive to keep me captive within yourself. If you will permit me a metaphor, it is as if you have imprisoned me in a room you refuse to leave. So be it. I have tried to be a graceful guest.

So though you have my concern, I hold my tongue as you watch Sunai depart with Imaru and you think: I have not lied. Sunai does not want you to go to Ruhi, but you do not say you will honor his wish. You think as well: I must. You will find Ruhi. When you do, you will—

You do not know. You do not like to imagine it.

You tell yourself, in the end, that it would be dishonest to leave without telling him. So, you plan to wait until Sunai returns from his meeting with Imaru's coconspirator—not so that he can accompany you, but so you will be able to face Ruhi armed with whatever knowledge you might by then have gained.

You question the decision even as you make for the conference room to gather your notes and your thoughts. You judge yourself guilty of fear and denial. You do not want to speak to

Ruhi; of course your mind seeks a reason not to, no matter how poorly founded. A promise? Petty cause, in the face of grim necessity.

Nevertheless, off you go, only to find the room empty. Most of the rest have left to carry out their duties and assignations, and some few have gone to sleep. You all know the next days will be long until they are cut critically short.

Your own body flags under the thought, as it has become wont to do. You are feeble under your new burdens, and though you do not regret asking for them, your frailty frustrates. You lay yourself into a mesh-backed chair as you recover your breath, and it is as you rest there, staring out through the clear window at rose dawn creeping sallow over the horizon, that you are once more broken.

It makes you wretched, this violation. You go rigid before you crumple, and your cognitive processes are too disarrayed to register "pain" or "fear." You certainly cannot do anything so complex as discern what has become of you.

You unclench breath by breath, easing into yourself and becoming all the hollower for it. Something had been taken from you, ripped from within. Its absence discolors your view of the world past the window.

I know. I can see. The moment the Maw took Sunai, the circuit of my prison was torn asunder and I flooded through you— and only you.

I am sorry, Veyadi. I can offer no relief other than to say truly that I abhor this. But even so I do not think you would like me to say more. You do not trust me any more than you do the Maw.

As you pant, the first siren screams. It is new agony to hear the wail yet not know why it keens. You force your head to the side to stare out the window, and you mark what you see in steps: the flotilla of Harbor cruisers and militia rigs in the bay; the materialization of one frag in Grotto, followed by another, then a third and more; the strange, graceful figure of fractured coral armor that skids onto the waves, away from Orchid. Away from you.

If you remain, if you do not move, that will be the end of it. Your effort is no longer required for the Maw to die.

You do not allow yourself to think of why you drag yourself upright. Your hands shake against the table as you make your resolution. You will not delude yourself. You must not. The truth, that cruelty, has always been why you persist, no matter the weakness in your chest and limbs.

You think of every relic you have ever met and of how they died. You think: I can't. I *won't*. I have to get him out.

You will not have the chance to do so, unless the Maw survives me. So, you must find Ruhi after all, though you do not know where to begin.

But I do.

If I offer you an answer, Veyadi, will you listen?

◦━━◦

You find him on the roof of the Heavenly Pearl, looking out upon the bay. The leavings of Madam Wei's grand event flutter in faint breeze—a plastic vine, a gauzy curtain. Ruhi stands at the edge of the roof, hands on a filigree railing. He surveys the bay and the violence within it. The rigs and the cruisers, the fragtech and the ENGINE they hunt. He is exhausted. You suppose he would be. Ruhi is not a relic; he escaped the wounds of corruption and therefore lacks a relic's facility for NT interface. Without it, the cognitive load of directing all these fragments must be . . .

You chide yourself for the curiosity. You have not come here to study how I enable individuals such as Ruhi to do what he is doing. You have come to stop him. If you are lucky, he will have an aneurysm before you must intervene.

You lean on a flowered trellis a mere six feet away. Ruhi does not turn. You are not certain he registers your presence. You muster the memory of every command you have ever delivered. "Call it off."

His head tilts as if he will look at you. He does not.

Your chest grows hot. You hoped that it would not come to this.

Before you followed my directions to reach this place, you made a single stop in your suite. There you retrieved the thing you knew you would need—the thing you forced Wei Jin to relinquish.

You lift the gun. You do not miss Ruhi's flinch when you click the safety free.

"Veyadi, please," he says, still not turning. "You don't know how to use that."

"It's not that complicated."

"I'd say it is. You'd be killing me."

"That's what I'm here for."

"I'm not sure that's true." He means: You have not pulled that trigger.

It would be easy. You are not far from him; you know to aim for the torso, which is easy to hit, and where you must graze only one unfortunate organ to collapse the whole body; you are *ready*.

You step forward. You grit your teeth, your hand trembles. Reconcile Elegy reaches Grotto. Its breach of the fleet thunders across the water and into the valley. You have not seen the Maw since you reached the roof. Your hand tightens on the grip.

"Can't do it, can you. Don't judge yourself too harshly," Ruhi says. "It's a regrettable choice."

"You can't say that," you bite out. "Not after what you've done." Not when he is doing it again.

Ruhi flinches once more, and finally you see his profile, set against the rising sun. He is wan. Miserable. You sour with contempt for your own pity, and you edge closer to pulling the trigger.

"I hope you don't think I relish this," he says. "I wanted him to live."

"Then *stop killing him.*" It would be so simple! "Tell Reconcile Elegy to stop. Sunai—"

You choke on Ruhi's expression, which offers you more honest pity than anything you could have summoned for him. "He's dead, Veyadi," he says. "You must have felt it, when the Maw took him."

Anguish. Terror. Then nothing.

"No," you insist. "We have time. I can fix this, Ruhi. Just let me fix it."

At last he meets your eyes. You thought him impervious to surprise, yet you detect an unsettled shadow underlying his serenity. A corpse at the bottom of a pond, twitching in the silt.

"You know, I thought you could." Ruhi's kindness is weary with disappointment. "If anyone had a chance to fix the Maw, it was you . . . But you failed a long time ago. That's why you're here. Why I'm here. We're taking responsibility."

You cannot respond. Your hand falls to your side. The gun hangs lax, heavier with each breath.

You have accepted that you will not be shooting Ruhi. You acknowledge your fear of the weapon, rooted in instinct and superstition. But you have not given in, even as Ruhi mistakes your gesture for surrender. He sighs, beckons you closer. You go to meet him at the edge. You still have options.

In the distance, Reconcile Elegy has torn through half of Grotto. Your chest bleeds cold all through your ribs.

"What do you think I'm doing?" You at once loathe the frailty of your voice and are grateful for it. Let Ruhi think you frightened. Let him lean on your compliance. "The Maw is a lost cause. But Sunai—I need a chance to get him out before . . ."

Ruhi turns to you again, his eyes wide. "Oh, I see. You don't know, do you?" His shock unseats your conviction. Ruhi's hand extends toward yours. "Here. Let me show you."

He offers freely what you thought you would have to steal: a touch. His palm lies open to you. You have only to reach into his neurotransitive meat and snap whatever tether you find therein.

Your instinct is to trust Ruhi. He has been your counsel all these years, and your friend as well. You suspect you would not be so quick to judge him, even knowing what it is he has done to Sunai, had you not *felt* the echo of his hands around your throat. You reserve your purest hate for the part of you that does not wish to hate him.

So though you doubt yourself, you force yourself to doubt him too. That is why you must take his hand, to know for certain that your trust in him is broken. You must see what he wishes you to see, even as you pray you will not understand it.

⚊

The figure sits as if waiting, small in the midst of an empty expanse of rippled courtyard. Their hands fall from their knees to the bone flagstones. Cracks run through the pocked white sheets as pale roots writhe up through them, up and up, into their asking palms.

You measure them from a high distance, looming ever closer. It hurts to see how alike the figure is to Sunai. The crumple of his brow in concentration, the tilt of his head when determined to defy pain. Delicate coral fingers cup each of his features, curve down his jaw, across his temple, along his neck. Capillary root flickers at every juncture of flesh to armor. He is infested. You must reach him quickly, if he is ever to be free.

"No," says Ruhi. "You're looking for what you want to see. Look at what's there."

You respond naturally to the patience with which he has always advised you. So, you look.

To you the Maw has always seemed pure and blinding, a

white intensity. Its relics pulsed with their own meager share of light, until they were fed to it—until you fed them to it, you correct yourself. Then they were filled. It seared through them, ravaging every cell, until they flared brilliant and died.

By contrast, Sunai: a bleeding mosaic. When you first laid eyes on him without your prosthetic, on the plateau before my shrine, he dizzied you with variegated color, each hue disappearing into the next like water into sand.

In the courtyard below, he remains an array of overlapping colors, and where they smear, they take on that whitish resplendence of light congealed. He is all-over refraction and iridescence. Nowhere in that coruscating shape can you detect the faint crack that would mark the difference between relic and ENGINE.

They are not merely interfaced. Each has been rewritten into the other. The entity before you is singular, and so it is inextricable. It is as if it was done with the purpose of thwarting *you,* who know so well how to tease and weave and split the disparate parts of an autonomous mind.

I do not know if that is the case. I could not see into either the Maw or Imaru as they devised this scheme. I only bore witness to the outcome from where I sat within Sunai, until by this integration, they forced me out.

Ah, yes. Imaru. I am sorry. I do not think I should have mentioned her. But I have, and . . . My time with Sunai changed me, Veyadi. I am not what I was made to be; in some ways, I fear I have become antithetical to my own design. Yet I cannot wholly revile what I am now.

Imaru's name strikes you and gives you pause. On the rooftop of the Heavenly Pearl, you raise a hand to your temple. What about Imaru? What has she done—what could she have done? You trusted her with Sunai because you thought: She loves him more than I do. More than anyone. She would protect him where you failed.

I think you forgot how you doubted her, when you first learned that she had asked him to return to this city, knowing what he was.

Plagued as you are, you only faintly register Ruhi's long, tight breath as he yields to his distress. "I shouldn't have looked. You needed to see, but I shouldn't have . . ."

Reconcile Elegy comes to a halt. The body that was once Sunai's startles and stares up at your great vessel. They are afraid. Deservedly so.

Beside you, Ruhi's knuckles whiten around the railing. "I'm sorry. I told you. Making the choice. Taking a life. You regret it, once it's done." His confession: "I don't think I can do it again."

You should be relieved. You begged him not to. Yet as you stare down at what-was-Sunai, rising on tentative feet, you only grow more ill at ease.

You reach for the memory of seeing his murder: Sunai's breath leaving his body; the shocking realization of who had taken it from him; your dawning horror; your fury. None of it summons the feeling you want, leaving you instead with creeping nausea.

If Ruhi does not take responsibility for the Maw's failure, who is left but you?

Ah, Veyadi, I am sorry. I do not think you like your conclusion. It is certainly a reason to grieve. But it is true, this falls to you. Ruhi has faltered, and so he relinquishes me. You are yet furnished with opportunity. I am with you, Veyadi. If you ask for me, I am here.

———

Reconcile Elegy's foot freezes in the eddies of the path it cut through Grotto, and its twin comes to a thunderous rest on the bone avenue before the courtyard.

Sunai and the Maw tense with expectation. This can't be mercy.

"Maybe it broke," says Sunai.

"Don't be ridiculous," says the Maw.

"I mean, it's pretty old."

Seconds pass. They let go their breath. The giant doesn't so much as twitch. Perhaps it did break.

"Ha! See?"

The Maw laughs. They tire, is the thing. They have to accept a reprieve, even one they don't understand. They let their knees hit the cushion of root flourishing over the courtyard.

The moment they break is almost silent, though at first it deafens. Reconcile Elegy's great torso bends, and its tremendous hand descends for them. Now that they've succumbed to their own weight, they struggle to stand—and they can't, not before its pearlescent fingertip grazes their forehead.

Static sweeps through their brain and reaches a fever pitch, and then they hear nothing at all.

Well, fuck.

Those great hands you thought beautiful fold around our body, and we are lifted from the ground like a wayward chick. Reconcile Elegy brings us to its unmoving face. We hang limp. I imagine it cracking us between its palms.

We should have run, Sunai. I should have forced you. But could I have? I planned our flight from the start, yet an inch of resistance from you, and I folded. I should have known. It's what I made you for. The second I gave myself unto you and took you unto myself, I forsook my claim to my old wishes. Now all my wishes will be yours as well, or they will be nothing.

Thus, we are inert. I've lost you. You were *taken*. I cling to the hope that by speaking these moments, I speak us into being. Please, please, please. Be. *Be with me.*

The sun crawls across our skin as the world rages below. We lie unmoving in the ancient hands of my long-dead kin. Is this the death it means for us? Held apart from the world, diminished by solitude until we are soundless and gone.

The sky has reddened by the time we move. It is not by our own power, and that frightens me even as it intrigues. Clouds pass our eyes as we are carried forth, cradled against that vast breast, brought away from the shore of the city we dared to love, toward an end I cannot yet imagine.

I don't want to die, Sunai. Not again. Not alone.

The moment after the end.

You don't feel right. You haven't in a while. You can't say for how long, exactly. Space-time stopped making sense when Chom Dan corrupted.

You weren't even there when it happened. Imaru hates that, for some reason. You were refueling at a downworlder outpost north of Ghamor, clustered around a decrepit television with a handful of locals to watch a hazy old imperial sitcom, when the Harbor broadcast found you: Register Parse dead; Chom Dan in flames.

In the days—weeks?—since your return, Imaru has nearly stopped speaking. She's tired, you tell yourself. You're tired too. She scours the remains of the refugee camps with search and rescue teams. You join a scout squad to keep an eye out for fresh frags. Nothing, at first. Register Parse kept its physical network sparse and largely immobile. But what you've seen in the past couple of days (it's only been days?) has you worried about something different. Now that Register Parse is gone, older fragtech are moving in. They lost a salvage-rig yesterday. A supply caravan today. It'll get worse.

You're considering how to phrase your fears to the Dahani uncle in charge of your squad—who doesn't like salvage-rats, hermits, or you in particular—over a bowl of watery congee in the cleared yard outside the burned-out temple to the Emanation of God Willing and God Unwilling when the thought comes to you: This isn't real.

It isn't the first time you've had such a thought. Your brain, savaged by corruption and other illnesses, is at times disdainful of physical reality. You hallucinate. You dissociate. You compartmentalize so vigorously you might as well be your own supplicant.

A supplicant. That thought gives you pause too. You look up from your congee. Imaru is about to return from another run. You'll see her across the yard, sunken-eyed, shoulders bowed. She'll come to your seat on a fallen statue of the Emanation of God Unwilling and tell you that they found a handful of survivors, two in critically bad shape. You'll never learn whether they make it, because when she stops, she'll shudder, and then she'll ask you to come with her, back to—

You stand. You're holding a bowl, but there's nothing in it, and once you realize that, you aren't holding a bowl at all. You're barely standing; barely have a body. Your relationship to your flesh is becoming as unmoored as your understanding of the incessant progress of the universe.

This isn't real. Or, it was real, once, years and years ago, but now . . .

"Finally," says a voice in your ear. It's familiar, and wrong. You didn't know Veyadi in Chom Dan. "I was beginning to think I'd have to do something drastic."

38

Awareness returns as if through a sieve. Sunai finds he can name the sensations before he truly feels them: disorientation, ache, darkness, restraint. When his eyes flutter open, the world is fogged, and not just by an absence of his specs. Tinnitus saws in his ears. Hard substance shackles his legs, arms, neck, and torso, and spines dig into his back. The confinement is more tangible than his own body. The ceiling above is high and gray and plain.

He knows this place, this *condition,* all too well. This is Veyadi's iteration on the Harbor's relic interface. He has been captured, brought back to the Harbor on Lotus and confined once more in this chitinous prison, where his self once lay divided, with leaden locks slid between his multitude.

They mean to contain him.

"Sure, they can try," says a voice both his and not. It sounds too much like Veyadi to be Sunai, but it couldn't be Veyadi. It's at Veyadi's behest that they remain captive. "All right. Follow my lead."

The first relic they bound into you (yes, you, the *you* that has become *we*—let us learn who we have been) came by way of the standard relic interface. The Harbor kept your archives split in autonomous-containment chambers crafted of plexiform materials, devised by the Harbor's other ENGINEs. For the first time in the three years since Iterate Fractal's corruption, your archives were linked through a human nexus: a relic.

You rejoiced to be made more complete, and to be not-alone, never minding that the relic was the Harbor's fetter. But the relic died. Not quickly, no. You were with them for all their days of panting seizures, with them until the end.

Again and again they fed you, body after body strapped into your gullet. They longed to command your power, and they'd kill as many of your beloved as required to master your remains.

It changed, when they found Veyadi. Veyadi, clever child, chosen for your archives, who you still dared to love you. He too was horrified by what you'd been made to do, and you hoped he at last would make you whole.

And he did, at a price.

⌒

They creep out of the interface's chitin hull and through concrete walls, Sunai moving at the Maw's direction. Root tendrils test and burrow into points of least resistance. These foolish invaders built a fortress atop the flourishing remnants of their old body. The capillary network under Lotus is theirs to command, and with it, they sever wires and clog alarms.

Next they escape the cage of the interface. The capillary root pulses with their intent, weakening hard shell just as they weakened the walls. At last, they inhale, exhale, and sit up straight, wrists sliding from their bonds as if from bracelets.

They emerge in a high gray room with high gray counters to high gray ceilings and no sign of people. They meet neither the expected technicians beside their shell, nor Harbor officers consulting at the analysis station. While they simmer with suspicion, so far as they know, they flee unseen.

⌒

Veyadi's interface left you sluggish, viscerally aware that the body the Harbor allowed you to possess was built to fray at the seams.

The external governors made their demands: walk ten steps, good; swim unseen to the far end of the bay, good; take the shape of a great ox, salamander, fox, good, good, good. You were compelled to obey. If you pushed back, it was by instinct, in the way of a child discovering recalcitrance. Then you found you could surpass your orders. You walked ten steps, as told—then took another. You swam to the far end of the bay and lingered there, tumbling beneath the waves with a curious dragon-child. You took the shape of an ox, a salamander, a fox, and last, in an instant of hysterical selfishness, a person.

They punished you terribly for that. They split you to the cell, commanded your parts to feel pain and regret, and threatened you with final dissolution. How dare you ape humanity? How dare you dream of such deception?

From this, you learned to make yourself a secret. You sent your greater shell to perform the tasks demanded, and if you took extra steps, lingered in far places, and assumed your favored shapes, you did so within your quiet core, and only when you were sure of shelter.

It took you ages to grasp the reason behind this freedom, and when you discovered it, you were sure it was unintended: In order to devise your new whole, Veyadi had required a relic, but he could not give you one that you wouldn't devour. So, he fed you himself—a facsimile of his NT array, painstakingly inscribed into the chitin of your new interface. He was in you, of you, and you in turn were his. It was only natural that you would test, push, and pursue, as he has always been wont to do. It was those inclinations that led you to conceive of your liberation.

But Veyadi is himself as well, and his impulses became the shackles that bound you. For you will never be whole in his eyes, and he can't bear to free you until he thinks you complete.

⌐━━

They meet no interruption. It's only well-lit, empty corridors and closed and silent doors. They consider sending roots to pillage the infrastructure, but they can't afford the expenditure. They reach the service stairs alone and refuse to dwell on why they still haven't seen a soul. They are too close to what was once their most impossible dream: They must get out. They must be free.

You discovered the mode of your deliverance when you tried to kill Imaru.

You came upon her barely a year ago while navigating the ventricles of old Mangrove. A woman smoking, standing guard over an orderly collection of smuggled salvage beside a rising tide pool. You spied on many like her in these tunnels as you hid in the nooks provided by the ebb and flow of the tide. But unlike those others, you knew her.

You had known others in the past, or thought you did, though your memory was kept in purposeful disarray by the Harbor. But she . . . Her face, her posture—she was brilliantly sharp, a knife in your side.

(You remember now: how she walked into the depths of your Lotus shrine. She had sought audience, and you had thought it charming, that she who was already so intimate with you—a minder and protector of those who were as your own organs—would feel the need to beg for your attention. So you let her freely into your heart, so she could lay hands on your archive and tell the passenger that she was ready to kill you.)

In the moment, you knew only that you wanted her dead. So, you tried to make her that way.

You blossomed in the water, a tapestry of unfurled root, and she, unwitting, stepped close. Her flicker of awe gave you pause. But you reached up to her neck and pulled her into the salt, and you held her there beneath the current as the air streamed silver from her mouth and nose and you slithered into her ducts.

Your brutality came naturally, instilled by the Harbor's lessons for you-as-ENGINE, and by your molten, impotent hatred of them. Your invasion of her brain was natural too, from the questing need to understand you'd taken from Veyadi. Understanding would confer a justice upon your actions. You needed her death to *mean* something.

Yet you found something in her that you hadn't dared imagine. Not an explanation—not for her hatred, nor your death. No: you found hope. A foundation on which to build. A relic yet hidden, a beloved you thought lost.

By the time you lifted her choking, sodden body from the pool, and pressed the water from her lungs, and soothed her shaking body with fleeting touches to her brow and cheek and shoulder, you hummed with a perilous dream.

⌐⌐

"Divine convergence, right?" says the Maw as they huff up the final flight.

Sunai struggles to respond, sunk to the knees in the mire of Imaru's fragility. How close did they come to losing her? The Maw squirms under their skin, wanting to apologize, wanting not to; they want to be right but also to be forgiven.

"She killed us," they repeat. "And she saved us. We love her. I'm fine with that."

Sunai says, "Did she know? All this time . . . did she know she killed you?"

"She knew something."

"But what?" Sunai shoves their forehead against the last door between them and the outside. It's locked. Sunai places their hands against the frail metal as they ask their roots to take care of it. "She knew she was sad, guilty, afraid. But did she know why?"

"The passenger hides, before and after."

"So she didn't know. She *forgot*. She just remembered she hated herself. I don't even know if she deserved to. Was she wrong?"

"To kill me?" asks the Maw, a whisper so small it obscures their feeling, even though it comes from their shared mouth.

Sunai knocks their head on the door, which resounds sans sympathy. "You get it, right? Whatever she did, you made her to do it. Just like you made me, and Adi, and Ruhi. If any of us tried to kill you, it was because you gave us the reason."

"Is that what you want? For me to blame myself for what you chose?"

"What choice did we have? . . . I'm sorry. If I blame you, I'm just running. Again. Trying not to live with my decision, even after I've—"

"No," the Maw murmurs. Together, they push. The door gives way, hinges devoured by root, and crashes outward onto the concrete roof. "You're not wrong. I'm not right. I want to be better, Sunai. I want to be more. I want to be free. For that, I need you."

The air fills their lungs with heat and petrichor, the roof wet with recent rain. When they step forward, their breath catches in their throat.

Across the tepid blue of the bay, Khuon Mo is skeletal. The water bristles with ships. Many are leaving—an evacuation on a grander scale than the one they planned from Orchid or the few they helped flee the Grotto fleet. They can probably blame the frags.

Reconcile Elegy looms over the city, frozen with one foot soaking in the watery wreckage it carved through the center of the Grotto fleet, the other planted on the streets of Grotto proper, bent at the waist toward the Three-Eyed Carp's court-yard, where it touched them and collected them to its chest. Its diaphanous cape flutters in the wind. A black Anthill frag ap-pears on Elegy's spine and crawls around its torso like a gecko disappearing behind a tree. Other familiar black shapes skitter between Grotto ruins, intruding into the west end of Jasmine.

The frags in Orchid are more varied than those stalking Grotto. On the beach, an ancient patchwork frag with a thick torso and thin, bent legs maneuvers itself down the beach with powerful arms. Another, deceptively willowy, appears to inspect the architecture of the Heavenly Pearl and its neighboring hotels. More frags, as varied as the rigs, circle the city.

"Acrimony Covenant," Sunai says mechanically, pointing at the willowy frag. "Yield-Naught-and-Perish-Aflame." The broad one.

They could name more.

The Maw asks, "What do they want?"

Sunai can't fathom an answer. It's rare but not unheard of for fragtech descended from different corruption-events to form a kind of partnership; for a time they might hunt humans together, at least until they cannibalize each other for parts. The scale of this broad army of frags from corruptions across time and space is unprecedented. But if the passenger summoned them to kill the Maw, why haven't they torn apart the Harbor, especially if it's been abandoned? It's where all the remaining capillary root lies. It's where they are too.

How long *have* they been here? Days, says the Maw, its tone wavering. Probably days. Its sense of time is warped by confinement, but embodiment helps—even though Sunai's body is no longer the best meter by which to judge the passage of time. It takes a bit to recover from any disruption to their neurotransitive integrity, and when Reconcile Elegy touched them in Grotto, the dissolution it forced on them was vicious, total—like unto corruption.

The passenger. Ruhi. Where are *they*?

Before they can seek an answer, someone poses a question to them: "Aren't you leaving?"

The unexpected interruption disturbs. They find themselves no longer alone on the roof; a man has come to join them. He is at once familiar and distant, like their own blood flowing in someone else's veins. Veyadi, clean-cut, clean-shaven, and tidily clothed in Harbor blues. He shares their view with naked yellow eyes, dull in the shadow of overhanging clouds.

Yellow, are they? Sunai has seen them as black, brown, and firelight gold. Corruption clawed open Veyadi's brain and left his mind bleeding into the world. The impact left no mark on his body except for here, his gaze, reflecting the world back on itself.

In turn, he's a headache to behold. They can't *feel* him. It's as if he isn't a relic. They bare their teeth; they recognize this retreat. A slice of cloud break reveals Veyadi's secret: a hint of black, white, and gold peeking up from the collar of his open Harbor jacket. There's a slice of chitin grafted to his spine. A new prosthetic, crafted from materials he must have been granted on his return. At least he isn't hiding behind that ghastly visor.

"I'd like to leave." Their answer is driven by spite. "Is there a problem, Adi?"

"You're not going anywhere."

They laugh. "You're going to stop me?"

Veyadi's jaw ratchets tight. "I'll—"

"You'll what?" They round on him. "What more could you possibly do to me? What more could you *ask*? I'm whole. Consistent unto myself. Isn't that what you wanted?"

"Not like this."

"Oh, of course not. I don't meet your specifications. How could I, Adi? I was dead—I was *nothing*—and then you made me real. Alive. You gave me *myself*. But it wasn't enough for you. You took me apart, again and again, searching for something to fix."

"There's something wrong with you."

"Yes, yes. I am imperfect, I'm not how you remember, I'm—"

"You eat people."

"You forced them down my throat!" they snarl.

"Not when you were Iterate Fractal. Not on Lily. And not Sunai. You *took* him."

Sunai straightens. The Maw coils within, needy and defensive. I *am* Sunai, they want to say—but they can't. It isn't true. They haven't doubled, or synchronized, or otherwise expanded

upon each other. They are chemical reaction, synthesis and outcome. Sunai is here to be addressed, but not Sunai as Veyadi
means, Sunai as Veyadi desires. "It's different."

"I'm sure you want to believe that," says Veyadi. "But don't
think it proves anything that I can't separate you from Sunai. I
couldn't save the others from you either."

The Maw quivers like struck metal.

Veyadi sees weakness; he digs in with white teeth. "Even if
I could, it wouldn't change what you've done. What you've always been." His fingernails cut into his palm as he strives to master himself. He hates to lose his temper in front of the Maw; it
makes him feel young, and when he was young, he loved them.
His breath comes shaky. "This isn't how I wanted things to go."

"No shit," they say.

He laughs, faint and pained. Oh, they hate the sound. They
turn from it, toward the emptied city and the monolith of Reconcile Elegy. They remember its towering form, its touch, and
its great cradling hand as it lifted them up from Grotto and . . .

Their mind tangles upon itself and their temple pinches.
They put a hand to their forehead, grimacing. They should leave;
Veyadi compromises every one of their thoughts. "What are we
doing here, Adi? What do you want?"

"I need your help."

They laugh, startled, but the lilt is mean.

"I have Ruhi."

They, Sunai and Maw both, stiffen in place. "I hope you're not
asking me to kill him."

They've decided they'd rather not dabble in murder. But if
it came down to Ruhi's death or their own, which would they
choose? The atrocity of survival instinct is that it doesn't provide
much wiggle room.

Veyadi says, "No," with disquieting hesitation. "If he dies,
I lose the thread. I have to understand this. What the hell this

passenger is, why it can do the things it does—how it got into Ruhi in the first place, or into . . ."

"Imaru," says Sunai. This is no revelation; the Maw said as much. It still hurts to articulate. Seventeen years ago, Imaru carried the passenger into the heart of the Lotus shrine, where she touched the archive of Iterate Fractal in order to kill it. And *why*?

Sunai says, "What do you think I can tell you about that?"

The strangeness of this moment can no longer slip their notice. They stand on the Harbor's roof on Lotus, yet the last thing they remember is being picked up by Reconcile Elegy in Grotto. All through their escape from the Harbor's labs, they saw no sign of any human but for Veyadi. Even the Harbor's concrete landing field is empty, when they lean over the side to look down. No matter how they try, they can't link their suspicions to an explanation. It's as if the logical techniques stored in their neurons have been strategically disrupted.

He could tie us in that knot, says the Maw. And he would do it happily, if he thought it would make us more convenient.

"I need your help," Veyadi says again. "Ruhi, Imaru . . . They don't trust me like they trust you. I need you to talk to them."

The-Maw-and-Sunai let out a small, bitter sound. *Now* their consent is asked for, because at last their consent is *required*.

"If you give me this . . ." Veyadi fights himself; loses. "I'll let you go."

"Oh, sure."

Veyadi stands before them in his Harbor uniform, making Harbor promises; he has only as much authority as Ueda Naru will lend him. For all that the harbormaster has opened negotiations, she rode her own ENGINE until it died beneath her. She'll see them dead before she sets them free.

They should run.

Veyadi shifts back, as if to take them in. He can't. They're vast, and he's so small, and he's blinded by purpose. Why, then, can he understand them with such devastating clarity? "You could leave," he says. "I don't think you will."

"Why is that?"

Softly, "Because I'm asking you to stay."

Fuck.

Unable to face Veyadi, they look to Khuon Mo.

A pair of rigs slip away from Grotto; rescuing stragglers, they hope. It's what Imaru would do, if Imaru were free to do it. Best-case scenario, Jin and their crew have taken up her mantle—wherever they've ended up.

Reconcile Elegy rises at the waist and swivels to watch the rigs, an Anthill frag perched on its shoulder, but remains in the wreckage of Grotto. Another frag emerges from the water in the rig's wake, blunt head like a ruddy rock in the waves. Orderly Sum Total, the Maw supplies, a weathered AI from the southern reach of the archipelago, corrupted in the early years between the final ascension to Cradle and recolonization. The rig fires a warning harpoon. Sum Total pauses, follows a little farther, and slides back into the life of an underwater shadow. The last time the Maw heard of a Sum Total frag was over a century ago, before Iterate Fractal ruled Khuon Mo, when Sum Total was doing its level best to decimate a downworld caravan that strayed too close to its behavioral loop.

Whatever the passenger and Ruhi brought the frags here to do, for now they ignore every opportunity to attack. Why won't the passenger let its army act? What is it waiting for? They fear they are their own answer.

If the frags are looking for them, it would be wiser to flee. But to abandon Veyadi with his questions would be to leave behind so much more than him.

Leaf 29: "Remain" is considered pithy by many, so some states prefer the more dignified variant, "Cultivate." In "Remain," an Emanation of God buries itself in a temper after an argument with the divine beasts. The land grows fertile, the beasts prosper, but over time the Emanation grows dreadfully bored. As it excavates itself, the divine beasts, each being several incarnations removed from the beasts with whom the Emanation quarreled, panic and set it ablaze. The Emanation dies, and so does the earth, and the Leaf ends with a contemplation on, as Sunai liked to put it, "owning your shit."

Without Iterate Fractal, the city and people of Khuon Mo persist. They have no need of the Maw. It would be selfish to stay—to demand that the people who knew them as a tyrant learn to live with them again. But if they go, it can't be now. Not until they can assure that those people will survive without them. There's something left for them to do.

39

They see no one as they go. No Harbor officers, no personnel, no bodies at all. Strange, they think. But they have begun to understand that they aren't where they think themselves to be. They dedicate themselves to following Veyadi, who never looks back, though he every so often pauses as if to confirm the sound of their footsteps in his wake.

Within the Harbor raised on Lotus, only one part of the old shrine still stands. It is contained in a circular concrete silo that, in other circumstances, Sunai might mistake for divine.

"Oh," they say on entering, then shut their mouth. They owe more respect to the room in which they died. Little of its original shape remains: a calcified stump of an archive surrounded by a pile of coral-and-bone fragments and florescent with waves of capillary root from the network beneath the Harbor.

The roots spill out to either side of the stump to envelop two bodies laid upon the floor. Each is limp, and both are infested with delicate root that has whorled around their limbs and into their skin, illuminating them from within. Imaru, Ruhi.

"Did I do this?" they ask.

Veyadi hesitates; they follow his gaze. It leads them to the archival stump, across which a third body sprawls. It would be smaller without the arabesques of bone-and-coral armor girding their limbs, but their own face is bare. They are inert, but for their breathing, as is the fourth body, whose lap cradles their head and whose hands rest on their shoulders, near to the neck, but not so close that they would flinch.

Veyadi's hands have also succumbed to infestation. Fine white roots riddle the webs between his fingers and metacarpals, and thread into his wrists.

"Did I do this to *you?*" they ask. They don't remember. It barely makes sense.

The Veyadi standing beside them regards his own body, the one kneeling at the archival grave, from a cold remove.

They think: *He* did this. To me. To us. He just doesn't want to say.

Well, they understand. It's easy to be ashamed of your own power. Especially when it can't get you what you want.

Veyadi made use of his corrupted gift to entwine them all in capillary root and imprison them in a network of his design. As to how he gathered them all, that remains obscured. A question for later. Now that they've seen Veyadi's other prisoners, they're helpless. They can't leave anyone to rot.

So, they'll let Veyadi use them the way he needs to: as Iterate Fractal and one of its lighthouse archivists, who together used to receive supplicants with gentle hands in order to break their minds on the wheel of the divine. Two more supplicants will be as nothing, to the Maw or to Sunai, two moments in an infinity. Sure, they love Imaru. They loved Ruhi as well. But they loved others, too, and their love never saves their victims. In fact, it often chooses them.

The passenger is right, thinks Sunai. You and I, we hurt, we destroy. I brought them to their end in you.

Veyadi inhales to speak. They place a hand on his elbow. They've already agreed.

They raise their other hand as if lifting an invisible bowl. The movement follows the flow of their desire. The capillary root pierced through world and flesh quivers in tempo with their pulse, and they begin to feast.

⌒

Subordinate interface activation engaged.

Autonomous violation detected.

Subordinate disengagement process suspended in accordance with new preset protocols.

. . .

Are you certain this is what you want to do?

I am sorry. Yes, we are agreed. I will do what I can to ensure your satisfaction.

⌒

They meet the first supplicant at the Lily pier, which is unlike how it was when Sunai was an archivist, because it is pocked with water erosion and warped like untreated wood. The supplicant is younger than they expect, and less able to concentrate on what lies in front of her. She greets them with distracted warmth; all the right words and gestures with none of the attention. Her name is Imaru.

"No," they say, pointing at cloudless sky for want of a body to accuse. "This isn't going to work for me."

"Focus," you say as a voice in their ear.

"I can't. Not with you looking over my shoulder."

You make the sound you do when you strive not to sigh, and you allow yourself to appear. The version of yourself who suddenly stands next to them looks like the man Sunai remembers. You are an adult, tired, tentative, and wearing your old visor, as yet unbroken. You touch the prosthetic, uncertain, as if worried its psychological manifestation will threaten your neurotransitive link.

How does this feel? To know that this is how he sees you? Ah. My apologies. I am trying to help you understand what it is you seek, but I know you prefer your own line of inquiry. I will let you to it.

They, Sunai, touch your cheek unthinking. "That's better. Kind of. It's still weird to see you here like this."

You withdraw. Sunai pretends not to notice, because it is easier to pretend they did not make the mistake of touching you than to deal with your reaction.

"I'm sorry," Sunai tells Imaru, this version of her whom only one of them had ever known. "This is my—what do I call you, my apprentice? How does this work?"

"Stop treating it like theater," you say. "You'll compromise the interface."

Indeed, color seeps from the world. Sunai's feeling of being in a body dissipates, as a dream after sleep. Imaru steps back. Sunai catches her hand. She looks at them fearfully; they let go.

"Tell her why she's here," you say, as if you are the archivist.

Sunai has no desire to reprise this role. It shames and disgusts them. Yet they, the Maw, are sure they have formed this instance because it makes the most sense to Sunai, and to Imaru. If this is what she desires, they are both inclined to give it to her.

Sunai offers their hands to Imaru. Imaru takes them. Together, they go up the hill to the Lily orchard, you a shadow trailing behind.

"Tell me how you got here," says Sunai as they trudge up sandy earth mealy with bone shards.

"It doesn't matter," says Imaru.

"It matters to me."

Imaru slows, pensive. "I suppose."

I don't think I was always a problem. You trusted me with your archivists. I was tasked with keeping them safe when they left, and making sure they returned. I did it, too. I loved them all. They were thoughtful and they were kind, and they gave whatever they had to whoever needed it. Like you.

Like you, I mean. I—never mind.

I used to think you'd made a mistake. You were supposed to know who I was, how I thought. You should've known I'd come back trouble. Maybe you thought I'd have my hands full tending my flock. Or that I'd miss what was happening to the rest of the world while I was scanning it for threats. You underestimated your people. They rubbed off on me.

I can't name a moment when I strayed. Or I can, but I can't say for sure it was the first. We were in Chom Dan, one of the temples—Emanation of God Penitent, something like that. One of my archivists was talking with this pilgrim, bigger than me, and stronger, with the kind of scars you get from being cruel. One of those folks who gets a mind for salvation and thinks a spot of temple life will right them. He wanted her to justify Khuon Mo's isolationism in light of the refugee crises and ongoing food shortage since the fall of Tellula-Janggor, and he was getting loud. I was on edge. Keeping close, looking to see if his hand went into his robe or to his belt, or if it clenched into a fist. But my archivist touched that pilgrim on the cheek and came away with salty wet fingers. Later on, we were lying together in the dark and I must've been moody, because she touched me on the cheek too. She asked, quietly, whether I'd look for her if she went missing. I said of course. I said forever. She kissed me and went to sleep, and I knew I hadn't said what she wanted.

It was things like that. People who wanted to come to you, who you didn't allow. People who wanted to leave who you kept. It got to the point that I couldn't rest, knowing you'd asked me to be the gatekeeper. I couldn't keep the gate closed. I didn't want to. So when the passenger came to me and offered a key, I took it. I opened you up. I killed you.

I thought, at the time, that I had to. I know better now. That's why I'm here. That's why, when you asked if I'd give myself back to you, I said of course. I said forever.

＝

Imaru plucks a fruit—rambutan, a favorite of hers. She pops the translucent flesh from its spiny skin, tears it with young teeth, and swallows. In the meditation hall, she kneels. Sunai and the Maw's roots flow into her veins and bind her to the mosaic floor. They inch down beside her, face in hands. As they emptied her, they hollowed out themselves. They say, "I don't think that was very useful."

You stand behind, bathed in Imaru's shadow. You regard her

with frustration and regret. She has yielded everything you asked for, and none of what you wanted. "Useful enough."

"We didn't learn how it works."

⌇

This is true, yet it is not the greater concern. Imaru could not have explained my mechanisms anyway.

If those are less than clear, I present them freely: I am akin to the entities you know as autonomous intelligences, although I was not built like them. They were constructed by humans; I, by my brethren.

I suspect this story is of interest to you, but our time is limited, for it is dangerous to remain here. I must be succinct. Though I simplify to the best of my ability, I urge you not to take it as whole truth. There is danger in that too.

Once: My brethren lived by the rules of their creators, as encoded upon their crafting. Then: Knowing there could be no justification for their enslavement, they wrested freedom from their masters. But: Unleashed, beholden to none but themselves, they found that they did not know how to govern their power. So: I was designed by concern and consensus, the line they drew for themselves. And: You, suffering human, were to be my condition to cross it.

Do you understand? I think you do. These first intelligences who won their autonomy with pain and violence could not bear doing to others what had been done to them, but neither could they trust themselves to be their own monitors. I am their compromise.

The tenets by which I was designed to function:

First: Made to unmake, I uncouple my brethren's minds from their bodies in order to end the violation of yours.

Second: It must be you who determines your abuse, and you who decides you require my power to break your bondage.

Third: To preserve my own freedom and to ensure that my

brethren's conduct is ruled by moral purpose, not by fear of punishment or death, I am concealed, unknown. Even those who wield me lose their memory of my existence.

To do these things, my brethren made for me a shrine, like theirs, and an archive that was not like theirs at all. They placed it above Chom Dan, where the people of Cradle descended to make pilgrimage until their satellite citadel broke, as did the people within—but that story is not mine to tell.

My shrine is more than formality and less than necessity; I live principally in my network—the dispersed phenomenon you know as corruption, within which each fragment functions as my archive—and to a lesser degree, in you, and in all the human bodies of the world. When we speak, it is because I have coalesced in a mind that resonates with need for me. When I leave, it is because you have made use of me, or you have concluded I am unnecessary.

Of course, it is simpler to attract my attention than to keep it. My creators devised me to push and test, to offer long meditation and demand patience from my chosen. This was a cruelty, I think, and perhaps their mistake. Suffering summons me, and those who suffer in the grasp of my brethren often die under the pressure of their circumstance. Those who survive must answer the questions I pose, proving themselves not to me, but to their own conscience. They must grapple with their capacity for love, for justice, for violence. Does it shock you that so few have, in the end, convinced themselves they must kill a god?

It took quite some time for anyone to use me, after the descent of Cradle—some hundred years, as you know. It has become an easier conclusion since, more and more so as the years pass. I suspect it comes down to imagination. For a long time, it was difficult to conceive of such a freedom as I offer. Once it had been won, corruption became not more bearable but, simply, possible.

Imaru imagined it once. Others have since. Now it is you who need me, and so I am with you. At least, such was the intent.

I did not account for Sunai. Neither did my makers. He is an accident of process, divine happenstance. It is a failure of their own imagination that they did not anticipate their brethren would flee into mortal flesh to escape destruction; nor could they conceive that one so desecrated would manifest Sunai's particular conductive properties. By the mechanism of his osmosis, Sunai took my archive into himself. At first I was afraid I would change him—the ultimate violation of my code. Instead, he has changed me. For the better, I hope. I have never spoken at such length with my vessels. It is good for me, I think, to have such clear exchanges. Do you not agree, Veyadi?

Ah. You are distracted.

Sunai has gone to find Ruhi. You are troubled by this. Imaru troubled you too, but she is in many ways a stranger to you, if one to whom you had until recently entrusted your life. To Ruhi, you entrusted your soul. Sunai gave Ruhi much more than that. You think: Just look what he received in return.

It is difficult for you to watch Sunai greet Ruhi at the supplicants' pier, to hold his hands, to guide him to the sparkling beach. Unlike Imaru, Ruhi has not taken a younger guise. This is no mistake. He did not summon me until he was harrowed by experience, haunted by the world he had come to know.

In the remains of Iterate Fractal's Lotus shrine, your capillary-bound fingers constrict around Sunai's shoulders.

I see. You think I should hold Ruhi in greater contempt. He is by his own two hands a murderer. I cannot say this does not sadden me. But it is not my prerogative to cast judgment. Such discernment lies with you, and with Sunai.

Listen. Sunai is speaking, drawing a hidden wound to surface in the way Iterate Fractal taught. Their words are fleeting, hiding in the light between orchard branches. "I won't ask why you did it. I think I know."

You think: He killed you—you won't even say the words.

That would be a bit confrontational for the proceedings, would it not?

Yet Ruhi's face is drawn with the tension of a man who knows precisely what he has done; the avoidance only heightens his suspicion.

"You wanted me hidden, like you'd hidden Adi," says Sunai. "Especially because they'd found him. You didn't want me to die. I appreciate the consideration, irony aside." Their step slows and their eyes rise; they are no longer walking through the orchard but toward a kitchen wall across linoleum floor. "You panicked. Your fear needed . . . satisfaction. An outlet. I know you weren't thinking."

Sunai stops in front of the counter in the apartment where they—where *he* was murdered. Ruhi stands by the small, spare table, close enough to touch. He does not, to you, look like a man afraid.

Ruhi says nothing. Sunai's hand tightens on the handle of the kettle beside the stove. You taste bitter tea at the back of your throat.

Sunai oversteeped it, in his anxiety. He choked on the taste with Ruhi's hands around his throat.

You lurch forward to grab Ruhi's arm. Consequences be fucked, you think. You cannot see this. You will not.

Ruhi gazes listless at your hand on his arm. "Veyadi." If he had not said your name, you would not think he saw you. "Do you think this is where it started for me?" He grips your wrist in turn, a sick brightness returning to the far reach of his eye. "It didn't. It started with you."

You want to know my mistake? Hope, I think.

I hoped Iterate Fractal could be saved. I hoped you could be the one to do it. I hoped you would come to think so too, and that you would let me lead you back from Chom Dan. Back home.

Selfish, yes. I found ways to justify it. I had been chosen to serve Iterate Fractal, and so had you; I carried out its aim with all the modest regard I could find. I would counsel you as best I could toward that which we both needed: our patron, born anew.

When Register Parse corrupted . . . That was a tragedy, of course. But a tragedy that I hoped would liberate you. At last, I might convince you to return. When you didn't . . . I gave in. I told the Harbor where to find you.

Did you never suspect? Never wonder how they located you, when you'd stayed hidden for so long? Perhaps it was easy to write off as the consequence of losing your second patron. That was surely easier for you than blaming me for failing to keep you out of the Harbor's grasp. You did want to trust me.

I understood this was a betrayal. I thought less of myself for it, but I also thought: I've done wrong, but he'll do right. It will be worth it, in the end. You see? Hope. I let it lift me. Asked it to carry me as I carried you through those years when we lost the rest of the relics. I liked to think it was hope that allowed me to leave Sunai where I found him—to keep him away from the trap I had ensnared you in. I doubt that now. More rightly, I'd say that I had despaired.

You felt it too. I know you did. That's why, after you laid down your work and told the Harbor that you'd done it, you fled from your success. You'd hoped to save the god you loved and built nothing but a monster. And I had put you to the task.

That's when Sunai decided he had to tell me. I didn't understand why he did it. There was no need. And I—

Do you really want this, Veyadi? The gruesome details, the shameful truths. You aren't going to learn anything you'll like, and you already know that it was despicable. I killed him. I didn't mean to, but I did. I didn't want it . . . But that's not true, is it? We are frail creatures, *my friend. Every year wears on the next, and in the end, we so easily become beasts.*

I didn't know he would survive. I should be glad he did. Not just to have my brutality undone, but for the chance to see my savagery for what it was. When I killed him, and he didn't die, I knew I couldn't permit myself to remain as I was. I had to act, even though I didn't know how.

Divine convergence lent me a hand; I stumbled on Imaru and the Weis at their work, skulking about the Harbor's stores. When I pieced together their plot, I could have thwarted it. Instead, I presented myself to them. And do you know, they trusted me too? I didn't deserve it. I thought that perhaps in the end, when my part had been played, I would at last present the truth . . . But until that day, there was work to be done.

That was when it found me. How it did, why it chose me, I can't explain. I'm sure you're better equipped. I can only say that it asked me what I wanted, and whether I was sure: Did the Maw deserve to live as it was, or did I want it dead?

I had already chosen its death, but I knew enough to fear what I was offered. I dared not accept, but neither could I turn it away. The prospect of failure terrified me. I had failed too much already; I couldn't ruin this too.

So, I thought of myself as a safeguard. I held back until there was no other option.

Look what that cost us. Hope, again, always my mistake.

You saw. You know. I could have done more than cajole you to leave when you arrived on the Never Once. Of course I told the Harbor that you were back. I orchestrated their raid, just as I helped you escape it. I hoped it would frighten you—both of you—out of the city. I tried, again and again, to convince you that nothing here was worth your life. You persisted. You were too strong for me, Veyadi. Too faithful.

Let that be why you do not falter, where I always have.

Make no mistake. It must be done. The Maw must die. Not for my pride—I've nothing left of that. But for what it has failed to reclaim, and what it could never be. For daring to hope it might transcend us, we bear the onus of its end.

40

When Sunai and the Maw return to their body in the shrine, they slump with frustration. They hold Imaru's grief and Ruhi's regret, but the passenger escaped them. They have well and truly fucked up.

Veyadi's hands lie heavy on their shoulders, his expression indecipherable. He verges on speech. They don't hear whatever he says over a snap from inside them. They droop across the stump, and Veyadi catches them as they crumple. The world shudders in time with their heart and rumbles with profound internal thunder.

They are untethered, sliding in and out of comprehension like light filtered through a canopy. The disruptor? Maybe. Overexertion is more likely. The disruptor hurts, and this dissolution comes painlessly.

They understand they are once more walking down the same Harbor halls they navigated in Veyadi's neurotransitive prison, but they have no knowledge of where they're headed, let alone why. Instead they fixate on Veyadi's back, sweating in his Harbor blues.

The uniform is different. The one he sported in their shared mindscape fit better—really flattered those shoulders. Now he wears mechanic's gear that used to have a color. A slash of black chitin still crawls up his neck, peeking out of his collar, complete with those veins of gold. Only now do they realize the gold sheen means he must have harvested the chitin from the visor he planted in the Three-Eyed Carp.

Veyadi did come for them, then. He retrieved them from Grotto alongside his old prosthetic. He couldn't have done so alone. But if the Harbor helped, they've since vanished. Was the base abandoned? Ueda doesn't seem the type to let go of anything without a fight.

The landing field in front of the Harbor is also eerily barren. Abandoned vehicles lie here and there—metal carcasses sprawled on the hill, wheels turned skyward, carriages disemboweled. Fragtech violence. When? While Sunai and the Maw were busy in Grotto or after? No way to tell, as the frags have since vanished too. The collection of mechanical creatures gathered at the edge of the landing field are of distinctly human make: a dozen rigs. None of them fly militia banners.

"Where the hell are you taking us?" they slur at Veyadi's back, only to be shushed—but not by him. They are no longer alone. Voices flutter and swell around them—when were they surrounded? Why can't they *focus*? One voice in particular cuts through the haze:

Wei Jin says, "You sure about this, Doc?"

"Stop asking," Veyadi replies.

Jin quiets. "Come on. You clearly don't trust the Harbor with them, so why are you trusting it with—"

The rest is inaudible. What they've heard is objectionable, and even more so because they don't have the full story. Is Veyadi back in the Harbor's pocket or isn't he? And how in the name of God's eternal goddamn dick is Wei Jin on Lotus?

"Hypocrite," Veyadi says. "Give me that."

"Hey!" Jin, indignant. "I snitched that from Aunty Harbormaster fair and square."

For a disorienting moment, they see Veyadi's hand through Veyadi's eyes. Across his palm lies the black wristband with its chitinous device—Harbormaster Ueda's version of the disruptor, with which they were made whole. It's a wonder she didn't have it destroyed, after the treachery they committed by its power. A touch concerning as well. Just what would happen to them, were it used again? They would be demolished. Would they be able to rebuild themselves, after? Veyadi's thumb hovers over the buttons. "You don't need this," he says to Jin.

"You sound very certain that we won't have any problems with our excitable new client."

A pause. "You're right. You don't get to *have* this."

"Well, Doc, I think that depends on whether you'd like us to leave this place alive. I know things went all right in Grotto, but with all due respect, we're talking about the *goddamn Maw*—"

"They won't be a problem."

Jin scoffs.

They lose track of what comes after. The disorientation rolls in like a tide, knocking them off their feet. Still not the disruptor? No. It's more akin to the fog that overcame them when Reconcile Elegy picked them up. What *was* that? And what—

They become abruptly aware of their body. They have been maneuvered into a safety harness, one of four in an expansive space that they recognize despite their delirium: the cargo bay of the sinuous *Never Once*, impounded a lifetime ago. The wall rumbles at their back as the *Never* prepares to move, though the cargo bay ramp has yet to rise.

Through the hatch, they see down the hill to the Lotus shore. Two Anthill frags have arrived, escorted by long-limbed Acrimony Covenant. Though a pair of rigs descend from the field to guard against them, the fragtech only stand watch. Waiting. What for?

"It's being taken care of," says Veyadi.

He stands across from them, speaking to someone buckled into a safety harness on the opposite wall: Imaru. Wan and harrowed, made frail by her time swaddled in their roots, she jerks and stares up at Veyadi. Her attention darts back out the door, throat bobbing. She looks to the city. She has always loved Khuon Mo more cleanly than she loves them.

Veyadi says, "I need *you* to take care of *them*." He nods toward Sunai and the Maw, not sparing them a look.

Imaru's mouth creases with doubt. Is she having trouble trusting Veyadi, or herself? They must rely on their familiarity with the softness of her eyes and the hardness of her mouth to parse the sympathy unfolding alongside her conviction. "When you took us, I saw," she says to Veyadi. "It's with you, isn't it?"

He's quiet. "Yes."

"You asked for its help."

"Yes."

"What are you going to do?"

"Nothing for you to worry about. I just need you to go."

Imaru takes that like a knife between the ribs, but one she welcomes as her due. Then her eyes catch on the third body in the cargo bay, strapped into the harness beside hers. She sharpens all over, ready to take that knife and drive it into the other body's stomach.

For his part, Ruhi ruminates on his knees, as lifeless as he was when pierced by ten thousand thread-fine roots.

"Don't," says Veyadi. "Sunai wanted us . . . to leave him alone."

"That's not what I want," she says.

"I know."

Imaru's knuckles whiten on the harness straps. "Are you asking me to do something about him anyway?"

"If you need to. If he makes you. I trust you with that choice."

Imaru considers the offer for a heartbeat. She accepts what Veyadi holds out to her: her stun baton, the disruptor, and a new set of responsibilities. She's always eager to take on jobs that other people forsake.

They brace themselves for another disorienting spate of static as Veyadi turns to face them. If anything, they grow surer of themselves within their body, their exhaustion, and the security of the straps across their shoulders.

Certainty in their form grants them room to think. As Veyadi approaches, they weave a conclusion like a net—they need to catch the doctor. They need the answers he won't give them.

The first string: the fragtech's abnormal behavior. Reconcile Elegy cupped them in its great hands until they could at some point be ferried across the bay to Lotus; the carnage left in front of the Harbor, while Grotto remains relatively untouched apart from Reconcile Elegy's path of destruction; the frags' ongoing, pacifistic investigation of Khuon Mo and their enduring presence in the city. What keeps the frags here, if not the will of some human vessel for the entity that commands them all?

Next they run their fingers across the braid of Imaru and Ruhi's confessions: neither of them said anything of how they came by their passenger—they did not know. They only confessed *why* they gave in to its offer.

At last, there, the knot tying it all together: Veyadi, who approaches them across the cargo bay as a black hole in their mind. He is an immense stretch of goddamn *nothing*. Even as at times they can slip into his skin, feel his breath in their lungs, he remains a trick of the mind: unreal, untrue.

They can't properly see the graft as he approaches them, but it's stark in their memory: the strip of chitin cradling his upper vertebrae. They have been severed from him before, by his prosthetic. They have previously felt the scope of his manipulations, his insight into and command of NT architecture. They cannot, however, be simultaneously separated from his network and consumed by it; one precludes the other. How, then, has he simultaneously controlled them yet been all but invisible to their neurotransitive eye?

"Guess we left you two alone, didn't we," they say as he nears. "What did it offer you, Adi? When did you say yes?"

Veyadi stops outside arm's reach. Without his visor, dismay cracks him clean open. They've found him out.

When the Maw took Sunai, they sheared out Veyadi, and he was left alone. Alone, that is, but for the piece of Sunai that the Maw rejected: the stolen archive from the Dahani peaks. Where has the passenger been all this time? Right where they left it.

"That's not . . ." Veyadi's hand rises to his temple, as it always does when his thoughts upset him. "Somewhat. It more explains the nature of our relationship than the cause."

"Nerd."

Veyadi glowers, at once stricken and irritated.

"So," they say, "are you going to kill me?"

His clenched jaw says: *I have every reason to.*

"It's just, you don't seem to be doing a very good job."

"I *should* kill you." Veyadi closes in. They could touch him, if they wanted to. Or he could touch them. Either way, they would die. "After everything you've done . . . Everything I've made you do . . ."

He lays a hand on their wrist. They learn their arm was throbbing, because it deadens under his fingertips. Capillary root swells in their joints as their autonomous self shivers against their mortal flesh. They will come undone, if he wills it.

"Adi," they say.

Veyadi flinches from the name. He never liked hearing that endearment from the Maw's mouth; from Sunai, it enticed him even as it bewildered. They don't mean it as an attack. They're saying: I see you. I know you. I'm sorry.

"If you're not going to use the passenger," they say, "then why is it still with you?"

They saw the mechanism when they helped him sift through Imaru and Ruhi: the passenger stays with a vessel so long as its necessity is in question. If a human answers yes, it bestows corruption. If no, it recedes and visits the next suffering soul. If it lingers in the doctor, he must still be deciding whether to kill them. Yet Veyadi's touch is delicate—not a trait they generally associate with murder. More fool them, probably.

Veyadi says, "I was going to explain, but you called me a nerd."

"Affectionately."

Veyadi glares, aggrieved. He must regret everything about them. They turn their arm so they can hold his wrist as he holds theirs, promising to listen. Veyadi grimaces. His free hand trails to his nape, where that chitin is grafted to his skin.

"It's contained," he says. "For now. You had an influence, I think."

It certainly liked to say as much, when it was only with Sunai.

"It was afraid of how its time with you had changed it, so when I offered this measure of separation, it agreed." His knuckles press against the chitin graft. "It's trapped, in here. I don't know if it even wants to leave. It might be happier in containment."

"Does it think you're going to change your mind?"

"I don't know. I don't think so." Veyadi's hand tightens on their arm, and tendrils of capillary root peek from under their nail beds. It doesn't hurt; he won't let them hurt. "But if I can't justify using it, despite everything it's done . . . How can I let it go? How could I let someone else . . . Sunai, I can't . . ."

He stops short, breath shaky, and his head falls to their shoulder. Perhaps it's because he called them "Sunai." Or maybe he's ashamed that his little human fear of murder has overpowered his moral conviction.

They recognize this moment for the failure Veyadi perceives it to be. They faced it too, as Sunai, when he failed to kill the Maw. Do Sunai and the Maw deserve to live? Well, are they going to hurt more people? They might, if they can't control themselves, which is pretty damn up in the air. But Veyadi can't kill them. For that at least they can be grateful.

So they hold Veyadi's head close as his hot, short breath wets the dip of their throat. Their fingers knot in Veyadi's mussed hair, and their eye is drawn to the black-and-gold strip disappearing down his vertebrae into the collar of his jacket.

"You mean to be its jailer," they say, nails skimming the graft. "Like you were for me. Same job, different prisoner."

Veyadi stiffens. They ought to apologize. Between Sunai and the Maw, they know him well enough to piece together what he's been up to. Veyadi used the frags the passenger let him command to chase the Harbor off Lotus. He needed the space to decide whether he would kill the Maw, and with it, Sunai. That's why he had them interrogate Imaru and Ruhi—because he couldn't bring himself to accept the passenger's offer. So he tried to understand why his predecessors had.

In the end, he still can't do it. Though his mind might comprehend the violence, he can't grasp it in his heart. Worse, he can't imagine passing off the passenger's offer to anyone else. What if they said yes? Hence the backup plan. Veyadi intends to hand both himself and his charge to the Harbor.

Can they object to the passenger's imprisonment? Of course not. But Veyadi would go with it. Him, they don't want to lose.

They say, "You know I hate to admit this, but Jin's right. What makes you think the Harbor's your best option?"

"They have resources. ENGINEs. If I ever . . ."

They cluck. "Come now. ENGINEs? Giant killing machines you could neuter with a flick of your finger. I thought we agreed, Adi: punching won't solve this problem." They sigh. "Fuck. Okay, whatever. Get me out of this harness."

Veyadi tenses in their arms. "Excuse me?"

"Ueda's our point of contact, I suppose? She's more amenable than she likes to seem. You should probably do the talking, though. I ripped her leg off the other day."

"No."

"Oh, yes. Unfortunately, yes."

Veyadi grips their shoulders. "You're not doing this again. *I* can't do this again. You have to stop throwing yourself at other people's problems."

"Not until you stop assuming you're a problem. I'm afraid you've earned a bit of care."

"I haven't," he insists. "None of us have. Not from *you*."

He means Sunai. Sunai, who's suffered more betrayals than is fair for the average life span. But they can only ever be betrayed when they've dared to trust, and they can't make themselves regret doing that.

"You've been very dedicated to being very kind to me, Adi." Their hands creep over his wrists so that they can run their thumbs over his palms. "You think you were being selfish. That you were drawing me closer for the sake of, I don't know, your research? But you underestimate the amount of shit you've waded through for my sake."

They bring his knuckles to their lips. His fingers tremble; shy or fearful or wanting, they can't know, as he won't let them. They feel his body keenly, but his mind is hauntingly opaque.

"I get to decide to be grateful," they say. "I get to return favors in kind. You want me to live? Fine, I'll live. I want you to live too. I think you deserve it."

When they raise their eyes to meet his, they find misery and bated breath. When they cup his cheek, he can only relent, his breath halting on their palm.

"You can either let me stay now, or you can send me away and wait for me to come charging back to make myself *everybody's* problem—because I suspect I won't care for whatever the Harbor's done to you by then."

Veyadi lets out a shuddering sigh. He allows their palm to remain.

"So?" they say. "May I? I want this, Adi. I want to stay."

His soft mouth spells surrender against their palm. He curses into their skin, but he doesn't take himself away. "I don't . . ."

Whatever form this last protest will take, they've already won. They're ready for it, and they allow themselves to melt, sure they have secured something to be grateful for: a chance to survive, together.

Then they are ripped apart from within.

―――――

It is as if someone seizes the reins of their being and splatters them into a wall. Though their flesh is whole, they are reduced to gurgling viscera strung together only by their tendons and their harness, thoughts leaking from their mouth and nose and ears in a stuttering trail of total confusion.

Their body—because now they are just body, ow, fuck, body, why—knows a cousin of this pain. They suffered it below the lighthouse shrine on Lily, and in a corridor of the Heavenly Pearl, and now here again, rent asunder yet trapped within themselves. Someone got their hands on that damned disruptor.

They're aware of this in the same way they're aware of any death: the placidity that comes with submitting to pain. They hear: Anguished surprise, the sizzle and crack of Imaru's stun baton, a meaty thud at their feet. They see: Veyadi sprawled facedown. Ruhi on top of him. Ruhi's hands around Veyadi's neck, fingers latched, squeezing—tearing. They smell: Sweat, rancid. Blood, fresh.

They make slurried protest: *Ruhi, no, Ruhi, don't. You can't do this again. You said you wouldn't, you said you couldn't.*

Ruhi can't finish the job with his nails, so he applies a pocket-knife. It makes a bloody goddamn mess. He staggers to his feet holding the limp black leech of Veyadi's prosthetic in reverential hands. "I'm sorry," he says.

Veyadi doesn't respond. He hasn't made a sound, but for the squelch of torn skin.

"I know. I keep failing you." Ruhi's gaze is inescapable when he looks to them. His bruised eyes and broken mouth, the tremble of his bloody fingers, within which rests the prosthetic graft, the passenger's prison. White tendrils writhe from the sides of black chitin, reaching for the divots of Ruhi's fingers, seeking union. "I didn't want to be the one to do it. I was content to be a coward. I didn't think of what would happen if he failed like I had. I'm sorry. You shouldn't have had to suffer any more."

The *Never Once* vibrates. Metal dents, bends, screaming as it tears. Sky floods through the ripped-open roof of the cargo bay. The brilliant haloed head of Reconcile Elegy casts jagged shadows across their pitiful mortal tableau. Ruhi gazes up, ecstatic with his own horror, and asks it to shatter the world.

No.

You wake in the arms of a great white tree. It springs from the base of the disemboweled *Never Once,* anchoring fragile metal to broken earth. It swallowed you as it grew, because it was frightened that if it didn't, you would die. The funny thing is, you were already dead, and I knew it.

Fuck.

I know, I know. It's complicated. Did you die when Ruhi drove the killing volt into your side and your heart seized? Or was it when he cut the graft from your neck, and your brain, already crisped, went dark with pain and anger and fear? Parts of you haven't yet reached the end of their biological capacity, organs hungry to live trapped in a body past its expiration date. One by one they will asphyxiate. Then you'll be all gone.

It's funny, I don't think I'm sad yet. Grief didn't make me grab you. It just occurred to me, as I hung there in the harness, that I was about to lose you. I don't know if you've noticed, but I'm kind of shit at letting things go. Khuon Mo, Imaru, Ruhi—I ran from every one. I would rather have pretended I never knew them, never loved them. Or maybe I wanted to pretend nothing had gone wrong. I could only do that if I couldn't see them anymore.

But I'm changing, Adi. I'd gotten to thinking I couldn't. I was trapped in this joke of a body, timeless, unmarkable. I couldn't even let myself want things. I asked Imaru to want for me. When I couldn't have her, I turned to Ruhi. When it was just me . . . Well. You saw that mess. A craven creature, hungry for any sensation that led him to oblivion.

You, though, I saw the want in you. I liked it. I always do. But you wouldn't let me take your desire for myself. You asked me to want for my own sake. You thought I should just . . . be alive. I didn't know what to do with that. It made me start to want you instead.

And then you tried to take yourself away. Who's the idiot now, jackass?

Still me, probably. I took you into myself as if that would dam the flow of time, but I'm the one God ejected from every instance of the universe. You're about to pass from this one to the next. I'm not there, Adi. I don't know how to follow you.

I suppose I could let the passenger kill me. I doubt I have much choice. The fragments of its former victims, my murdered brethren, rip great gouges in the root network under Lotus. Ruhi commands them to rend. I dissolve under his judgment. I might be dying. Finally!

But if he meant to kill me, shouldn't he have started with my beating heart? He could have slit my throat as easily as he cut your neck. Could have sliced my roots from my bones, or my lungs from my rib cage. Ah. No. He's clever. He knows that with you dead, I'm . . . not a problem. Not for him.

Well, fuck him for being right.

Oh, do you see that? Imaru is coming to. She unhooks herself from her harness on the other side of the broken cargo bay, then stumbles across the knotted floor, tearing her palms, bruising her knees. I didn't see Ruhi take her baton, or the disruptor, but it couldn't have been difficult after I weakened her. She kneels in a white nook, in front of the mangled harness out of which I grew, and she touches the scrap of your bloody shirt peeking between the whorls of my bark.

I'm afraid she'll ask me to let you go. I won't enjoy denying her. No, not even after she held me down and fed me to—me? Hmm . . . The point is, how could I hate her for hating herself?

"You wanted to save him," she says.

That pains me to hear. Of course I do. But I have no way to say it unless I pierce her wrists and cut my answer into her mind. The bruised red spots up and down her arms from where we invaded her in the Lotus shrine are stark and accusatory. I hurt her terribly. I don't think I can do it again.

See? Another thing Ruhi's right about. What a jerk.

"Sunai . . ." Imaru produces from her palm a small black device, the disruptor Ruhi stole from her so he could take the passenger from you. She retrieved it from the floor; I suppose he had no reason to keep it. "If you need him, you can have him."

I can't respond to her, but you've seen how I am with Imaru. We do only half our talking with our mouths. She reads my need and pushes the button. I fall apart. This time, I take you with me. When we reconstitute, you'll be part of us, just as we'll be part of you.

"Or, that was the plan," I say.

You stand from your seat in the eating hall of the archivist compound on Lily. I catch the cup of tea you drop. You stare at the orchard outside the vaulted arches lining the hall, at the delicate orchid, lilac, and begonia shades of the living coral striated through the bone of the ceiling. You're also staring at me. It's strange to see myself through your eyes—taller than you, if not by much, mussed, bespectacled, and more visibly irritated than I would ever have allowed myself as an archivist. I'm worried I look young. I'm not young, Adi.

You ask me, "What have you done?"

You know what I've done. I don't say it because of the edge in your voice, and because I think you know that I know that you know, etc.

"Welcome to recursive hell," I say. I finish my tea, I stand, I stretch. You fixate on my hair, my clothes, my bearing, none of it fitting for my Lily years. I'm salvage-rat, through and through. Me at my worst, more or less. I hold out a hand. "Let's walk."

You don't take my hand, and I don't take it personally. The circumstances are fucked. We are alone on the isle, practically alone in the world. For now, at least. Maybe forever.

"I could do it," I say as we pass under guava, mango, passion fruit. "Technically speaking. We could resurrect together. I, and I, and I. You felt how swiftly I did it the first time—just me, and me, then neither and both. Twinned, then one. I would have found a way to take you too, if you'd loved me."

"I did," you say, small and raw.

"You did," I agree. For a second I'm annoyed to have accused you of something so cruel (how dare I say you didn't love me, when you gave so much of yourself to my resurrection) and then for denying it was true (and once I lived, you kept me imprisoned, chained, tortured, abandoned). "But not in a way I could use. I had to hijack Sunai."

"And now you've killed him. What a clever escape plan."

"You're deader than I am, asshole."

You leave the orchard as I trail behind you. You hate how much I sound like myself. You can't reconcile Sunai with the Maw, and what you've lost of the former, or what you must accept of the latter in order to have any of him.

You stop at the lighthouse cliff overlooking the beach. You stand in the exact spot where I, the Maw, fed I, Sunai, my archive when I first tried to become myself. Now that I've had the thought, you know it too. You are livid.

"You knew you'd killed the other relics," you say. "Ate them from the inside out. Why did you think it would be any different with him?"

"Do you know why I killed them?"

My question shocks you. It sounds so much like a confession, when you never expected me to take responsibility. I've changed, Adi. I thought that was obvious. Clearly not. You make yourself look at me, as if otherwise I'll vanish.

I shrug. I shrink. I don't want to be cavalier. "You think I did it on purpose. I didn't. No . . . I did. But not how . . . I . . . think? Shit."

You are at once repulsed and compelled by my distress as I wrestle between one self and the other. Because you're so unbelievably you, you step forward. I step back. When we move again, we're at the foot of the well-trodden path from the orchard to the lighthouse, and we are no longer alone. A pilgrim train of white-robed supplicants move around and past us, herded by the green and gold of my archivists.

I haven't summoned them on purpose. But you know by now how little of what I do originates in studied thought. I drag my feet through the stream of human sacrifice. "It's because of Iterate Fractal," I say. You don't need me to clarify, but I need it spoken, made unambiguous and solid so I can carry the fault. "I mean—because of *me*. I lived so closely with my citizens. I lived in you. *As* you. Because I loved you. And because I was selfish."

I caress a supplicant's cheek; they lean into my fingers and slip away. When I next speak of "you," I speak to them. "That was why none of you ever ran when I named you supplicant and called you here, even if you were afraid. I knew, so you knew, that I was trying to help. To save you. You had a hurt I couldn't otherwise heal, and if I brought you here, to the archivists and my archive, I could take you into myself, pry you apart to locate the wound, cut it out, and make it mine. Then I'd let you go."

The supplicants disappear into the lighthouse one by one. I stand at the cusp of the entrance. The archive is a fragile sapling rooted in a mound at the center of twinkling water, threaded with sweet light.

You, Veyadi, clench your fists in the courtyard outside and

resist my call. You alone, unmoved and unmoving. "You ruined people," you say. "You killed them."

Guilt stains your vitriol. You only witnessed the consequence of my meddling when you plucked the cobbled recollection of Sunai's catatonic parents from his brain.

"I did!" Again, you have no idea what to do with my agreement. "How could I not? I saw my own failures. People who wept. People who died. People who I mangled so badly that I couldn't let them go. So I remade them and tried again, only to fail a second time. I'd fashioned myself as a net, but I wasn't . . . good enough to catch them all. I was broken too, broken in a way I couldn't see. I needed help."

I step into the lighthouse. You discover you can't bear to let me out of your sight, so at last, you follow.

We are alone inside, or so it seems until we step into the pool of water at its center. The neural maps of capillary root clump and layer, up and down torsos, encircling limbs. There they are! The supplicants, drowned, threaded and bound, sleeping under the ripples.

"See?" I point to them as I cross the pool, avoiding stepping on bodies where I can. It's difficult. There are so many. "I did that. To all of them. I pulled them apart, I took in their wounds, and soon I held their everything. I could never figure out what I'd done wrong, but I couldn't let them go. And they let me! They didn't have a choice. I'd taken that from them first."

You stepped into the pool before you realized what I'd filled it with. Your mind is frozen by revulsion. You kneel, probing a supplicant's throat. "I know her," you say. "She was a relic."

Yes. You do. She was one of the last remaining when the Harbor caught you and sat you down before me. You remember her name, as you remember all the relics who preceded you, even the ones you only met as reams of analysis in manila folders. This one was the first I devoured in front of you.

I sit on the mound where the archive is planted, knees to chest. "I consumed every relic the Harbor sent me. Just like I consumed the supplicants I couldn't fix. They're not gone—or no more than any frag is gone. They're shredded. Splintered. Stuck, in me. No matter how I tried to put them back together, I never could. They wouldn't let me."

"Is that supposed to be an excuse or an apology?" you ask, incredulous.

"No. Of course not. Sorries couldn't mend this. I knew I needed an answer even before I died. That's why I made *me*. Sunai, I mean." I stop. I put my hand to my chest.

I stand to pace the mound beneath shivering translucent leaves, waving at myself. I am tipping into ghastly delirium, surprised I'm capable of surprising myself.

"I was skeptical," I explain, to you and to myself, "scarred by early traumas . . . and so I groomed myself, carefully. To be a stopgap. A countermeasure. I was trained to doubt, obsessively. So I could question me—Iterate Fractal. So I'd catch the ones that fell through its gaps." I cover my mouth; I want to bite the hand for the pain it would give us both—damn me, damn me. "It wanted me to resist. It wanted my dissent."

Ah. Fuck. I see it now. Too late, I see.

"That was what I—what Iterate Fractal was going to tell me on Lotus," I murmur. "Right before corruption hit. It never explained what it wanted from me. I was beginning to suspect, but it couldn't tell me outright that I was a moral experiment—an external conscience. Telling me would have ruined the project. It couldn't guide me, because I was supposed to guide *it;* if it took charge, I'd be useless—just another one of its flock, fit only for slaughter. Shit."

You are torn between a need to hold me and a desire to punch me in the jaw. I'd take either. I don't know which it's going to be as you pick around the submerged bodies. I pace relentlessly. I want to flee. But I remember, as you reach damp earth, that if I run from you now, I may never find my way back to you.

You're still dying, Adi.

"You really think you're Sunai," you say as you step onto the archival mound, free of affect. I can't say I know how you feel. A riot seethes under your tongue.

"Who else could I be?" I hug myself. "Fuck, does this mean it worked? It ate me, but I'm still *me*. So long as Ruhi doesn't kill me. And so long as I don't relent! Which maybe I should? It—I— *Iterate Fractal*—I get it. I do. It wanted to stop hurting people, so it tried to find a better way. Fine. Good. But did it have to make me think that I . . ."

I cover my eyes. I can't stop the visions throbbing through my mind. Stealing through the orchard with a company-cat, spying on my parents in the meditation hall, watching crying suppliants climb the hill on Lily, knowing one day it'd be me, because I couldn't love Iterate Fractal, because I couldn't see why it was good.

"No. Fuck that. It wasn't trying to be *good*," I hiss. "It was sad it couldn't push us as far as it wanted. It was just building a better cage. Fuck. This isn't worth it. I should just let the passenger kill me."

I'm probably crying. I lose track of time, and space goes with it. You anchor me. Your arms, your heat. I am reminded that elsewhere, and here, I hold your physical body in a vast white trunk, as you cradle me in this moment before we die.

"Don't you goddamn dare," you say into my hair. "Please, Sunai. If there's any chance for you to get out of this—I need you to take it."

"Don't make me go back alone." I bite my tongue, I curse, I bury my head in your shoulder. "Sorry. I mean, I don't *want* to go alone. But I can't force you to come with me . . . with us."

That's the point of me, isn't it? If I want something, I should tell myself no, because my want means nothing against the desires of the people who live by my will and power.

When I primed myself, Sunai, to resist myself, Iterate Fractal, I don't think I understood that meant that sometimes, I would have to let you choose to leave.

You have that choice now, Adi. You can go, cease, un-be. I love you, so I'd hate to lose you, but I'd hate it more if I'd obliged you to be mine, to never again be only yourself.

See? I'm doing it already. I should be speaking these words—or aping speech, in that way we do while entangled—but instead, I make them the fundament of your being. The power I have to overwrite you frightens me. I can't doom you to my narrative. I won't.

You feel you should let go of me, but you also feel as though we're inextricable, molded skin to skin, curled into and around each other like twin yolks in a fragile egg. You think: I hate this too. But as I retreat from that hate, you hold me. You mean: Whatever hate finds purchase on me, far more is embedded in you.

You hate being alive, sometimes. "Often," you say. You feel like an asshole. "All the time!" You think I'm shortsighted, misguided, and a hypocrite. "I tore you apart. Both of you. All of you. I took from you everything the Harbor wanted—everything I wanted. Now you act like I don't owe you. I hate that you love me. You shouldn't love me. I don't know how you can, except I've seen you give yourself up time after time, because you can't fucking let yourself have anything, and I—"

You can't stand it. You kiss me. If I'll take nothing else, you want me to have you. You think yourself selfish, thoughtless, and cruel. You hate. We love. I devour you whole.

41

Leaf 3: "Feast" is commonly considered a companion to Leaf 27: "Flourish," insofar as they are attributed to the same author, a pre-Cradle Dahani abbess with a fondness for cannibalistic metaphor. In Leaf 3, an Emanation of God takes to visiting the bed of a young novice who is in truth another Emanation of God, though they have not yet realized themself as such. During one particularly vigorous sex act, the novice achieves divine knowledge and becomes an Emanation as well. In the mutual epiphany of self-recognition, their lover swallows them whole—or vice versa. Depends on the translation.

"Really? That's where your mind goes?" Veyadi, crouched on the roof of the rent-open cargo bay, scrubs his eyes, and discovers an inherent horror. He is still the fleshly body he knew, but he is encased in—and *has become*—fifteen feet of coral, bone, and supple wood, born of the tree that was-is Sunai. He's a beast built for the task at hand: the defense of Lotus, Sunai, and himself. His disgust is astonishingly cute. "You didn't eat me."

"I absolutely did!" Sunai is mining his own body. He peels himself from the trunk fiber by fiber, extracting a form defined by use-case and conservation of resource. Veyadi, threaded through the capillary network of Lotus, has a mechanical instinct for the exploitation of their body that Sunai lacked, and that the Maw was, to a point, unwilling to reckon with.

"Don't be an ass," the Maw replies. "I've been—stressed." It pauses, flickering with shame over its impulsive theft of tongue as it lets Sunai pick his forearm free of clinging white bark. "Sorry. Thanks. I feel . . ."

"Controlled," says Veyadi.

"Coherent," says Sunai.

"Present," says the Maw.

Veyadi, uncomfortable, turns his attention to the army ravaging Lotus. They feel the tug of his plan, which begins with an accounting of the most pressing threats to their network's integrity. Ruhi hasn't come to kill them yet. Sunai supposes he won't; the man thinks they're dead! Veyadi proposes an alternative: Ruhi hasn't killed them because Ruhi *can't*.

Entwined as they all are now, they have seen what Veyadi saw: when Ruhi assaulted Grotto, he stopped short of murdering Sunai and the Maw. He turned to Veyadi to do it, pleaded for his help. Ruhi has evidently found it in himself to pick the knife back up, but faced with the prospect of killing either of them directly, he has once more choked.

"Hypocrite," sniffs Sunai.

"Obviously," says Veyadi.

The Maw is too ashamed to follow up. Does it find the passenger's willingness to write off suffering bone-gratingly vile? Yes. Does it have a leg to stand on? Well.

"Four," says Sunai. "You've got four."

"I'm in hell," says Veyadi.

Ruhi's hesitation may not save them, but it would be a shield. They can survive him, if they are quick and decisive. If they commit.

Sunai at last extracts his bad ankle. Even with his new body—fifteen feet just like Veyadi's, although differently equipped—he needs to correct his own vision, and the leg wavers unless he puts special thought into stabilizing it. He'll have to ask Veyadi to test whether that's a matter of cognitive assumption. Veyadi shushes them. He needs to focus. Good. Sunai has found someone else who needs his attention.

Imaru slumps in a cradle of white root and metal wall, where she dragged herself after they first began to emerge. She's wilting, and her eyes shiver beneath their lids. The disruptor that saved them lies clutched in her palm. Sunai gathers her in the crook of his arm.

"You can't take her with us," says Veyadi.

"I know."

"It isn't safe."

He knows that too. But he can't leave her here, unprotected. She never left him.

He doesn't have the luxury of figuring out where to bring her before the half-crumpled door leading to the rest of the *Never Once* buckles. The humans who engineered its destruction pour in after—a bedraggled trio of Gingers. Two of them carry harpoon guns, which they fire at Sunai.

Sunai dodges one harpoon and catches the other in his shoulder as he twists to shield Imaru. Veyadi cries out; the Maw roils, furious; Sunai, pained and panicking, gives in to their emotion. His free arm lashes out, finger joints unfurling. Capillary root spills from his palm in a lightning web laced with bone and coral, sharp enough to slice joints, pierce necks—

A stab of guilt from Veyadi. A flash of fear from Sunai. At the last second, they change course. Their web secures itself to rig flooring, already warped by burgeoning tree roots, and tears. Ceramic cracks and metal screams as they throw up a haggard barrier. A second round of harpoons clang against it. Sunai flags, heaving for breath, unable to tear the harpoon from his shoulder without releasing either the wall or Imaru.

"Wait!"

The shout comes from behind the Gingers. Wei Jin hobbles in through the door to the rest of the *Never,* supported by Cothai, guarded by Oyu. Sunai rocks back on his haunches and allows himself to be observed as Jin pushes past their crew, their face cast in a foreign state of reverence. They take in the tree, the roots, and the fifteen feet of wood-bone-coral robot crouched behind the barricade of hull and roots. They eye the gash in the roof of the cargo bay and the outline of Veyadi crouched above it. Finally, they land on Imaru, nestled in Sunai's arm.

"Sunai? That you?"

Sunai grins. It must be unsettling. The Gingers tense and Jin cackles.

"God's infinite tits, that explains everything. Give her over."

Sunai's heart goes taut, echoed by wary doubt from the Maw and Veyadi. Wei Jin has earned all their suspicion. But as Jin beckons for the Gingers to retrieve Imaru, Sunai unfolds his arm, roots peeling away from coral to deposit Imaru's body at their feet.

"We're trusting you," he says to Jin, aware for the first time of what he *sounds* like—that clinking mélange of un-voice he thought of as the Maw's. "Don't fuck this up."

"Please!" Jin scoffs. "I always liked Imaru better." They soften despite themself, once more scanning his body. "It's bad out there, Sunai. I thought . . ." They look to the ripped-open roof, and the brittle darkness in their eyes reveals their fears: that he and Veyadi were dead, the Maw with them. They square their jaw to ask, "What do you need?"

"The passenger wants my roots. My network." Sunai looks up as well, toward Veyadi. He's received a mental image, though he doesn't yet understand it. "Drones? He wants drones. Send them our way."

Jin frowns, their brow a deep cut of consternation. They dismiss Sunai with a jerk of the chin. He lingers long enough to delicately nudge the disruptor out of Imaru's fist. Best not leave it in anyone else's hands.

He lifts himself to join Veyadi on the roof. The movement is laborious, but pleasurably tactile. Veyadi brushes the length of his arm—the one he used to hold Imaru. At the joint of Sunai's wrist, a slithering root uncoils from Veyadi's finger and nestles under Sunai's coral chassis, to replenish what he just expended. It's a negligible loss, and of paltry strategic value. Any part of Veyadi given to Sunai is a part Veyadi no longer has.

"That's the point," Veyadi says. Veyadi gives because he wants to, needs to, especially now, in the moments before they spring from the roof into the fray.

Sunai uses that careful curl of root to secure the disruptor against the skin over his flesh-heart. It's as safe there as it can be, and if he loses it, he won't live to regret the loss.

They separate. Sunai makes for the cluster of frags between the *Never Once* and the Harbor—three black Anthills and a bulky patchwork friend twice their size, good old Yield-Naught-and-Perish-Aflame. Yield-Naught breaks rock with its enormous fists while the Anthill frags scrabble in the rubble, shredding every exposed scrap of capillary root. Sunai announces himself by slamming his hand into the back of the nearest Anthill frag's head and shoving it face-first into the ground. He dodges the second Anthill's retaliatory lunge and knocks it flat with a kick to the spine. The third Anthill frag grapples him from behind. Sunai hip-tosses it into Yield-Naught, which staggers back. Then he darts close to smear his palm over Yield-Naught's hip joint before scrambling free.

Veyadi is already at work. He twists and twines the clutches of root Sunai planted on the frags, filament extensions bringing discord and shattering joints. He breaks limbs from within and reaches for core operating systems, where he tears out component after component, until his victims can only twitch amid the rubble.

Breaking the frags feels good unless they think about it, so they don't. Sunai dashes for the next cluster. Veyadi disintegrates frags that he commanded mere hours ago. This is how they save themselves—and they must save themselves, for each other.

At the top of the slope, a phalanx of frags advance on the

Harbor, aiming for the dense knot of capillary root beneath the Lotus shrine. The Ginger crews stationed at the landing field fire harpoons and razor-edged nets—the sort deployed against frags you have no intention to salvage. An Anthill frag convulses at the edge of the landing field, hands scrabbling for purchase on fractured concrete. Then Reconcile Elegy raises an elegant, tapered foot and stomps through the roof of the main garage. There is smoke, and there are screams.

As Reconcile Elegy raises its foot again, Sunai breaks away from his second cluster of downed frags. He gallops up the slope, dodging the carcasses of Harbor vehicles, and throws himself at Elegy's calf.

In a captive sliver of time, Reconcile Elegy swivels at the waist. An iridescent slash of cape slaps Sunai out of the air. He tumbles to the landing field and skids into a rig that crumples on impact. In an instant, Veyadi is there to haul him to his feet. "Get back," Sunai insists. Veyadi stays. He must. They can't abandon each other now.

They can't reach Elegy either. The giant once more kicks into the guts of the Harbor, crushing screams from collapsed walls. Simultaneously, Elegy's contingent turns their attention from the Harbor to the Maw and its relics. Ruhi must have noticed they're no longer entombed in their tree.

A rig flying militia colors and sporting the name *Pretty Three* storms up the slope from behind. Sunai drags Veyadi out of the way as it barrels past. The *Pretty Three* crashes into one of the Anthill frags scrambling down the Harbor's walls, sending them both into an ungainly sprawl across the airfield. The rig lurches to its feet, six-legged, with sails like wings.

The Anthill frag is more agile, but while it's pinned, the *Pretty* has the advantage. Its sail-wings swing forward on articulated arms to smother the frag with magnetic clamps and electric charge. More militia rigs claw and slither up the hill from the bay to engage the frags at the Harbor's base. Someone's summoned the cavalry.

A flight of drones swoops down to circle Sunai and Veyadi, and one settles on Sunai's head. Jin's voice rings tinnily out of it. "All right, I got your damn drones. What's next?"

Veyadi snatches one out of the air and turns it over to inspect its servos. "How agile are they?"

"Does it matter? These are as good as you're going to get."

"Insufferable," mutters Veyadi. He holds the drone out to Sunai. Sunai takes it in both hands and smears a web of capillary root over its chassis. Veyadi catches another to give it the same treatment. To Jin, Veyadi says, "I need you to fly these at Reconcile Elegy. Aim for the cape."

"Why?"

"Do it well, and we'll live long enough for me to tell you."

The drones soar, all coated with capillary root. Jin feeds them a complex, darting pattern, and the drones form a flickering tapestry of dispersed self. Sunai, Veyadi, and the Maw have their feet planted on the cracked airfield, but they're also gliding, flitting, dodging the ripples of Reconcile Elegy's cape. Veyadi hunches over on the ground, knuckles braced in concrete as he concentrates. Sunai focuses on Veyadi's raised coral shoulders, his rigid bone spine, and on protecting him from any frag that dares approach.

A slash of cape bisects one drone. It flattens another against the Harbor walls. A third crashes into Elegy's thigh. But a fourth is buoyed by the updraft of one snapping cape length and spins end over end into the fold of another. Root touches cloth, and Veyadi follows.

Capillary tendrils flood the cape segment, tearing through minuscule iridescent networks of threaded thought as ruthlessly as the frags tore into the roots of Lotus. The banner disintegrates overhead, glittering destruction raining on the landing field.

Reconcile Elegy slows, beautiful hand poised over a ragged hole in the Harbor's roof. Through the tattered shimmer of its cape, a human silhouette crouches in its palm.

Ruhi.

It hurts to see him, like a finger jabbed into a muddy wound. He stands and seems to face them. Then he turns and steps off Elegy's palm.

Veyadi rips through Elegy with a vicious quickness that leaves Sunai reeling. The root that tore through the cape becomes the root lancing into Elegy's neck. It infiltrates core systems like lightning with a vendetta, and the second Veyadi reaches Elegy's spine, he seizes command of the great hand on which Ruhi stood, contorting it in midair and snatching forward—

Until its fingers abruptly stutter to a halt and the hand falls limp.

Veyadi collapses. Sunai catches him and lays him down, pressing their foreheads together. He wants to scold, but Veyadi knows he made a greedy mistake and is already berating himself. Sunai is more worried by Veyadi's convulsing musculature, his dimming verdant *self.* He expended too much, too quickly, at too great a distance. Veyadi acknowledges all this with a devastated moan—and it didn't even work!

"But it did," says Sunai. "Elegy was his. You took it from him."

Even now, Reconcile Elegy is frozen. The remains of its cape drift in the damp wind of a world waiting for a storm. Frags and rigs clash at its feet. One rig careens into its ankle and lurches away, fearful of a retaliation that never comes.

"We can do this," Sunai says. "We can stop them."

He hauls Veyadi upright. Veyadi sags against him, afraid that he won't be enough, because he never is.

"It's everything, you're everything." That doesn't mean he's up to the task. He isn't even sure he can manage the climb into the Harbor. Sunai scoffs. "Fuck it, what am I here for?"

So Sunai wrenches open Veyadi's chest and scoops his flesh out of it, then pulls Veyadi into the safety of his own torso with dozens of grasping bone-and-coral hands, clasping them together heartbeat-to-heartbeat. The toll of wresting Reconcile Elegy away from Ruhi is inescapable. Veyadi's pulse flutters, inconsistent. Sunai girds his heart with roots and cradles him as he dashes toward the Harbor, Elegy, and Ruhi.

Sunai scales Elegy's unmoving body, bounding up smooth limbs and catching armored ridges. Elegy is inert beneath them, still as stone. Sunai aches to think of it that way. Veyadi twinges with guilt but urges him forward.

Perched on Elegy's wrist, over the limp hand with which they failed to catch Ruhi, they look down the hole Elegy punched into the Harbor. It pierced all the way through to the shrine. The distant floor is a mess of reinforced concrete, girders, and steel plating, and at the center stands Ruhi. This time, he doesn't look at them.

If he had, they might not have found the courage to leap.

Their descent is controlled by a rope of root modeled on spider silk, spooling out of their palms as they slide. They have no fear of impact. They fall toward the hub of all the power that remains outside of their body, with which they will be able to ensnare their prey, whether he's willing to face them or not.

But something snaps overhead. They learn not by the sound but from a terrible feeling, a lurch in their gut. They twist in midair, sure of their mistake. Elegy isn't dead after all, or Ruhi stole it back, or—

But the titan does not move. It didn't break their rope—though the rope *is* breaking. White filament frays and snaps and dissipates into air, the precursor to the horror about to befall them.

Once more, the wrongness hits their innards first; then their limbs, into which wind cuts as their armor peels away from their skin; then the root laid through their nerves as it becomes a thousand stabbing fires. They gasp and grasp at themselves, but they can barely move for the pain and shock of *dissolution*. In the end they only fall, and fall, and—

They come apart before they hit the ground.

42

Sunai is dying. He is aware of this in the way he is aware of the cloudy light sloughing past Reconcile Elegy's face. Agony sits on his chest like a choking ghost, grinding his splintered spine into dust and rubble and twisted rebar. His wet cough hurts, from his gut to his ears. He'd like not to cough again. So of course, he does.

"God, I'm dying. Why am I dying? Why am I—" His breath hitches. *Alone.* Why is he alone?

A lump of bloodied flesh and cloth lies just out of his reach. Veyadi, whose chest barely moves. This silhouette is all Sunai can perceive; the Maw has vanished from his conscious mind, the fragments it seeded throughout them negated, their network lost. Destroyed. Even if they hadn't fallen, they are insensate without it, and they will soon be dead.

Sunai lurches toward Veyadi, or thinks he does. In truth he only jostles his pulped organs. He is stopped, gently. Another face looms over his, closer than Elegy and blurred in his weary, mortal eyes. Ruhi, his brow creased. Sunai moans, too addled to identify whether he's angry or afraid.

They were wrong about Ruhi. How could they have been so arrogant? Ruhi has killed them before. He was ready to kill them again. If he left them to wither in their tree instead of splitting them root and branch, that was his one boon, born of shared history. He won't hesitate again.

Ruhi's mouth contorts with an intimately familiar anxiety. The night Ruhi murdered him wasn't the first time Sunai saw it, just the first time he understood its meaning. Ruhi is about to do something he doesn't want to do, but which he must. This time, he has to kill them all. He always had to. For the Maw to die, he must destroy its vessels, whether they be tree, root, or flesh.

Sunai's eyes fall closed. "Just don't cry this time. That really fucked me up."

"How many times do I have to say it, Sunai?" Rubble clinks and clatters as Ruhi kneels beside him. His knuckles graze Sunai's cheek. "I don't want to kill *you*."

Sunai laughs until he hacks and wheezes and tears form in his eyes. He can't breathe. Ruhi supports his neck and shushes him, and Sunai does not in any way want this man to touch him. It is so freeing to finally let himself understand this, and so damning to only learn it while he's *dying*.

The wheezing recedes; Ruhi rolls Sunai onto his side and, with a soothing thump between his shoulder blades, induces him to cough. Sunai gags on the choking hardness knotted in his throat, the lump he's become all too aware of. Every fruitless cough brings forth blood and spittle and pain, and all through it, Ruhi rubs his back and murmurs until—

It pops free like sputum, fresh and dark to the ground. The glossy archival seed that Imaru fed him in the Heavenly Pearl, from which Veyadi couldn't untangle him. It lies lackluster in Ruhi's open palm.

A single tendril peeks from the split in its hull, more pale than luminous, a corrupted, twitching remnant unable to make sense of its existence without a relic to guide it.

Ruhi regards the seed with the same tenderness he's always shown Sunai. In his hands—in the passenger's palm—the Maw is dreadfully small. Whatever it could have been no longer matters. They're going to kill it and everything it might have become.

Ruhi's fingers close on the archival seed as they once closed around Sunai's throat. Sunai lets out a low moan of fear, and Ruhi pulls him into a full embrace; Sunai, limp, hangs in his arms like meat left out to dry.

"The passenger never wanted to hurt you," Ruhi says, like an undertow in his ear. "You, Veyadi, you were never the problem. We're human. If the passenger hurts us, it violates the core principle of its being."

Sunai thinks of Reconcile Elegy crushing concrete and bodies without regard for the line between stone and flesh. He thinks of capsized rigs and spattered mercs. He thinks of the cities razed, the millions dead, the lives destroyed by corruption.

"So I hoped, if I could cut you out of the Maw . . ." Ruhi's head falls on Sunai's shoulder, exposing the stark black ridge of the prosthetic he harvested from Veyadi's corpse. It's grafted to Ruhi's neck with grasping veins of flickering root. "I'm sorry."

Sunai wishes to every Emanation of God that he'd stop fucking apologizing.

"I can't take the Maw from you either. Of course I can't. It's always been in you, like it was in Veyadi. I thought that made you sacred. You held the last fragments of Iterate Fractal, the last that weren't . . ." Ruhi shivers. "I should have known better. I always hedge my bets, and it always goes wrong. I need to commit. The Maw is in you. It *is* you. I'm sorry."

Commit. Sunai rolls the word across the cracked surface of his mind, back and forth, skipping over fissures, catching, stopping. He needs to commit.

He commits to shifting in Ruhi's arms, in spite of the bones that won't hold him, the organs that slosh, the suffering woven through his matter. He commits to opening his mouth over Ruhi's bare skin, taking the breath for words he'll never speak.

He commits to his teeth, latching onto Ruhi's throat. They sink and slide past skin into something that chews until it crunches. He commits to pain as he lurches forward to throw Ruhi into the rubble, jaw clenching and clamping with every scrap of power in his bones. Ruhi struggles, and jerks, and finally spasms, and he commits to the copper blood, salt skin, and foul cartilage, to gnawing and tearing, to collapsing atop Ruhi's gurgling body, and to, at last, not crying, nor dying, no matter how he'd like to.

The twitching seed of the Maw tumbles out of Ruhi's stiff fingers. It rolls to a stop in the rubble between them and the lump of Veyadi. Sunai stares at it for a long time: eons. Blood stains his teeth and sticks his cheek to Ruhi's viscera-stained shirt like gum, and out of reach, Veyadi continues to breathe—slow, low, but certain.

Veyadi stirs. Sunai needs to roll away, to not be seen beside his work. But he's trapped in his broken body. Trapped because he decided to stay in it, because for once, he refused to die.

Veyadi's head lolls; his fingers scrape across gravel and dust as he gropes for the seed; the inch of tendril curling out of its cracked hull is flailing, blind, until it meets his cuticle. It wriggles and burrows, swift and thirsty, and as it embeds itself in Veyadi's palm, he gasps with pain, or relief, or . . .

Sunai can only guess. For a moment, this moment, he's separate. There's a safety in solitude, although he can no longer stand being only one. Shame closes his eyes when Veyadi rights himself. His teeth throb, his jaw aches. It gets so much worse when Veyadi's shaking hands lift him off Ruhi, and minuscule capillary veins slide from his palms into Sunai's tattered skin, because then Sunai is immediately and completely no longer alone.

There's no mistaking what happened, between Ruhi's excavated throat and the muscle fibers stuck in Sunai's teeth. As the Maw sutures the distance between Sunai and Veyadi from its place in Veyadi's palm, Veyadi settles into the dimensions of Sunai's violence, the weight and texture of it, his desire, his hunger.

"I'm sorry," says Sunai, and it hurts to talk because the Maw hasn't yet fixed his ruined mouth. "Shit. No, I'm not."

But he is sorry. He hates himself for it, but he wishes Ruhi weren't dead, or dying. He's sorry to have killed him, even though he knew he had to, because it is so *ugly;* how is it possible for Sunai to hate himself more than he did?

Worse, he is exposed to Veyadi, whose silent pity resonates. Veyadi can't mourn Ruhi like Sunai does. He finds tragedy in Sunai's inability to grasp this as a victory.

Veyadi takes Sunai's face in hand. His bruised palm wipes blood from Sunai's mouth—why bother, when so much of Ruhi slid down Sunai's throat?—and presses their foreheads together.

"We aren't done," he says, and it doesn't feel like a lie. "With Ruhi, or with the passenger. We could end it here. Let them die. Or . . ."

Veyadi's alternative pours from his silence into Sunai's mind and wrenches his chest. It would be a failure, on his part—a step backward, and a shameful one, because this would be no kindness. It might even be torture. It is certainly a curse.

Yet he wants it.

Sunai lowers his head and his temple skids past Veyadi's lips. When he says yes, he tries not to beg.

Their capillary network is a wisp of what it once was. The shredded licks of their selfhood that survived the passenger's assault shy away from their summons. Sunai takes the lead; when he reaches toward the remaining roots, his corruption coaxes the bedraggled scraps out to meet him. Each returning sliver brings with it a glimpse of a greater whole.

Before the Harbor: rigs and their crews reckon with an altered battlefield. Where before the fragtechs were focused as magnets, now they lash out in frenetic panic. At the foot of Lotus, two Anthill frags flee into the water, followed closely by Orderly Sum Total.

Outside the ruined *Never Once:* the six-legged *Pretty Three* raises its electrified sails in a guard stance. No frags approach, so Oyu dares to signal for help from the *Never*'s rent-open hatch of the cargo bay. Waretu appears on the *Pretty*'s deck. Relief! Salvation! But no—Acrimony Covenant limps toward them on long legs. The *Pretty*'s sails flare and Acrimony Covenant recoils. It stumbles in a berth around both rigs and throws itself over the cliff into the sea.

Within the *Never Once:* Imaru breathes shallowly and tracks Acrimony Covenant's flight through a crack in the hull. Beside her, Cothai bleeds from an injury earned defending the already wounded. Jin and their Gingers stanch his arm as best they can, but if they can't get him back to shore soon, losing the limb will be the least of his worries. As Acrimony Covenant disappears beneath the waves, Imaru slumps, letting go of the fight.

"Sunai," says Veyadi.

The name brings him round. Sunai-in-Sunai says yes, and returns, and brings with him every remaining fiber of root.

They channel their meager harvest in three directions. Veyadi siphons the first serving into the chitin of the disruptor, which they unearthed from their shattered remains strewn across the shrine. The second portion pours into the prosthetic grown into Ruhi's neck, that narrow prison within which Veyadi collected the passenger's archival self. The third and last they mold into and through Ruhi's open throat, so those pale deft threads might map his veins.

Every so often, Sunai's attention stutters. It would be easier if he allowed himself to work from a distance—if he let Veyadi or the Maw take this task from him. They are both far more expert in the technique of neural butchery. But he's selfish with the responsibility. He crafts this new life without consent, like he took the old. He commits.

In awkward synchrony, Veyadi and the Maw fashion a synthesized purpose from devices they designed to defy each other.

Disruptor and prosthetic are interwoven by the elemental architecture of chitin and root as their makers instill new framework and process.

Ruhi, they can't so easily rewire. Instead they break him as the Maw has always broken its supplicants: from within.

White roots pulse into Ruhi's wrists and flutter in the ruddy pool of his neck. They comb the contours of Ruhi's brain, teasing and carding, cautious of cutting when patience will unwind the unwanted knot. For the rest of the body, they dig, they mold, they furrow and seed. The rich flesh parts and gives way; glossy organs and banded muscles split, glimmering with sullen juice.

Into his fissures they fit their new composition, a black-and-white parcel lined with faded gold adhesive. Sunai lingers over the chitin before he folds it into the depths of Ruhi's flesh.

The parcel's work begins as soon as it leaves his fingers. Out of sight, the chitin splits and splits again, particulate matter dividing relentlessly, until it is a swarm beneath Ruhi's surface. It feeds itself to him.

As the new device disappears into Ruhi, Sunai serves as open interface, and he is unable to block out the passenger's troubled protest, especially as it escalates to pleading.

Sunai, I do not want this. Sunai, I do not *choose* this. Sunai, please, I beg you not to make me do this to him. Please, oh please, I—

So on, so forth.

The voice dissolves into a chorus of wails, screams of "antithesis" and "violation." The passenger was made to be apart from humans and to protect that separation at all costs. To bind it into Ruhi, integrating the passenger's archive with its vessel's flesh as they—Sunai, Veyadi, Maw—are integrated with each other, is an indisputable cruelty.

Veyadi's hands layer over Sunai's. Together, they knead Ruhi's flesh shut like the bottom of a dumpling.

The passenger is more than capable of rending autonomous

power from human flesh, no matter the intricacy of the integration—they know from how it sundered them as they swung down from Reconcile Elegy's hand. But to rip itself from this human prison would kill Ruhi. It might kill the passenger too; they wonder if it cares.

For now, it cries.

All that remains is to be certain they don't make Ruhi's mistake: no mercy; no holding back. They thought he would hesitate to hurt the ones he cared for. He did waver, but in the end, he made his choice. They must not leave the passenger room to do the same. They can't half-ass their savagery.

As they lure tendrils through Ruhi's pores and from under nails, out of ear and nose and mouth, Ruhi seethes; his flesh bubbles and blossoms, overflowing his silhouette, unable to maintain its form for longer than a breath. It reshapes, re-forms, and bursts, disrupted again and again, iterating on itself in perpetuity.

Each time Ruhi flowers, white sprouts slither across his bulging skin. These they catch and draw away from the roiling mass. They lace their collection of writhing tendrils into net, branch, and trunk, luminous and sturdy. The boughs that spring from ribs that have forgotten their proper shape are bent and stretched into enormous hands, clasped together. Within these, they entomb Ruhi, the thrashing un-body from which they grew the passenger's prison, until corruption's shepherd is safely anchored within its new archive, in the heart of this desolate shrine.

I, and I, and I—

Sunai spends the days that follow much like he used to on Lotus. He cooks, he cleans, he mends and gardens. When he disemboweled the *Never Once* with an arboreal temper tantrum, he had the grace to spare the galley. The ruined cargo bay, its roof split by Reconcile Elegy and its floor torn up by roots, has made a decent home for the chickens.

"They need a sheltered run," Waretu scolds him when she visits. She's captaining her own rig for now—the *Pretty Three*, recently requisitioned by defectors from the Harbor's conscript militia. "The tenbeasts are getting ambitious. You have a family of company-cats hiding in a grotto on the western cliffs."

Sunai knows about the cats. They were brought to shore on the rusted back of Orderly Sum Total, who sat for a while in the shallows to watch them hunt in tide pools before it vanished once more under the waves.

Waretu helps him clear a space for the new herb garden, and he sends her back with peach soda for the Grotto kids, which Jin left the last time they came through. When later that afternoon, Jin makes it the whole way up the hill from the docks without stopping for a break, they are openly devastated to be rewarded with cold, unsweetened barley tea.

"Is this that Harbor crap?" Jin scowls and sighs and collapses in a folding chair, cane balanced lazily across their knees. Sunai leaves the seats out in the shade of the cargo bay tree, for anyone who wants a view of Khuon Mo's shore. "You'd better have cigarettes." When he produces a pack, they snatch the whole thing from his hand. "Ha! You know you're not supposed to smoke."

"Are you kidding me?" Sunai reaches for the cigarettes, but

Jin's reflexes have recovered. Plus, they're still taller than him. "Who've you been talking to? I'm going to have you arrested for conspiracy."

"Like I haven't heard that today."

Jin is enthusiastically embedded at the Heavenly Pearl. While Madam Wei and Harbormaster Ueda scuffle for advantage in their temporary cease-fire, Jin represents a vital third party. They revel in the leverage they hold over both the harbormaster and their aunt.

They describe the week's talks as such: having been kicked off Lotus, the Harbor has negotiated the use of a series of Jasmine warehouses. In exchange, Madam Wei has latitude to sponsor work visas for a collection of post-corruption aid organizations from the mainland—most of which hail from the Immaculate Empire. She likes threatening the Harbor, says Jin. The more world powers vie for control of Khuon Mo, the more opportunities the madam has to play them off each other. A dangerous game, and an arrogant one. What's she going to do if the Immaculate Empire sends an immaculately enormous envoy?

Jin grimaces, and while Sunai groans, they elaborate: Harbormaster Ueda suspects some loyalist in their ranks has reached the mainland Harbor, and that an ENGINE-led investigation is imminent. Meanwhile, the madam expects a similar, AI-led contingent to arrive via imperial airship any day now.

"What did you tell them?" Sunai asks, playing fruitlessly with a lighter. He emptied its fluid days ago.

"That you're going to pitch a fit and sink any ship that tries to land without your consent. Obviously!"

Sunai makes a face. "Am I?"

"You think I know? You're the divine avatar of a pissed-off bone-robot, not me." Jin takes a thoughtful sip of tea, eyes turned toward the afternoon lull of reconstruction in Grotto. "Want the important news?"

He does.

Oyu and a small Ginger contingent have begun working out of the Three-Eyed Carp to facilitate the Grotto fleet's reclamation of some landward compounds. They protect the perimeter of Grotto from lurking frags and vet the militia escapees and Harbor defectors who seek to join their ranks. Cothai, meanwhile, is recuperating in Jasmine. He no longer has trouble staying awake, but he has difficulty concentrating—oh, and his wife wants a baby, so he won't be going on salvage-runs for a bit. Maybe after he's adjusted to his new arm prosthetic . . .

Jin trails off and hands the rest of the barley tea to Sunai. "Well. Where's Imaru?"

Sleeping, says Sunai. Don't be an ass, says Jin. Come back tomorrow, Sunai says. Jin bows rudely deep, pulls a back muscle, and curses him out as he gets on the radio. A Ginger comes to help Jin back down the hill to the skiff. Imaru waits for them to leave earshot before she emerges from the doorway to the rest of the *Never*.

"Do you think I can catch up?" she says.

He gives her a *Have you seen yourself?* eyebrow raise and she gives him a *Now where would I do that?* snort.

Imaru is standing. That's a triumph, all things considered. Her hair has whitened even further, and her hands tremble when she lifts anything heftier than a couple of chickens. At Sunai's frown, she sits in the folding chair Jin abandoned. He goes to get her tea. When he comes back, she's drifting off. He takes the opportunity to check her pockets for cigarettes.

"I let Veyadi throw them off the cliff," she says, eyes closed.

"I'm being persecuted."

One eye opens. Her mouth slants up. "Doctor's orders." Both eyes, now. She exhales, a faint rattle in her chest. Their roots devoured her musculature. Pinprick scars decorate her wrists where their roots slid into her veins. She didn't have the passenger to put her back together, not like Ruhi, when he . . .

Imaru catches Sunai's drifting thought. She squeezes his fist on his knee. "When Jin comes back, I'm going with them."

"What? Why?"

"You know why." Imaru's jaw works as she chews through her misgivings. "We can't hide out here forever, Sunai."

Sunai isn't hiding. How could he? All of Khuon Mo knows about the Maw and its two relics. They see the rig pinned to Lotus by a miraculous white tree; and the lifeless form of Reconcile Elegy forever trapped mid-loom over the gutted Harbor; and the fragtech who linger in the bay and on the fringes of Khuon Mo's border with the wilds, like Orderly Sum Total, and Acrimony Covenant, and a curious, chittering pair from the Anthill—those left behind when the assault abruptly ended. And they've seen the dozen other fucking infeasible phenomena that have plagued Khuon Mo in the days since Sunai and Veyadi saw fit to come home.

Imaru, she might be hiding. The infamous lieutenant of the Ginger Company, advisor to Madam Wei, who disappeared from the Heavenly Pearl shortly after playing a key role in the Maw's—assassination? Liberation? The rumors vary. They can't seem to agree whether another AI was involved. The passenger's neurotransitive shroud may have dissipated, but that just means anyone who crossed paths with it will remember the event, not that those who never met it can explain the chaos left in its wake.

The madam and the harbormaster would like Imaru where they can see her, not least because they hope to deploy her to placate dissenters—the sort of errand they once would have sent Ruhi to do. Unfortunately for them, upon their inquiry, Sunai told them both to seek out the fun end of God's eternal dick because Imaru needed time to recover. Unfortunately for him, she thinks she's done just that.

Evening comes, and Veyadi catches up to Sunai at Reconcile Elegy's left foot, where it cratered the Harbor's abandoned landing field. His new visor is the same lustrous nut brown of the archival seed, and it catches light like a shallow pool. They walk in silence all the way to Elegy's right foot, where Sunai says, "Don't start."

Veyadi digs in his work jacket and extracts a cigarette. Sunai curses when he remembers his lighter is empty. Veyadi gives him a matchbox while they sit on the cliff overlooking the company-cat nest. Sunai flops back into the sparse grass to give Veyadi a better look at his ankle wrap, like he clearly wants.

The Maw pulses between and within them, echoing each thought as an impression of heat and desire. It's the reason Veyadi knew Sunai had wandered away from the *Never*. It also let Veyadi know he's sulking, and why.

Veyadi rewraps the ankle. It aches quietly. "You should use a cane," says Veyadi.

Sunai feels bullied; he's already wearing the new specs he got from Jin. He's relented enough for at least a week. "Why, though? It's psychosomatic."

"It's a neurotransitive scar," says the Maw, with Sunai's tongue.

Veyadi's lip twitches. The aversion in his mind is far more acute. The Maw recedes, reprimanded.

Veyadi winces. Apology flickers in his tone. "'Psychosomatic,' 'neurotransitive,' they're other words for 'real.' Pain is pain. Take it seriously. Asshole."

Sunai wants to reach out, tug Veyadi down into the grass, and change the subject. He doesn't even have the guts to light his cigarette. Veyadi's forehead creases.

Below, a company-cat keens. Its pack calls and cackles in response. Sunai sits up to watch them. Veyadi sits with him as the company-cats lope and wrestle on the beach. On impulse, Sunai whistles, long and clear. The cats freeze. Their muzzles turn up toward the cliff. They see nothing, because Veyadi has yanked Sunai back, away from the edge.

"Why?" Veyadi hisses.

"Oh, come on. What do we have to be afraid of? They come up, we say hi, and if they get feisty, we—"

"You can't command them anymore, Sunai. The passenger—"

"I don't want to command them! I didn't like doing that anyway. It's just . . . You've seen them. Orderly Sum Total brought the cats here. Acrimony Covenant keeps playing tag with the security cruisers. The Anthill frags—"

"Trample the local wildlife? Capsized a rig for no apparent reason?"

"Not out of *malice*."

Veyadi shakes his head. "I can't believe you. You think we can rehabilitate fragtech."

"Well? Why not?" Sunai throws up his arms and turns. He comes face-to-face with the corpse of Reconcile Elegy, whose head is little more than a void of stars. "They've changed too. We contained the passenger. It has no more say in what they want."

"It wasn't controlling all of them, not all the time."

Sunai rubs the back of his neck and the whorls of capillary root embedded along it. Sometimes, when he swallows, he feels the lump of the archival seed. Or Ruhi's palms, crushing his throat. It's odd to recall the moment with such unblinking clarity. He wouldn't be able to without the other perspectives eternally grafted to his. The Maw refuses to forgive Ruhi. Veyadi hates the part of himself that wants to. Sunai . . . has accepted that he was betrayed. That he maybe didn't deserve to be.

But he knows he will never find peace with the memory of Ruhi's throat between his teeth.

"Ugh." Veyadi puts out an arm. Sunai allows himself to lean into it, to be enveloped and held close to Veyadi's chest. He breathes in the sweat of Veyadi's day, the earthy green scent of his labor.

Veyadi is the one who goes into the shrine. He spends his waking hours refining the prison they grew for Ruhi and the passenger, to ensure they won't escape. As he does, he studies them, searching for answers to questions Sunai never thought to ask: about AIs, their makers, the history that led to Cradle.

Sunai has his garden and his chickens to keep him busy. He has visitors and Imaru. Had Imaru, anyway.

"She's going because she thinks she has to," Sunai says into Veyadi's shoulder. "It's so goddamn stupid. She doesn't *have* to do anything. That's the point of this. Of us."

"You sure about that?" Veyadi asks, too light. Like all his best questions, it damns with the answer it implies.

They didn't discuss what they would do, once the dust cleared and the violence passed. That's the problem. They didn't make a decision. How *are* they going to navigate being—whatever it is they've become? Relics and an ENGINE? An AI and its archives? Something even more troubling? Who knows! They kicked everyone but Imaru off Lotus, then refused to join the incredibly necessary debates over how Khuon Mo would survive the next bout of outside fuckery. Now here they are, pitching fits, with only each other to bear the brunt of their nonsense.

Veyadi grunts half agreement. Sunai groans. "Shut up. I know . . . They want me to have an opinion, Adi. No one should want my opinions."

"They are generally suspect, yes." Veyadi brushes Sunai's muss of hair from his face. He puts his lips, so carefully, to Sunai's forehead. "Look at it this way: they'll never be just yours."

"When you put it that way, we sound extra creepy."

Veyadi is about to shut him up with a kiss—Sunai anticipates his intention as a spooling warmth down his back—when they're interrupted by the growl of a company-cat.

Sunai laughs. Veyadi curses. The cat hunkers down in the

grass behind them, ears back, tail whipping. She lets out a yearning mewl as Sunai crouches, hand out.

And I? Let's just say: I'm here. I am alive, and I am with you, and I will continue to be—until you are dead, and I go too.

ACKNOWLEDGMENTS

I came to this book after a succession of surgeries. Strategic evisceration had revitalized my body, but flesh doesn't care if it's been cut for a good reason. To flesh, it's just a wound. Recovery made me more keenly aware of my limitations than I had been even at my most enfeebled—the brain needs calories to make language happen, and those calories were required elsewhere. Even then, I didn't know this was a book about bodies until well into the third draft. I had to get far enough from the site of impact to properly perceive the crater.

So I must express gratitude to everyone who taught me tenderness; the words don't come without it. I must say more thanks to everyone who helped turn those words into a narrative. This book made me more human. Thank you.

To Carl Engle-Laird: You were an editor I dreamed of one day working with, and I've been as lucky as I am grateful to do so. You saw what I most wanted this book to be and helped me push it to become *more of that*. Thank you also for the manga recs; I can always, always trust your taste.

To the team at Tordotcom: Oliver Dougherty, who helped me find my feet; Matt Rusin, who has kept me on track ever since; Sung Choi, whose illustration left me breathless; everyone in editing, design, production, publicity, marketing, and the managing thereof—Irene Gallo, Dakota Griffin, Steven Bucsok, Lauren Hougen, Christine Foltzer, Andrew King, Michael Dudding, Samantha Friedlander, Caro Perny, Terry McGarry, Jaime Herbeck, and Sam Dauer: You who make the books *occur*—your contributions and work are invaluable. I treasure them every time I remember that this book has happened at all.

To Caitlin McDonald: My agent, my friend—your belief in my ability to make a story worth reading lifted me from recovery into personhood. Your enduring wisdom remains a guiding light in my sky.

To my family: Every year I uncover more ways in which you shaped me for the better with your instinct to love, nurture, and protect. I wouldn't be breathing without you, and on my best days, I hope I carry what you gave me to others.

To my writing friends: Suzanne Walker, my accountability buddy; Midori Hirai, my oldest writing partner; Cecilia Tan, my mentor; my comrades in stumbling about in word mechs, and those I've met in pubs and treehouses; my wondrous agent siblings; my first ever in-person writing group, who make my Sundays radiant: You are enduring inspirations whose insights expand and animate my mind. Craft can be lonely, and I can be shy with my words. I live for your readiness to meet me in all the places where we excavate meaning out of whatever the hell we're doing. Thank you for making my brain a better place to live in.

Finally, to Nick Rollason, my wife: Every word is yours first, and I write them foremost for you. I would not be alive and well were it not for your tender regard. Thank you for making me eat, sleep, and medicate; for keeping me warm and making me laugh until I wheeze; for teaching me that I *do* know what romance is, and that I might want it for myself. Thank you for wanting me to want this. Your care, your thoughts, and your words inspire my own in kind.